OVERKILL

ALSO BY TED BELL

FICTION

Patriot

Warriors

Phantom

Warlord

Tsar

Spy

Pirate

Assassin

Hawke

NOVELLA

White Death

What Comes Around

Crash Dive

YOUNG ADULT NOVELS

The Time Pirate

Nick of Time

OVERKILL

TED BELL

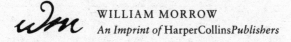

WILLIAM MORROW
An Imprint of HarperCollins*Publishers*

HarperCollins books may be purchased for educational, business, or sales promotional use. For information, please email the Special Markets Department at SPsales@harpercollins.com.

FIRST EDITION

Library of Congress Cataloging-in-Publication Data

Names: Bell, Ted, author.
Title: Overkill : an Alex Hawke novel / Ted Bell.
Description: First edition. | New York : William Morrow, [2018] | Series:
    Alex Hawke novels ; 10 |
Identifiers: LCCN 2017053351 (print) | LCCN 2017056120 (ebook) | ISBN
    9780062684547 (ebook) | ISBN 006268454X (ebook) | ISBN 9780062845672
    (Large Print) | ISBN 0062845675 (Large Print) | ISBN 9780062684516
    (hardcover) | ISBN 0062684515 (hardcover)
Subjects: LCSH: Hawke, Alex (Fictitious character)—Fiction. | Intelligence
    officers—Fiction. | Kidnapping—Fiction. | BISAC: FICTION / Espionage. |
    FICTION / Action & Adventure. | GSAFD: Adventure fiction. | Suspense
    fiction. | Spy stories.
Classification: LCC PS3602.E6455 (ebook) | LCC PS3602.E6455 O94 2018 (print)
    | DDC 813/.6—dc23
LC record available at https://lccn.loc.gov/2017053351

ISBN 978-0-06-268451-6

18 19 20 21 22 RS/LSC 10 9 8 7 6 5 4 3 2 1

I should like to dedicate this book to the memory of my maternal grandfather, George Blaine Howell. I owe him all that it means to be, not only a man, but hopefully a gentleman as well. After Dartmouth College, after Captain of the Artillery in France. After Cornell Law School, a brilliant career in banking, after huge success in the world of offshore ocean racing aboard his beloved schooner "Rambler," George Howell and his dear friend, my godfather and World War I fighter Ace, Captain Eddie Rickenbacker went on to create their first startup, Eastern Airlines. He died too young at sixty-six. He loved his wife, Mary Trice, and he loved life more than any man I ever knew. And, god knows, it loved him back.

At least when you're dead,
people stop trying to kill you.

—V. PUTIN

Part One

Antebellum

PREFACE

Switzerland is one weird country. In an odd assortment of ways. But most especially when it comes to their military. Most people, including their neighbors to the south, the Italians, would be surprised to learn that Switzerland even *has* an army. One Italian banker, bragging about the size of the Italian army, was told by his Zurich barber that "Switzerland doesn't *have* an army, signore, Switzerland *is* an army!"

"No! It cannot be true! We never see them! How big they are, this army?"

And the Swiss gent says, "One million men under arms, Signore Buttafusco!" The Italian, in shock, came up out of his chair so fast his barber nearly took his right ear off with the straight razor.

"A *million*?" he exclaimed. "*Non è posibile!* It cannot be!"

But it's true. At any given moment, there are in excess of one million men under arms in the country. Switzerland has been steadfastly neutral for centuries. But truth be told, it has one of the largest armies in the world on a per capita basis. All Swiss militia soldiers take their rifles home and keep them loaded under the bed for the rest of their lives!

One could say, quite rationally, that Switzerland has a national paranoia about defense. Where does this come from? Historically, it stems from the fact that Switzerland is at the very heart of Europe. The crossroads of all the important routes through the Alps—directly in the crosshairs of any invading emperor, Nazi despot, or, just possibly, a deposed Russian president desperate for Swiss gold.

The Swiss Theory of War: "Know all about how to fight a war . . . so that you never have to, you know, fight one."

Little-known facts: In case of nuclear war, they've got it covered. The Swiss have underground bunkers capable of fitting *a hundred percent* of their population inside. Think of it! A national building code requires every single home to either have an underground bunker or pay into a fund to maintain community bunkers—so every Swiss citizen has quick access to a shelter.

Only the Swiss could be paranoid enough to even think of doing that! Let's begin with the Swiss air force. These flyboys are out there. Above and beyond. Check this out. First of all, there are no air force bases inside the country. Nada, zero, not one! So where do they hide all the planes? Inside mountains, of course, all over the country. And what about the runways, so fighter jets and bombers can take off and land? Well, for that they use the international highways system, of course. Hmm, why didn't we think of that?

That wide four-lane highway down there, snaking along through the Alps beside that sparkling river? That ramrod-straight country lane through heavy forest? Late at night and into the wee hours of the morning, all these roads and highways actually convert to Swiss air force runways! And it happens in no time. Military Police halt all traffic in both directions and then quickly remove the grade separations between the lanes.

And the Swiss air force has office hours—you heard that right, *office hours*. So despite all the "heavy iron" they've got lying around within the mountains, squadrons of F/A-18s, F-5E Tigers—should you ever decide to invade the country during the nighttime, you'll find all the Swiss air force pilots are tucked in bed! Zzzzz. And get this: due to the noise levels, which could harm the all-important

Alpine tourist regions, Swiss pilots have to go abroad to fly super-sonic training missions.

During the Cold War, the Swiss built a giant militia-based national defense system that rivals that of any country in the world. If any country should be foolish enough to invade Switzerland, they would find an entire nation armed to the teeth and ready to fight to the death . . .

Always keep your guard up in this picture-postcard-perfect land! That charming little chocolate-box mountain chalet you are hiking toward? On closer inspection, you'll probably notice it has machine-gun slits beneath every window. That lovely old hotel across the river? The one with red geraniums filling every window box? The press of a button and the entire front wall retracts to reveal a Howitzer cannon and a nest of machine guns.

The Swiss army maintains vast defense networks of huge fortified cannon placements—mainly howitzer cannons, some of them well positioned enough to attack an approaching enemy well beyond Swiss borders. These cannon placements are extremely well hidden, completely enclosed within fake rock formations, and you can imagine it would be a nasty surprise for an invader to find himself within firing range of one of those cannons.

The Swiss army builds countless fake rocks to hide things besides cannons inside. Rocks conceal machine gun nests and light artillery. Also, thousands of Swiss tunnels and bridges, highways and railroads are built with tank traps and wired with demolition charges. Bridges are blown instantly at the approach of hostile forces. And, well, you get the idea . . . attack Switzerland and all you will get is your hat handed to you!

Late at night, when all those secret highways are closed down so the fighter jets and bombers can land and take off, you can hear the roar, the thunderous rumble down through the sleepy Alpine valleys . . .

Welcome to sunny Switzerland!

Hope you enjoy the show.

PROLOGUE

In the skies over France

Vladimir Putin closed his eyes, smiled, and zipped up his trousers. "*Spasibo, Kat,*" he whispered, thanking Ekaterina for her services. He had distrusted the woman at first. Far too familiar right from the beginning. But over time she had worked her magic on him. To the point that by now he felt he could not live without her. "What would I do without you?" he would find himself whispering into the perfect shell of her ear in the heat of passion. And in fact he meant it.

The former Miss Ukraine looked up at him from beneath long black lashes and smiled. "No, thank *you*, Excellency," she said, playfully snatching the white linen handkerchief from the breast pocket of his suit. With a coy little smile, she delicately patted at her full red lips.

Her confidence was not ill-founded. She'd long ago realized that not only did she have the president of Russia hooked, she had him in the boat. She had him fileted. She had him *on ice.*

She had him *sautéed.*

The president of Russia reclined his seat, put his head back, and closed his eyes. A few moments later, feeling suddenly tired, he motioned for Ekaterina to get to her feet and return to the galley.

"Cup of tea, please, my dear," he whispered, cracking one eye, "the Lapsang Souchong."

"My pleasure, Excellency," she said with a small bow before heading aft to brew his tea.

"Sorry, Kat?"

She paused, turned, and said, "Yes?"

"I suddenly feel so tired," the president of Russia said. It was true. Lack of energy was never his problem. Could he possibly be getting sick? No. Not now. Not possible.

"No, *Volodya*, I think you just feel a little bit more relaxed, yes?"

He laughed at her little giggle and the way she wiggled her hips and broad fanny while walking away. What was it about pleated skirts? Was it a Russian thing? Probably not . . . he and the American president, Donald Trump, had once addressed the pleated skirt issue at Davos. Trump had said he fully shared Putin's views on the subject of pleats when it came to skirts.

In fact, the two men privately shared a great number of views. They didn't need any plastic reset button. They instinctively saw each other as equals. Both strong and proud men, two willful leaders who put their own countries first. And, rightly so. Putin knew he would never like many of the American president's actions, but he would understand the man's motivation. And vice-versa.

He willed himself to do as she said and relax.

It was difficult. The explosive sounds of screeching brakes, high speed collisions, and cacophony of heavy gunfire was still ringing in his ears. Less than an hour ago, en route to a hastily arranged secret rendezvous with Andrei, his pilot, his convoy had been ambushed by successive carfuls of paid assassins, firing heavy machine guns. And not once, mind you, but twice on the deserted country road to his private airfield just north of Moscow.

His tank-like state limousine, a cocoon of lead and steel, had roared through the field of fire each time, the limo's structural integrity intact despite the hail of bullets. He'd been well-defended by the men in his convoy, of course, but still, it had been a very close thing.

The oligarchs had made it clear he had a target on his back and time was running out. That's why he was getting the hell out of town. But, with any luck at all, he'd be back in the ring shortly.

His once unthinkable decision to vacate the Kremlin had been a long time coming. But, after repeated assassination attempts by his enemies both within and without the Kremlin walls (read the traitorous oligarchs) he'd finally opted for this midnight getaway. He planned to disappear, soon after planting rumors of a terminal cancer diagnosis. Fake his death. The good thing about being dead, he'd told Kat one night on his yacht, *Tsar*, was that no one was trying to kill you.

And all this crap, courtesy of the fucking oligarchy! The very men he'd made rich beyond anyone's wildest dreams, men who had tens of billions upon tens of billions in gold. Gold, he knew from his private sources in international banking, that was now hidden away deep inside vast caverns in the Swiss Alps. And these bastards who'd turned on him in these last few years? They'd been methodically stealing the few gold reserves that he, Putin himself, still had left!

This had been an extraordinarily rough year, even by his standards. The oligarchy, it finally became apparent to everyone in the Politburo, in the Federation government, was now wealthy enough and thus powerful enough to seize the reins of the Kremlin. Then, through powerful paid stooges loyal only to them, they could rule Russia in a way that suited only their interests. That's the future he was abdicating. A kleptocracy. He was leaving his people in the hands of a government of thieves!

Plots conceived and executed by bands of roving criminal thugs, men now working for his betrayers. He'd endured poisonings, threats of a coup d'état, many assassination attempts (one that left him severely wounded), and hellish riots outside the Kremlin walls. Food riots that seemingly went on for weeks, the ruble dropping to historic lows, oil prices in the toilet, U.S. sanctions over the annexation of Crimea and his recent actions in Syria. And very little money for food in the stores. Hell, very little even for vodka, for Christ's sake!

And that really *was* an economic crisis. "Little water," as the alcoholic staple was called in Russia, was no luxury. It was simply indispensable in Russian society.

Even his state media was openly daring to question his fitness to be president, saying perhaps if Putin was gone, Russian citizens would fare better under the oligarchy leaders in the Kremlin . . . Christ.

Well, it would be good to get away. Disappear off the face of the earth. Possibly fake his own death if the opportunity presented itself. As he'd joked on the phone with Andrei that day, "At least when you're dead, people stop trying to kill you!"

He'd have time to do some serious thinking about his political future. And whether or not he had one. It was debatable, whichever way he chose to look at it. Now that his beloved motherland was almost flat broke, his once loyal base was turning on him in droves. Sooner or later, unless he was able to come up with a massive injection of capital into the system, Russia would go the way of Venezuela. Like the chaos now, at the hands of that idiot bus driver, Maduro.

He glanced at his new Patek Philippe watch. Nearly noon. They'd be touching down at Aéroport de Nice in one hour. Then a quick hop in his chopper over to Cap d'Antibes where his beloved yacht *Tsar* was moored. His wife was with her mother in Vladivostock for a month. So a brief respite of bliss lay ahead.

He and Ekaterina would have the world, *his safe, private* world, all to themselves without interruption. Tonight, at dinner aboard the yacht, he would give her the emerald and diamond necklace, the one he'd pocketed during a midnight visit to the Hermitage Museum last week. The necklace Catherine the Great had worn to the palace the night she . . .

He must have dozed off!

He opened his eyes and looked around. Everything was fuzzy. It was like waking up in the morning in a room you don't recognize.

He was barely able to lift his arm—what the hell? Heart attack?

He called out for Ekaterina. No response. When he swiveled his seat to see where she was, he saw both she and Irina slumped forward in their seats. And the oxygen masks dangling over their heads! Were they incapacitated? Or dead? He looked up in horror at his own mask. Did he even have the strength to get the damn thing on?

He reached up and yanked at the mask.

Yes. Okay. Calm yourself, Volodya, breathe! Breathe!

A wave of panic swept over him when he finally got the mask in place.

There was no fucking oxygen flowing to suck down into his lungs. No. Of course not. It was just one more betrayal! Andrei, his trusted friend and pilot, had initiated a gradual depressurization of the cabin and was now withholding the oxygen supply. Enraged, he calmed himself and gathered his wits about him. He would need them, those pilots.

He was dying of hypoxia.

THE PRESIDENT ALWAYS TRAVELED WITH his "end of days" backpack. That, and an emergency parachute. The large black backpack was filled with cash, jewels, weapons and drugs, survival clothing and a little dried food, Imperial vodka, a few books, and everything else. He keyed in the code for the lock, trying to shake off the dizziness that threatened to disable him. Clouds were forming at the perimeters of his vision and he knew he was rapidly running out of time.

He grabbed his old KGB Makarov 9mm because it was loaded and its weight was reassuring in his hand. He staggered to his feet. For once in his life he wished his Ilyushin II presidential aircraft wasn't so fucking huge. From his private resting area amidships, the cockpit looked a million miles away.

He knew if he ran he would fall; a feeling of severe vertigo had gripped him. He walked, using both hands to hold on to anything solid. He knew the cockpit door would be closed and he knew the traitorous two bastards inside had locked it.

He'd get only one good kick . . . but he was a lifelong martial artist, a full black belt in judo, and he fucking well knew how to make his kicks count.

The aluminum door flew inward and he was inside, covering the pilot and copilot with the Makarov.

"Andrei, Andrei, Andrei," he whispered, putting the gun on the pilot. "You cunt-hearted bastard. I gave you everything . . . hands up and turn around!"

"But I . . . please, sir, don't kill me! They said they would kill my wife and children! They left me no choice but to—"

"Et tu, Andrei," said Putin.

The Makarov popped softly, creating a smoking bloody hole in Markov's forehead. He pitched forward against the controls, dead. Putin leaned down and snatched the bloodied, gore-filled oxygen mask from his late pilot's head. With a grimace of disgust, he fitted the disgusting device over his head, covering his nose and mouth. He inhaled hungrily, savoring the bite of the cold oxygen sucked into his starving lungs. He glared at his copilot, breathing deeply.

He felt himself slowly coming back, his terrified mind settling back into some semblance of normalcy.

"And, what am I to make of you?" he said, now aiming at the terrified copilot. "I don't even know your fucking name. Listen carefully. Do exactly as I say and you may live another day. Descend and maintain three thousand meters."

"Roger that, sir," he said, throttling back and easing the airship's nose downward. "Descend and maintain three thousand."

The big four-engine Ilyushin quickly shed altitude.

"Reduce your airspeed to two hundred kph."

"Reducing airspeed to two hundred kph."

"Go to full autopilot. Lock it in."

"Engaging full auto . . . and . . . locked."

"Good work."

"Thank you, sir."

"Now. Get on your feet, you nameless little fuck—I said, on your feet now!"

"But, sir, someone must fly the airplane! I cannot just . . ."

"Do as I say or die where you sit. Take off your oxygen mask and hand it to me."

The terrified and trembling man did as he was told, then unbuckled his safety harness and stood on legs that felt like jelly. Putin ripped off Andrei's bloody mask and replaced it with the copilot's.

"Please, sir! I have a young family! I didn't know what Karpov was planning until we were aloft and I would never have—"

"Have come back and warned me? Put your hands on your head and turn around. Don't move . . ."

The doomed man did as he was told.

Never once taking his eyes off his would-be assassin, he said, "Bang, you're dead," and shot him in the back of the head, spattering the cockpit windows with strings of gristle, grey matter, and gore. He lowered the gun, struggling for air. Something wrong with the late copilot's mask! Then, inhaling deeply, sucking what little oxygen he could into his starving lungs.

He had an overwhelming desire to lie down, curl up, and go to sleep right there on the cold metal cockpit floor.

But two far more powerful desires dictated otherwise. The twin instinctive needs for survival and revenge. He left the two dead men on the bloody floor where they lay and staggered back to the wide fuselage door just aft of the galley on the port side of the aircraft. He cast his eyes to the back of the lounge, just briefly. It was the last time he'd lay his eyes on his beloved Kat. The bloody oligarchs had snatched her from him. They would pay.

Shaking his head violently to maintain consciousness, he somehow disarmed the door, swung the big lever to the open position, kicked the door away, and stepped out into the dirty sherbet skies over France.

CHAPTER ONE

Christmas Day, St. Moritz

Two heavily armored Range Rovers, black, with impenetrable inky black windows, emerged from the underground garages at Badrutt's Palace Hotel in the sleepy little town of St. Moritz. Perhaps the most celebrated hotel in the world, the palace had sadly seen better days. Much better days.

On the other hand, it was one of those clear, clean days in the Swiss Alps, when the Alpine skies above were shot through with blue and brimming with bright promise. Everything seemed to have been washed clean by the frothy overnight snowfall. Every window in town gleamed.

The very air itself seemed to sparkle. A foot of squeaky powder had fallen on the rooftops, parks, and ski areas. The black ice of the famous town's narrow twisting roads was now especially treacherous. Early morning drivers had to mind their speed and brake at every intersection.

After a long pause for surveillance, the first vehicle, known as the Beast because of its heavy armaments and studded as it was with external gunports, turned left into the snowy white streets of the old town. The second car followed on its heels. Bristling with antennas, this was clearly the communications vehicle. It maintained a distance of precisely fifteen feet from the lead car at all times.

The twin vehicles did not attract much attention. St. Moritz was no longer the glitzy playground of paparazzi, movie stars, and jet-setters it had once been. Now it was the haunt of Iranian arms dealers, filthy rich Chinese, and bullyboy Russian oil oligarchs. Also, there were people here who simply didn't know any better, unwitting American tourists who naively believed the town was still home to the chic, the beautiful, and the truly famous.

It was not.

All of that jet-set luster was long gone—all of the evanescent golden girl glamour, all of the flashy aristocratic playboys, all the louche old men with their bosomy Parisian nieces, gone. Fled to Gstaad or Courchevel or Cortina d'Ampezzo in the Dolomites. The only thing here now was money. Cold, hard cash. Gobs of it. And most of it, if not all, was in the wrong hands.

The duplicate Range Rovers, now making their cautious way up the slippery slopes of the Corviglia mountain, were a case in point. You didn't ride around in cars like these unless you were a man with countless millions in cash and nearly as many enemies.

The casual observer, upon spotting this little caravan passing by, might simply say, "Bloody Chinese" or "Russian billionaire bastards" or something similar, and look away in disgust. A true member of the Old Guard—or what was left of them, anyway—might punctuate an epithet with the international single-digit salute.

The radio in the second car crackled. "Arriving in five minutes, sir," the lead driver said simply.

"Thanks, Tristan," came the reply from the rear seat of the trailing car. "A rosy picture out there?"

"Beautiful day for it, sir."

"Indeed. Can you get us any closer to the base station of the lift? Take the service road if you have to."

"Done and done," Tristan replied.

Now the lead car slowed to a crawl, approaching a turn into the bustling car park. The looming gondola base station was visible on the far side. It had begun to snow again, and the cheery skiers bustling about on this Christmas morning were elated. The Swiss Ski School instructors, all in their signature scarlet snow gear, were all smiles as well. Another powder-packed day, for sure, and the mountain was already bristling with children of all ages.

Since 1932, Swiss ski schools have maintained a presence at all the winter resorts in Switzerland, providing lessons in all snow sports to learners. Just above the gondola station, one could see the Swiss Snow Kids Village, the Swiss Snow League, and the Swiss Snow Academy. These gentle open lower slopes formed a near-perfect nursery area for ski school children first learning to snowplow and gaining confidence, without the threat of snowboarders and more accomplished skiers whizzing scarily by.

Christmas Day was the ski school's big day of the year. A hundred or more excited children were already visible up on the slopes, all decked out in their red parkas. More were crowded around the base station, waiting with their parents or nannies or siblings to board the aerial tramway.

Children were there for a morning rehearsal for tonight's festive holiday event. At dusk would begin the annual children's Christmas torchlight parade. It promised to be a grand spectacle, with the children, carrying torches, snaking down the broad slopes of the main run as gracefully as they could manage. With their newfound skills, they would create a river of fire flowing down from the summit to the base.

The lead car slowed, turning into the car park at the gondola base station.

The lead Range Rover's driver, having navigated a lot crampacked with tour buses, cars, and pedestrians, now used a narrow road leading up to the base station itself. It slowed to a stop as close to the gondola as possible.

Upon seeing the second vehicle come to a stop a few feet behind the first, many of the ski school children and their parents paused and had a look-see. The big black cars had used a service road forbidden to members of the public at large.

Someone very important, or at least extremely rich and famous, would soon emerge from the car. Royalty? Celebrity gangster? English footballer? Snoop Dog?

The lead car's heavy rear door opened very slowly with an audible pneumatic hiss.

First out was a tall blond man wearing mirrored Ray-Bans and dressed head to toe in the famous scarlet ski kit of the Swiss Ski School. A private instructor? Yes, one hired for the day or the week, anyone would assume. And yet he had an imperious manner, an almost military confidence. And he wore an earbud in his left ear.

He seemed to be conversing with an unseen colleague, using a lip mike as he surveyed the crowds, systematically swiveling his head left to right and then back again. A ski instructor? Perhaps not. Rather, he looked to be someone easily capable of instantly brandishing heavy weapons plucked from inside his bright red parka.

The crowd, now sensing, if not unfolding drama, at least something mildly interesting, pressed in for a closer look. The "instructor" then turned his back on them, presumably to help one of his clients out of the big black car. He slowly swung the door open.

The client was not at all the great personage they'd been expecting. No movie stars here. No, emerging from the cavernous interior of the big black vehicle was a very small and beautiful boy.

It was a mere child, blinking in the brilliant sunlight, who fell into the waiting arms of the tall man in the red ski kit.

A radiant boy, not more than seven years old, with thick black hair, enormous ice-blue eyes, and a wondrous smile. Seemingly unaware of his effect on the crowd, he reached up and tugged on the instructor's parka saying, "Where is Daddy, Tristan?"

"Right behind you, Alexei!" The big man smiled as he placed the boy down on the well-trampled snow. "Look! There he is! Just now getting out of his car, actually."

The boy whirled, spinning around just in time to see his gallant father step out of the rear of the second Range Rover. Lord Alexander Black Hawke at your service. Commander Hawke, former Royal Navy fighter pilot and now a senior counterterrorist officer for MI6, British Secret Service. He had the look of a man who had taken in stride everything the world could throw at him. But one who had flung it all right back, smiling all the while.

This Lord Hawke was hardly anyone's picture of an English lord, plump and sheathed in tweed. He moved with a warrior's bearing, inherited down the centuries from the Knights of the Round Table as well as the proud pirates, the Brotherhood, who plied the waters of the Spanish Main. His lordship was in fact a direct descendant of the infamous pirate captain John Black Hawke, known and feared throughout the Spanish Main as Blackhawke.

Lord Hawke, addressing the House of Lords on frequent occasions, possessed the visible gravity of a man who had been there and back. Lords (and ladies) had come to know him as a pure and elemental warrior—necessarily violent, riveting, nature itself. Still, he was someone whom men would love to stand a drink . . . and whom women much preferred horizontal. He was, after all, devastatingly good-looking, not to mention, the sixth richest man in England.

The ski crowd was instinctively wary of this dark Englishman. Wary of the half-smile of certitude on his somewhat cruel mouth. Who was he? Where did he come from? What did he do? A murmur of excited speculation rippled through the crowd.

Lord Alexander Hawke was tall, well north of six feet. He possessed a full head of unruly jet-black hair, had a chiseled profile, and displayed the deepwater tan of a man who spent a good deal of his life at sea. He had the most astonishing eyes. A gossip columnist for *Tatler* magazine had once raved that London's most eligible bachelor had eyes that looked like "two pools of frozen Arctic rain."

He was lean but heavily muscled, as would befit a man who swam six miles in open ocean every day of his life that he could. He still performed the Royal Navy's exercise program upon awakening each morning. He kept fit and consoled himself with the only two vices left to him since he'd given up on women: Gosling's Bermuda rum and gold-tipped Morland's cigarettes. He moved with the jaunty confidence of a world-class athlete.

Like his child, he was almost impossibly attractive.

No one present had even a clue as to who this elegant gentleman might be. But it was immediately obvious to every one of them that he was *somebody*.

"Daddy!" the little boy cried, racing toward the open arms of his father beneath the pristine blue skies.

"Alexei, Alexei," the smiling man said, dropping to one knee to embrace his son. "It's finally Christmas Day! Are you happy, darling?"

"Oh, yes, Daddy! Ever so happy! May we go up the mountain now? With Tristan? My friends are all waiting for me up at the tram station!"

"It's going to be the best Christmas yet, isn't it, Alexei?"

"Oh, yes, Daddy! Hurry, let's go!"

CHAPTER TWO

As each arriving gondola discharged passengers, young and cordial Swiss aerial tramway personnel were there to help usher new ones aboard. They ushered ascending passengers through the wide pneumatic doors at the rear of the soon-to-depart gondola. The silver gondolas were state of the art. Luxuriously appointed and very spacious, each one could accommodate fifty passengers.

As they neared the front of the boarding queue, little Alexei's bodyguard, a fair-haired young Scotland Yard detective inspector named Tristan Walker, led the way. Walker was a highly respected officer of the Royalty Protection Group known as SO14. These were the men and women responsible for the safety and protection of the queen, her family, and her royal friends.

Detective Inspector Walker, studying the scene from behind his mirrored glasses, noticed that all the adults were being directed to the forward seating in the tramcar, while the ski school kids were being seated at the rear. He turned to the boy's father and whispered, "Bit of a problem up ahead, sir."

"I see that, Tristan. I don't want him back there alone."

"Adults to the forward end of the car, please, and all ski school students at the rear!" one of the two young Swiss tramway officials said as Alexei's father boarded first and addressed him.

"May I have a word?" Hawke said to him, lowering his voice.

"Yes, sir?"

"The child directly behind me is my son. I wish to remain with him here at the rear for the ascent."

"Not possible, sir. I'm sorry. All adults please move forward. This is so children can be first to exit when we reach the top. It's a very strict safety policy."

"I understand that policy perfectly. My name is Hawke, by the way. I am a British government official. I ask that you waive that policy so that my child remains in my custody."

The man shrugged his shoulders. "Nothing I can do. You'll have to return to the station office for written permission to waive official policy, sir. Sorry. Please move along."

He turned away to assist other passengers. Hawke put a firm hand on his shoulder.

"Listen to me. The man with my son is a British Royalty Protection officer. SO14. You understand what that means? Inspector Walker will show you his credentials. By international law, you are required not to interfere in his official duties as mandated by Her Majesty the Queen. I suggest you make it easy on yourself. This is no day for an international incident, is it, now? It is Christmas, after all."

The young man just shook his head and waved Hawke forward.

Hawke bent to speak in his son's ear. "Alexei, Daddy's going up to the front. Do you want to stay back here with your schoolmates?"

"Oh, yes, Daddy. These guys are all my friends from school. May I please stay?"

Hawke looked at the protection officer. "Tristan, this official knows who you are. If you have further trouble sticking with him give me a signal. We'll just have to disembark and get some kind of permission. Yes?"

"Of course, sir."

"Show them your Scotland Yard creds, Inspector. Tell them your orders from the British Crown require that you remain within a three-foot perimeter of my son at all times, anywhere in the world."

"Yes, sir. No worries, sir. It's a short ride at least, thirty minutes or so."

Hawke smiled and made his way forward with the surge of adults, looking back over his shoulder as Tristan pleaded his case at the rear. He was glad to see the young Swiss chap appear to be relenting. Inspector Walker was now all smiles and nodding at Hawke. Then he and Alexei took their seats side by side beneath the curved window at the very rear of the car. Alexei was plainly delighted, chatting and laughing with all of his newfound friends.

All was well.

THE REAR DOORS SNAPPED SHUT. Twenty-five children packed into the rear shouted cheers of joy, stamped their boots, and applauded as the gondola jerked into sudden movement. It shuddered a bit, then left the station, rapidly gaining momentum as it climbed the mountain suspended by the three overhead cables.

A thousand, then two thousand meters it soared, ever higher above the snowy white treetops, mounting toward the peak, dangling above a great ravine, six thousand feet below. Hawke, like most of the adults, had settled in on his steel bench, reading his London *Times* sports section, delving into the football statistics, highlights from the week's matches. What the devil had gotten into Manchester United?

He looked up and smiled.

This last-minute vacation had very nearly not happened at all. The man for whom he worked in London, Sir David Trulove, had nearly nixed it just three days earlier. Trulove, who was chief of British Intelligence, or MI6, had his hands full as the holidays approached.

The bloody Chinese were hacking at Sir David's electronic firewalls; a team of North Korean assassins, funded by the bloody Chinese, was even now somewhere in Britain, plotting his imminent demise. And then there was the beleaguered Putin, who wanted nothing less than to rule the world. A man whose bellicose belligerence was nothing short of—ah, well.

Bloody hell!

Hawke snapped back to his immediate reality. It was Christmas morn, after all, Christmas Day at last. The first one he and his son had celebrated together in years. It was his bloody work, wasn't it? He was a warrior, after all—it was what he did—roam the world, looking for trouble. It was his never-ending missions that took him from one exploding end of the globe to the other that—he put his paper down and looked up in alarm.

Something was wrong. The former Royal Navy fighter pilot could sense it. He could *feel* it, and it set his teeth on edge.

The shuddering vibrations of the cable car had subtly changed, shifted into a lower gear. The metal floor beneath his ski boots hummed and thrummed a different tune. Odd. He looked up through the curved plexiglass windows above him. The tram's two support cables and the thicker motorized one that carried them upward were all seemingly intact and seemed normal . . . and yet . . . and yet . . .

Hawke had long ago noted how passengers aboard big commercial jetliners exhibited signs of panic and fear when they became aware of small changes in the pitch of the jet engines. Almost everyone human had a nagging pinprick of fear when boarding an airplane. Or an aerial tram, for that matter—anything that had the ability to fall out of the sky or plunge thousands of feet into a mountain crevasse could cause palpitations and sweat.

He picked up his newspaper and dove back into the world of sport. What in god's name really was going on with Manchester United? And why on earth was he so bloody jumpy? If there was anyplace on earth he and his son should feel safe, it was here in his beloved Switzerland. He got to his feet and tried to catch Alexei's eye, but the boy was lost in the melee of shouting, shoving children.

Tristan was sitting quietly, focused on the crowd. His roaming eyes never stopped moving as he surveyed the myriad faces in the tram. His young charge was standing only inches from his left knee, well within what he'd long ago begun calling the "circle of love."

There were shrieks of laughter from the children as the swaying car approached the peak. As they approached their destination and saw their red-clad schoolmates already whizzing about the snow white slopes, the noise reached a raucous crescendo . . . and then, without warning, there came a loud mechanical popping noise overhead, and seconds later, a kind of muffled bang that silenced everyone inside the car, adults and ski-schoolers alike. The cable car slowed its ascent of the mountain and then shuddered to a jerky stop.

Eyes opened wide in shock. They were so close! But they were suspended in space. And still dangled thousands of feet above the jagged rocks below.

And then the unthinkable happened.

CHAPTER THREE

Provence

"I am become the plowhorse," the frozen man alone in the rocky field said aloud, gazing up at the heavens.

Standing there in the vast black night, pelted with icy rain, sick with a raging fever, exhausted, hungry, filled with dread. He knew now that he was perhaps near the end.

And if he was truly honest with himself, maybe it was a blessing. How long could he last, really, running for his life? Running for cover, looking over his shoulder at the latest assassin hot on his heels? Holed up in a hovel in Siberia or some foul hostel in the backwaters of Bogotá. Endure a life of humiliation lived in constant fear? No. That was no kind of life for a man like Vladimir Vladimirovich Putin.

He who had once bestrode the earth as if a god?

Now in his darkest hour, the courageous plans he'd been making for defeating the treacherous oligarchy that had turned on him, and a victorious return to power, seemed laughable. An epic march into Moscow rivaling Napoleon's triumphant return to Paris after his humiliating yearlong exile in Elba? If you didn't laugh at such folly, you would have to cry.

He had conceived of his grand plan last year in Davos, Switzerland, at the last meeting of the G7. That's where he'd first sensed it, world leaders once his equals, if not his inferiors, now treating him with a certain hauteur, eying the Russian president with shark eyes, sharks who sniffed Russian blood in the water. It was not so very long ago that he had said, "When I enter the water, the sharks get out."

Yes. Now in all his misery and despair, all of his wild dreams, all seemed the musings of a madman, clinging at straws, clawing at any dangling lifeline he chanced upon. And always, the brass ring, receding.

And now as he stood there somewhere in France, in the slanting rain, head bowed, he recalled another desolate farm in another country, another time. His grandmother's few meager hardscrabble acres outside Stalingrad in Mother Russia. And he remembered the Putin family plowhorse, Fyodor, long his grandmother's mainstay and salvation.

The year was 1953. Uncle Joe Stalin, that sadistic and bloodthirsty Communist fuckhead, was finally dead and buried inside the Kremlin walls. A feast even maggots could not abide.

Still, thanks to the fucking Nazis, Mother Russia's future had looked unspeakably grim.

This bleak, blackened landscape was the hideously cruel legacy of the Battle of Stalingrad. Death. Disease. Starvation. The one last horse remaining alive, Fyodor, was worked mercilessly. But the beast was dying before the boy's very eyes. When Fyodor was gone, so too was hope for survival. He was too young to help in the field. His grandmother too old and too weak to plow.

And now Vladimir Putin, who found himself standing alone in the darkness of an empty field, battered by freezing rain, remembered Fyodor.

The boy had tried to do what he could for the horse. Shared what little food he could steal or forage. This while the citizens of the city were reduced to eating boiled shoe leather and drinking their own urine to survive. He had hauled blankets out to the shed in the dead of winter and draped them over the broad flanks of the great black stallion.

How the mammoth dray horse would stand alone for punishing hours in the field when day's work was done. Stand there unmoving, as if constructed of marble, in the drenching downpour, absorbing all the pain the world could offer, unyielding, mute . . . heroic.

Fyodor still stood there in that hoary field, in Putin's mind. The

Putins' plowhorse was Vladimir Putin's stoic symbol for all the heroic Russian people had endured at the hands of the murderous Nazis in World War II. And a constant reminder of all they had suffered later at the hands of their other European enemies during that war. And more recently, the depredations and humiliations they'd suffered at the hands of the Americans and the British. And a reminder that his life's mission was to avenge those ancient humiliations. To return Mother Russia to her rightful place on the world's stage.

Front and center, and crowned in glory once more.

These memories, and there were many, had served him well over the years. Being small of stature, the boy had learned to defend himself through the art of judo, becoming a black belt. During his career, his steady ascent through the ranks of the KGB, the horrific lessons of his youth propelled him forward. He rose to the senior levels at his KGB post in East Berlin and was devastated when the Wall came tumbling down, and the Soviet Union with it.

He adjusted his sodden slouch hat, the one he'd stolen from the sleeping man in the little rail station on that first night alone on the ground in France. He'd taken the man's greatcoat as well, cowhide, but lined with bearskin. The temperatures at night hovered around freezing. The paltry bits of food he had eaten after his own supplies had been exhausted were pilfered or recovered from garbage at the farms and small vineyards that dotted the countryside of Provence.

It had been several long and brutal weeks since he'd stepped out of a doomed airplane flying nine thousand feet above the earth.

Since he had one of the most famous faces in the world, he would have to remain in the shadows. He slept by day and traveled on foot by night. Slowly making his way south to Antibes on the Riviera, where he hoped his yacht, *Tsar*, would still be lying at anchor. He would simply sail away from the world. He would seek refuge at some remote anchorage, lost in the lower latitudes, among the countless reefs and isles of Polynesia . . . lost in the comforts of the beautiful bare-breasted women who adorned those shorelines.

That was his great hope, at any rate.

CHAPTER FOUR

He had literally dropped out of the world.

The news sheets he'd scavenge for in the tiny deserted rural rail stations all had differing accounts of the president's fate. Some maintained he had been poisoned; others insisted he had been kidnapped by his enemies in the Ukraine or finally murdered by KGB dissidents or oligarch assassins from the People's Commissariat for Internal Affairs—killers who'd failed so many times before. Or in the end, some said, was he simply a suicide who'd decided his life was a living hell and he was through with living it?

No one, save one, had any earthly idea.

The Kremlin was, and would remain, mute on the subject. Despite rumors about what had happened to the president's airplane rippling through Moscow, the crash of his presidential aircraft high in the mountains, with the certain death of all aboard, the story had somehow been kept under wraps. As with the strictest of state secrets, it had been buried with the ashes of those who perished, their secrets never to be revealed.

But with the passing of time, the world had begun to believe the many alternative rumors. He'd been poisoned by his enemies, the powerful oligarchs in the Politburo. Or kidnapped by KGB thugs in open revolt, shot in the head, and dumped unceremoniously out of a chopper somewhere over the Black Sea.

That Vladimir Putin now slept with the fishes was perhaps the general worldwide consensus. Who knew?

And what of his former friend and protégé Dmitry Medvedev? His second-in-command? The prime minister had quickly seized the reins of power, becoming a puppet for the oligarchs who'd ousted him. But that was fine with Putin. He had found in recent days that he liked being dead. In fact, it suited him perfectly. As he'd often said to himself, when you're dead, people stopped trying to kill you. Instead of the dismal view over your shoulder, you got to peer straight ahead into what, after all, might yet yield a glorious future!

AS HE CONTINUED HIS SLOW slog through the journey south, the world's most well-known missing man had somehow sustained himself. He did it by returning over and over to what he now considered his grandiose notions of snatching victory from the jaws of defeat. Perhaps the improving weather had played a role. The cold front had moved out, carrying the rain clouds away, and the temperatures moderated a bit . . . and his spirits had likewise lifted with the morning sun.

And he regained, to a degree, a small sense of destiny.

As the days turned into weeks, and the world started to forget about him, he began reformulating his plans for his ultimate return from exile. He wasn't giving up the throne. He had left Moscow under existential threat. A man badly needing a break from the political noose tightening around his neck, still determined to save Russia or die trying. But he could see that now was not the time for that. That would come later. When he would have all the chips, all the pieces on the chessboard. And once more a vast fortune. Then, only then, would he be once more unstoppable.

Trying to prop up his regime, he had exhausted almost all of his own resources. The motherland itself was nearly flat broke. The cash and gold in Russia's formerly vast Swiss reserves were at a dangerous all-time low. So was oil income.

His beloved Russian people, a population starving on pitiful wages after all those years of adulation, had turned on him en masse. There was precious little money for the food on the shelves of the stores; there was hardly even any money for their "Little Water," the potion that fueled the nation. And kept them compliant.

Now there were riots everywhere. Kremlin Square. Theatre Square, inside the Kremlin walls of Red Square. It seemed they never stopped chanting.

"Putin, *nyet*, Putin, *nyet*, Putin, *nyet!*" Calling for his head.

Even his much-vaunted military leadership was no longer reliably loyal. Rumors swirled inside the Kremlin walls. The oligarchs! The oligarchs were seizing the reins of power! These were the words the cardinals of the Kremlin had taken to whispering, lowering their eyes whenever he passed by. There was simply no one left to trust. Literally no one. He'd made them all billionaires, and now they shunned him, detested him, spat on him in the street like the lowest of the lowest castes of Calcutta.

An Untouchable. But the hardest thing, the most painful realization of all, was this: *no one feared him anymore.*

And so, yes, now he knew what he had to do. Returning to his beloved yacht *Tsar* at this point would be the stupidest move he could make. How could he hide on a two-hundred-foot yacht with a bright red hull? It had most likely already been seized by the Kremlin! Polynesia? He'd been an idiot to even conceive of such a romantic fantasy.

No, he would simply evaporate, take himself off the world stage, to reappear only when the time was right. A time when he could recapture his stolen billions and even more! Amass another great fortune with which to build a new army and a new navy and do battle with the world on an epic scale. A new political class that feared, worshiped, and was loyal only to him. Militarily, an officer class that would lick his boots!

For now he needed a place to hide and bide his time. Time to plot every single one of his moves in exquisite detail. Cover every contingency. And slowly gather gold and glory and might back unto his bosom.

When the great warrior was ready, the world would take heed. And then he would strike a mighty blow that would stun the world into submission. He would break the oligarchy's ironfisted hold on the Kremlin. He would have every bloody one of them executed in Red Square! Impaled upon posts to rot in the sun! A little trick he'd picked up from Peter The Great. And he would make Mother Russia whole again, and under *his* restored leadership, ready to vie for *world* leadership once more.

The election of a new American president had given him added hope. Here at last was a strong leader who understood how the world really worked; a businessman who knew the art of negotiation and the need for decisiveness rather than coy evasiveness. Here finally was an opponent driven by hard reality rather than wispy dreams. He had dealt with this man, and he thought he could deal with him now. If not an ally, then at least a kindred spirit.

EVEN THOUGH HIS APPEARANCE HAD changed dramatically, he still dared not take the little local trains for fear of recognition. His thinning blond hair, usually neatly trimmed, had grown long and scruffy. He now, for the first time in his life, had a beard. It had grown in thick and black, peppered with grey. He did not mind that it was filthy, matted with dried food and saliva. It was a badge of honor, that beard.

He was the warrior. He was in the field. His brains and his courage were his only weapons now. But he knew that somehow he would cover himself in glory. And soon.

Nothing else mattered.

CHAPTER FIVE

St. Moritz

A jolt, then a jarring explosion somewhere above their heads. *Close.* Somewhere up on the rear rooftop of the cable car. The stable platform of those inside the tram instantly came unhinged. The floor beneath their feet dropped away—a sickening drop of a foot or two before jerking to a stop as the damaged cable somehow shouldered the shifting weight.

You could hear a pin drop inside. They all held their breath, men, women, and children alike, all fighting to gain control of the panic rising like bile inside them.

The rear cable most surely was severely damaged, barely able to support the weight of the rear of the car. The front cable was all that stood between them and plunging thousands of feet to certain death on the jagged rocks below.

In their guts, they all knew the essential truth of the thing: their very lives were now hanging by a thread, suspended ten thousand feet above the yawning ravine below. A sudden thought, like a runaway train, roared through Hawke's mind. The chasm that was the ravine was rumored to be thousands of feet deep. None of them would ever be seen again!

And then the nightmare began in earnest.

With a loud *twang*, the cable supporting the rear of the gondola snapped in two, cleanly severed. The floor below suddenly became a precarious slide to the bottom, with human beings, backpacks, ski equipment, and everything else plummeting downward.

The bottom had dropped out of the world, this time for good. They waited an eternity for the death plunge that was to be their end. No one dared move . . . nor even breathe nor blink an eye. There was an unheard roar of fervent prayer in the doomed tram, and though no one could hear it, they were all part of the chorus now beseeching their gods . . .

The front cable had held!

The violence of the car's instantaneous upending was particularly horrific for the children. All those formerly at the rear were now trapped at the bottom of the suddenly vertical tramcar. They were crushed and trampled upon and their pleas for help and screams of pain filled the air.

It got worse.

The wind was up, whipping snow off the mountain, particularly gusty at these higher altitudes.

The big tram was now wildly swinging back and forth. Benches ripped, tearing away from the thin aluminum flooring. All was tumult and screams for help. The bodies of the adult passengers who'd been seated at the front, now the top, hurtled downward onto the children's bleeding heads and broken bodies.

Hawke was one of the few lucky ones. Since he'd been seated all the way forward, he didn't have far to fall. And nothing and no one rained down on top of him from above. When he fell, he did have the misfortune of slamming his head into one of the steel benches, rendering him instantly unconscious and bleeding from a deep laceration on the forehead.

When he regained consciousness moments later, he awoke to hell. Or worse. Everyone aboard was crying, praying, or trying to keep their sanity. This was it. This was what they all feared, but what they'd been able to subdue: an image of themselves plummeting thousands of feet to their deaths, hurtling downward while sealed inside an aluminum tube . . .

Until this very moment, when the rocky earth would rush up to meet them . . .

The muffled but still heartrending screams of the terrified children filtered up through the pile of bodies from somewhere far below him. The tortured cries of parents calling out the names of their children, not knowing if they were dead or alive. Or how badly they might be hurt. He called out for his own son: "Alexei! It's Daddy! Can you hear me? Alexei?"

He heard his voice joining the pain-racked chorus. Hearing no reply from the boy despite his repeated shouts, he called Tristan Walker's name repeatedly. Nothing. Could Tristan have been killed? "Tristan! Can you hear me? Tristan? Is my son all right?" he shouted.

"He's injured, sir!" came the faint reply. "I'm doing the best I can! He needs help . . . he needs—"

"Good god, man! Is he conscious? Is he breathing?"

"Breathing, sir. But unconscious and—"

On the closest slopes below, horror gripped the skiers clustered to watch the unfolding drama. The wind was whipping the gondola, like a pennant on a stick, back and forth, and with each new gust, a cry of terror wafted up into the frigid mountain air. The worst part for those skiers below observing the imperiled passengers inside was imagining the poor panic-stricken children.

And then the whoomp-whoomp sound of rotor blades beating the air could be heard. Hearts lifted and people cheered at the sight of a bright red helicopter racing across intensely blue skies toward the upended gondola. Was a rescue even possible? The crowd on the mountain stood and waited, transfixed, as the chopper drew near.

Hawke must have passed out again, longer this time, because when he opened his eyes once more, it was to the sound of wild cheering. What had happened? He lifted his head to get a look out the windows.

His own heart lifted mightily within his chest. He saw a miracle in the making.

A helicopter. A beautiful red and white helicopter! Glory be to god on high! It was hovering just outside the upended tramcar. Red and white were the colors of the Swiss Red Cross. The pilots were clearly getting their bearings, deciding what would be the best way to approach the intended rescue. To begin the extremely dicey, perilous process of evacuating the wounded and panic-stricken passengers without triggering a disaster.

The chopper nosed down. After a momentary hesitation, it angled slowly toward what was now the bottom of the tramcar. Where the children were closest to the exit, Hawke thought, his heart suddenly gladdened. Yes. And Alexei and Tristan had been sitting right next to the sliding doors, near some of the strapping young ski instructors allowed to sit with their charges.

Surely his son had come through unscathed . . .

After the initial joy came a long period of agony in which the Swiss Red Cross rescuers (risking their own lives) searched for a way to pry the damaged pneumatic doors apart. Once this was done, they would then scramble on board and quickly transfer the children to the hovering helo . . . Hawke bent his head to prayer once more, felt himself drifting away . . .

Suddenly a Red Cross corpsman spoke loudly through a megaphone. *The Red Cross man was now inside the car!*

"We are now commencing a Red Cross rescue operation. Everyone, please remain where you are and remain calm. Do not move unless you are told to. Sudden shifts of weight are extremely dangerous! In order to begin transferring all of the children to the helicopter, we will begin with the most seriously wounded boys and girls. A triage. Doctors and trauma nurses are already standing by at the Klinik Gut hospital helipad in St. Moritz, about a ten-minute flight away, and—"

"My daughter just stopped breathing!" a woman cried out. "You must help me! Please, I beg you!"

"Please be patient with us, madam. We need to evacuate everyone as quickly and carefully as possible. Our situation is precarious, so there's no time to waste. But there are trauma medics aboard the choppers and there is plenty of room available in the helicopter. We believe we can transport all of the children in one flight. Be patient. For the adults, numerous Swiss army rescue choppers are airborne now and already headed this way. We will get everyone out. The forward cable appears to be holding steady. Be patient. Pray for us. Pray for all of us."

But in the panic, patience was in very short supply, as opposed to tearful prayers, which were abundant. Hawke cupped his fingers and swiped away the blood pooled around his left eye socket. Then he removed his Alpine climbing shoes and pulled off one of his knee-high socks, tying the sock like a bandanna around his head to stanch the bleeding from his wound.

He began carefully picking and choosing his route downward when his turn to go finally came. He knew those in the forward cabin would be among the last to escape. But he moved ever so slowly along with the other terrified adults as the children were evacuated.

Surely Alexei was already aboard the rescue chopper. Headed for the *Klinik Gut*. And trauma doctors were standing by at the helipad . . . not five minutes away, the man had said.

God help my son.

CHAPTER SIX

Provence

There came then a miracle, or at least so the president of Russia thought.

That very night, events started shifting in his favor. The traveler was passing through a deep valley beneath a starlit sky. The rocks and trees and twisting river all bathed in moonlight blue. He'd been following the slowly flowing river for hours. Keeping to the thickets of trees on its twisting banks . . .

And that's when he suddenly saw flashes of light through the forest ahead. And the scent of smoke was on the air. Yes! The pungent sweet smell of woodsmoke came drifting through the trees. And miracle of miracles, it was coming from a chimney.

And there it was, his miracle, his salvation.

The log cabin stood in the center of a small clearing. It was completely enveloped by deep wood. It was small, with an overhang for a narrow porch facing the river through the trees. On either side of the crude front door were large windows flanked by dark green shutters. And a crooked chimney made of river stones stood on the right side.

He pulled the Makarov 9mm from deep inside his overcoat. He'd never needed it before, and he hoped it wouldn't be necessary now. He shook off the backpack that held his two valises, leaving them at the base of a large tree, and crept closer to the cabin. He paused for a prudent moment, listening for sounds from within. Nothing save the faint melodies of *Rigoletto*, full of static, as if coming from an old LP record. Carefully and silently, he mounted the five weathered wooden steps up to the covered porch. And then, using all the stealth he could muster, he approached the window to the right of the door.

Inside, he saw a room lit only by fire.

There was a big blaze going in the stone hearth, sparks flying about, rising upward inside the chimney.

As to furniture, there was little he could see. In the rear to the left was a small iron bed. Beneath the window where he now stood was a round wooden table laid with pewter plates, goblets, and a bowl containing some kind of bubbling stew. There were only two chairs. The sink and cupboards were at the right rear.

There was an attic of some kind too, because he saw a rope dangling from the ceiling, the kind used to pull down a folding stairway ladder.

In the center of the cabin floor, facing the crackling hearth, was a large old leather wingback chair. Putin could tell that there was a man sitting in it because of the thin plume of pipe smoke rising toward the ceiling.

He kept one hand on the Makarov in his right pocket, grabbed the door handle with his left. He knew before he pushed that it would not be locked. It swung inward quietly, with nary a squeal.

"Hello?" Putin said, stepping inside, his index finger slipping inside the trigger guard on the Makarov. The man stood, his back still turned to the door, head down, gazing into the fire.

Putin, thinking it best to use what little schoolboy French he could muster, said *"Excusez-moi, monsieur. Aidez-moi?"*

Help me.

He hated the sound of his Russian-tinged French accent; his German was perfect—all those years with the KGB in East Berlin. But surely he knew just enough French to get through this encounter.

Without warning, the man whirled around.

When he turned, it was with a double-barreled sawed-off shotgun cradled in his arms, aimed at Putin's head. His voice was the plain-spoken French of the countryside.

"My name is Étienne Dumas. How may I be of service?" the squat little French woodsman said. He had an open face, shoulder-length white hair, and a great white beard that put the Russian president's to shame.

Backlit by the flickering flames of the fire, the man looked like one small ball balanced on top of a great big round ball supported by two pencil-thin sticks.

He wasn't an ogre, Putin, thought. No. His lack of physical beauty was incidental to the innocence shining in those wide blue eyes, gleaming in the firelight.

Putin smiled and said, *"Le fusil de chasse, c'est ne pa nécessaire, mon ami.* I'm not going to hurt you."

"It's not me I'm worried about, monsieur," the woodsman said, lowering his sawed-off shotgun to bear on Putin's mid-section. "It's you. Now. Take your right hand out of your pocket. Put the pistol you're carrying in that pocket on the table. Slowly, everything very slowly."

"Pas de problème, monsieur," Putin said. Calmly he put the gun on the table. This man, though very well armed, just did not seem like someone who might be acquainted with the arts of judo.

"Why are you arrived in my house?" the little Frenchman said, a quizzical cast to his blue eyes.

Putin had rehearsed his speech standing outside at the door.

"I'm in trouble, monsieur. On the run. Some people are chasing me who want to kill me. I've been out in the woods for a long time. I've nowhere left to run."

"You are a criminal?"

"No, no. Not at all. I'm a policeman. Well, former policeman. In Germany—Berlin. These people, they want to kill me. For my money. It's outside. I can show it to you. It's a great deal of money, sir."

"You don't look so rich, monsieur. Beg your pardon. And you don't speak German like a German."

"I don't?"

"No. You speak German like a Russian. And you look like a drowned rat, if I may be so honest."

"Ah, it's true. I am Russian. I'm a sick and cold and hungry Russian. But I used to be rich, believe me. Come, let me show you what's left of my once great wealth."

"Where is it?"

"Out there in the wood. Buried."

"You leave your fortune all alone out there in the wood? No wonder you're so poor."

"You may be surprised."

And so the little Frenchman followed Putin out into the chill of the still night, his sawed-off shotgun still pointed at a man who had been one of the last great emperors of the earth.

CHAPTER SEVEN

St. Moritz

Hawke had heard the word *heartache* used many times before, but he had never experienced it physically. His heart *hurt*. Buried in the center of his chest was a hollowed-out place from which emanated a pain so hot and so bright that it threatened to overpower him. He was sweating profusely and still felt dizzy. His brain was telling him to be calm, that surely Alexei had survived and that he would see his son soon.

But his heart told another story. A story of fear and impending loss of a magnitude that could destroy him. It was only by fervent prayer, putting himself in god's hands, that he could stem the onrushing tide of despair.

He was among the last to leave the crippled tramcar and board the rescue helos. As he finally stepped aboard the Swiss army Super Puma, he felt tremendous relief and grief at the same time. Along the starboard side of the aircraft's wide fuselage lay the most grievously wounded, bodies partially covered with bloody sheets. And some covered completely.

The looks on the faces of the passengers said it all: many of them were clearly in shock. They were huddled on the steel floor and swathed in army green blankets. All these parents had right now was hope.

A corpsman closed the helo doors. The pilots backed off, dipped the nose, and swung to the north, headed for the little village of Tiefenthaler. The big trauma center there was already processing the most seriously wounded adult victims from the first chopper.

A medic directed him to take a seat on the deck, his back right against the bulkhead, and offered him a blanket, kindly draping it around his shoulders.

Hawke looked around, getting his bearings. The interior was nearly windowless, and very dim despite the flickering fixtures mounted up on the overhead. There were bodies stretched out along the far side, two deep against the portside bulkhead. Many were wounded, some grievously, moaning with pain. And some, those with the sheets pulled up over their heads, were dead.

Where was Tristan?

He gazed up at the blood-spattered young medic, a fresh-faced boy who couldn't be more than twenty. He knelt down beside Hawke and began to cleanse the deep wound to his scalp, stitch it, and dress the wound with gauze and bandages.

"It's deep, sir. But clean," he said, very businesslike. "I don't think you've got a concussion. You'll live."

"Well, that's a relief," Hawke said, a very poor attempt at gallows humor that fell flat—as well it should have. "Anything you can do for my heart?"

With a sympathetic glance, the young corpsman said, "Sorry, sir. Try not to worry."

"All the children are safe at the hospital?" he whispered. "Yes?"

"Yes, sir. They are in good hands now, don't worry, sir."

"Was it bad?"

The youth looked away.

"Tell me," Hawke said. "My son was at the rear and—"

"I'm sorry, sir. I cannot say. I just don't have any information."

"But surely you—there are injuries? Among the children, I mean to say."

"Yes."

"Deaths?"

The young man looked down at him with pity. "I really can't say, sir. But I'm sure a great many survived without a scratch. Try not to worry, sir. As soon as you are released from the clinic at Tiefenthaler, you can make your way to Klinik Gut. Transportation has been prearranged for the parents. There you will find your son. In good health, I'll bet."

The kindly young man rose up and moved on to the next injured victim.

An elderly woman began moaning loudly. Her head swathed in bandages and clearly disconsolate, she was seated right next to him. She was whispering a name as she rocked back and forth on her haunches.

He put a gentle hand on her shoulder. "We're all right now. We're all right. Safe."

She shook violently, shaking her head back and forth.

"Please, try not to worry," Hawke said. "You're going to make it."

"Ingo!" she suddenly cried out, extending her right hand and pointing at a sheet-covered victim on the floor not ten feet away. "My darling husband . . . he . . . he's not breathing!"

"I'm so sorry," he said.

Hawke withdrew inside himself for the balance of the flight. Desperate for anything to soothe his misery, he let the throbbing of the helicopter's powerful engines and the sound of the rotors beating against the wind lull him into a state of mild hypnosis. It was a trick former Royal Navy fighter pilots had learned long ago whilst being medevacked with grievous injuries across great distances inside Royal Navy rescue choppers.

Someone was calling his name . . .

He had no idea how much time had elapsed since he'd closed his eyes. A minute? Ten? Had he been dreaming? He opened his eyes and looked around at the familiar scene.

A voice. A strained, gravelly voice, but still a voice *he knew.*

Intruding into his space. Someone repeating the same thing again and again . . . croaking as if barely able to speak.

"Commander Hawke . . . Lord . . . Hawke . . ." It was just loud enough to be heard above the din of the rotors inside the aircraft. Hawke craned his neck left, then right, searching for the source.

Tristan.

"Where are you, for god's sake, Tristan?"

"Portside bulkhead. Opposite and aft of your position, sir. I can't move."

"Hold on, don't try. Don't speak. I'll come to you," Hawke said.

He got to his feet and made his way to the rear of the gloomy bay, stooping to peer into the faces of the victims seated along the portside bulkhead. A pair of pain-ridden blue eyes looked up at him, pleading for recognition.

Hawke dropped to one knee beside the man. The Scotland Yard man's lacerated and bandaged face was barely visible above the edge of the sheet that covered his body. He was sitting, shivering with the cold, with his back against the bulkhead, his long legs stretched out in front of him.

"Tristan," Hawke said, nearly overcome with emotion. He reached under the sheet, found the man's hand, and squeezed it. "My god, it's Tristan, isn't it?"

"Yes, m'lord," he croaked.

"C'mon, Tristan, you know we don't use that title around here." Hawke smiled at him. It was his lordship's standing practice that he allowed no one save his aged valet, Pelham Grenville, to use his title, under any circumstance. He chalked it up to his firm belief, held since childhood, that he was far prouder of his pirate ancestry than of all of his aristocratic forebears.

Tristan smiled through his pain.

"Sorry, sir. I heard your voice. But I wasn't sure. I can't move, you see. My leg."

"Tell me."

"Fractured. Left one. Femur. Hurts like a bitch, sir, pardon my French."

"We should be on the ground soon. I'll get you morphed up."

"Thank you, sir."

"Tristan. Tell me. Is Alexei . . . is my son all right? He wasn't badly hurt, was he?"

"I'm so sorry, sir. You see, I was knocked unconscious when the bottom dropped out of the gondola. Landed on my head. When I finally regained consciousness, all of the children had already been . . . uh . . . evacuated. I never saw him subsequent to the moment the cable snapped, sir, I'm sorry. I'm quite sure he's all right, and . . ."

The man was plainly exhausted.

"Get some rest, Tristan. We'll land at the hospital soon. Just tell me one thing. Before the explosion, I mean when last you did see him, where was he located?"

"He was with his friends, not three feet away from the rear entry door, m'lord. He would have been one of the very first out, sir, I promise you."

"Albeit, at the very bottom of the heap," Hawke said quietly, his eyes drifting away.

"I'm sorry, sir."

"Thank you, Tristan. Get some rest. I'll see you on the ground. Soon as I've collected Alexei, I'll come straight round to see you. So. You've got your mobile? Call your family, tell them what happened. I'm sure this is all over the telly by now. Tell them you're alive."

"I will, sir. Thank you very much indeed. You'll call me when you see Alexei?"

"I will indeed," Hawke managed to get out.

Chapter Eight

Provence

"You like it, this little dish?" a smiling Étienne said to Putin, ladling another spoonful of the pungent stew into his pewter bowl.

The Frenchman filled both their goblets with good local claret and smiled. It promised to be an evening full of good talk, good wine, and good food. Étienne lived a solitary life, so nights like this were few and far between. He was relishing the company of the wayward policeman.

Darkness had come to the valley. The wind was rising. Cold, it had a bite that pinched your fingers if you stood outside too long. The two men were seated at the small, rough-hewn wooden table, now pulled closer to the warmth of the fire.

The little fellow had made a big fuss over his honored guest, setting the table with polished pewter tableware, cotton serviettes, and his best wine goblets. Even a loaf of warm bread fresh from the oven and a flickering candle for the table. The wind had picked up even more, whispering around the house and up under the eaves, where stark branches clawed at the windowpanes.

It was distinctly cozy here in the warmth of this room, Putin thought, with a shiver of pleasure. He felt better here in this tiny cabin, more comfortable and happier than he'd felt for all his years of exorbitant luxury. The yachts; Hôtel du Cap; his many glorious palaces; the mammoth bed aboard his plane, where he'd dallied with Kat, which was now nothing but burned rubble.

The modest attic bedroom above his head was all he wanted. More importantly, it was all he *needed*.

A lot of it was Étienne. The jolly fellow's good cheer, humor, and relaxed demeanor were a welcome contrast to the last few years trapped in the hell his enemies had made of the Kremlin. "Delicious stew," Putin said, "What is it?"

"Mutton," the Frenchman said. "My sainted mother's ancient recipe for mutton stew. Potatoes, parsnips, onions, garlic. Lots of tamarind. Good for you. Get your stamina back up."

"Another glass of that good red would be nice, too."

"I'm so glad you like it. I steal it from a vineyard a few miles from here."

"Ah, stolen wine is always best, you know. Like stolen women?"

Étienne laughed, filled his goblet, and said, "So, Volodya, I wonder—what does Volodya mean, anyway?"

"It's a nickname for Vladimir. Very common Russian name. A diminutive, you see, more friendly than the full name."

"Hmm. At any rate, Volodya, what I was wondering is what are your plans? Where are you headed next? Not that you're not welcome here, of course. I'm just a little curious, you see."

Putin smiled. "Thank you. Well, south, I think. I don't really know, Étienne. No place is safe anymore. Just keep moving until I find somewhere else to hide, I guess, is the only thing for me to do."

"Not necessarily."

"What do you mean?"

"So, why not stay here with me for a spell? You see that ladder pull? As I say, there's a small attic bedroom up there. I made it for my daughter, Sophie, many years ago. The room has very cheery wallpaper with flowers and a small four-poster bed. And a small window that floods the room with morning sunlight. Sophie doesn't come much anymore . . . she has a good job, and a lover, in Paris."

"Very kind of you, Étienne, but I couldn't do that to you—take advantage of your generosity."

"Oh, it's nothing to do with kindness, Volodya. And everything to do with loneliness. I would welcome your company, my friend. And, I could use your help with my logging. You look like a fellow who could swing an axe if you wanted to."

"Are you quite serious?"

"I am. You'll stay the night, of course. See how you like it here. We can just play it by ear, as the British say. Does that sound good?"

"Only if you let me pay for my room and board."

"I can't let you do that, Monsieur Volodya. You are an honored guest beneath this leaky roof."

"Well, as you wish. But when I depart, I want to make a small donation to the cause."

"We'll see, we'll see. Now, you're tired. Let me get the ladder down . . . and please take that candle with you. It goes on the table by the bed."

"You really have no idea who I am, do you, Étienne?"

"Of course. You are Volodya, a Russian policeman from Berlin who looks like he could use a shave and a haircut and some sleep in a real bed. Go on, up you go! There's an extra blanket and more candles in the cupboard if you need it!"

And so to bed.

PUTIN LAY FOR AN HOUR, hands behind his head, staring up at the flickering candlelight on the ceiling, celebrating his good fortune. He had begun to think of himself as a Napoleonic figure, like the great hero forced into exile on the little Mediterranean isle of Elba. Well, a woodsman's cabin would be his Elba. Etienne would be his Tallyrand.

And Moscow would be his Paris.

He smiled, rolled over, and blew out the candle.

Here at last he could live for a brief time in peace and serenity. Here he would begin to plot his magnificent return to Moscow. First, he would build a secret army of loyalists. He could begin now to envision a future day, one just as joyous as Napoleon's triumphant entry into Paris in 1815 had been. Once there, once he had regained the trust of his people, acquired legions of supporters and ranking military officers . . . and seized power once more.

"I shall ascend to the throne," he whispered to himself in the dim moonlight. "I shall ascend to the throne! As for those bastards who stole it from me, I shall do no less than reinstitute the guillotine in Red Square!" For the worst of them, nothing less than impalement.

"Ha!"

The fantasy of oligarchs' heads rolling into baskets was a good one to fall asleep with. But he had one more thing to do before he slept. He lay still for a moment, listening in the dark. He could hear the rhythmic snoring of his new friend below. He slipped from his bed, opened his backpack, and carefully removed the emergency satellite telephone, the smallest, but most sophisticated one there was, lightweight, yet encrypted and very powerful.

As he tapped in the number, his hand began to tremble. The number belonged to the one man who now held his fate in his hands. He was literally the only man left on the planet who could possibly save him from disgrace and dishonor and death. Not only save him but help him return to power and glory. He had been Putin's right hand a few years ago, a man he'd trusted with his life. But in the end, his own right hand had betrayed him.

His name was Joseph Stalingrad. A historic figure he bore an uncanny resemblance to. But to millions of Russians, he was the infamous Uncle Joe, the president's trusted hatchetman. And he now lived in, of all places, Hollywood, California.

And, Putin had heard, despite Joe's resemblance to an infamous mass murderer and his vertically challenged stature, the former actor had become something of a movie star.

CHAPTER NINE

Three years ago, Putin had been locked in a death struggle with a British spy named Alex Hawke—his sometime MI6 friend turned nemesis. Hawke was then trying to put an end to Putin's land grab in the Baltics. Near the end, Putin had the upper hand. He had Hawke and the famous detective Congreve and their men trapped inside a secret KGB compound in Siberia.

There was no way out.

Putin's men were moving in for the kill.

And then this funny little man known as Uncle Joe, short, round, and terribly pockmarked, like his namesake, had switched his allegiance to a foreign flag. He had called in two Russian army helicopters. The choppers were there in moments to ferry not only Ambrose and Alex and their men, but Joe himself beyond the Russian borders and Putin's reach to safety.

Treason. Of the worst kind. But times changed.

Putin could hear the call going through, then the memorably gruff and raspy voice of Uncle Joe on the other end of the line.

"Hello?" the voice said.

"Hello, Joe Stalingrad. This is the president," Putin said, reverting to Russian.

Silence.

"Who?"

"The president, Joe. Remember me?"

"The president of *what*?"

"For crissakes, the president of *Russia*. Joe, this is President Vladimir Putin and I need your help."

"You're dead, Mr. President. Haven't you heard?"

"So they say. You were very disloyal, Joe. And rude. Do you remember? You left Russia without saying good-bye. You and that fucking turncoat Alex Hawke, of all people. The man who betrayed my friendship and turned on me in my hour of greatest need."

"Leader, I beg to differ. I must tell you something about this man Hawke. I came to know him. He is a great man, and one with a deep sense of honor and the desire to do what is right. He thinks very highly of you. He told me so, more than once. He still holds you in the highest esteem, to tell you the truth. He still remembers the night you saved his life. Saved him from a horrible execution in Energetika prison and—"

"Then why did he turn on me? Betray our friendship? His son was born in Lubyanka prison, for god's sake! Were it not for me, they would have smashed the infant's head against the wall within seconds of his birth."

Joe said, "He is well aware of that and deeply grateful. But, in those hours when we were trapped within the KGB compound in Siberia, we spoke deep into the night about other things, the coming war with the West. It was Hawke's sense, his absolute *conviction*, that you completely underestimated the Americans. Yes, their president was weak. But their military was not. He was certain that U.S. and UK allied forces would crush us in very short order. He actually saw himself as a loyal friend, coming to your aid."

"Did he, now?"

"So when he asked to see you privately, it was in his heart to help you avoid catastrophe. Because of his friendship with you, to try to make you understand that you were about to make a tragic mistake.

Literally putting yourself and all of Russia at existential risk. He knew he might not come back alive. But he kept saying, 'Volodya and I are friends, Joe. Surely he will see that I'm only there to help him. Save him from disaster.' "

Putin held his tongue, letting his brain process all that he was hearing. Then he said, "Look here. There may be some truth in what you say. He is one of the world's great warriors. A man I still hold in high esteem. But you? You helped an enemy of the state escape. It's called treason. Death sentence. I've had KGB watching your every move for the last few years. I read the surveillance reports. You're living the high life in Hollywood, Joe, but I've got men out there who want to kill you for your treatment of their president. But so far I've stayed their hands. Why? Why would I do that, Joe?"

"I don't know. To be honest with you, I thought I'd surely be dead by now."

"After what you did to me, you should be rotting at the bottom of the Hole at Lubyanka. I'm only on this call because I have no other options. Make no mistake. I admire your gifts, and I despise your disloyalty. But desperate times call for desperate measures."

"Why me? Why now?"

"Because, Joe, we understand each other. We worked very closely together for a long time. Your Kremlin office was next door to mine. God only knows how many plots against my life you thwarted. You're a master of logistics. You finish my sentences, you're a natural politician. You know how I think and anticipate how I like things done. And you get those things done. Never a hiccup. Are you perfect? No. I've kept you alive because I always knew there might come a time when I'd need you. That time is right now."

"I understand, sir. Thank you, thank you. Thank you so much for your confidence. Trust me now and I swear I'll never let you down again. Tell me how I can help."

"All right, listen. I assume you have a bank in Los Angeles."

"I do. Wells Fargo."

"Give me your wiring instructions."

"Gladly," Uncle Joe said, and gave him the account routing numbers.

"In the next few days, you'll be receiving a wire transfer from a bank in Switzerland. Five hundred thousand dollars will hit your account. This will cover expenses, as well as the first part of your operation."

"Thank you, Mr. President."

"First move, you book a first-class flight from LAX to Zurich. Once there, you will check into the Baur au Lac Hotel. I have very few people I trust anymore, but the owner there is an old friend and he will discreetly help you with whatever you need. I will call him and tell him about you. He'll provide you with a suite on the lake and a car and driver during your stay. Am I clear so far?"

"Perfectly, Mr. President."

"Your new base will be Zurich. To that end, I have acquired a residential property for you. An island villa called Seegarten. Right on Lake Zurich. There is staff on duty. There is a large dock with many boats, and lovely gardens. Believe me, were it not for the fact that you'll be sharing the villa with a very important visitor, I would not be so extravagant."

"A visitor? May I ask whom? Female, one hopes."

"No. You will learn later. The entire property is surrounded by a high stone wall. This is to protect our visitor from prying eyes. The property will be patrolled day and night by dogs and armed guards."

"I understand."

"Do you, Joe? Perhaps. At any rate, there is another man I trust in Zurich. I'm sure you recall my old friend, Dr. Steinhauser? He's called the Sorcerer. We dealt with him during our efforts to remove some of the gold from Queen Elizabeth's Swiss bank accounts, remember?"

"Oh, yes, guy's a world-class financial genius. He and I got along."

"Just so. You need to go see him. He doesn't know it yet, but I'm going to be acquiring his home in the Alps. He tells me he's tired of the splendid isolation and wants to live out his days in a villa in the

South of France. As soon as he vacates, I shall move in. As will you yourself and the important visitor. Understood?"

"This house is in Zurich?"

"It's a mountain house. Literally, built inside a mountain in secret by Albert Speer and the Nazis. It was to be Hitler's Swiss residence after he'd conquered all of Europe. I'll make arrangements for you to call on Dr. Steinhauser in person to discuss the purchase. Bit tricky getting inside, as the main entrance to his home is a broad shelf at fifteen thousand feet on the side of a mountain. There is another, more secret entrance, but it may be closed now. Tell my old friend that I've decided I definitely want the property. But you will tell him also that I will go no higher than five hundred million U.S. dollars."

"Half a billion? For a house? Boss, you've got to be kidding me. Even for you, that's—"

"Joe, listen. I told you it was a mountain house. And that's what it is. This house is located at twenty-one thousand feet above sea level, and is usually covered with ice and snow most of the year. Do you understand me?"

"His house *is* a mountain, is what you're telling me. He lives inside a goddamn mountain?"

"Precisely. And not just any mountain, either. It's fucking Fortress Switzerland. The mountain is called White Death, because of all the men who've died there during ascents. And that is where I shall reign supreme in total secrecy: White Death will be my new address.

The president paused and then continued.

"Sorcerer's Mountain shall be the new mini-Kremlin. A bastion, one in which I shall devise my strategy for a glorious return to power in Russia. Where you and I and my new generals and admirals will lay the groundwork for our epic heroic return to Moscow. And re-assert Mother Russia's rightful place on the world's stage.

"It will be my new Kremlin in exile, the place from which I will wage war on my enemies of the state. Do you understand my vision, Joe? Do you?"

"I not only understand it, I fucking share it, Mr. President. I'm excited by this opportunity. You can count on me, sir. What else can I do?"

"When all is in readiness, when it is time for us all to move into the mountain lair, you will need to come get me."

"Where are you?"

"In the Provence region of France. Near the town of Aix-en-Provence. In a cabin in the woods. I'm very comfortable here, so don't feel it's urgent. Only when all the pieces of this massive puzzle are assembled will I come out of hiding. I want the world to continue to believe I am dead. Besides, I like being dead."

"Yeah? Why is that?"

"Nobody fucks with you anymore."

"That's a good one, boss. How shall I come for you when you're ready to make the move?"

"I want you to buy a car in Zurich. An SUV. Nothing too fancy or conspicuous. A medium-priced Mercedes will do. But with the big engine, four-wheel drive, and total blackout windows, understand? You know how to acquire diplomatic plates, so that, too. You'll take the back roads to Provence and you'll not exceed the posted speed limits. Understood? There is a sizable village near my location. There you will hire a chopper. Once that is done, you can sell the car. Understood?"

"Totally."

"We will then fly straight through from Provence to Switzerland. To the Sorcerer's Mountain in the dead of night. Once we have established ourselves there, I shall not set foot outside again for the duration. You will be my eyes and ears out in the real world. You will make sure I have everything that I need from the outside world. You will be my second-in-command and will execute any and all of my orders with full faith and fidelity. You see, I'm putting my faith in you once more, Joe, and you will be rewarded beyond your wildest dreams. But I warn you, failure is punishable by death. Am I clear?"

"Hundred percent, boss, hundred percent. Unlike you, I don't think I'd like being dead all that much."

"You'll be hearing from me, Joe."

"One thing before you go, sir. When you throw out a figure like, oh, 'beyond your wildest dreams,' what are we talking? I mean, you know, just talking round figures, you know, ballpark numbers is what I'm saying . . . hello? . . . Hello? Mr. President?"

Click.

CHAPTER TEN

St. Moritz

The big chopper hovered, then settled. The skids touched down soundlessly, dead center on the big red *H* painted on Tiefenthaler hospital's rooftop helipad.

"Please remain seated until we've shut down the engine and the rotor has stopped," the pilot said over the PA system.

Hawke instantly rose to his feet and made his way aft to where his son's guardian was seated. Tristan smiled up at him.

"Can't get up, sir."

"Yes, you can. Put your left arm around my neck. Let's get you to your feet, old soldier."

"Yes, sir."

It took a little effort, but Hawke was able to help Tristan to stand on the first try. With his strong right arm around the wounded man's waist, Hawke was able to get him forward to the wide-open exit bay. First out, first served. Tristan's injuries were far more severe than his own, but he was in an agony of despair, desperate to return to St. Moritz and find his son.

Nurses were waiting outside on the helipad with gurneys rigged with IVs. Hawke got Tristan to the nearest one and the nurses quickly whisked him away. "I'll be back, Tristan," he called after him. "Alexei and I will be back here to see you before you know it."

Hawke used the stairs to reach the ground floor and hurried to the exit. He pushed open the door and was greeted with a blast of frigid air.

It had begun to snow again, heavily. There was a line of black Mercedes SUVs idling nearby, waiting just outside the entrance of the emergency room.

He went to the closest one and addressed the driver behind the wheel. "Any room left?"

"Six in the back, just one seat left. Right up front, sir."

Hawke climbed inside, taking the seat right next to the driver. He buckled up, and the driver pulled away from the curb.

"How long a drive from here back to the Klinik Gut?" he asked the portly red-faced fellow at the wheel.

"In this weather? And traffic? Half an hour, sir. Perhaps closer to an hour if we don't get lucky."

"My son is there, you see . . . and—"

The driver gave him a look of compassion. "Look. We are all in the same boat here, sir. I will do my best to get all of you there as quickly and safely as possible."

"Thank you," Hawke said, feeling as if he was on the verge of a panic attack. He sat back and tried to calm himself. Patience was not a trait that came easily, but he made an extraordinary effort. He knew the men and women seated behind him in the van were just as frightened and anxious as he himself was.

He turned around and spoke to a woman seated directly behind him. She was weeping softly into her handkerchief.

"I'm sorry. But have you heard anything at all?" he asked her. "Any word on the children? Anything coming from the hospital? I lost my mobile in the chaos on the tram."

"My husband has been trying to get through," the woman said sympathetically. "The hospital lines are jammed. But the accident is on the news. Reporting only that there were injuries and deaths when the cable gave way. But no specific information or numbers. I'm so sorry. How old is your child?"

"My son is seven years old. He's all I have."

"I'm sure he's fine. Try not to worry."

The drive south to St. Moritz, normally half an hour's journey, took two hours. All courtesy of a jackknifed lorry blocking three lanes. Whiteout conditions prevailed and the road conditions were treacherous.

But Alex Hawke, who had been dealing with nervous anxiety for the last six months—hell, for most of his life—had found a new way to deal with the delay and distress, and he resorted to it now. Talking privately with his god, and beseeching him for the protection of his one and only child.

THE MERCEDES FINALLY MANAGED THE exit for St. Moritz. Twenty minutes later, the driver rolled up the broad sweeping drive to the hospital. Hawke leapt out instantly and ran up the wide snow-covered steps to the trauma center's emergency room. He dashed inside and made straight for the nurse busy taking questions from behind the information desk.

He waited patiently in the queue for the parents and relatives who'd arrived ahead of him, finally coming face-to-face with a pleasant-looking white-haired nurse of about sixty. Her tired and reddened blue eyes told him that she had already seen far too much suffering and tragedy this day.

He pulled out his UK diplomatic passport and placed it on the counter in front of her.

"Good day. My name is Hawke. Is this where the, uh, all the children from the gondola are being treated? My son was aboard, you see, and I must find him immediately. Do you have a list of those admitted? Of the children? I need to know where he—"

"Don't worry. You've come to the right place, mister—uh, sorry, is it Lord Hawke?"

"It is."

"The trauma center and pediatric wing are both on the top floor of this building, right next to the ICU, and—"

"Yes, yes. Do you have a list? Of those who were admitted?"

"They were not admitted to the ER, sir. The children were all taken directly from the rescue helicopter to the trauma center. It's located one flight down from the rooftop helipad. That's where they were all admitted earlier this morning."

"Ah, yes, of course. Thank you so much. Were any children admitted to other hospitals?"

"No, no. All here. The injured children are in surgery, intensive care, or the pediatric ward. All of them are being treated for shock. The clinic's chief of staff has ordered that all those admitted remain hospitalized for overnight observation and—"

"For how . . . I'm sorry . . . for how long?"

"Twenty-four hours, Mr. Hawke. Those who are able will all be released at nine A.M. tomorrow. Now, if you have no further—"

"So sorry. Thanks for your help," Hawke said, and sprinted across the wide lobby for the elevators.

CHAPTER ELEVEN

Los Angeles

Hollywood had been good to Uncle Joe.

But then again, he'd been good to Hollywood, hadn't he? He had a nice little bachelor pad just off Melrose where he entertained all the ladies, of whom there were more than a few. He'd earned himself quite a nickname among the women in his circle. They called him Playstation—for anatomical reasons, of course. And these were serious ladies. Ladies who if not all bold-faced names, were at the very least bold-faced liars.

Playstation had a car, the first one he'd ever owned. He loved it. He loved it with a passion he usually reserved for the bedroom. He sometimes went down to the garage just to stare at it. Rub its curves. It was the kind of car Americans sometimes called a chick magnet. It was a 1965 turquoise Corvette convertible with eighty thousand miles on the odometer. It ran a little rough, but it was still a Corvette. He called it the Getaway Car.

He had a cat too, the first one since he lived in the West Village five years ago in New York. Before his acting career had taken off. She was a Maine coon called Ninotchka, little darling.

He also had a job. A couple of them, in fact. One, he'd fast-talked his way into CAA, the most powerful talent agency in town. He started where they all started, in the mailroom. The personnel director had asked him why in the world she should hire him. He was almost forty years old, for god's sakes. "There are thirty people in here already and a zillion or two more out there banging on the door. What's so special about you, Joseph? And aren't you a little old for this job?"

Uh, I used to be Vladimir Putin's right-hand man at the Kremlin. Is that special enough for you, bitch? he thought but didn't say. Instead, he said, "Look, doll, I'm a very smart guy. I know I look older, but I'm still in my thirties. I can learn everything there is to know about being an agent in ninety days. I don't? I give you back every penny you paid me." She was laughing so hard, she probably doesn't even remember hiring him.

He figured out fast how to shake up the mailroom, get attention. The young dudes, the fancy pants East Coast grad students and the other guys, they came in at the crack of nine. Joe came in at seven. They'd leave at six, he'd leave at ten. He worked his butt off, reading every script that came his way. Volunteered for everything and was very, very, almost scarily aggressive.

He loved it there. When he wasn't there, he actually missed that old mailroom. That's why he wasn't all that excited about going back to Moscow or Switzerland or wherever the hell this gig with Putin would take him. But the half million upfront in expense money? And lots more where that came from?

Fuhgeddaboudit.

His other job, part-time, was movie star. Stage name: Joe Stalingrad. Well, maybe *star* is a bit of a stretch. Because of his CAA connections, he met producers, directors, casting directors, and even a smattering of stars. Jim Carrey is still a star, right? Right? So, early days, he got crowd scenes, walk-ons, and then bits in films like *Bitch on Wheels* and *Beverly Hills Butcher 3*. The bits just kept on coming, and pretty soon he was a featured player in the indie *Too Hot to Sleep*. It was a noir detective story set in the Florida Keys, sort of like a *Body Heat* meets *Key Largo* kind of thing.

His character, Cody Lazarus, was a two-bit Jewish mobster hauling product up from Havana aboard his rust-bucket trawler, the *Cindy Lou*. His death scene at sea in a hurricane at the finale was not exactly a vintage Bogart, *Key Largo*–type performance, but it wasn't chopped liver, either.

One reviewer on Rotten Tomatoes had him down as "Maybe the new Peter Lorre?" Deadline Hollywood crowed, "Stalingrad the new Danny DeVito?" Not bad company. Oh, and commercials up the wazoo after the movie. Last one was a McDonald's spot he'd shot out in Orange County. He played the manager, standing atop the counter and singing to the crew about his new secret sauce.

Now, where were the keys to his Vette? He was late. Today was the day he planned to visit his Wells Fargo branch on La Cienega Boulevard and set up the wire transfer from Zurich. He took the elevator down to the garage and hopped in the Vette. It had the 327-cubic-inch engine with the supercharger. Badass. He fired her up, startling citizens a block away, and burned rubber as he cranked the wheel of the Getaway Car and rumbled out onto Melrose.

Driving over, he smiled in anticipation of seeing the look in the eyes of the nitwit manager who ran the bank. That pillar of the L.A. banking community, Mr. Larry "Buttwipe" Krynsky.

"LARRY KRYNSKY STILL WORK HERE?" he said, a little too loudly to the babe at the reception desk. "You know, the white-collar criminal?"

"Well, well, well, if it isn't Joe Stalingrad, the semi-famous movie star," Larry said, grabbing his elbow and ushering him into his dipshit cubicle of an office. Larry had a big fake oil painting on the wall behind his desk, looked like a paint-by-numbers project one of his kids had done—picture of Lake Tahoe at sunset. Big whoop. This pussified manager, this Krynsky guy, was officially a member of Joe's Hall of Fame of Flaming Assholes. Man kept his butt where his face used to be.

Joe lit a cigarette, propped his Guccis up on Larry's cheesy faux wood desk, and said, "Hey, J. P. Morgan, how high up you have to be in this company to have air conditioning in your office? Or an ashtray? Seriously."

Larry sat back and forced a smile. "Hey, movie star. How's your long-awaited movie deal coming along? Universal green light that epic yet?"

"You mean *Uncle Joe and the Donald*? The Paramount picture starring yours truly as the evil dwarf Stalin and Alec Baldwin as the president? That one? The picture Deadline Hollywood says has the makings of this summer's number one comedy? That one, Larry, you dumb fuck?"

"Yeah, that one. When *are* they gonna green-light it? Never? Is never good for you?"

"Does the phrase *Go fuck yourself* have any resonance for you, Larry? Any at all?"

"What can I do for you, Joe?"

"Wanna arrange for a wire transfer of some funds owed to me."

"All righty, and where are these funds coming from?"

"My bank in Zurich."

"Your bank in Zurich. Right. Now, that's funny! Didn't know you had a bank in Zurich."

"That's what I said."

"And which bank might that be?"

"That bank might be UBS."

"UBS."

"Right. But it isn't. It's Credit Suisse."

"Roger that."

"Don't say *roger that*, Larry. It's such a douchebag Tom Clancy cliché."

"All right. And how much money are we talking about here, Mr. Joe Stalingrad, aka, Playstation, future A-list actor? A thousand? Five thousand?"

"We're talking a half mill."

"Half a million dollars?"

"Kee-rect. I'm doing some renovations at my apartment and I need a little extra cash, if you know what I mean. New fridge in the kitchen, new toaster. Redo the laundry room. Washer, dryer. Stuff like that. A makeover."

"Is this a joke, Joe? Because if it is, I don't have time to—"

Joe slid the Credit Suisse routing information and wiring instructions across Larry's desk. "Does that look like a joke to you, Larry?"

Larry scoped it out, his eyes bulging. "No. No it does not."

"When can I expect the funds to hit my account?"

"Usually, overseas, let's say twenty-four hours?"

Joe stood up. "Must be great sitting in here all day, Larry. Looking out on the lobby and all. All the fake plants and crap artwork. Not to even mention that redheaded teller over there, the one with the super-huge tits you told me you were fucking. Mr. Larry Krynsky, vice-president of all you survey. See you around sometime, loser."

Joe walked out onto busy La Cienega and headed to the lot where he'd stowed the Getaway Car, the smile on his face a mile wide.

Game on, motherfuckers.

CHAPTER TWELVE

St. Moritz

Reaching the hospital's top floor, Hawke immediately spied a sign that read ADMISSIONS mounted over a wide arched corridor tiled in hospital green. Just inside the arch was a table where two pretty young nurses in white were busy at their computer keyboards.

"May I?" Hawke said, taking a seat on one of the two wooden chairs.

"May I help you?" his nurse said, offering him a warm smile.

"Yes."

Hawke pulled two passports from the inside pocket of his jacket and said, "Yes, you can. My name is Alexander Hawke. British citizen, as you can see, but currently living in Switzerland as an official representative of Her Majesty the Queen regarding some financial matters."

"What can I do for you, your lordship?" the younger one said, looking at his passport. Sometimes having *Lord* in front of your name didn't hurt.

He picked up the second passport and handed it to the nurse. "And this is my son, Alexei. Age seven. We were both aboard the gondola this morning. He is a member of the ski school, his class is called the Donald Ducks or something like that. There were twenty-five of them on the gondola. So can you direct me to wherever he is? The pediatric ward, most likely and—"

"Lord Hawke, it's understandable that you are upset and anxious. But let me assure you that all of the children who survived are receiving the best care possible under the circumstances. Now, if you'll just be patient, I'll try to locate Alexei's admission paperwork . . ."

"Survived."

"I'm sorry?"

"You said the children who survived. Is that correct?"

"Yes."

"How many . . . uh, sorry . . . how many didn't make it?"

"Two of the twenty-five children aboard the Silver Arrow gondola died of their injuries en route to the trauma center."

"I see. How unspeakably sad."

"Indeed."

"And . . . have the parents been notified of the loss of their children?"

"I cannot provide that information, Lord Hawke. I'm very sorry."

"Please tell me that my son was not one of the fatalities. Please tell me that. You've got to do that for me. I'm going insane . . ."

"I'll see what I can do. I need a word with the head of admissions. She's just down the hall. Can you excuse me for a few minutes?"

"Thank you," Hawke said. "Thank you very much indeed."

"May I have your son's passport? His picture could be helpful."

"Yes. Yes, of course you can."

He handed it to her as she got up from the chair. He knew he was on the verge of tears and fought them back.

Suddenly she was back at her desk, speaking to him in a soft voice. "Lord Hawke? Are you listening?"

"What?"

"Do I have your full attention?"

"Yes. Yes, of course. I'm sorry. What were you saying?"

"I was saying that, unfortunately, I am forbidden by hospital policy from giving you any information regarding the disposition of parent notifications of the deceased or seriously injured. I'm sorry."

Hawke lowered his head. "I understand."

"Lord Hawke, if I may speak to you in the strictest confidence, there is one thing I can tell you that may help . . ."

"Yes?"

"Lord Hawke, the two deceased children were both little girls. Twins, as a matter of fact. Age six."

"My god."

"There's something else, sir. I'm afraid we can find no record of an Alexei Alexandrovich Hawke being admitted to this hospital."

"Of course he was admitted!" Hawke leaned forward, aware that he was raising his voice.

"You say there were twenty-five children aboard your gondola? The Silver Arrow?"

"That's correct. Twenty-five. The instructor made each of them count off after the doors closed. I heard them! I heard my son's voice call out 'Nine!' I heard him. 'Nine, sir!' he cried out!"

"I'm terribly sorry, Lord Hawke. But only twenty-four children disembarked from the rescue helicopter up on the roof. And only twenty-four children were admitted. We have no record at all of your son."

"But he has to be here! For god's sake, look at his picture! He's here!"

"I showed his picture to all of the admitting staff, sir. No one recalls seeing this boy or taking his information. I'm very, very sorry. I don't know what more we can do—"

"There's got to be some mistake. I'm going to walk through the pediatric ward, look for him there and—"

"No one save staff is allowed to do that."

"I pity the man who tries to stop me."

"Besides, there are some children in intensive care and some still undergoing surgery. There is no Alexei Hawke in either place. I don't know what more we can do."

"Where is he, then? Maybe he wandered off after getting off the helicopter. Maybe he was dazed and just wandered off, a concussion perhaps . . . Isn't that a possibility?"

"Lord Hawke, I understand how difficult this must be for you. I will make an exception. You are free to search the other floors and the grounds of the hospital. That's really all I can offer. I have to tend to my patients. I wish you all the luck in the world. I'm sure you'll find him. He's got to be somewhere. It was rather chaotic up on that helipad. Perhaps he really did just wander off into the streets . . ."

"No. My son is gone, do you understand me?" Hawke said. "Someone has taken him."

CHAPTER THIRTEEN

The Cotswolds

After a quiet supper with his wife, Lady Diana Mars, Chief Inspector Ambrose Congreve repaired to his small study. Up on the second floor, his refuge was located in the oldest wing of Brixden House, the great manor house above the Thames that once belonged to the Astors.

On a chill night like tonight, during these frigid wintry months, there was always a cheerful fire, dry pinewood crackling in the low stone fireplace. The book-lined room was redolent of beeswax and old leather books, spilt whiskey on ancient woolen carpets, and whiffs of woodsmoke from fires long gone cold.

"The smell of pine—god, how I do love it!" the chief inspector said to himself, sniffing the air. Deeply satisfied, he settled blissfully down into the worn leather armchair situated behind the walnut desk. His dear friend Pelham, a man not given to polysyllabic turns of phrase, had once surprised him by saying of the room that he "admired the catholicity" of his library. Meaning, of course, its breadth and general inclusiveness, not its religions orientation.

He got the old churchwarden briar pipe going, expelling great plumes of blue smoke, and dove back into his beloved Holmes. This small room was the favorite of the passionate Sherlockian, an eminent student of all things Holmes. His library housed, among its many treasures, not only his leather-bound collections of Dickens, John Buchan, Eric Ambler, Dorothy L. Sayers, Zane Gray, Rex Stout, and C. S. Forester, but the first complete collection of Conan Doyle bound in red leather! And a considerable collection of Sherlockian memorabilia.

Tonight, Congreve was diving once more into Conan Doyle's *Hound of the Baskervilles*, turning its pages for what was perhaps the eleventh time. A rare Morocco-bound edition, it was one of his priceless treasures . . . let's see, where were we? Oh, yes, here we are . . .

That merciless fiend, Sir Hugo Baskerville, was pursuing the beautiful country lass he'd captured and imprisoned at his estate, chasing her across the boggy moors. It was a night so foggy that not even a scintilla of light could escape from the mist, and now the fiend had her in his clutches—

A noisome jangle pierced his reveries.

The bloody telephone again! Who on god's green earth could be calling at this ungodly hour? Good heavens, it was nearly nine o'clock in the evening! What manner of man would dare disturb him at this late hour?

"Hullo?" he said into the receiver, stifling the urge to say what he really wanted to say, which was *"This better be good."*

"Ambrose."

"Yes? *Alex?* Is that you? You sound awful."

"Very perceptive. I am awful."

"Where are you, boy?"

"Hoosegow."

"What?"

"It would appear I'm an overnight guest of the St. Moritz constabulary."

"What? Seriously. Tell me where you are, Alex?"

"I am bloody well serious. I've been thrown in jail. I'm allowed only one or two phone calls. Lucky you."

"Jail? That's ridiculous. On what charge?"

"Trespassing, apparently. Breaking and entering. Aggravated assault."

"Tell me what's happened. I'll make some phone calls and get you released forthwith."

"Alexei has been taken."

"Taken?"

"Kidnapped. Lost. I don't know. He's disappeared. There was an accident with the gondola this morning. We were all picked up by Swiss Air-Rescue choppers. Alexei boarded with the rest of the children and hasn't been seen since."

"No! My god, I'm so sorry, Alex! I'll be on the next flight to Zurich. I shall come immediately. Tell me exactly what happened."

"We were on the aerial tramway up near the summit of Mount Corviglia. The rear support cable failed, some kind of malfunction—hell, I don't know. The car upended vertically. Utter chaos and panic. Alexei and the other children in the rear suffered the worst of it. They were at the bottom of the heap. Two girls died, six-year old twins, many were injured. All were evacuated by a helicopter rescue mission and flown to a clinic."

"Was Alexei hurt, Alex?"

"I have no idea. I was at the front of the bus. He was in the back with his Royal Protection officer when it happened. Tristan, you know him. Badly wounded and still unconscious when the children were off-loaded, no idea of my son's condition. He and I were taken to a separate hospital from the children. When I finally got to Alexei's clinic, he was nowhere to be found. They said he was not among those who'd been admitted."

"Good heavens, man. And how did you end up in the hoosegow?"

"I was in a blind rage leaving the hospital. I searched every floor, every ward. I walked the grounds outside and the surrounding streets for hours. Thinking maybe Alexei had suffered a concussion. That he'd somehow gotten separated from the other children disembarking on the helipad. Wandered off unseen. It was my only hope as I searched. Exhausted, I went to a neighborhood pub and had a scotch or two to calm my nerves. Once I had time to think, I knew then exactly what I had to do."

"Find the man in charge of the rescue mission helicopter and you'll find your son."

"Bravo. You've not lost your much-vaunted powers of deduction, Chief Inspector. Yes, all I wanted to do was find the pilot of that rescue chopper. There were twenty-five children aboard that tram. And twenty-five children were transferred to hospital in that helo. But only twenty-four arrived at the clinic."

"That's not possible."

"No, it isn't possible. Not even remotely so. I drove out to the airfield where the Swiss Air-Rescue has its operations center. I demanded to see the pilot who'd flown the children to the clinic. The duty officer was no help at all. Drunk. I'd had a few, but he'd had a dozen. He told me I was crazy, which I suppose I was."

"Two scotches, Alex?"

"Right. Two. More or less. I told him what had happened. The accident, the children's rescue by his number four chopper. At any rate, Waldo Pfeffer, this trumped-up air rescue chief of staff, said he didn't know what the hell I was talking about. That none of his helicopters had participated in the rescue. He said I was in the wrong place and get the hell out of his sight before he called the police."

"Good lord. What then?"

"That's when I broke his jaw."

"Always a sound strategy."

"Right. At any rate, I ran out into the night. Drove round and around the field until I located the Swiss Air-Rescue crew's dormitory. Door was locked and I kicked it in. The pilots and crews were watching news of the accident in the lounge. I walked in and demanded to see the pilot who'd flown the Corviglia gondola rescue mission. When they too said I was crazy, that they didn't know what I was talking about, I started swinging and—woke up in a jail cell. You know, Ambrose, losing that boy will kill me, and I just cannot imagine how he—"

"Alex, stop. You need to calm down. We will find him and we will bring him home. Do you understand me? No matter where he is, no matter who has done this terrible thing. We will find him. All right? Are you with me?"

"Of course. How soon can you be here?"

"I'll catch the first flight out of Heathrow."

"No, you won't do anything of the sort. I'm sending my plane for you. My pilots will be waiting for you at the Banbury Airfield at first light. I'll book a room for you here at Badrutt's Palace. Anyone else I should call?"

"Yes. You need to call your friend Stokely Jones in Miami and get him up to speed. I will call Scotland Yard and alert them. I'll also ring up your pal Brick Kelly at CIA and tell him everything. Something tells me we're going to need a lot of help before this thing is over."

"Yes, I agree completely. Anything else?"

"Hmm. I've been thinking. Is there more than one Swiss rescue operation? Not civil, a military one, perhaps? In addition to a national one? Or even a privately owned and operated service?"

"I have no idea. The chopper that carried Alexei away had a bright red fuselage and white markings. The colors of the Swiss Air-Rescue teams, as far as I know. There was a big white number painted on the sides. Four. That was the number I recall."

"Righto, that's the number you said earlier. All right, Alex, that's good, we'll start there."

"We've got to locate that helicopter."

"And that's just what we're going to do. Now get some sleep, damn you. I'll come straightaway after landing to the police headquarters and get you out of the hoosegow as you call it. Then we'll go find your son and get him to safety."

"What would I do without you, you old dickens?"

"I wouldn't even hazard a guess, Alex. See you tomorrow. As soon as we ring off, I'll put in calls to both Scotland Yard and Langley to spring you from jail first thing in the morning. Now. Try to get some sleep, and for god's sake, try not to break any more jaws."

"You're right. Thanks. G'night."

CHAPTER FOURTEEN

Key Biscayne, Florida

G et in the damn pool, big boy!" Stoke's wife, Fancha, cried out. Wearing an emerald-green bikini that did little to camouflage her spectacular figure, she was sitting at the business end of the diving board, sunning herself and wiggling her toes in the sun-sparkled turquoise water. "Water only hurts you if you're made of sugar!"

Stoke looked over at the beautiful café au lait redhead and laughed. He was watching his pal and colleague Sharkey Gonzales-Gonzales doing lightning one-armed push-ups beside the pool. So named after an encounter with a big bull shark down in the Keys, the Sharkman had yet to break a sweat. Already had fifty under his belt and gone to get himself a cold one when Stoke said, "Uh-huh, which I clearly am and which you clearly are *not*. Sugar."

She laughed, her white teeth gleaming, and dove for the bottom, surfacing moments later at the shallow end.

"I love the shallow end!" she cried out, laughing. "It reminds me so much of you, darling, you and all of your little friends!"

"Wait!" Sharkey said, returning with a Bud tallboy. "She include me in that? She calling me shallow? Shallow? Hell, I don't even know what that means, shallow." The man, like Stoke himself, was wearing a bathing suit and a big floppy red Santa cap. He was a wiry little guy, not quite five and a half feet, but tough and sinewy as old cowhide.

"Uh-huh," Stoke said. "Me either, Shark. That's because your ass needs to be *deep* to understand why you're shallow. But, according to that woman over there, we so damn *shallow*, we will never understand. Know what I'm sayin'?"

"What?"

To call Stokely Jones Jr. shallow may or may not have been entirely accurate. But his wife's calling him *big* was the grossest form of understatement. This man mountain—this ex-U.S. Navy SEAL, ex–New York Jet linebacker, ex-NYPD detective—was *huge*. His best friend, his comrade-in-arms, Alex Hawke, always joked that Stoke was "about the size of your average armoire." To call Sharkey anything at all was to risk getting your ass handed to you. As Hawke once said, "He's only got one arm but one arm is all he *needs*."

A decade ago, the little Cuban fishing guide had taken the George W. Bush family bonefishing out of Cheeca Lodge on Islamorada. Diving into the water in hot pursuit of the president's dropped Ray-Bans, the man so nice they named him twice lost his left arm to a bull shark off Ramrod Key. The shark was having a run at a big swordfish the president had just caught for lunch, snacking on chunks of it as the fish surfed and bounced and rolled in the boat's foaming wake, trailing at the end of the starboard outrigger.

Sharkey, tired and cross at the end of a long day of too few bonefish, slowed the old bucket to stop, dove off the transom, and went after that shark with his machete. It was not an epic struggle.

The shark won.

Sharkman still lived in his "office," a battered old Hatteras fifty-foot Yacht Fisherman he'd named *Maria* for his estranged wife.

Sharkey, a legend among the fishing classes in the Keys, was up in Miami a lot. He often did part-time work for Tactics International, Stoke's soldier-of-fortune outfit based in Coconut Grove across the bay over in Miami. The two men did freelance counterterror operations around the globe, working for CIA on an as-needed basis, which lately had turned out to be very frequently. And profitable. All of which made Alex Hawke, who'd put up the capital for Tactics's formation, very happy.

The two warriors weren't working today. It was Christmas Day, after all. And also Shark's wife, Maria, had left him a month ago, on Thanksgiving Day. That morning she'd gotten a call from a friend that her husband had been seen around town with a six-foot-tall three-hundred-pound Seminole woman named Florence Lawrence. Apparently, Florence Lawrence was a checkout queen at the local Publix supermarket.

Also, to add insult to injury, it turned out that Sharkey had met the Indian princess just one week earlier, while he was at Publix buying their Thanksgiving turkey, a big bird Maria had just put in the fucking oven when she got the heads-up call from her neighbor! Shark discovered the half-baked bird full of stuffing under the covers at the foot of his bed when he climbed into the sack that night.

Shark screamed, remembering that they had watched "*The God-father*" two nights earlier. Since the suddenly single Sharkey had no children and no other family of any note, Stoke had invited him up to spend the holiday at *Casa Que Canta*. This was the luxurious waterfront estate compound of Mr. and Mrs. Jones on Key Biscayne in Miami.

"You looking good, brother man," Sharkey said, watching Stoke now keeping up his own rapid-fire push-ups poolside. The big man was still a little banged up from his last mission. He and Hawke had gone to Cuba, sailing right into the harbor at Isla de Pinos. There, Stoke, Hawke, Harry Brock, and a combined force of CIA, plus British and American forces, had assaulted a Cuban KGB compound, reducing it to rubble.

It was here, at the site of the Russian's Cold War spy compound, that the Russians had stored WMDs, weapons of mass destruction and other explosive devices. These with the intent of attacks on America's southeastern coastline should the current détente between Moscow and Washington turn into a real-life shooting war.

"Getting there, getting there," Stoke said, talking comfortably despite his fierce exertions. "More you sweat in training, less you bleed in battle."

"You got that right," the Sharkman said. "By the way, I got you something for Christmas. Put it under the big tree in your front hall."

"I got you something, too. Put it in the trunk of your Camaro. You're going to love it."

"I'm going to get another frosty. Get you another eggnog while I'm in the kitchen?"

"Why not? It's Christmas, ain't it, Sharkbait? Got to live a little."

Sharkey got up and sprinted up the wide white marble steps to the main house, a sprawling white British Colonial mansion. Sitting atop the highest piece of land on Key Biscayne, the place had spectacular views of the sparkling blue bay by day and the twinkling lights of Miami by night. The house had been left to Fancha by her late husband, Momo Marino. He was a Sicilian with deep ties to his Brooklyn crew and the Cosa Nostra back home in Sicily.

The husband, a smiling fat man who used to call himself the Mayor of Miami Beach was in reality a brutal little thug, a made man, a kingpin in the South Florida rackets and cocaine trade. The night death finally rang his bell, Big Momo was sitting between two hookers on a banquette at the Alhambra, a classy Miami Beach nightclub.

Onstage was the Alhambra's shining star, his wife, Fancha. Hailing from the Cape Verde Islands, the elegant beauty was one of the most successful crooners in the music business, having had two of her more recent Cape Verde fado albums go to the top of the *Billboard* charts.

"Mr. Mayor?" a small man with a big gun said. Because the man was swarthy and wore an impeccable white dinner jacket, the mayor took him for a new maître d'.

"Fuck you want?"

"This is for you, Señor Hijo de Puta," the tiny gangster said, putting a bullet hole the size of a quarter smack-dab in the middle of the son of a whore's forehead.

And from that day forward, at least until the day that she met and fell in love with one Stokely Jones Jr., the beautiful nightclub singer Fancha was known around Miami Beach as the Merry Widow.

The Merry Widow with a hundred million dollars under the mattress.

CHAPTER FIFTEEN

Hawke couldn't sleep.

After he had spent a solid hour trying to find comfort on a steel cot with no pillow and one threadbare blanket, a copper came to his cell to say that he was being released. Congreve's calls to the Yard and the CIA had resulted in his swift release. He'd immediately gotten permission to make one phone call.

He called his good friend Blinky Schultz, MI6 chief of station in Zurich.

"Come get me, Blinky."

"Alex? Good god. Do you know what time it is?"

"Too late or too early, for sure. I'm at the bloody jailhouse in St. Moritz, they just released me."

"Christ. What did you do now?"

"Got into a bit of a brawl with some helo pilots and lost. Blinky, you've got to help me. Alexei has been taken."

"What do you mean, taken?"

"Taken. Kidnapped. Stolen away from me."

"Do you have any idea who could have done it?"

"No. It was during the aerial tramway disaster. He was lost being transferred to hospital."

"All right. Try to calm down. I'll leave now and can be there in under an hour. No traffic this time of night."

He said thanks and sat down on a hard wooden bench to wait. He must have fallen asleep because a second later, a copper was grabbing him by the shoulder saying, "Wake up, sir. Man's waiting outside in the car."

Walking out into the deserted snowy streets, he'd almost hoped to a see a nondescript sedan parked nearby, with two invisible grey men sitting up front, men who would follow them wherever they went. Kidnappers who knew the whereabouts of Alexei, men whom he could confront in an alley and beat the living daylights out of.

It didn't happen that way.

He'd climbed into Blinky's Volvo and they drove across town to Badrutt's Palace Hotel. The lobby bar was still open, a few patrons at one end of the long bar. More desperate for sleep than alcohol, he bade his friend good night and trudged up the wide carpeted steps to the third floor. At the end of the corridor were two heavy mahogany doors, his suite.

He'd gone straight to bed but had lain awake for hours, staring up at the dark ceiling, waiting for the pink spread of dawn to appear in the windows of his bedroom. He'd left the television on with the sound muted, scouring coverage footage of this morning's accident before finally falling asleep.

Local news was naturally chock-full of coverage of the tramway accident. TV crews at both hospitals, survivors covered in blankets, weeping parents; plus aerial footage of the damaged gondola being whipped about by the high winds at that altitude. Terrorism had been ruled out.

But, not a mention, not a single bloody word, about one of the children having gone missing during the rescue operation! Only a brief report of a violent disturbance at Swiss Air-Rescue head-quarters that had resulted in the arrest of a foreign national. A man whose name was being withheld by the police for diplomatic reasons.

Well, that was good news, wasn't it? On this most hellish of days?

He looked at his watch. "Christ in heaven," he said and reached up and lit the sconce on the wall above him. It was nearly four A.M. He saw the smudgy nightcap glass from the bathroom on the bedside table. He winced at the sight. There was still a little whiskey remaining in it, and he started to reach for it.

Yes? No?

No. He grabbed the nearly empty pack of Morland cigarettes, plucked one out, and stuck it between his lips. His old steel Zippo flared and then, greedy for the smoke burn, he inhaled deeply. Ah. Better. Stirred by the sudden explosion of warmth inside him, he waited for the nicotine to kick in, gathered what was left of his wits, and took an accounting of matters where they stood.

His mobile was buzzing on the bedside table. He picked it up, saw that it was his pilot.

"Good morning," he said cheerfully. He felt like his day was finally under way.

"Morning, sir. Just a brief update. I have Chief Inspector Congreve aboard. We are out on the tarmac, on a brief hold before wheels up in ten minutes."

"Excellent, Chris. The old man is in good form?"

"Raring to go, sir. Happy to be back in the saddle, I'd say."

Hawke laughed. "That's him. Already donning his cloak and clutching his dagger. What time are you anticipating arrival in St. Moritz?"

"Touching down at SMV-Samedan in just about three hours, sir. No weather on the way, lovely morning for flying."

"Good, good. See you then."

He shut down his phone and lay his weary head back against the pillows. Reflected that a few moments of quiet contemplation were always helpful in times like these.

Finally sleep came. It came with nightmares.

But it came.

CHAPTER SIXTEEN

The second Stoke saw the Sharkman emerge into the sunlight and sprint down the steps to the pool, he knew something was very, very wrong.

"Stoke!" Sharkey called as he ran, "you gotta come inside, man! The boss is on the landline for you. Whatever it is, it's not good, man! He sounds terrible."

Stoke leapt to his feet and grabbed Sharkey's arm. "Shark, it's Hawke?"

"Yeah, it is."

"What did he say?"

"You gotta come, man, that's all, you gotta come!"

Stoke dashed up the broad marble steps and into the cool of the long center hall, where a real live phone sat on the sideboard.

"Boss?"

"Stoke. I've been calling your mobile."

"Oh, shit. Yeah. Left it on the charger up in the bedroom. Sorry. You okay? You don't sound so good."

"Somebody's taken Alexei, Stoke."

"Fuck."

"I'll tell you the details when you get here."

"Ah, Jesus, boss. Ah, shit. Alexei? Oh, man."

"We need to find him. Fast. Who knows what these people are after?"

"Ransom note?"

"No. There was no ransom note, nothing. He just . . . disappeared."

"All right. I'm on it. On my way right now, you know that. Tell me where I'm going."

"I'm in St. Moritz. There's a nonstop Swissair flight in the morning. Miami International to Zurich. There'll be a driver waiting in baggage claim."

"Hell happened, boss?"

"No idea. There was a tram accident. He literally disappeared. Ambrose is on the way here right now. If anybody can figure this out, it's him. Then we go get him and bring him home. Right?"

"Right is right, boss. Right is right. I got Sharkey here with me for Christmas. Want me to put him on the payroll?"

"I'll leave that one up to you. Sure, bring him. Listen. One more thing."

"Shoot."

"We're going to need a war room here in the hotel. So as soon as you two have checked in, get on that. Encrypted communications, two coffee pots, whiteboards, iPads, you know the drill. I've taken one of the meeting rooms on the top floor, already booked it in your name. All clear?"

"State of the art, coming up, boss."

"Good," Hawke said, and he was gone.

FANCHA SAID GOOD-BYE TO SHARKEY at the front door, giving him a big hug. Sharkey smiled and said to Stoke, "Hey! Don't forget your Christmas present, man! It's right there under that sparkly white tree."

"Aw, man, you didn't have to get me anything," Stoke said as he opened the box to find an enormous red cashmere V-neck sweater. He said, "That's beautiful! Lemme put it on . . . I love red sweaters, how'd you know that, man?" He pulled it over his head and it actually fit.

Sharkey gave Fancha a peck on the cheek. Then the two men strolled down the walk to the sweeping circular drive, where a large white fountain filled with spouting mermaids spewed jets of water twenty feet into the air. A flock of brilliantly colored tropical birds swooped in and took up residence in the trees surrounding the fountain.

Stoke said, "That your new Camaro over there, Sharkbait? Hot damn. That's some serious weaponry right there. "What engine you get?"

"A 6.2L V-8 Direct Injection."

"Hot shit, man. Let me see inside."

He walked Sharkey over to his new car. First automobile the little Cuban had ever owned that had both a roof and a floor at the same time. He was going to miss Christmas dinner, a royal treat, prime rib rare at the Jones household, but there was nothing to be done about it. Man had to race down to the Keys, return to *Maria*, and pack a bag for the mission to Switzerland. Pack his shaving kit, his clothes, his machete and his Duran Duran CDs.

"What you think, bossman?" Sharkey said, running his hand lovingly over the gleaming purple flanks of his new car. "Something else, right?"

"Nice Camaro, Shark. Unusual color. What color is that?" Stoke said to his friend, who was just now donning his trademark yellow porkpie hat.

"Old blue jean, the guy at the Chevy dealer said. Something like that. Damn if I know what it is."

"Say what? What color he tell you?"

"I told you, man. Old blue jean."

"*Old blue jean?* You mean, like Levis?"

"What he said."

Stoke laughed as Shark got in the car and fired her up.

"It ain't old blue jean. It's *aubergine*, buddy."

"Ober-what?"

"Aubergine. That's what fancy white folk call eggplant."

"Eggplant? Wait. My car is eggplant-colored?"

"Yeah, it is. But you don't have to tell anybody that. Just tell people it's old blue jean, man. They won't know! Hey, want to see your Christmas present before you go?"

"Hell, yes, I do! Where is it?"

"Get out the car, man. It's back here in the trunk."

"Don't tell me you got me a new tire jack . . ."

"Just pop the trunk, Shark, you'll see. Gonna love it!"

Shark held out his key fob and pushed the remote lock button, bending forward to peer inside. He nearly fell down as he jumped back to avoid the giant breasts and garish face of a huge, overly inflated sex doll. He backpedaled as the super realistic woman came exploding out of the Camaro's trunk and flew ten feet up in the air, landing on her back atop the Camaro's rooftop.

"Ain't she beautiful?" Stoke said, grabbing her by the ankle and pulling her down to eye level. "Lookie here, she floats! I had them fill her with extra helium just for fun. Her name's Angelique. Someone to keep you warm on those cold lonely winter nights on your boat, brother! You like her? Very realistic in every way . . . and, I mean *every* way, and, as I said, she floats!"

Shark was staring at Angelique, unable to put her into some kind of context.

"I—I don't know what to say, Stoke. I mean, yeah, she's great and all, but how do I smuggle her aboard *Maria*? All my crew down on the docks, they'll be laughing and—they bound to see her, right? Think I'm some kind of deviate or something, a sick puppy or something."

"Shark, listen up, that's part of the fun of the present. She's a natural born conversation starter wherever you go! Put her up front with you on the drive down to Islamorada! Relax. Get to know her a little bit on the trip to Cheeca. She'll grow on you, I promise. Hell, I thought about getting one just like her, but you know Fancha would kick my ass."

Shark, climbing behind the wheel as Stoke stuffed Angelique through the passenger side window said, "I don't know about this blow-up chick thing, man . . . It's a little weird, right? Perverted?"

Stoke smiled and buckled Sharkey's new girlfriend's seat belt, strapping her in tight.

"I just don't want you to be lonely, man. Get back up here as fast as you can, man. Boss needs us bad."

"*Hasta luego, amigo*," Shark said, cranking the Camaro.

The happy couple drove off into the sunset side by side.

Stoke, still smiling as he strode up the drive to the entrance of Casa Che Canta, put his arm around his wife and ducked into the cool of the tiled interior hallway.

"You got to love that little dude," he said to his wife.

"No, you got to hope he can help you find Alex Hawke's little boy, Stokely Jones, Junior. That's what you got to do."

"WAIT. YOU MEAN I GET my own room?" Sharkey Gonzales-Gonzales said next morning as they boarded the Swiss Air widebody. It was the Sharkman's first transatlantic crossing, and it was in first class, no less. Stoke had gotten lucky, got the last two seats available.

"That's right, brother man," Stoke said, smiling. "And you see that seat?"

"Yeah."

"Turns into a bed."

"No."

"Good evening, gentlemen," the stewardess said. "Can I help with anything? Champagne?"

Sharkey plucked a glass of champagne from the tray and knocked it back. Then took another. Stoke smiled at the pretty girl in the light blue uniform.

"He doesn't believe me that the seat turns into a bed."

She smiled at Sharkey, "Oh, but it does, Mr. Gonzalez-Gonzales. Watch. I'll show you."

She pushed all the right buttons and Sharkey's jaw dropped as the seat unfolded itself like a Swiss Army knife.

"*Fuck me, amigo!*" an excited Shark shouted, way too loud for the confined space. "It *is* a bed!"

All the air was sucked out of first class. Stone silence. The little one-armed Cuban fisherman in the yellow porkpie hat and purple sport coat realized that all the rich folks were looking at him in various states of semi-shock.

"Tell the nice people you're sorry, Sharkey," Stoke said, smiling at all the passengers. "These folks unaccostumed to such profanity."

"Damn right, I'm sorry! I am so fucking sorry it's unbelievable! Okay. I'm sorry."

"Sit down, Sharkbait, sit down and shut up and drink your champagne."

"Thanks, Stoke. This is really nice up here, man. First class! Like a palace . . ."

"You're welcome. Hey, you bring Angelique with you? She in your carry-on bag?"

"Who?"

"Angelique. Your new blow-up girlfriend."

"Oh, no, no, man. I didn't bring her," Shark said, his voice a fierce whisper.

"Why the hell not?"

Sharkey whispered in Stoke's ear. " 'Cause I would've had to deflate her to get her through security! And, if I deflated her, I wouldn't have known how to reflate her, that's why. Plus, her left leg has a leak. She sorta whistles all night. I put a band-aid on it and tried to blow her back up last night and I . . . And I . . . ah, shit. I'll be honest. I already miss that woman, amigo."

"True love," Stoke said, "is a wonderful thing."

And the two amigos were off to sunny Switzerland.

CHAPTER SEVENTEEN

St. Moritz

Alex Hawke's midnight-blue Gulfstream VII came sliding up the wide valley, soaring over snow-covered fields and white mountaintops, picture-postcard towns of rooftops and steeples and flower-box windows that would be bursting with red geraniums come next summer. Hawke watched her land and taxi toward the observation platform, where he waited for the arrival of Ambrose Congreve. His best friend since early childhood.

Chief Inspector Ambrose Congreve of Scotland Yard was a world-renowned criminalist, a giant brain of a man the press usually referred to as Britain's Demon of Mass Deduction. He was, Hawke thought, an almost supernaturally ingenious detective, a man whose entire life had revolved around finding a great mystery and then using his razor-keen intellect to bend that mystery to his will. Between the two of them, they'd cracked some of the toughest cases on record in the last decade. And had stopped even the deadliest evil dead in its tracks.

Now someone had taken his boy. It was the worst possible nightmare, the one thing that kept him awake at night, figuring new ways to protect his son. And he'd failed. But at least he now had hope. Now if, as he prayed, Alexei was still alive, Hawke had a fighting chance to foil his captors—whoever they were, however powerful they might be, and wherever on god's earth he might find them.

Because, now Hawke had the ultimate weapon in the fight to help get Alexei back. He was in the process of assembling what was perhaps the best hostage rescue team in all of Europe. It was comprised of Hawke, Congreve, and Stokely Jones Jr. Three unstinting warriors who had joined together to take on the worst the world had to offer. And they were still standing, still ready to fight for the weak and the helpless, wherever they might be.

This was the team that had once stormed Balmoral Castle, the royal summer residence of Her Majesty the Queen and the entire Royal Family. All of Britain had been riveted to the telly as the story unfolded. Al-Qaeda were holding the Queen and her family in the basement, threatening to execute them one by one until their demands were met. Their lives hung in the balance until help arrived, just the three of them. Hawke, Congreve, and Jones saved the Queen this time, not god.

And now the stakes, at least for Hawke, were even higher. The life of Hawke's only child was at risk.

As his plane drew closer, he felt a weight begin lifting from his shoulders. Now that he had managed to grasp thin shreds of hope, Hawke felt he might be able to breathe again. The clouds of fear and doubt that had been obscuring his mind and his heart since the accident began to clear away.

If he was to find his son and get him to safety, he would need his mind back, clear and strong. He would need to hone his innate warrior instincts.

He was now sure of one thing, however. Hawke, Congreve, and Jones, god help them, would now mount a hostage rescue operation like no other in order to bring his boy safely home.

HAWKE WAS OUT ON THE tarmac, waiting at the bottom of the aircraft steps. The wind and freezing rain whipped at his navy pea coat. The sight of his gleaming midnight-blue airplane gliding majestically to a halt never failed to move him. Hawke, the former Royal Navy fighter pilot, was on the phone with Artemis Cooper, his captain, as the plane taxied to a halt, going over some recent issues with the aircraft's avionics systems.

Hawke hoped any repairs necessary would not delay his pilot's quick turnabout, keep the plane grounded a moment longer than was necessary.

He finally told his chief pilot, "Keep me informed, Artemis. Whatever needs fixing, fix it. And be on standby with the tank topped off. When I need to go, it will be right away. Are we clear?"

"Roger that, sir. Oh, hold on, sir. Chief Inspector coming out soon . . . along with our other passenger."

"Other passenger, Artemis? What *other* passenger?"

"It's a lady, sir. Very pretty, I might add."

"Lady? He didn't mention anything to me about anyone else coming. Is it his wife? Hold on, here he is in the doorway now."

Chief Inspector Ambrose Congreve, who was godfather to his son, stepped out into the cold, blustery weather. Upon seeing Hawke below, he raised his infamous black umbrella in greeting.

This was the famous brolly Hawke had nicknamed Mary Poppins, a steel mesh contraption that, when extended, was entirely bulletproof. It had been designed by some gimcrack genius at Scotland Yard. Mary Poppins had once saved Congreve's life during the Dragon Lady Affair, an iffy incident involving killer ravens. But that's a tale for another time.

"Halloo! Halloo!" Congreve shouted above the wind. "Be right down . . . hold on a tick," he called down to Hawke, pausing to look back inside the aircraft, as if he'd forgotten something or someone.

A moment later, Hawke got a wholly unexpected shock.

Sigrid.

Sigrid Kissl. What the hell was she doing here?

The tall ash-blond Swiss beauty, in her late twenties and wearing a full-length sable, was standing up there beneath the umbrella with

Ambrose, smiling down at him and waving as their cabin luggage was being handed down by Hawke's uniformed air hostesses.

Fräulein Sigrid Kissl. Of all people.

Hawke had met the former Credit Suisse banker in Zurich a couple of years before. He and Congreve had been looking into a case involving the Chinese or the Russians and some gold mysteriously gone missing from the Queen of England's vast Swiss reserves. Hawke had enlisted a senior banker at Credit Suisse, Sigrid Kissl, to help him ferret out the thieves.

Who turned out to be both the Chinese *and* the Russians.

In the end, Sigrid had helped Congreve crack what was a very difficult case. She'd also helped identify the names of the Russian perpetrators and talked Congreve into taking her on as his personal assistant. He had even invited her to take up residence in the gardener's cottage at Brixden House, his country home in the Cotswolds.

She'd also broken Hawke's heart.

The two had become romantically involved that first Christmas in Switzerland. Two years ago now. In the early going, as she was settling into the idea of living in the English countryside, turning the little cottage on the vast rolling estate into her home, she and Hawke were inseparable.

And she'd spent countless weekends and overnights at Hawkesmoor, the Hawke family seat, some fifteen miles away from the Congreves. In those happy months, Alexei had bonded with the beautiful woman. The three had become, in Hawke's mind at least, like a family.

They traveled the world together, spent holiday weekends at Sandy Lane in Barbados, and then one spring weekend in Capri, there came, from out of nowhere, a weepy declaration: "Darling, I love you, but I simply cannot do this anymore. It's impossible. I'm so sorry."

Sorry?

And that was the end of it. She was gone from him. She refused to see him or speak to him, and the long sunny weekends she'd spent at Hawkesmoor with him and his son suddenly were no more.

That there had never been anything by way of an explanation—something, *anything*, he could offer his son by way of comforting him—was to this day a source of deep anger.

She came down the stairs first, her fur coat collar up against the chill rain, her eyes never leaving his. As she neared the bottom, he offered a hand and managed a brief smile. He couldn't help but notice she was wearing the gold-and-blue Hermès scarf he'd bought her on their last trip to Paris.

She smiled back. "Now, don't you dare be angry with Ambrose, darling. All my fault. It was a last-minute thing. I talked him into letting me tag along just this morning at breakfast. I'm so sorry about Alexei, Alex, so terribly, terribly sorry . . . and I felt that if I could be of some help to you, you would let me stay on."

She swept a gloved hand across her brimming eyes. He had read into them that she was truly sorry, not just for his son's disappearance, but perhaps for the abominable way she had treated him as well.

"Thank you for that."

"Oh, come on, Alex. Give me a hug, damn it, and tell me you're glad to see me. I'm your old girl, here to help, you know."

He hugged her. How could he not, inhaling the ridiculously intoxicating scent wafting up from her generous cleavage. She was, despite his various issues with her, the most spectacular woman he'd ever admitted inside the heavily guarded defenses of his lonely heart.

"Thanks for coming, Sigrid," he said, mulling the situation over in his mind. If the most cunning detective in Scotland Yard's modern era thought she could help, perhaps she could help.

"I deeply appreciate your offer, Sigrid. I accept."

"I knew you'd see things my way, old chap," Ambrose said, putting a hand on his shoulder. "I think it's time you and Sigrid buried whatever hatchet is between you once and for all."

He turned to embrace his old friend.

"God, it's good to see you, Constable," he said. "I cannot tell you how much this means to me."

"Alex, my dear, dear boy, don't be ridiculous! Tell me, how are you bearing up?" Ambrose said, giving him a good squeeze.

"As well as can be expected, I suppose. There's still been no word, no ransom note or . . . I don't even know if he's alive!"

"I know you cannot help but worry night and day, Alex. But I do want you to know that Miss Kissl and I are already chewing on this kidnapping case like dogs on a bone. I've not a doubt in the world regarding a happy ending. I hope you're not cross with me about Sigrid. But truth to tell, she's been invaluable to me . . . and I just felt that we, at this juncture, needed all the help we could get."

"Friends?" Hawke said, smiling at Sigrid.

"Friends." She smiled back.

"All right," Hawke said. "We're all standing out here like sentries at Buck House, freezing to death. Let's get you two to the hotel so you can—"

"We don't have time, Alex," Congreve said. "We've got a meeting in twenty minutes at the Air-Rescue operations center with your new friend Waldo Pfeffer, the Swiss Air-Rescue chief who had you thrown in jail."

"Lovely," Hawke said. "I look forward to seeing see his face when I walk through his door once more. See how is jaw is healing."

CHAPTER EIGHTEEN

Zurich

Uncle Joe had been a very busy boy.

He found his shiny new Mercedes 450 GLC right where he'd parked it, under a foot of fresh snow on *Torsten Strasse*, about a block from Scheherazade, the Zurich restaurant where he'd just lunched with Heinrich Rosenstiel, the Swiss banker—Putin's buttoned-up Swiss banker, to be more precise about it. Buttoned up so tight he might pop any minute, Joe thought, as he swept the snow from the windshield, pondering the Swiss mentality. No sense of humor, these guys. Zilch, nada.

But if you were a billionaire recluse like the currently semi-dead president of Russia, you weren't looking for some kind of Pal Joey, right? Buttoned up was a plus with these financial types.

Herr Heinrich Rosenstiel was very, very discreet. Joe had dealt with him before, back in his salad days as Putin's henchman at the Kremlin. Back then, Heinie was just another of the countless grey men he'd dealt with in Switzerland, nothing more than a glorified bagman, moving vast amounts of money and gold and art around the planet for Vladimir Putin. Joe, the middleman, had worked directly with the guy. He'd made countless trips to Zurich to ensure there were no snafus or fuck-ups of any kind.

Joe once took Heinie to his favorite bar, try to loosen him up a little. Joe ordered two ketel martinis, straight up. Heinie was ordering a third while Joe was finishing his first. "I didn't know you like to drink, Heinie."

"Only on special occasions," Heinie said, polishing off his third see-thru.

"Like what?" Joe asked.

"Only when I'm alone or with somebody."

The cat was actually *funny*! Who knew?

Heinie, mainly because of his Russian connections, was now a big shot at Banque Pictet. But luckily for Joe, Rosenstiel still knew what side his bread was buttered on. He knew Joe and the late president had been tight, thick as thieves, like *thistight*. Knew better than to ask Joe any questions or probe into any areas better left unprobed.

Questions like why the hell Joe Stalingrad, a man who had been infamously banned from the Kremlin, now had access to all of the late president's accounts? Yeah, that was a biggie, but Heinie was smart enough to keep those troubling thoughts to himself.

So when Joe provided working account numbers and the correct access codes and transactional summaries, and had said he wanted a hundred and fifty million in cash and gold bars ready to be shipped to an as-yet-unspecified location on an as-yet-to-be-determined date, it was "No problem, sir."

Joe had been hard at it on Putin's behalf for some weeks now. Working on the complex infrastructure, the underpinnings of what would one day become Vladimir Putin's military stronghold in exile. Secrecy made everything exponentially more difficult, but Joe was no one if not someone accustomed to keeping secrets.

Why, under Joe's aegis, entire Chinese squatter villages deep in the Siberian border forests had disappeared. Send a signal to all the inhabitants of northern China that crossing the Russian border to steal Russian timber was a very bad idea. And Ukrainian fighter squadrons had flown off the radar, never to be seen again. Into the

"Crimea Triangle," he and Putin used to joke after pulling another fast one on the world.

Joey himself was sitting atop a very large secret at this very moment. Today was the day he would finally have an audience with Dr. Gerhardt Steinhauser himself, the notorious Sorcerer. He was actually going to see this incredible "mountain house" that the boss was so excited about. Gaining entry, the boss had told Joe, was a bit iffy. "There are two entrances to the complex inside the mountain," Putin had told him. "Built by Swiss engineers secretly working for the Nazis near the end of World War II. One of the entrances is near the bottom of Lake Zurich. A hundred yards offshore, and about fifty feet below the surface. The other is a giant secret door at fifteen thousand feet, camouflaged by faux granite boulders."

Unless you were willing to scale something called the Murder Wall, a mirror-smooth face at fifteen thousand feet, your only other option was the hidden underwater entrance below the surface of Lake Zurich. The one Hawke had believed closed, apparently, was not.

Transport across the lake to the air lock was via a trip in a two-man sub from the western side of the lake to the eastern side. Putin had supplied the phone number of Horst Becker, a man in Zurich who worked as a sub jockey for the Sorcerer. And he had given Joe a code phrase, "I'm a friend of Johann's," to which the reply from Horst would be "What kind of dogs does Johann like?" The correct answer from Joe was "Johann doesn't like dogs."

He climbed into his new car, took a big gulp of that deliciously exhilarating new-car smell, fastened his seat belt, and cranked it up. The resulting *vroom-vroom* was not exactly up to Vette *vroom* standards, but what the hell. He wasn't exactly living in a shitty one-bedroom walk-up on Melrose Avenue in L.A. anymore, now was he?

No. He was back in the Big Show now, no doubt about that. And if he played his cards exactly right, he'd be a zillionaire when this was all over.

HORST HAD TOLD HIM THE pick-up would occur at a pier in the tiny village of Riga, about an hour's drive north along the lake. Meet him at midnight, to be exact. So Joe had a late supper in the hotel dining room at Baur au Lac and called for the Mercedes at ten thirty. The roads were extremely icy, and after a few skids going into corners carrying too much speed, he slowed way down. He didn't want to end up in the icy lake prematurely.

He was excited about the trip across the lake in the two-man sub. It wouldn't be his first rodeo, either. Putin had a sub and he'd taken Joe down more than once when he'd been aboard the presidential yacht, *Tsar*. His favorite dive? Two years ago. The time off the coast of France when he and the president had discovered a sunken Nazi freighter, a massive thing sitting upright on the bottom. Putin had brought him along for the ride for a reason. To stage a demonstration of his new secret explosive *Feuerwasser*.

"I like it," Joe said. "I'm on it. Boom!"

HE SAW THE SIGN FOR Riga and exited the highway. The little picture postcard town on the lake was dark and deserted. A pale moon hung high above a lit church steeple in the blackness above the mountains. He glanced at the dashboard clock: 11:46 P.M. He was a little early, but that was all right. When you're doing any kind of business in the midnight hour, it was always prudent to arrive a little early.

He climbed out of the Mercedes, locked it, and walked out to the end of the pier, where a dim red light glowed. It was below freezing, but he had his mainstay bearskin coat and the sable hat Putin had given him and it was enough. There was a bench. He sat down to wait, lit a cigarette, and thought about how dramatic a life could be if you had the appetite for it.

And, indeed, he'd known few men hungrier than he.

His lust for life was *insatiable*.

CHAPTER NINETEEN

Zurich

W ell, well, well," Hawke said, staring at the loathsome Air
Rescue chief. "If it isn't the Great Waldo Pfeffer!"

"Ah, good morning, Chief Inspector, Miss Kissl, and uh . . . and
yes, you too, Commander Hawke," the Swiss Air-Rescue chief of
staff said as soon as they were all seated. He'd had obvious trouble
getting Hawke's name to pass his bruised and broken jaw and rubbery
red lips. His attempted smile hid an obviously imperious demeanor.
He was "Germanic Swiss official with a penchant for schnapps"
personified.

"What can I do for you this morning?" he asked, never meeting
Hawke's eyes and speaking only to Congreve. "I understand you
have some questions?"

Hawke crossed his long legs, smiled, and said, "Yeah, I've got a
question. How's your jaw, Waldo?"

Congreve, never one to miss a beat, jumped in, "We deeply appreciate your taking time out of your busy schedule, Chief. We shan't
be long."

"Good, good, I am a busy man," the chief said, glaring at Hawke
as he reflexively rubbed his sore jaw. The two men stared at each
other until Sigrid mercifully interrupted the awkward silence.

"Good morning, Chief. I'm Police Constable Sigrid Kissl, Scotland Yard. I work for Chief Inspector Congreve. We are here on official business, conducting an Interpol criminal investigation with which you are required by international law to cooperate. I am speaking of the recent disappearance of Commander Hawke's seven-year-old son, Alexei Hawke. Do I make myself clear?"

"Ah, yes," Pfeffer said, "the unfortunate gondola affair."

"Unfortunate, did you say?" Hawke said, his icy blue eyes firing white-hot bolts of anger at the man. There was nothing in the books to say he couldn't break this bastard's jaw *twice*.

"Ah, I mean to say tragic, Commander. Yes, tragic. But still and all, I'm not sure how I can help you."

"I told you all of this last night. Let me refresh your memory. My son was on that gondola. So was I. It was a good deal more than tragic, it was a nightmare of pain and suffering for the children. Not to mention the agony of those of us parents aboard. We worried and prayed for our children's very lives and safety for hours. I, as it happens, am still worrying and still praying. And I am not leaving here until I get some answers. Do we understand each other? Verstehen-sie? Capiche?"

The man stared at Hawke but could supply no further dialogue.

Hawke said, "All right. My son was seated next to his Scotland Yard Royal Protection officer throughout the ordeal. We all were eyewitnesses to your rescue helicopter. We saw it arrive and off-load the children. And later, two other helos showed up for the adults. There were fatalities, by the way. Twenty-five little boys and girls were loaded aboard your helicopter. But only twenty-four were disembarked on the roof of that hospital. Do the math. My son boarded, but he did *not* disembark atop that hospital!"

"Impossible."

"But true!" Sigrid said, leaning forward. "His lordship went to the hospital immediately to find his son. He wasn't there. And there was absolutely no record of him being admitted."

Pfeffer said, "I'm sure you're telling the truth as you know it,

Police Constable Kissl. But I myself can offer no rational explanation. It doesn't make any sense. None at all."

"No, it doesn't. But you need to deal with it and deal with it now," Sigrid said, her sentences welded with steel.

"What do you suggest I do?" the florid fat man said, exasperated.

"Commander Hawke," Sigrid said, "wishes to speak to the pilot of the first chopper at the scene. That's why he came to see you the first time. According to his lordship, you were intoxicated and extremely unhelpful. That's why Chief Inspector Congreve and I set up this interview. Lord Hawke still wishes to speak with the pilot."

Congreve stood up and began pacing back and forth by the windows, hands clasped behind his back. "Then I would inform you," he said, "that Lord Hawke is here in Switzerland as an official representative of the Crown. And you, sir, are giving testimony as relates to an international crime of vital importance. Dwell on that thought, Chief."

He did not dwell long. "Then I will say again what I said that night. We did not effect that rescue. We got the alert, launched a helo immediately. En route, our pilot was told to stand down. He was notified by rescue officials already on-site that there was a rescue chopper in the immediate vicinity and en route. My pilot was waved off and returned to base. That's all I can tell you."

"I saw the damn thing with my own eyes!" Hawke said, his overwrought temper flaring. "It was an AW169. It was a Swiss Air-Rescue Rega helicopter. It was one of yours, damn you!"

"And how did you know that?" Pfeffer shot back.

"I saw it! It was red and white the length of the fuselage. Red cross and number on the flank, Swiss Air-Rescue insignia, for god's sake!"

"So, Commander, you would recognize it if you saw it?"

"I most certainly would."

"Well, there's nothing else for it, is there? Shall we go to the hangar, then? As it happens, our entire fleet is on the ground at the moment. Routine maintenance and bad weather, mostly. We shall settle this matter here and now."

"Most kind, Chief," Sigrid said, her short leather skirt riding up on her thighs as she rose, giving the man the high-beam smile as she got to her feet. "Lead the way, sir."

"No, no. After *you*, Police Constable Kissl," he said, blushing pink and bowing slightly from the waist.

He actually thought she'd been flirting with him, poor bastard.

THERE WERE TWENTY OR SO identical red-and-white helicopters parked in three lines inside the cavernous hangar. All with the big red cross on the flanks. The place was a beehive of activity. Many of the helos were undergoing mechanical inspections and repairs.

"Let's split up—faster that way," Congreve said.

Pfeffer said, "Yes, good idea, Chief Inspector. I'll leave you to it, then? I don't see how I can be of further assistance."

"Yes. You're free to return to your office. But I must insist that you not leave the base until I've spoken to you after our search of the hangar. Do you understand?"

"Perfectly. Chief Inspector, Fraulein Kissl."

He turned and left without, Ambrose noticed, saying good-bye to Alex Hawke.

"Alex, do try not to let that little toad get under your skin. He's just not worth the effort."

"If you had any idea how vile he was to a desperate father that night, you'd understand."

"Hmm. Tell me, what was the number on the side of the helo that picked up Alexei?"

"Four."

"Off we go! Let's meet back here at the door in, what, fifteen minutes?"

"Yes," Hawke said.

They went their separate ways, Hawke deciding to investigate the aircraft on the far left side of the hangar. The first one he saw had a large red number, but it was a nine, not a four. He kept striding down the line. Ten minutes later he was back at the door, joining Ambrose and Sigrid.

"No number four on my line," Ambrose said. "Sigrid?"

"Sorry. No number four, Alex?"

"Nor mine. What the devil?" Hawke said. "I think I need another word or two with my good friend Waldo."

CHAPTER TWENTY

The mood in Waldo Pfeffer's office was decidedly somber. Hawke was on his feet, hands clasped behind his back, staring out the window at the hangar on the far side of the field. He lit another cigarette and spoke without looking back at Pfeffer, who was seated at his desk, his normally pink face now a bright red. Hawke was at the point where he literally couldn't stand the sight of the little fat man.

"You're short one helicopter, Waldo," Commander Hawke said.

"Don't be ridiculous."

"Number three is there. Number five is there," Congreve said. "How do you explain the absence of number four?"

"I don't know what you're talking about."

Hawke whirled and barked: "Let me ask you that question another way. *Where the bloody hell is chopper number four?* It's not out there in that hangar with the other nineteen helos! Just tell me that, damn it. Where is it?"

"I told you, or tried to tell you that last night, Commander. But let me say it one more time. Number four is offline. Not in service at this time. Period."

"So what the bleeding hell did I see up on top of that mountain? I saw it and so did a whole lot of other people. I've got video, Waldo, on my mobile phone! Shot by skiers on the side of the mountain! Want to see it?"

"No, no. I believe you."

"Then answer my question!"

"I can't account for it."

Hawke shook his head angrily and was silent.

Sigrid's voice was next. He heard her say, in her silkiest tones, "Chief, I'm sitting here wrestling with your answer. In particular, the word *offline*. What does that mean exactly? To a layperson like myself."

The rooster puffed himself up. "Look here. I'm running out of patience with you people and—"

And then again came Congreve. "Let me know when your patience is completely gone, Chief Pfeffer. That's the exact moment when I arrest you for obstruction of justice and impeding an Interpol criminal investigation, and for disobeying the direct order of an officer of Her Majesty's Government. That would be myself and Lord Hawke over there."

"Lord Hawke is it now?" Waldo snorted.

Hawke looked at him coldly and said, "You'll know when my patience is exhausted, Chief Pfeffer. You'll know because that will be the moment when I stick my hand down your bloody throat and rip your still-beating heart out of your chest."

"Boy, boys, stop this," Sigrid said, genuinely worried about the possibility of violence. "Chief, you can end all this. Just tell us what *offline* means in your parlance."

Pfeffer sat behind his desk, literally shaking and sweating profusely. Few men would not be. Hawke was a creature of radiant violence. And the chief could see for himself that he'd meant every word of that threat.

"All right, all right. I'll tell you. But I must warn you that I am violating a strict code of silence imposed upon us by the police in this matter until it is . . . resolved. Swiss national security is involved." He paused and mopped his face with his soggy handkerchief.

"What matter?" Congreve said. "I want the truth."

"Number four helo has disappeared."

"Disappeared? What do you mean, *disappeared*?" Congreve said.

"No one knows where it is."

"What? What are you talking about?" Hawke said, astonished at the news and its implications in the disappearance of his son. He'd seen the bloody chopper with his own eyes, less than twenty-four hours ago!

"It was stolen."

"When? After the rescue?"

"No. About six weeks ago."

"By whom?" Congreve said.

"We've no idea. The aircraft had been damaged during the rescue of a trapped climber near the top of the Eiger. In severe storm conditions. It was deemed not to be airworthy and was grounded for repairs. At some time during the night after its return here to base, a truck carrying two men penetrated the security gate and killed three military policemen who tried to stop them. The men had had no chance to even sound the alarm. Five minutes later, the chopper was airborne and flying a course due south toward Italy. It was never seen again."

"Right," Hawke said. "Until I saw it yesterday morning."

Sigrid and Congreve eyed each other. This was it. This was just the kind of break they'd been hoping for.

A doorway into the investigation had just cracked open.

Ambrose said, "And what was the justification for this national security blackout?"

"It was believed in some circles that ISIS terrorists had stolen the chopper and were planning to use it in some kind of aerial attack on the Swiss Parliament. Striking a blow at the heart of Europe . . . the government imposed a black-out on the story while they tried to find the chopper and the Iranians. They never did."

"Ah, I see. Well, that's most interesting," Congreve said.

Ambrose got to his feet, as did Sigrid. He said, "Thank you for your candor, Chief Pfeffer. You know you might have saved all of us a whole lot of trouble by paying attention to what Commander Hawke first told you that night. Upon learning that he was an officer of British Intelligence, investigating a major international crime, we had every right to know the truth of the chopper's theft."

"I would have told him! But we took no part in that rescue! Had he bothered to tell me the number on the fuselage and—"

Hawke was already halfway out the door. "I did tell you the bloody number, you little prick. Four. I said it more than once. But the Great Waldo Pfeffer was too drunk to even know what the hell I was saying."

And they were gone.

When they got back to Badrutt's Palace, there was a message at the concierge desk for Mr. Alex Hawke from Mr. Stokely Jones Jr.

It read:

We're here at the hotel, boss. The war room on the top floor is up and running. Hope you don't mind, but we started without you. I got a call from my pal Harry Brock at CIA, Miami. CIA says mountain hikers in Italy have found what looks to be the wreckage of a small aircraft in a mountainous region of northern Italy. Could be our missing helo? Who knows? CIA is keeping the site secure until we get down there to investigate. Love, Stoke. Oh, and one more thing. Harry says Putin may not be dead. PS: hope you like cold pizza.

CHAPTER TWENTY-ONE

T alk to me some more about Harry Brock," Hawke said to Stokely
Jones Jr. "Start with the crash site." The lobby bar they were
using was closed and Hawke had asked his friend to come down-
stairs for a one-on-one conversation. They sat side by side at the
darkened bar, speaking barely above a whisper.

A match flared as Hawke lit another cigarette and said, "So
what's he got?"

Stoke turned to him and said, "Okay, but first of all, lemme tell
you the good news. According to Harry's intel, your good friend at
CIA, Director Brick Kelly, is all over this case."

Brick Kelly was one of Alex Hawke's closest friends, and the two
of them had worked together on many difficult operations with joint
U.S. and UK involvement. Their first meeting had not boded well for
their joint futures, however.

Commander Hawke, who'd been a top-gun Royal Navy fighter
pilot before joining MI6, had been shot out of the skies, captured,
and frog-marched through the unrelenting heat of the Iraqi desert
to a prison so bleak and cruel as to defy description. There was an
American being held there, a young U.S. Marine colonel named
Brick Kelly.

He took his name from the color of his hair, a reddish gold that recalled that of Thomas Jefferson. Brick was tall and lanky, the perfect Virginia gentleman, and he and Alex struck up a friendship that would endure. But Hawke, lying in his cell night after night, was worried. Kelly had been there for too long a time. He was starved, dehydrated, and the victim of countless beatings and worse. One night, he'd managed to overcome his guards, escape his cell, and snatch Kelly away from his torturers. They raced out into the nighttime desert and never stopped running.

"You say Brick's on the case. Which case?" Hawke asked Stoke.

"Alexei's kidnapping."

"Seriously? Brick's in? Who brought him into the loop?"

"Your buddy Brock."

"Harry? Really? Didn't know he had it in him, god bless him."

"Yeah. He made sure all the CIA station heads in Europe are now aware of Alexei's disappearance Christmas Day. Shared with them all the details of the kidnap operation. And every last one of them has vowed to make it a priority, do whatever they can to help us in a hostage rescue."

"Thank god for Brick Kelly," Hawke said, his voice resonant with relief. He was finally amassing the necessary resources to mount a serious hostage recovery operation against world-class operatives. And it wasn't a moment too soon.

"And thank god for Harry, Boss. Look, I know you don't like him and I know you don't think we need him, but I think you're wrong. Besides, he's our de facto liaison to CIA until we get Alexei back. And anyway, he's put himself on the case until you kick him off."

"Christ, Stoke, you know Brock makes me crazy. Bloody annoying on a lot of levels. You never know what the hell he'll do next."

"I know, I know. Tell me about it. But listen. There's stuff here you need to consider. You remember that KGB sting operation we pulled in Moscow a few years back? Blew up their shit, right, their fancy mansion on the banks of the Moskva River? You, me, and Harry?"

"Of course. We were waiters serving bombs in chafing dishes to those bastards."

Stoke laughed.

"Well, it seems like while we were in Moscow, Agent Brock recruited a mole. A well-placed ranking member of KGB, apparently. Former leader of a Spetsnaz special forces team from the Russian GRU. His name is Oleg Rostov. Code name Rasputin. Remember?"

"Harry brought this guy in?" Hawke said, one bushy black eyebrow lifted. "You're kidding, right?"

"All I am saying is that Harry, all by his lonesome, suckered an experienced Russian military officer into trusting a young American agent from Miami. And Rasputin has given us a way into Putin. If he's still breathing. Which Harry believes is true. Gotta admit, boss, as Ambrose says, that's pretty good gravy."

"Point taken. I will temporarily adjust my attitude about Mr. Brock accordingly."

"At any rate, Harry's still working the guy. And yesterday, on a deserted stretch of South Beach in Miami, Rasputin delivered a nuke right into Harry's lap."

"Tell me."

"Like I say. Your pal Putin may not be dead after all. According to Rasputin, anyway."

"What? Don't be absurd. Pure disinformation. C'mon, Stoke, somebody took him out. KGB assassination. A bloody Kremlin coup, for god's sake. We all know that. Volodya's probably buried right alongside Jimmy Hoffa by now. Under some stadium in New Jersey."

"Well, here's what Harry knows from his source. Okay?"

"Okay? Of course, okay! You think I don't want to know?"

"Okay, here's what. Apparently in the last few months Vladimir began to see the handwriting on the Kremlin walls. He knew his time was short, the axe was swinging his way. So he made plans to disappear for a while. Plot his next move. Go to the only location where he felt like he had any margin of survival. The safest place he could go, right?"

"Right, right, just tell me, Stoke. Cut the drama. Tell me where he is."

"His yacht, that's where, according to Rasputin. *Tsar*. You've been aboard her many times."

"I have, yes."

"Heavily armed, heavily armored, that big boat, would you say? A floating fortress."

"Not up to the standards of my Blackhawke, but, yes. Of course."

"Even SAM missile-protected, and anti-submarine defenses, yes?"

"Yes," Hawke said. "Even back then, a couple of years ago, *Tsar* was where Volodya felt safest. He never said as much, but I always knew he thought of that yacht as his ultimate getaway car."

"So, according to Rasputin, the last anyone saw of Putin was boarding the presidential aircraft at his private airfield. Five passengers. Putin, plus the pilot, copilot, and two stewardesses. One of them being Putin's favorite mistress, a former Miss Ukraine named Ekaterina. Kat for short.

"The flight plan had them heading east and south on a direct course for Nice. *Tsar*'s chopper had been ordered to be waiting out on the tarmac to ferry Vladimir and Ekaterina to the yacht anchored in Cap d'Antibes. Anchors aweigh and they've vamoosed. We don't know where they were headed, of course, but it doesn't matter anymore."

"Why not?"

"The plane never made it to Nice, that's why not. It just dropped off the radar. CIA did a sat recon of the flight path between Moscow and Nice. Nada. No sign of any wreckage, no mayday distress calls from the cockpit, nothing. Up in smoke."

"Oh, the mystery of it all."

"Yeah. But two days ago, we got lucky. Head of CIA in Paris, under orders from Brick Kelly, sent two of his top encrypted communications guys to go out in the field and listen for any sign of radio activity. Even a beep generated by Putin's encrypted sat phone could be traced. For weeks, nothing. But then Monday night, Putin popped his head up and took a look around. Not just a beep. He made a call to Los Angeles. A long call. Who it was and what they talked about, we don't know. But he's alive, and still on the move."

"He's got a friend in L.A. His former right-hand man . . . Uncle Joe . . ."

"Who?"

"Just thinking out loud." Hawke thought for another moment. "Wherever he is, he'll head for France. His best bet is still the yacht. But somehow he has to travel below the radar and board the boat unseen. Then they sail straight for the back of beyond, right? That's what I'd do."

"Right. So here's the deal. Harry's in the air. On a CIA Gulfstream flight to Nice. He wants me and Sharkey to meet him there. Get in position to surprise Putin when he arrives at the yacht."

"So I've got Harry whether I want him or not."

"Afraid so. But right now he's way ahead of the rest of us, don't you agree? We're all playing catch-up?"

"Agreed."

"Best use of my time right now, boss. Have a face-to-face with old Vladimir, see what he knows about Alexei?"

"It certainly is. I'll get my pilot back here tonight. You and your Sharkman can take off at first light."

"Thanks, boss. This is maybe a necessary first step to finding Alexei."

"I know. Okay, good luck. Let's get back up to the war room and debrief everyone on these new developments."

"Do I get Harry?" Stoke said.

"You get Harry. Jesus," Hawke said, shaking his head. "Harry 'I don't give a shit about anybody but me' Brock."

"Right. That Harry," Stoke said.

CHAPTER TWENTY-TWO

Hawke sat back in his chair, sipped his tepid coffee, and looked around the room. His gaze lit on each one of the team members seated around the war room table. After the Rasputin debrief from Stoke, they'd been at it for hours. It was now nearly midnight and everyone was running on caffeine; tobacco smoke swirled about beneath the recessed ceiling lights.

Ambrose had his pipe going full blast and Hawke and Sharkey were gulping coffee and chain-smoking Hawke's gold-tipped Morland cigarettes.

Stoke had booked the private meeting room in the hotel, one with a round table to encourage free-flowing discussion and argument. They were all here now, his team of five reunited. And facing a huge challenge once more. Chalkboards and easels with whiteboards now covered with scribbles, overflowing ashtrays, pungent room-service trays with half-eaten sandwiches and stone-cold pizzas.

Congreve and Sigrid were in deep discussion, arguing about who should and should not be included on Hawke's enemies list. The current list was too long, spanned continents around the world. It had all of the usual suspects and then some, and it needed to be whittled down, especially in light of the new intel regarding Putin's sudden reappearance among the living.

Stoke was talking to Sharkey about logistics. They would be departing for Nice on a Hawke Air plane at first light. Now they were discussing what the team would need in the way of weapons, body armor, transportation, accommodations, passports, encrypted sat phones, et cetera, for the hostage rescue mission to come.

All of which left Hawke alone with his thoughts.

There was still no sign of a ransom note. And his dwindling hopes that Alexei, having suffered a concussion, had simply wandered off after landing at the hospital had evaporated into nothingness. It had been forty-eight hours now, and the absence of any sign of the boy now led him to an inescapable conclusion.

Alexei had been kidnapped.

But why? How? No demands for cash. No threats against his life.

So how had they managed to take him? A snatch on the roof of the hospital when the chopper landed? Too public. Way too public and incredibly complicated to coordinate and execute.

But someone might have torched the rescue helicopter in Italy. If true, that was the key to it all.

They would have to find out if it actually was number four. If it was, all the evidence was pointing him in one direction. If he was right, his enemies list could be shortened considerably. Whoever orchestrated Alexei's kidnapping had enormous resources. And was an extraordinarily powerful adversary. One with the ability to project its reach anywhere on the planet and pull off a spectacular crime in broad daylight.

Three powerful nations on the planet had very good reason to hate him. The Chinese loathed him because he'd slipped into their country and killed a wildly popular rogue general who taken control of the Chinese Communist Party.

The Russians despised him because a couple of years ago he'd humiliated Vladimir Putin in a showdown over Putin's putting troops and tanks on the borders of his Eastern European neighbors.

Putin had disappeared shortly after that final confrontation with Hawke. Nobody knew what had happened to him. Hawke strongly believed it was a suicide. Or even more likely, a KGB murder. The very public humiliation had been the last straw in the man's descent into desperation at the fall of Russia from the world's stage. Under his aegis, they'd gone from superpower status to also-ran.

He closed his eyes, remembering that night, the very last time he and Putin had spoken. The two of them had been alone together, drinking heavily, by the fireside at Putin's private dacha, Rus Lodge outside of Moscow . . . Putin's beloved Russian wolfhound, Blofeld, puddled at his feet, sleeping . . .

IN THE TALL EASTERN WINDOWS of the lodge, the watery thin light beyond took on a vague pinkish cast. Hawke, bleary-eyed, had finally had enough of the endlessly combative conversation. Putin was unapologetic about trying to start World War III by his aggressive actions in the Baltics. Hawke got to his feet and started pacing back and forth before the fireplace, just to get his blood flowing again. He finally spoke.

"Look here, damn it. You don't seem to understand that the Americans have already gone to DEFCON 3, Volodya! A state of war with America already exists! America and Britain are on a war footing, do you understand me? Just waiting to get rid of you once and for all. Don't give them that excuse, Volodya. Don't have history record you as the one who bet it all and lost."

"Fuck you," Putin said. "You hear me? Fuck you, Hawke!"

Putin was plainly drunk now. Hawke knew he had to hurry. The last vestiges of sobriety were now evaporating and, with them, any hope of amelioration or a peace with Russia. Hawke, desperate, said, as forcefully as he'd ever said anything in his life:

"For god's sake! Look at yourself! You're up to your armpits in shit. And now that Western economic sanctions have brought you to your knees, where do you think that leaves you, damn it? Plummeting oil prices have emptied your coffers. You're broke. Your gold reserves are down to twenty tons. And now you would go to war? You don't want to be remembered by future Russian schoolchildren as history's number one fool, do you? Hell, I know you. We're friends, remember?

And you don't want that and I don't want that. You're far too bloody narcissistic for that. Am I wrong? That was a question, damn it. I said, Does the great Vladimir Putin want to be remembered for all time as history's fool? Or not? Now is the time to decide."

Putin paused a moment. Then he rose, quite wobbly now, to his feet. He threw back his head, drained the last of his vodka, and hurled the crystal vodka tumbler against the stone. More shattered bits of glass scattered on the hearthstone, glittering in the firelight.

Everything was broken now. It was all broken. And the end, his end, was very near.

"How long have I got?" Putin said, his voice cracked and shaking. He was a broken man, Hawke saw, one perhaps not long for this world.

Hawke had told him forty-eight hours. In the end, Putin relented. He signed the treaty papers Hawke had brought with him. The next day he told all his commanders in Eastern Europe to stand down and begin withdrawing back inside Russian borders. The threat of imminent world war was over. Hawke had won. Putin had lost.

Hawke would never forget what had happened next. What Putin had told him that night, at the very end.

An unsteady Putin backed up against the wall, rubbing his bruised throat, his eyes glaring and red.

His voice was raw when he finally spoke in a harsh whispery croak. "Oh, what a noble image of yourself you've always had, Alex! The valiant Arthurian knight on his black charger. But you hear this, Hawke. The second you walk out that door, you will no longer enjoy my benevolent protection. Nor will your beloved son, Alexei, be safe, Alex. Nor even the Russian whore who bore you your bastard child. So I suggest you run for the woods once you step outside my door. Run as fast as you can. Do I make myself perfectly clear? Now get out of my sight!"

Nor will your beloved son, Alexei, Putin had said, *be favored with my protection.*

And now his old friend had somehow arranged for a miraculous resurrection . . .

CHAPTER TWENTY-THREE

Riga, Switzerland

Joe heard the sub before he saw it surface. She was moving slowly closer, fifty yards from the end of the pier. It was a monochrome yellow Triton 1000, a smaller version of Putin's personal exploration sub aboard the yacht *Tsar*. Great machines, these Tritons. Capable of diving to a thousand feet, about thirteen feet long, weighing in at about 18,000 pounds, and equipped with two powerful thrusters, it was the real deal.

Joe got to his feet, picked up his leather overnight bag, and headed for the steel ladder at the end of the pier. The night was cold and very still. The delicious smell of the freshwater lake wafted up from below. The night was ready-made for the adventure his life had suddenly become. He was back in the game, all right, and this time he would play to win.

He could see Horst plainly inside the bubble of plexiglass, his face illuminated by the light of his instruments. The little sub slowly approached the pier, and Horst used the submarine's extendable claw to make the craft fast to the ladder. The hatch popped open.

Small lights embedded in the foredeck illuminated it for boarding.

"Careful coming down," Horst said as Joe began his descent to the sub. The dock rungs were coated with thick ice and it was hard to keep his boots from slipping off as he climbed down the ladder. Last thing he needed tonight was plunging all the way to the bottom of a cold dark lake!

"Careful!" Horst shouted again as the Russian slipped again, then caught himself.

He stepped off the bottom rung of the ladder and boarded the Triton. He couldn't help but admire the sub. If ever there was a perfect toy for the man who had everything, the Triton was it. A high-tech masterpiece, the sight of it gave an already freezing Joe Stalingrad a little extra chill.

"Hey, how you doing?" Joe said, sliding down into his seat. "I'm Joe."

"Glad to hear that. I'd be worried if you weren't, my good sir," Horst said, extending his hand. He was a Swiss guy, sure, but one who talked like a normal person trying to sound like a fancy person.

"Glad to be aboard," Joe said. "I love these damn things."

"Subs, you mean?" he said, hitting a button that lowered the hatch with a soft whoosh. He then reversed the props and backed slowly away from the dock, before bringing her around to port and beginning their descent. Stoke watched, fascinated, as the dive began. Horst smiled at him.

"Ready to go? Venting the ballast tanks now. Commencing our dive. All very simple, you see."

The sub nosed over and began to submerge.

"Damn right, subs. Love 'em."

"Not your first voyage to the briny deep then, I take it, sir?"

"No, an old friend of mine has one of these Tritons. We've explored just about everywhere in it . . . off his yacht, you see."

"Then I don't have to give you the safety briefing?"

"I'm good. How long a trip?"

"About an hour, he said, his eyes taking one last look at the weather here on the surface. "We're crossing the lake at its widest point. You saw the Eiger over there, the mountain on the far side, on the horizon?"

"Which one?"

"The highest one, Mr. Stalingrad. Most people know that."

"Really? Is that the Eiger from *The Eiger Sanction*? Clint Eastwood?"

"Indeed, it is. The tall mountain just beside it is Der Nadel. The Needle. Not as famous as the Eiger, but well known just the same. The climbers all call it White Death. There's this vertical face up there that—"

"White Death? Really? Why?" Joe said, as the sub dove deeper.

"A short history lesson, Mr. Stalingrad. In the 1930s, sporting climbers from all over the world began flocking to Switzerland as word of Der Nadel and its impossible vertical face, called the Murder Wall, spread. They came in droves, they did, all determined to conquer the wall. Topping out at 25,430 feet, Der Nadel ranks with Everest and K2 as one of the deadliest mountains in the world. In storm conditions, it *is* the deadliest."

"Holy shit. And I'm going up there?"

"You certainly are, Mr. Stalingrad. Since the first climbers attempted to climb the north face in 1933, over seventy-five men have died up there. Countless more have been severely injured. And here's the thing. Almost everyone lucky enough to survive the climb never went anywhere near that nasty bitch again."

"Oh, goody. Can't wait," Joe said.

"And that mountain, Mr. Stalingrad, is the home of Professor Gerhardt Steinhauser and our destination."

"Can't imagine why the hell anyone would want to live up there, Horst."

"No. You can't. But the Sorcerer does, and it's been his home for decades. When he disappeared, he was the most powerful man in Swiss finance. He ruled the roost. And nothing happened or didn't happen in the great Swiss financial institutions that did not have his blessing or his fingerprints on it. Since the world relies on Switzerland to maintain global financial security, not to mention protect eighty percent of the world's gold reserves, that makes the Sorcerer a one-man world power."

"So why does this genius hide inside a mountain?"

"He cherishes his privacy, you see. Walked away from the outside world and never looked back. Some people, though the professor would never agree, claim he's the most powerful man on earth. Presidents and kings come to kneel at his feet."

"So, what, there's an underwater air lock or something over there, on the other side of the lake? The way we get inside, I mean."

"Air lock, exactly."

Joe smiled. When you were rich, everything was simple. Or something like that. Outside, in the dark underwater world, a single brilliant shaft of light illuminated the route ahead.

Joe was in heaven.

AN HOUR LATER, THE LITTLE sub slid silently inside the submerged air lock. The thick steel and plexiglass doors hissed shut behind it. This secret entrance was located at the base of the mountain, some fifty feet beneath the surface of Lake Zurich. The underwater structure was a steel and glass compartment with controlled pressure inside. Two parallel sets of doors permitted movement between the two areas at different pressures.

Joe looked up. The water inside the airtight compartment began to recede, revealing a white ceiling above with bright recessed lighting.

"Know what I'm thinking about, Horst, old shipmate?"

"No, sir, I do not."

"Groceries."

"Ah. Groceries. Canned goods, et cetera."

"Exactly. So, what? You deliver groceries to the guy this way?" Joe asked, unfastening his seat-belt harness. "I mean, otherwise, how's he eat?"

"The boss told me I can speak freely with you. Says you work for a very close friend of his. So I don't mind sharing a few details."

"Great."

Horst said, "Two larger subs deliver groceries, fresh flowers, and fuel oil, the daily mail and newspapers, firewood, wine, whatever he needs. He owns three of these Tritons, you see. Another pilot—Jurgen's his name—drives the other passenger boat, and the freighter runs every other week. We're on call twenty-four hours a day, seven days a week."

"He lives alone, I suppose."

"My god, no. Has a private army inside, in fact. Not to mention an air force."

"Air force?"

"Small squadron of six F-18s, sir. Pilots, crew, maintenance."

"Jesus Christ. Inside a goddamn mountain?"

"Hmm. You may get to see for yourself. Professor Steinhauser gets very few visitors. I don't know who you are, Mr. Stalingrad, but you certainly must be somebody. To have this kind of access to a man like this, I mean, and—"

"Nah, nah. I'm only an actor," Joe said. "Studied at the Stella Adler Studio in New York. Lived in the West Village for the last couple of years, then moved out to L.A. Got into pictures. Maybe you saw me in *Kill, Baby, Kill!* or my favorite, *The Tipsy Gypsy?* Tarantino helmed that first one. I played the killer."

"Sorry. No. I must have missed those."

"No biggie. My stage name is Joey Stalingrad. I'm all over Hulu, places like that."

"So you're here because . . ."

"He's a huge fan, this Sorcerer. What can I tell you? Seen everything I've ever done. Says my latest, *Too Hot to Sleep,* and *Forrest Gump,* which I was not in, are his two favorite flicks of all time. Of course, he's never seen my star turn in *Tit for Tat.*"

The water level inside the air lock had drained to almost floor level, emptying fast. Horst popped the hatch open and said, "Nice to meet you, Joey. We don't get a lot of actors. So now you exit through that sliding door over there. Press the silver push plate on the wall. There's a well-lit corridor to your left. At the end, directly beneath the mountain, you'll find yourself at an elevator bank. We have four—two for freight, two for people. You take the third one from the left. That's the express that goes straight to the top. It's fifteen thousand feet straight up, but that thing is a rocket. Hold on to the handrail until you come to a complete stop."

Joe said his farewells, climbed out of the Triton, and made his way to the gleaming stainless-steel elevator bank. He pushed the button for one of the center lifts. It opened immediately and he stepped inside. It was cavernous. The door slid silently shut and he looked at his options. The keypad listed different locations: cafeteria, dormitories, aircraft hangar, communications control, weapons command, and, at the very top, residence.

He used one hand to push that top button and then held on to the handrail for dear life. He was expecting something like a Disney World Atlas Rocket Launch, the g-forces contorting his face as he was thrust into zero gravity . . .

It didn't happen.

The elevator was a little faster than normal, but it was certainly no rocket to the moon. It took what seemed like forever to reach the top. Hysterical people, these Swiss. And that Horst!

What a character.

Very Chatty Cathy, as they say in L.A.

CHAPTER TWENTY-FOUR

St. Moritz

I think I know who might have him, and by god, we need to get him out of there fast," Hawke said.

"Who's got him, Alex?" Congreve said, leaning forward while he rekindled his pipe.

"Despite all rumors to the contrary," Hawke said, "Putin apparently might still be alive. And, if so, he's the one who's got Alexei."

Ambrose looked at his friend, studying his face intently. Hawke was desperate to put a name to whoever apprehended his son and to move heaven and earth to find him. Even if it meant jumping to an unwarranted assumption about Putin's involvement.

"How, Alex? Really? Are you so sure? And even if it is him, how in god's name did he do it?"

"God help me, that's what I've been trying to think through! A KGB operation? It almost has to be. And if it's not Putin, if it's not the KGB, then it's the Chinese secret police. Bloody bastards. Those are the only two services I know of capable of mounting such a complex operation."

He paused, and Congreve said, "Keep talking, Alex."

Hawke seemed to have left the room. He did this when he focused intently on a mission.

"Oh, right. Sorry, thinking the whole damn thing through while I speak. This is all conjecture on my part, but here goes. Or how it could have gone. They had early intel about Alexei and me spending a Christmas skiing vacation here at St. Moritz. They had us followed. Learned our routines, Alexei's ski school activities, for instance. Once they had that, they had the genesis of a plan for the kidnapping. Think about it. The boy and his father alone on vacation, far away from the Royal Protection officers at Scotland Yard who keep them safe day and night. They looked for something in the daily schedule that left us the most vulnerable. Then they stole an Air-Rescue chopper."

Stoke said, "Yeah, a gondola a mile or two high is a vulnerable place to be. But, boss, they couldn't know your plans in such detail. How'd they know you two would be on that gondola Christmas morning?"

"They've been monitoring calls going in and out of the hotel. They've been watching our every move since the moment we arrived in St. Moritz. They knew all about the Christmas Day program. And Alexei's participation in the ski school event. Somehow, during the night of Christmas Eve, they attached a small explosive device to the gondola cable."

"Not impossible," Sigrid said. "Minimal security when the tram-cars are out of service."

"My thinking exactly," Hawke said. "Next morning—"

Ambrose sat forward, puffing furiously on his pipe. "Hold on a tick, Alex. You've just lost me."

"It was bound to happen sometime."

"Righto, here's the thing. They knew ahead of time that you'd be arriving at the gondola station fairly early on Christmas morning, yes? Because of the ski school's printed Christmas Day program, I mean."

"Yes, yes! Of course they would. It's child's play for these KGB thugs. I'm sure they had someone out in the car park waiting for the arrival of the two Range Rovers."

"But, Alex, what they did *not* know—indeed, had no way of knowing—is precisely which gondola you'd be taking up the mountain. Yes? That was all up to chance."

Hawke's face fell. "Yes. You're absolutely right. God, I hadn't even thought of that."

"That's why I'm here, dear boy, remember? The Brain that came from Outer Space, as you once so eloquently described me."

Hawke smiled. "So, Constable, where does that leave us? Adrift and clueless once more?" Hawke said, disappointment coloring his words. How could he have been so stupid?

"Not at all!" Congreve said happily. "To the contrary. If my theory proves correct, we are now in the most fortunate position of being able to prove that this tram accident was no accident!"

"Elucidate, Constable," Hawke said.

"A plastic explosive of sufficient size and power to separate the cable from the car's roof would have to be no bigger than a golf ball. A small wad of Semtex and a remote radio fuse would do the trick, right, Stokely?"

"Absolutely."

"So they were faced with a simple solution as to which car you would eventually take. Install explosive devices on *all six cars*!"

Hawke smiled. "Which means there are still five devices left on five gondolas."

"Indeed it does! Miss Kissl," Congreve said, "could you please shoot an email to our friend Blinky at CIA Zurich? Tell him to get a team out to the Corviglia tramway straightaway. I mean tonight, not tomorrow. Check out our new theory. If I'm right about the remaining five, have them remove them and get out of there before daybreak. We won't be talking to local police about this."

"Why not, Chief Inspector?" Stoke said.

"I have little interest in our enemies knowing that we may be onto them. And what our next steps may or may not be. Yes?"

They all nodded.

"So, Alex," Congreve said, "Please continue with your fascinating narrative."

"Well," Hawke said, "let me back up a bit. KGB agents are inside the station. They're monitoring passengers arriving and the gondolas leaving the tram station, waiting for Alexei, Tristan, and me to arrive. They wait until we've boarded and the doors are closed. Then they radio the two Swiss KGB pilots circling above in the stolen helicopter. They tell them exactly which gondola we're aboard and that we will depart momentarily for the top."

"Where exactly is the chopper at this point, Alex?"

"Already on station. Circling high above. Swiss Air-Rescue choppers are always flying about. Wouldn't arouse any undue suspicion, I wouldn't think."

"No, it wouldn't, boss," Stoke said. "None at all. Folks would think they were out looking for somebody got lost, that's all."

"So our tram starts its slow climb upward. The pilots descend to an altitude where they can observe exactly what's going on. At a prearranged moment in our transit, they trigger the bomb via radio signal. After the explosion, they hover above, monitoring the emergency radio channel. When they get the emergency alert, they radio other rescue services to stand down. Then they descend and fly in to effect the rescue. And there you have it."

Sigrid said, "What about our friend Pfeffer at Swiss Air-Rescue? Wouldn't he send out a helo?"

"No," Hawke said, "as I said, because the on-scene chopper pilot tells them he's an Alpine rescue helo with two additional rescue helos en route. Additional help is not needed. As soon as the pilot of the fake rescue helo gets the children aboard, he radios the other rescue services. He requests assistance off-loading all the adult passengers. He then sets his course for the hospital and no one is any the wiser."

"Very good, Alex," Congreve said. "Couldn't have laid it out any better myself."

"Thank you."

"He lands on the hospital roof and then what?"

"When he lands at the hospital, he makes sure one of the children doesn't get off. It's the only possible explanation."

"But why do it now, boss?" Stoke asked. "Kidnap Alexei?"

"Putin's obviously in exile somewhere," Hawke said. "Nearly broke and alone. He's in financial disarray. He may demand money from me, but I don't think that's it. Nearly broke for Putin means he's down to his last few billion."

"What do you think it is, Alex?" Sigrid said. "What do you think he wants from you?"

"Alexei is his de facto insurance plan. Whatever he's up to, he knows he can keep me out of his way as long as he has the power to kill my son. He wants me to leave him alone. He's planning something big, and the last thing he wants is me coming after him again. Especially after what I did to him last time."

"Putin thinks the threat to Alexei will keep you from going after him?"

"Yes."

"But it doesn't?"

"Yes. It does not. And that's where he's made his first mistake. He's underestimated us. In this very room, I've got the best hostage rescue team on the planet. With an uncanny ability to locate hostages, get inside, and get them out to safety."

Congreve thought for a moment before he spoke. And then said: "Well, hopeful news. But none of us can even begin to assume that Alexei is safe. Putin will of course ultimately assure us that no harm will come to him. That the boy is insurance against our intervention. At least until Putin has succeeded in whatever it is he's planning. At that point, I have no idea what he'll do. Anything's possible. We need to move fast, and we need to move smartly. The clock and the calendar are not our allies in this."

Hawke was staring at the famous criminalist, nodding his head in assent. "After all, he's slightly crazy," Hawke said. "His fall from grace has been spectacular. We can't afford to underestimate what he might do or promise at any given moment. Where he is, I've no idea. But we will find the miserable bastard."

"Is the bar still open?" Sharkey asked, having remained silent throughout the meeting. "Tell you what, I could use a cocktail along about right now."

Stoke smiled, but Hawke did not. He still wasn't sure about what the Sharkman brought to the party.

With that, Hawke declared the meeting over, saying they all needed to get a good night's sleep.

Tomorrow was another day, another chance to find his son.

CHAPTER TWENTY-FIVE

It was well past midnight when there was a soft knocking at his chamber door.

Three knocks . . . a pause . . . three knocks more. A signal that only one other person knew.

Hawke slipped from his bed and donned his red flannel robe. Experiencing a sudden shiver from some nameless anxiety, he collected himself, then padded out to the darkened living room to answer. For some odd reason, he thought he knew who might be waiting there.

Hoping his midnight premonition was wrong, he reached for the latch.

"Who is it?" he said in his sleep-roughened voice, cracking the door.

Sigrid.

Yes.

"It's me," she said, smiling up at him. "Sorry to disturb you. I can't sleep. Can I please come in and talk to you? It's very important."

"Really? So important it can't wait till morning, Sigrid? I'm trying to get some sleep. I'm driving Stoke and Sharkey to their flight at first light, remember?"

"Alex, listen. Don't be angry with me. I've been going insane. I want to explain, to tell you why I was so horrible to you and Alexei. The truth is, I can't stand being apart from you another day. Hell, another hour. Please let me come in, Alex." She looked like hell and she'd been crying.

He swung the door open, stood back, and motioned her inside. She was oddly dressed, wearing a nightgown and a bed jacket with the Hermès scarf tied round her neck.

"Thank you," she whispered, sliding past him, avoiding his angry eyes.

He went to the mahogany sideboard and picked up a crystal decanter. "Would you like a drink?"

"Yes, thank you. Can we sit over there by the fire? My room up in the tower is freezing. May I borrow a blanket?"

"Sure, there's a throw rug on the sofa. Pick a chair and I'll bring you whiskey. Rocks, right? I seem to recall that was your poison of choice."

"No, neat tonight."

He poured her a drink and one for himself, neat—not that he needed another, but on the off chance it would help him get back to sleep. His hopes for a restful night's slumber had just gone up the chimney like smoke from the fire.

"There you go," he said, handing her the whiskey and adding another log to the fire. He collapsed into the deep leather chair opposite her, gave her a wan smile, and waited for her to speak.

"Thank you for letting me stay here in Zurich, Alex. I was afraid you'd take one look at me getting off your plane and put me on the next flight back to Heathrow."

"Don't thank me, thank Ambrose. If he thinks you can help me find my son, that's good enough for me. I seem to find myself in the rather unusual position of needing all the help I can get."

She tried on a smile of her own. "Ambrose and I are a pretty good team . . ."

"Hmm."

"Please don't be angry. Not now."

"Why not? I've been angry for months. A year! Why the hell shouldn't I be angry now?"

"Because finding Alexei and getting him to safety is the only thing we should be concerned with right now. Right? I came here to help, Alex. I hope you'll let me? We'll find them and then, who knows? Maybe we'll be reunited again . . . just like . . ."

She looked tired and bruised and as if tears were near.

"I'm glad to see Alexei's well-being is something you're concerned about, Sigrid. You could have fooled me that night at Casa Morgano on Capri. You didn't give a good goddamn about him then . . . or me, for that matter. Even Pelham was horrified by your behavior."

"I know, I know. I'm so sorry, Alex. I want you to know that I come to you with a deeply repentant heart. I only hope you can find it in yours to forgive me."

Hawke, wrestling with his demons, stared balefully into the fire. "Why, Sigrid? Why now? I'd finally erased you. And now you come back? If you only knew the pain your disappearance caused my son, you would—"

"Of course I know!" she said, "Do you think I'm a monster? Does nothing at all remain of the feelings we had for each other? The love I gave so freely? My devotion to you both?"

Hawke got to his feet and went back to the sideboard and the whiskey. "Devotion? Is that what they call it now? Not good enough, damn you, Sigrid. Not good enough by any standard of decent behavior. One minute there for us, all of us, the next not. No explanation. Look, it's late. Maybe you should just go back to bed like a good little girl."

"Or maybe I just need a reminder . . ." she whispered, not lifting her head.

"Reminder of what?"

"Reminder of how good little girls ought to behave—a much-needed attitude adjustment, you used to call it. Remember, Alex?

The orange riding crop you bought for me in Hermès that time in Paris? The one you carried around the big suite at the Ritz like a Prussian officer's swagger stick, slapping it against your thigh and swishing it about over your head and . . . making me crawl round and round the dining room table on my hands and knees, swatting at my rump and telling me to—Is that what you want? Because, if it is, then—"

"Enough! For god's sake. Have you really sunk this low? After all this, do you now turn out to be just some cheap trick? How low can you really go? That's a question, Sigrid. Answer it."

"No!" she cried out, sobbing. "That's not how I turn out. I turn out to be someone who is madly, wildly, deeply in love with you. Someone who can't go another day without you. Someone, Alex, who would do anything, *anything*, to get Alexei back!"

"Sigrid, will you please calm down? Stop crying. It's not working!"

"Shall I take my clothes off? Stand in front of you with my head bowed and remove them article by article? Slowly and with great—"

"Shut up!"

Furious, he was out of his chair and standing over her in a blink. He grabbed a handful of her hair and scarf and yanked her head back. He was shocked at what he saw. The pain and fear in her eyes. The pallid skin, the badly applied makeup, the faint bruises under her eyes. The buttons on her frilly white blouse mis-buttoned, lipstick smeared on the collar, her breath hot and not sweet . . . and the yellowed bruises on her neck.

She'd come undone. "Don't hit me, please," she whimpered.

"*Hit you?* I've never hit you. You've got me confused with someone else. Who *has* been hitting you, Sigrid? Someone has . . . Look at these bruises on your neck. What the hell is going on?"

"Oh, Alex, it's been a nightmare. A thousand times I wanted to pick up the phone to call you and explain everything—but I couldn't do it. I couldn't, that's all."

"Explain it to me now, or back to your room and to bed with you. All right? I'm listening."

He got up and walked over to the drinks table, adding a splash of scotch to his glass.

"All right, I'll tell you everything. But when I'm done, you may not want me anymore, darling. Do you still want to know?"

"Yes."

"I have to go back to the beginning for you to understand, Alex. Please be patient with me."

"I'm listening," he said, feeling the hot thrill of good hot whiskey down his throat.

CHAPTER TWENTY-SIX

S till listening," Hawke said, crossing his long legs. "Spit it out, Sigrid."

He watched her carefully, saw her make a huge effort to compose herself before launching into her tale of woe.

"My father, Jurgen Kissl, was a sheep farmer. My mother died in childbirth. I grew up an only child on our small farm high in the mountains above Teifenthaler. Think Heidi and her grumpy grand-father, about sixty kilometers from here. He was a mean drunk, my dad, and when he'd had enough schnapps, he came after me, scream-ing that he hated me when he beat me, telling me that I had reminded him of my mother."

Already morose at this tale of impending woe, Hawke found himself staring bitterly into the flickering firelight while he sipped his whiskey. As much as he had wanted an explanation for her abject behavior, he loathed the idea of sitting up late into the night hearing another sob story. He had a sob story of his own if he wished to be depressed—

"Heidi after the fall," Hawke said, trying to avoid the irony in his tone.

She looked over at him, shaking her head sadly. "Curb the sarcasm, please. It hurts."

"Sorry."

"Do you want to hear this or not? God knows I don't want to hear it myself telling it."

"Please. Yes, I want to hear it."

"All right, then. Be kind. When I turned eighteen, I escaped. I took what little money I had and went to Zurich to look for work. I'd always been interested in art, I guess, so I took a job as receptionist in a very fancy avant-garde gallery on Grossmünster Strasse. It was called A Clean, Well-Lighted Place, like the Hemingway story, remember? I didn't get much of a salary, but it was enough to afford a one-room walk-up and food on the table.

"Everyone liked me. I was pretty and bright, knew my art, and I was good for business. As well as the artists we featured, and the best customers from around the world, you know, our biggest clients. Soon I was promoted to a sales assistant, one of four. A year later, to a sales manager, one of two.

"It didn't hurt that the gallery owner, Felix, had fallen madly in love with me. He was married with two children, but he kept me in a side pocket. He was an artist too, but his paintings never sold like the Picassos and Pollocks and Dalís I was selling for him.

"Then one sunny day, my ship came in, as the Americans say. I managed to sell a large Pollock to a handsome young Russian oligarch for five million euros. That night Felix took me for dinner up at the Dolder Grand hotel. For dessert, he gave me a check for five hundred thousand dollars and a big diamond from Van Cleef & Arpels. He said he was going to leave his wife and marry me. But he was almost fifty and I was not yet twenty and I had the presence of mind to put him off of that notion.

"We stayed together, Alex, but it was never the same after I refused him. I think my rejection of the marriage proposal humiliated him, although that was never my intention. He had a cruel streak and he often took it out on me. *Plus ça change, plus c'est la même chose, n'est-ce pas?* And so I . . . I . . . oh, hell, I don't know if I can do this!"

"Do you want another drink, Sigrid?" Hawke said, feeling how hard this must be for her.

"Oh, yes, that would be lovely, Alex. Just a small one, please. Are you bored? Please tell me if you are and I will—"

"I'm not bored."

"Anyway, for the next six months, I treated myself like a queen. Trips to Venice and Cap d'Antibes on the weekends. Suites at the Ritz when I went to Paris on buying trips. Then one day the police came to the gallery. They arrested me, and Felix as well. The Pollock was in fact a fake, beautifully forged by Felix himself. His real fortune stemmed from his brilliant forgeries of the modern masters. The Russian mobster had incontrovertible proof of the crime, including a damning appraisal by MoMA in New York. I appeared in court and was sentenced to one year in prison."

"You served time in prison?"

"I did."

"Did you include that fact on your Scotland Yard application?"

"No, I didn't, Alex. How could I have?"

"How could you not? Surely you were innocent, Sigrid," Hawke said, giving her his full attention. "I hope you had a lawyer, for god's sake. It takes an expert art historian to spot a first-class fake. And, surely no one could accuse you of that . . ."

Silence.

"Did you know the paintings you were selling were forgeries, Sigrid?"

"Yes, I did know it—I'd watched Felix in his studio all that time. I'm so embarrassed and it was shameful, my behavior. But I was so young, and all that success and money clouded my judgment."

"Not all that innocent, it would appear."

"I deserve that, I guess. And worse. But I spent the whole time I was imprisoned beginning to formulate what my life would be when I got out. I pictured myself as a tiny leaf, shiny and new. I read every book in the prison library. I discovered the miracle of books for the first time—that a ship is a book that can ferry you away to distant worlds. I studied history and economics day and night."

She paused a moment, sipping her drink in silence, collecting her thoughts for the next chapter of her tale.

"Then what?" Hawke asked her, anger and disbelief blowing through his mind like a raging storm.

CHAPTER TWENTY-SEVEN

Okay. When I got out, I applied to the Universität Zürich. I was accepted. I devoted my entire being to scholarship, soaking up wisdom and history and economics and finance like a dehydrated sponge. When I graduated, it was with honors, Alex, first in my class. A month later, I was offered a spot in the training program at Credit Suisse. I was fast-tracked to the top. I rose to the level of senior vice-president, international banking in no time. And then I met you and fell in love for the first time in my life. The only time."

"And then?"

"And then I broke all of our hearts."

"Tell me, Sigrid. The most painful part for me has been not knowing why you did what you did on Capri. Left me and my son without so much as a good-bye."

"Okay. You'd been in hospital for complications due to surgery to remove that bullet from your spine. We'd had a fight and then you stopped talking to me. I was still in love but most unhappy. Then two days before you and I went to Capri, Felix came to my apartment in Zurich. I had not seen him in over ten years. It was obvious that a long stretch in prison had not had the same salutary effect on him as it had on me. He'd been living in Morocco, he said. He was a wreck, unrecognizable as being the beautiful sophisticated man he'd once been. He said he'd been ill, that he had a heart condition . . . and—"

"What did he want?"

"Money, what else? It was awful. He'd been stalking me. He said he knew I was involved with someone very rich, but he wanted me back. That he couldn't live without me. That he wanted me to take care of him. That his wife and children refused to even see him anymore. Even talk to him on the phone. I tried to get him to leave but he wouldn't. He struck me. And then—and then he kept asking me questions about you."

"About *me*? What the hell about me did he want to know? For god's sake, Sigrid?"

"He said he'd been following you for weeks. And that—and that—"

"And that what?"

"He wanted to know how rich you really were because he—he'd been thinking about kidnapping Alexei. Getting a million-dollar ransom out of you. And that he wanted my help."

"My god, Sigrid."

"I told him no, of course. Never! I told him you were a powerful man in the UK secret service and that you'd find him and kill him. I screamed at him to get out or I'd call the police. I picked up the phone, but he ripped it out of my hand and began to hit me with it. I begged him to stop. It was no use. He said he wanted me to help him another way. Find a way access your accounts at Credit Suisse."

"Bloody hell," Hawke said, his blood aboil.

"Yes. I refused, obviously. And then he said, 'You'll find a way to help me, Sigrid. Or I will make your life a living hell. Understand? I want fifty thousand Swiss francs on the first of each month. I don't care how you get it from that rich boyfriend of yours. But you will be very, very sorry if you miss a payment. You will wake up wishing you were dead.'"

"He threatened your life?"

"No. Worse. He said that if I refused to take him back and give him the money, he'd find a way to kill you or kidnap Alexei on his own. Send a ransom note that included the details of my sordid little story. Tell you about my secret life and ruin me for you forever. Tell you that I was a convicted criminal. That I had lied about my police record on my applications to the university, to Credit Suisse, and even to Scotland Yard when I applied for the training program. I would be humiliated. My life would be effectively over."

"And then?"

"He said that I had forty-eight hours to make up my mind. If my answer was no, then he had nothing to lose. If he couldn't have me, no one could. He would find a way to kill you and Alexei. Then he left. Next morning you and I flew to Capri and checked into Casa Morgano. I was a wreck, completely distraught, but I tried to hide it. I was in panic mode. I had no idea how to handle this situation."

"I see. You're quite a little actress, aren't you?"

She had no answer. She sat and stared.

For a time the room was filled with silence save the crackling of the logs. Finally Alex spoke into the gloom. "I knew something was wrong, Sigrid. You put on a brave front. But nothing made sense. We'd been so happy on Capri before . . . and then you just disappear? The only plausible things I could think was that I was *hors de combat* sexually because of my back surgery. Or that you'd been diagnosed with some deadly disease and didn't want to me to suffer along with you . . . What did you do about the money?"

"I went back to him, god help me. Straight from Capri. But only, and I mean *only*, to keep him away from you and Alexei, darling! Please believe me, it's the truth! I've been paying him of course, every month, ever since I left you. Out of my savings. I've spent all these years investing what I make, saving every penny. I've done incredibly well in the markets, but I could not go on forever . . . I went back to him to buy some time. Keep him out of your life, get him to forget about you somehow. Be there for him, make him believe I cared."

"And now what, Sigrid? He'll know about us sooner or later."

"Don't worry, darling. Felix can't hurt us anymore."

"What do you mean?"

"He's dead."

"Dead? What happened?"

"A month ago, I couldn't take any more the depression, the drinking, the beatings. I left him and went to hide in Paris. He must have followed me. I don't know. But one night he broke into my flat and tried to kill me. My screams brought the neighbors and the police banging on the door. He went out the window and down the fire escape.

"A week later, distraught, I flew to Casablanca. I had a plan, insane though it was. Talk to Felix. Try to help him stop drinking and regain his confidence. Make him swear to leave us both alone. I rented a car and drove to the little village where he lived in squalor and found him.

"He was very violent at first. Screaming that I'd ruined his life. He threw me to the bed, ripped open my blouse, and started beating me, choking me. I felt close to blacking out and knew if I did, he would kill me. I started kicking him, got him to let me go. I just kept talking, trying to soothe him until I could see he was ready to listen.

"I told him I'd come to a realization. I now understood how much he needed me. I would take care of him, nurse him back to health. And then I—"

"Stop. What was the name of the village? Where he lived?"

"Just up the coast from Casablanca, called Asilah."

"Please go on, Sigrid."

"I told him that I'd rented a little cottage. That it was right on the sea. Beautiful, pristine white with a peaked red tile roof. We could take long walks by the sea. I wanted him to see it. He agreed to come with me. But there was an accident on the way to the cottage. He was driving like a maniac. He went into a hairpin turn too fast and lost control."

Hawke got to his feet and began pacing back and forth before the fire. "I cannot believe this, Sigrid. I feel like I'm losing my mind. First Alexei, and now, now this nightmare bedtime story of yours . . . it's just about unbearable . . ."

He poured himself another scotch and went to sit in the window seat, as far away from her as he could get. "Finish it, for god's sake. End this."

"We went off the road. Smashed into some rocks on a high cliff overlooking the sea. The car flipped upside down and halfway over the edge and we had to get out. I tried to pull him out, undid his seat belt, but he was unresponsive. Unconscious. He was too heavy and trapped behind the steering wheel. I climbed out the broken rear window . . . and jumped. Five seconds later, I watched the car go over the steep cliff and all the way down. It exploded when it hit the rocks at the bottom."

"It was an accident? You're sure he didn't do it deliberately? Because I'm not so sure."

"Yes. I believe it was. It doesn't matter anymore."

"I've been meaning to ask you about those terrible yellow bruises on your throat, Sigrid? Thinking maybe you tried to kill him yourself and that he put up a hell of a struggle."

"What? From the seat belt in the crash, of course! Damn you, you don't believe me? How dare you! You think I killed him? Oh my god, Alex, I could never do a thing like that! You've got to believe me. I love you. And I love Alexei and want to help you find him! I could no more murder a man than—than—"

"I'm going to bed. Please see yourself out. I will say this. I hope to god you're telling the truth now, Sigrid."

"Will you at least give me time enough to convince you, darling? Please do that for me, won't you? I beg you . . ."

"I'll see how I feel in the morning, Sigrid. I'm not promising anything. By lying your way into a Scotland Yard position, you've already put me in the god-awful position of having to conceal the truth about your past from Ambrose Congreve. A man who thinks the world of you. A man whose trust I cherish. Good night."

CHAPTER TWENTY-EIGHT

Hawke, sleepless, rolled over and reached for the bedside telephone. "Ambrose, it's me. You awake?"

"I am now. Good lord, what time is it?"

"Sorry. Sorry, I can't sleep. I keep thinking about that wreck of the small aircraft in Italy that CIA satellite picked up. If we're right, and it's the Swiss helo, and it's Putin who has Alexei, we need another entry point in Putin's world to find my son. I just called my pilot, told him I needed a gas-and-go. Right now. I want to go to that crash site down in Italy, give it a fine-tooth comb. We may come up empty, but we need a place to start."

"I can't argue with that, dear boy."

"Thanks. And I want to go now."

"Right, copy that. I'll meet you in the lobby café in ten minutes. We'll grab a quick coffee."

"See you then," Hawke said, and that's when he noticed a large yellow envelope slid beneath his door.

"HAVE A LOOK AT THIS," Hawke said, pulling up a chair at the corner table where Congreve was sipping his coffee.

"What is it?"

"I haven't opened it yet. Better you do it, as it may be evidence ..."

"Appeared out of nowhere?"

"Slipped under my bedroom door during the night. I've no idea who—"

"Never mind. We can check the hotel's CC cameras in the hall ..."

"Open it, for god's sake, Ambrose."

Congreve slit the envelope, withdrew the contents. He stared bug-eyed at the eight-by-ten black-and-white photograph.

"He's alive, Alex! Your son is alive! Look at this!"

Hawke was almost afraid to look. "Oh, dear god. He *is* alive, isn't he?"

It was a picture of Alexei, apparently in good health, standing before a wall covered with stick drawings, unmistakably created by his son. In his hand, a copy of yesterday's *International Herald Tribune*.

Hawke failed to stifle the muffled sobs that came up from his heart.

Congreve looked up at Hawke, saw his face, and said, "Alex, this is the best news. At least now we know that Alexei is *alive*, Alex. You don't have to worry about that anymore. Try to calm down. I can hear the weariness in your voice. Are you getting any sleep?"

"Not much. I don't have time for it. I'm not going to slow down, I'm never going to relax. Not until I've found my son. Do you understand me, Constable?"

"Yes. And we will find him, Alex, by god and all that's holy." Hawke was staring at the photo in his hands.

"Look! There's a note scrawled on the back."

Congreve turned the photo over. This is what he saw handwritten there in fat black letters:

The wolf still has razor-sharp fangs.
Stay far, far away or he will die ...
Der Wolf

"What the hell?" Hawke said, staring at the signature.

"You know this man, Alex? Der Wolf? German chap, obviously."

"I do. Not German. German father, Russian mother. We met in Cuba. Der Wolf is a powerful KGB general named Sergey Ivanov. He managed to capture Stokely and me on that joint MI6-CIA mission to Cuba to assassinate him. We nearly died from the torture, but escaped to Guantánamo Bay, where I ordered a drone strike on his headquarters. His seaside hotel was flattened in the attack. I was told that bastard Ivanov was dead."

"Perhaps not, Alex, wouldn't you say?"

AN HOUR AND A HALF later, just before dawn, Hawke's sleek and darkly blue Gulfstream G650 touched down near the lovely town of Lugano on the shores of Lago Maggiore. Half an hour after that, they were in a hired car, making their way up into the mountains that loomed over the lakeside town.

"Surely you're aware that someone is following us, Alex," Congreve said casually.

"Yes, I noticed that," Hawke said. He'd never sounded more cheerful. There was a lightness to him now, one that Congreve had not seen since that terrible Christmas Day. Knowing for certain that his son was still alive, healthy, and apparently unharmed had made a world of difference in his friend's take on life. Some of his former jauntiness had now reappeared in the determined set of his jaw.

"Now, who in the world could that be, Alex? Following us here? Any idea? We just got here."

"KGB? Which would mean they're still following my every move?"

"Hmm. Got hold of your flight plan somehow and rang up their man in Lugano."

"Meaning my room phone at Badrutt's is tapped."

"Something like that."

"Are you armed, Constable?"

"Well armed, in fact. Heckler & Koch MP5. You?"

"Packing heat, too," Hawke said.

"Please tell me it's not that Walther PPK peashooter of yours."

"Kimber 1911 LAPD Swat, actually. Highly recommended by Stoke's friend Harry Brock. CIA Miami."

"Good news. There's a turning up ahead there. Top of the next hill. Let's get there first and set up an ambush? Yes?"

"No. Let's lead them to the crash site and see what they do. At this point, I'd rather chat with them than kill them. See what we can learn. Who knows, maybe they work for whoever is now calling himself the Wolf."

"Agreed."

"The wreckage site is just over that rise. Speed up. We want to be there first, find high ground."

They turned into an off-road glacial ravine that widened out into a boulder-strewn field at the bottom. And there were the charred remains of what looked to have been of some kind of aircraft. Hawke hit the brakes and raised a small pair of high-powered binoculars to his eyes, surveying the scene below.

"See anything interesting?" Congreve asked.

"Yes. Yes, I certainly do, thank god."

"What is it, Alex?"

"I don't see any evidence at all of human remains. None."

"Let's go down and have a closer look, shall we?"

THERE WAS CRIME SCENE TAPE surrounding a roughly circular area strewn with boulders, perhaps fifty feet or more across—rotted ice, ash and blackened wreckage. Hawke parked the car behind an outcropping of rock and the two men climbed out. Then he and Ambrose quickly scrambled to higher ground.

Hawke put his binoculars to his eyes. He did a quick but careful scan of the wreckage.

Something seemed very odd about the crash scene to Hawke, who quickly recognized what it was. "There's no surrounding debris field, Constable. Beyond the tape. None."

"Right. Whatever it was, it didn't crash here. It landed here and exploded later."

"Yes. The Russians flew that chopper and Alexei somewhere first, stashed him in a predetermined location, then flew the helo back here to destroy the evidence."

"Bloody hell. So it's got to be a helo, not a small airplane."

"Correct. Hold on—here they come," Ambrose said, squinting in the brilliant sunshine and pulling his side arm from the holster under his left arm. Hawke swung the binoculars in the direction Congreve was pointing his weapon.

"Yeah. There're four of them in the car," Hawke said, bringing the mini-binocs back to his eyes. "Get ready."

To their surprise, the four men inside the car didn't follow them on the snow-rutted road into the ravine. They kept going and appeared moments later at a much higher vantage point. Hawke trained the high-powered binocs on them.

"They've pulled over and parked. Four men inside. Not getting out of the car. Two in front, two in the rear. The guy in the passenger seat has his high-powers on us. You don't think they could be CIA, do you?"

"Protecting the crash site? Maybe. They did guarantee they'd keep it sterile until you'd had a chance to do a recon. But I'm not picking up CIA vibes here, as your pal Harry Brock might say."

"So what do we do?" Hawke said.

"Do what we came here for. Comb the wreckage for physical evidence and clues to the identity of the pilots. See what happens. If they start shooting, we can be pretty sure they're not from Langley."

Hawke said, "You're right. Let's go. Keep a weather eye on that car there, though. Here, take my binoculars."

Hawke picked his way carefully through the rocky cover. Congreve quickly followed right behind him. Both of them were exposed periodically, but there was no gunfire from the car, at least not yet.

"Bloody hell. Look, let's divide the scene in half. You take from here to the fuselage, I'll take the rest of it. That's got to be what's left of the cockpit right there. You take that locale, oh great master of forensic science."

"Alex, please. This is not funny. Let's get this over with before we start to take fire."

"They're not getting out. They're still sitting up there in the car. They get out or I see a rifle, we make for that nest of boulders over there, right?"

Congreve didn't answer. He was down on his knees, turning a blackened object over and over in his hands. "Look here, Alex. See this? This is—it's a piece of the chopper's fuselage . . . blackened, but with visible paint remaining."

Hawke stared at it. The visible paint was red. With a partial white marking that could well be the lower half of the number four.

A sharp retort cracked the air wide open. High-powered rifle, Hawke knew instantly.

"Damn it to hell!" Congreve shouted, his left hand clutching his shoulder.

Congreve, hit, was spun all the way round, a bright red blossom of blood on his right shoulder.

"Ambrose!" Hawke cried, firing his weapon up at the two men as he raced back toward his friend.

There was a lot of blood—too much blood.

CHAPTER TWENTY-NINE

Zurich

Mr. Joseph Stalingrad of Los Angeles, California, stepped out of an enormous elevator and into the strange and exciting new world of Professor Gerhardt Steinhauser and his Magic Mountain.

Alias the Sorcerer.

Joe found himself inside a mammoth cave carved out of rock. He now understood the true meaning of the word *cavernous*. Holy shit. Joe'd been meaning to drive the Vette over to Carlsbad Caverns in New Mexico, but hadn't made it. But he'd seen the postcard and those caverns had nothing on this joint.

And this was only the ground floor!

The interior dimensions of the damn thing were nearly those of a United Airlines hangar out at LAX! There was a funny smell too, one that he didn't recognize at first and then he did. The whole place smelled of engine oil and grease and heavy machinery. He moved deeper into the interior.

That's when he first saw the squadron of fighter jets. Four perfectly aligned rows of them in the hangar. F/A-18s too, pretty hot-shit aircraft. Silver fuselages with a mountan peak emblem on the tails, and the words *White Death* near the nose. They were in tiptop condition, looked just like they did sitting out on the deck of an aircraft carrier, waiting in line for the catapult shot. He walked over to the nearest one and—

"Can we help you?" a voice in the darkness said.

Four beefy characters in black uniforms materialized out of the gloom, carrying serious assault weapons. "Can we help you?" one repeated, and Joe, who was no slouch at recognizing sarcasm if not irony when he heard it, didn't hear any. He's just being polite, Joe found himself thinking. He's *Swiss*, for crissakes.

"Yeah, I guess so." Joe said. "I think I pushed the wrong button or the wrong elevator. Something."

"Which button did you mean to push, sir?"

"Um, let's see. Residence? Yeah. That was the one."

"Yes, well, this isn't the residence. Nobody's allowed on this level unless they've been cleared by the air boss. Who hasn't cleared you."

"No, no, I understand. Just a simple mistake. I have an appointment and—"

"An appointment? Really?"

"That's what I said."

"Just who are you looking for, sir?"

"I'm here to see Professor Steinhauser."

"He's not receiving visitors at the moment. Perhaps you could stop by again? Say, next year, or the one following?"

"Look here, pal, I got—"

"Are you expected?"

"I sure as hell hope so. I just took a long ride across a frozen lake in a submarine to get here." Joe looked around. "Say, is this a natural cave? Hand-of-God kind of thing?"

"God had nothing to do with the inside of this mountain, Mr. Stalingrad. As you will soon hear from the professor, everything you will see during your visit is the work of Hitler's best Nazi engineers. Hitler had the entire complex, all twelve levels, built in total secrecy."

"He actually lived in here? I've never heard of him living in Switzerland."

"No. But it was his plan throughout the war. After conquering

Europe and the successful invasion of Switzerland, *der Führer* would rule his glorious new Nazi empire from right here at the top of the world. Zurich was to be the new capital of the New Europe, and this was to be the ruler's palace. When Berlin fell, Hitler and Albert Speer were working on a Nazi aerodrome here in Zurich, one twice the size of *Tempelhof* in Berlin."

"What the hell is that noise?" Joe asked. Suddenly, hearing a deep rumble from somewhere far back in the cavern, he looked up. Something really enormous was on the roll. You could almost feel it moving forward toward them through the darkness. The vibration beneath his boots told him it was on the rail tracks laid in the stone floor, tracks that stretched away into the blackness of a large tunnel.

"Seriously? What the *hell* is it?" he asked the guard, upon seeing the approach of a hulking silhouette.

"We're moving some of our heavy artillery around," the lead guard said. "Keeps the wheels greased, you know."

"Of course," Joe said, enchanted with the whole layout and the nazified over-the-topness of absolutely everything inside this mountain. He could hardly wait to see the other levels.

Seeing the gaping maw of the huge black muzzle emerge first, Joe held his breath. It simply wasn't possible, but there it was. A massive German cannon, the most famous one, called the 88, was now rolling down the tracks straight toward them. He'd seen only one like it before, and that was in the movie *The Guns of Navarone*. Anthony Quinn had really rocked that role, his opinion.

"Are you guys serious?" Joe said. "What's an eighty-eight doing up here at fifteen thousand feet?"

"Part of our home defensive systems," the lead guy said. "A small part, yes, but an effective one if it's ever needed to dissuade an attacker. Hasn't been fired in anger since Hitler made a brief foray into Switzerland in World War II. Operation Tannenbaum, it was called."

"A deterrent, you're saying," Joe said, admiring the big gun.

Suddenly a giant section of the rough-hewn rock wall began to slide silently to the left. It was, Joe now saw, the rock-clad hangar door, now open to the freezing air of the cold and starry night.

"Over here, sir," the lead guy said.

"Sure, what's up?"

"I think there's enough moonlight for you to see those two high mountains standing side by side over there to the north. See the crotch between them? Well, that's the pass an enemy tank division would have to take to get anywhere near us here at White Death. Any commander foolish enough to try and get a division up this mountain and through that pass? The second he started taking fire from Big Bess here, he would very quickly realize he'd made a seriously bad decision."

"But I was told that nobody knows this complex is even here. Europe's best-kept secret kind of thing."

"Well, there are rumors of our existence. Always have been."

"I should introduce myself. I'm Joe Stalingrad. I live in L.A., by the way. Movie business when I'm not doing this kind of thing. Couple of pictures under my belt. You ever see a flick called *The Good, Bad, and the Naked*?"

"Doesn't ring a bell. Sorry."

"No biggie. Just sayin'."

There was a bit of eye rolling and then the guy said, "Welcome to to our world, Mr. Stalingrad. Please follow me. Professor Steinhauser has a high-speed private residential elevator right over there by that fire extinguisher. Express to the top level."

"Thanks, guys. Catch you later," Joe said. They were still staring at him, wondering what business a Joe Stalin look-alike actor could possibly have with the most powerful man in Europe.

A STATUESQUE BRUNETTE IN A tailored emerald-green suit was waiting outside when the elevator doors parted. As she walked toward him, he thought she was perhaps the most voluptuous woman he'd ever seen. And that face! Except for the auburn hair, she was living, breathing Diana, Princess of Wales!

"Mr. Stalingrad." She smiled. "I'm Emma Peek. So lovely to meet you!"

Her accent was a very posh, Mayfair, London, Joe thought. "We're ever so delighted to have you with us," she said. "Please give me your bag. I'll have your belongings unpacked and placed in your room. You're in the Blue Room in our guesthouse. It's a separate structure, just a short rail trip away."

"Wait, there's a railway inside this mountain?"

"Well, not exactly a railway. More of a tram. A system of trams serving all twelve levels."

"Twelve levels? You gotta be effing kidding me."

Joe felt like a kid who'd stumbled onto the ultimate Disney World ride. Space Mountain had nothing on the Sorcerer's little mountain getaway.

"Question. Does my room have a view?"

She laughed. "It would if it had a window."

"I'll take that as a no. Are there any windows at all up here in outer space?"

"As a matter of fact, yes," she said, leading him to a mammoth pair of carved oaken doors inlaid with ivory. "Please step this way, Mr. Stalingrad. This is Professor Steinhauser's private office. And yes, it has a large, lovely window out onto the world. Make yourself comfortable in that green leather chair over by the fire. He won't be long—just finishing up a call to London."

"I'm fine, no hurry."

"Would you like a drink? Brandy, perhaps? Schnapps?"

"I love schnapps. I even like the way the word sounds . . . schnaaaaaaps!"

"I beg your pardon, Mr. Stalingrad?" Emma Peek said. "Are you ill?"

"Uh, no. Not ill, Miss Peek. I think I'm in love."

CHAPTER THIRTY

A few minutes later, Joe was sitting alone with his coffee in a high-ceilinged office with lamps burning low on various tables. Faded Persian rugs of rose and pink covered the polished hardwood floors, and the walls were studded with Old Masters. Floor-to-ceiling bookcases bulged with leather-bound collections of authors from Goethe to Voltaire to Dickens to Hemingway and Twain.

An enormous carved partner's desk stood beneath the giant window, through which moonlight poured in. Now, this was an office a man could be proud of. Larry Krynsky, Wells Fargo on La Cienega? Eat your fuckin' heart out, Larry. You lousy scumbag.

Suddenly feeling just a smidge antsy, he got up from his comfy chair and walked around a bit, sipping his drink. Intensely curious about what made the Sorcerer tick, he went over to the source of the pale blue glow that filled the whole room. A soaring window reached from the floor clear up to a twenty-foot ceiling, lead-paned and crystal clear.

The view of countless snow-covered mountaintops, a pale blue in the brilliant moonlight, was staggeringly beautiful.

He was wondering if that massive window was such a good idea, especially for someone trying to remain invisible to the world. That was, until he saw the massive sliding steel doors built into the rock to either side. Studying them more closely, he saw that their exterior surfaces were sheathed in hyperrealistic fake rock. Doors that would instantly slam shut and seal tight at the press of a button hidden somewhere.

Trying unsuccessfully not to be a total nosey parker, he surveyed the rest of the surreally beautiful office.

He checked out the desk first, mahogany with carvings of Alpine and forest scenes on the drawers and dark green leather covering the top. There were papers casually lying about but he chose not to look. None of his business. But a recessed LED light high up in the ceiling illuminated a shiny desktop object that definitely caught his eye.

He bent and looked closer. It was a mounted piece of sculpture about a foot high, carved out of a solid block of highly polished steel.

It was a Nazi swastika.

He picked it up, feeling its hefty weight. What the hey? He's a Nazi, this Steinhauser guy? A Nazi Jew hater who—

"Good evening, Mr. Stalingrad," a voice behind him boomed. "So good of you to come."

It was the Sorcerer, he knew, no question. His big voice had an otherworldly quality that sent chills straight up Joe's spine.

MR. JOSEPH STALINGRAD WHIRLED AROUND, holding the swastika sculpture in a death grip as if he been caught snooping. Which was only fair. Since he *had* been snooping.

"I am so sorry," Joe said, hastily putting the artifact back on the desk where it belonged, and feeling ridiculously guilty, he added, "Beautiful piece of art, Professor, beautiful," and then he felt really dumb. A Jew calling a swastika paperweight beautiful? Really, Joe?

The Sorcerer smiled and said, "Not really beautiful perhaps, Mr. Staligrad, but surely a powerful and iconic reminder of the evil that dwells in the hearts of men. That's why it's there. Keeps me honest."

"I can't help but ask who the man was who built this . . . uh, this mountain fortress. German, I imagine, based on the big black eighty-eight cannon that welcomed me."

"Not to mention that controversial paperweight I caught you admiring?"

"Well, that, too."

"The man who constructed this vast complex for the Swiss government left behind this and many other Nazi mementos when he died. And a German and a Nazi, indeed he was. Until Hitler tried to assassinate him for political crimes he never committed. His name was Maximillian von Stroheim.

"A submariner and former Nazi Kriegsmarine chief of staff, Von Stroheim was a polymath who dabbled in engineering and architecture. I'm sure you've heard of, or perhaps seen his work, Hitler's Eagle's Nest in Berchtesgaden, for example. Von Stroheim and Albert Speer created that majestic lookout first, and then they based this mountain fortress on what they'd learned from building Eagle's Nest. The need for high-speed elevators, camouflaged entries and exists for example."

"Why here, Professor? In Switzerland, I mean."

"Good question. Hitler, who hated the Swiss people, was intent on the success of his impending Operation Tannenbaum, the triumphant Nazi invasion of Switzerland. And he wanted Von Stroheim to create a vast military/residential complex worthy of the man who would now rule the planet from the top of the world. He and his architect, Speer, had discussed the idea for years. Hitler wanted an impenetrable fortress built inside a mountain here in the very heart of Europe. One gloriously appointed domain where he could both live in comfort and safety and rule the New German Europe he planned to create.

"Secret construction was completed shortly before Von Stroheim's escape from Nazi Germany and subsequent defection to Switzerland in 1938. That monstrous death machine you just saw? The eighty-eight? The big gun was smuggled by train out of Berchtesgaden before people were paying too much attention to the Swiss-German border, you see. Hitler's idea was for the conquering Wehrmacht to use the eighty-eight in the event of an Allied invasion that never happened. Now it's mine."

"I don't mean to ask so many questions, Professor. It's just that it's all a little overwhelming. Our mutual friend gave me no idea what to expect. But Der Führer on steroids was certainly not on my radar."

"Not at all," the elderly gentleman said. "Sorry I'm tardy—been a busy day, you know. Please, have a seat. It's late. You must be tired. My thought was just a quick hello tonight and then to bed. We'll get down to cases tomorrow morning?"

"That sounds great."

"You've come to me with some kind of business proposal, is that correct?"

"More in the nature of an offer, Professor. But yes, that's right. It's a business issue."

"Well, I shall toss and turn all night long in wild anticipation," the professor said with a wicked smile, a jolly old fellow.

Steinhauser strode across the priceless carpets and collapsed into the leather armchair at his desk. He was now sitting with his back to the spectacular nighttime views. Joe, who had a keen eye for character, an actor's eye, sized him up very quickly. He was no banker. No, he was a philosopher, an economist, a scholar, a university professor, possessed of a keen intellect. He had a natural way about him, cheery, you know, and that too suggested brains and a quick wit.

"You bring news of our friend, the late president, I understand."

"I do, sir. He asked me to give you his kindest regards."

"You say he *asked you*. So he really is alive, is he? That old fox. Rumors of his premature demise a bit exaggerated, are they?"

There was that spark of humor again, in those big blue eyes fringed with bushy white eyebrows. His head was bald and he wore a pair of thin gold pince-nez eyeglasses. Glasses that gave him a slight Santa thing going on. But he was dressed like a banker. A three-piece navy chalk-stripe suit from Kingsman, a very good London tailor on Savile Row. A crisp white shirt, and a blue-and-white polka-dot bow tie like Churchill used to favor.

"He's very much alive, sir," Joe said.

"Ah, I thought as much," Steinhauser said, and sat back and placed his folded hands on the expanse of green leather. "Where is he, Mr. Stalingrad?"

"Somewhere in darkest France."

His smile brief, Steinhauser said, "Fine, fine. No need to be coy. I don't really need to know."

"Professor, you and I are the only two people on the planet who even know he's alive. Even I won't know where he is until the moment I get his GPS signal to extract him."

"Well then, I suggest we all get a good night's sleep and resume this fascinating conversation on the morrow, shall we?"

"Of course."

"Good. I'm an early riser. You are staying in the guesthouse, Joe. A brief tram ride to another part of the mountain. I think you'll find it very comfortable. Breakfast is at six sharp in the main dining room here in the residence. Just show up. Frau Emma Peek, whom I believe you've met, will lead you to it. Good night, Joe."

"Good night, Professor. Oh, before you go, would you like to hear the last thing I heard from our friend before I left for Switzerland?"

Steinhauser paused at the door, the moonlight on his face. "Of course."

"The president said, and I quote, 'I'm going to build a million-man army, Joe. And you, Joe, are man number one.'"

"God in heaven," the professor said as he left the room. "Whatever will that man do next?"

"I think he's already done it, Professor."

"Done what?"

"He's planning to make you man number two."

Steinhauser laughed heartily and said good night.

"God save us all," Joe whispered after the professor had closed the door. There was a grandiosity about Putin's already erratic behavior that was beginning to make him a tad nervous.

He knew Putin better than anyone on the planet. And a wounded, humiliated, narcissistic Putin was a greater threat to mankind than anything he could think of. He was truly capable of visiting the horrors of hell on an unsuspecting world.

That was the bad news. The good news was that little Joey stood to make countless millions of dollars orchestrating Putin's glorious return to power.

He got up from his chair and went to the drinks table filled with cut crystal decanters. About to pour himself another dollop of schnapps, he paused a second, looked around, and then slipped the entire decanter inside his woolen topcoat.

And so to bed.

CHAPTER THIRTY-ONE

A shot whistled past Hawke's head. He dropped to his knees. "Hear that crack? Makarov nine millimeter, dead cert. These are KGB boys, all right." Then he shoved both hands under Congreve and got to his feet, his portly friend now cradled in his arms.

"Hold on, old son, we're going to run for it," Hawke said.

He then carried the man the length of the shallow ravine at full speed, twisting and turning, zigging and zagging through the field of boulders as shots rang out above his head, rounds ricocheting off the rocks as he dodged this way and that. That a man could perform like this, running flat out while carrying someone weighing in at two hundred pounds on his shoulders, was astounding.

Congreve, the beneficiary of this rescue, knew it wasn't just strength and training and iron will, nor was it simply adrenaline at work. Ambrose knew that Alex thought he'd bleed to death if he didn't get him out of the firefight. Find better protection and some-place where he could stop the bleeding and apply a field dressing to that bloody wound. Just ahead! Up a small hillock where a free-form sculpture of large boulders would offer higher ground and sufficient protection. A place where they'd have a good field of fire when the gunmen came to finish the job.

"Constable, you're a mess," Hawke said, breathing hard as he lay the man down on a patch of soft snow in the shadows of huge boulders. Congreve's pained face, a white moon, gazed up in supplication at Hawke.

"Just get us out of this one, Alex," he said in ragged tones. "We've got a boy's life to save . . ."

"I will. But you are hurt, you know. May have nicked something, internal bleeding. Here, I'll give you a bullet to bite on while I do my worst."

"Just a bee sting, my boy. Don't get yourself all exercised about it."

"A bee sting, he says. A B-52 bunker buster to the shoulder, perhaps. No, wait. Spoke too soon. A flesh wound, clean entry and exit. Now stop talking while I stanch the bleeding and bind you up."

"I think I got one of them," Congreve said, attempting to sound conversational as Hawke went to work on his shoulder.

"Well, sorry, you didn't."

"Are they coming?"

"Yes."

"You can see them?"

"Yes."

"How long have we got?"

"A few minutes. Good thing it's your left shoulder, you old fossil."

"Really? Why?"

"Because you might well be able to use your right to get off a few shots when they come up that hill. Unless you're busy, of course. Otherwise engaged."

Having cleaned the wound as best he could, Hawke stuffed his clean white linen handkerchief down into it. He then quickly sliced a few long strips of khaki material from the right leg of his trousers. These would act both to seal the wound and stop the bleeding.

"Here they come," Hawke said, working furiously.

"How many?"

"Three."

"See! I did nail one of those bastards!"

"All right, all right, so you did. Done. How do you feel? You may be *hors de combat*, I'm afraid."

"Splendid offer, but no, thank you. Now let me get up, damn you!"

Congreve was pale and his breathing was shallow, but you'd never know it by the look of determination in those normally kindly blue eyes. "C'mon! Give me my revolver! I need to reload."

THE TWO MEN GOT THEMSELVES into position. The heavy boulders would provide solid cover, Hawke knew. At this point it was just a shooting match involving strategy.

"Well," he said, "at least we now know they're not CIA."

"How do we know that?"

"Lousy shots."

"Speak for yourself, dear boy."

"I just did."

Congreve laughed and said, "Any last thoughts?"

"Hopefully not *last* thoughts, Constable, but here goes. Their only chance is to try and flank us. Send one guy to either side while the middleman—the big boy in the red snow cap down there—advances straight up the hill. He's the least dangerous to us, so concentrate your fire to the left. I'll take the right-hand guy, primarily, and give the man in the middle enough entertainment to keep him occupied."

"Alex, I shall dispatch my target with authority."

"Of that I've no doubt, Constable. And don't wait till you see the whites of his eyes. Okay, get ready. They're moving again."

"I can't see from here. How long?"

"Take them five minutes to get within range. Maybe less."

The two men now sat and Alex watched the approaching gunmen in silence. The Russian thugs were taking their time coming up the hill, sprinting between areas of cover until they got within shooting range. Ambrose was startled to hear the flick of Hawke's Zippo.

"Hold on. You're actually having a cigarette? Now?"

"Why yes, it appears I am, doesn't it? What are you on about?"

"I mean really, Alex, sometimes you do drive one to distraction."

"A balm for the nerves, that's all. Quiets the hand that holds the gun, you see, the finger that pulls the trigger. By the way, change of plans," Hawke whispered, expelling a plume of blue smoke into the frigid air and taking a quick look at Red Cap's sneaky upward advance.

"All ears."

"They're getting close. I think I may have wounded your guy in the left leg. See how he's dragging it a little?"

"Yes."

"So in the opening salvo, I'll focus on Red Cap, lay down suppression fire, then we both go for Lefty."

"Check. Here they come!" Congreve said, opening fire on his man.

Hawke took aim at his man and fired three times in quick succession, trying to pin Red Cap in place. It was enough to make him drop to the ground and scramble for better cover. Hawke then turned his attention to Lefty. His attempt was to wing the man. Keep at least one of them alive so he and Congreve could interrogate them later.

But the big man on the left had a little surprise for Hawke. He jumped up suddenly and threw his nine-millimeter automatic to the ground, reached inside his windcheater, and whipped out a Heckler & Koch MP7 submachine gun. The smoking barrel started throwing lead their way immediately and the man pulling the trigger continued to advance rapidly up the hill toward their position.

"He's not dragging his leg now!" Ambrose shouted above the gunfire.

"Good actor," Hawke said, firing. He saw a flash of movement, Red Cap on the move, covering ground rapidly and coming right at him. "Heads up! My guy's trying to storm the gate! You stick with Mr. Right, I'll take this bastard to the left."

Hawke's target, who apparently did not have an H&K submachine gun tucked inside his jacket, had gotten a good deal closer. The rock he was taking cover behind was just below him, roughly a few hundred feet away. With his next move up the hill, Hawke's position would be exposed.

Suddenly the guy's head popped up. Couldn't miss him. His bright red woolen cap was pulled down over his ears against the frigid wind. Hawke took dead aim three inches below the red pompon that adorned the top of the cap. He squeezed the trigger and the explosive crack jerked the barrel up.

Damn it.

He'd overshot him.

He'd failed to account for the quirky windage up here and their differences in elevation! His man ducked again, probably unaware that his silly red pompon was still visible above the lip of the rock. Hawke waited till he saw it start to bobble upward again. He took careful aim and fired, neatly separating the pompon from the cap.

That would give the Russian bastard pause for a moment, Hawke knew, and he used that precious moment to his advantage. He'd spied two large boulders to his right, maybe twenty feet away.

He jumped up and dove into a tuck and roll, coming to a stop behind the big rocks. He'd gained a twenty-foot altitude and distance advantage and no shots had been fired at him. Maybe he'd gotten away with it. He could see the crown of the crouching gunman's head. He aimed, thinking it was a low margin shot, and the guy popped up and fired two rounds, still focused on Hawke's old position while firing.

Hawke took careful aim and fired one round.

Head shot.

Red Cap never saw it coming. He crumpled, dead before he hit the ground.

MEANWHILE, CONGREVE WAS HAVING A hard time with his guy, Mr. Right. He had climbed swiftly upward too, and now he was almost flanking Ambrose's position. Lefty too had advanced a good hundred yards up the hill, unaware that Hawke had moved. If Hawke was very lucky, both remaining gunmen had missed his move to higher ground to the right.

They were both focused on Congreve at the moment. Perhaps if

Hawke could keep his head down and make a swift dash right and down the hill, pivot, maybe he could come up at them from behind. What the hell . . . why not? He was up and running.

The thunderous chatter of Righty's HK machine gun masked the crunch of Hawke's footsteps approaching him from behind. Hawke was closing. He was able to get close enough to reach out and touch the gunman's shoulder.

Instead, he raised his weapon and fired two rounds into the back of the man's head.

"Ambrose! Over here!" Hawke shouted, diving for cover as he began taking fire. "Over here!"

Instinctively, Lefty had turned his submachine gun at this noisy new threat. But Hawke was nearly invisible on the ground, lying behind a corpse, the only available cover.

Hawke, knowing Congreve only had maybe two seconds left, cried out. "Ambrose! Take the shot!" Lefty was already firing again, swinging the muzzle of the machine gun back toward Congreve . . .

"Take the bloody shot, Ambrose!"

Hawke saw his friend Congreve rise up, raise his weapon, aim, and exactly one second before dying in a swarm of whistling lead, take the shot and duck for cover.

The KGB thug dropped soundlessly to the rocky ground. Dead? Hawke wondered.

Hawke, his gun at the ready, ran up and knelt beside the fallen man Ambrose had shot and started going through his pockets methodically . . .

"This one's still alive," Hawke said. "I'll call EMS and get an ambulance up here."

"Is he going to make it?" Ambrose said. "Let's hope so."

"Shot in the chest, but it was high and shallow and there's a clean exit wound. Pray we get lucky. Call the carabinieri and tell them what happened up here. Full report."

The Arma dei Carabinieri was a military corps with police duties, the Italian version of the French Gendarmerie Nationale. "What's up with EMS, for god's sake? You called them, right?" Congreve said, aware that his own wound was beginning to throb painfully.

"Not picking up the bloody phone."

"Oh, right, I forgot. We're in Italy."

CHAPTER THIRTY-TWO

An hour later, EMS and the military police had finally arrived at the scene. They'd administered first aid to Congreve and rushed the sole survivor of the gun battle to the nearest hospital. Once the man Congreve had shot was stable, Italian police would interrogate him and forward the results to Congreve.

A squad of carabinieri had assisted in that process, taken Hawke's report of the incident. CIA officers from Rome had done only a cursory investigation before taping the scene for Hawke. So the Italian police investigators were more than happy to help Hawke and Congreve comb the burned-out wreckage. For nearly an hour, the team scoured the site for evidence with the proverbial fine-tooth comb. There was zero evidence of human remains, leading the chief inspector to believe that this was indeed the stolen Swiss chopper.

Minutes afterward, the two men were back in the car and headed for the airstrip where Hawke's airplane was waiting.

En route, Hawke sat back in the passenger seat and said, "You're sure about this, are you?"

"I am indeed," Congreve replied.

"You saw irrefutable proof of arson? An accelerant being used?"

"I did. And we've now got unmistakable evidence that it was the stolen number four Swiss rescue chopper. Next step?"

"We call Brick Kelly at Langley and tell him what we found on the ground. And about the four KGB thugs who just tried to kill us. We ask him to go back channel to the Russian Federation embassy in Berne, Switzerland. Threaten to issue a formal demarche to the Russian embassy and warn of an impending and very public criminal investigation into Russia's role in the kidnapping. That is, unless the Russian ambassador agrees to meet with a member of Her Majesty's government. Namely you."

"Me?"

"Yes, Constable, you. Having gained access, you will then lay out the incontrovertible case for Russian involvement in a Russian-orchestrated kidnapping of the child of a British intelligence officer in service to Her Majesty the Queen."

"Then what?"

"Then we let the bloody bastards stew in their bloody juices for a few days . . . Putin's wandering in the wilderness, on the outs with all those oligarchs turned traitors these days. Here's my theory, or my hope, anyway. I think the Kremlin might just throw Putin under the bus in order to make us go away."

"Good plan, Alex. How'd you come up with it?"

"I made it up. While I was waiting for those gunmen to come up the hill and try to kill us."

"Well. I'll certainly be busy. And what about you?"

"I'm going to fly over to Cap d'Antibes tomorrow morning with Stokely and Happy Meal Harry Brock. You ever watch that chappie go through a Big Mac? Not a sight for the faint of heart."

"What's happening at Cap d'Antibes?"

"That's where *Tsar*, Putin's getaway yacht, is moored. At the harbor at Juan-les-Pins. That's always been his ultimate escape plan, if foes got too close on his heels. We're going to set a trap for Volodya if and when he does try to sneak back aboard his yacht. Have a little man-to-man conversation about giving me the precise whereabouts of my son."

"I've been thinking about the timing of the abduction," Ambrose said, puffing away at his old briar pipe.

"And?"

"And Alexei was snatched shortly after Vladimir dropped out of sight. If alive, he would have been on the run. And being on the run with a seven-year-old boy at your side would be extremely difficult. I mean to say . . ."

"Yes, I understand. Wherever my son is, he's probably not being held by Putin himself. Who could Putin possibly trust with keeping him alive? You've given me a whole new train of thought, Constable. I appreciate it."

AFTER THAT, THE TWO MEN rode in silence for a time, each content to be left alone with his private thoughts. Hawke was running down in his minds the places Alexei might have been taken. His first notion: the KGB's Winter Palace in Siberia. That's where Alexei's mother had long been held captive. And that's perhaps the only place where Putin would know his little pawn was safe. With his mother, and waiting to be played on the big stage of the world should Hawke interfere in his plans. He turned to another subject on his mind lately, one that was the source of a great deal of anxiety.

"Ambrose, let me ask you a question," Hawke said, coming to the surface about ten minutes later. "On an entirely different matter."

"Fire at will, my boy, fire at will," Ambrose said, the very soul of jollity. Nothing pleased that celebrated brain of his more than the contemplation of all things cops and robbers.

CHAPTER THIRTY-THREE

Have you ever done anything in your life that you're deeply ashamed of?" Hawke said to Ambrose.

"Hmm. Probably. That golf sweater I gave you one Christmas? The bright green one from Harrods with little red golf balls all over it? I shall never forget the look on your face when you opened that box . . . I felt so, what's the word? So *small*."

Hawke smiled. "No. Please be serious, Ambrose. I mean something that you are deeply ashamed of. Something that you would never reveal to anyone . . . that you would take to your grave."

Silence.

"Well, Alex, yes. There was that brief time at Cambridge. I was only nineteen and I thought I was in love with my rugby—"

"Stop. I don't need to know and I don't want to know."

"Why do you ask, Alex? Rather an odd question, coming from you. You're hardly the introspective type."

"I have a friend who's in trouble. It's all about fear and guilt and shame about the past."

"How can I help, Alex? Sounds bad."

"It is. And I don't know what to do to help. I'm dancing with demons I don't need in my life right now, given my priorities at the moment."

"You have my rapt attention."

"All right. How best to do this? I'm going to tell you a story. It's about me, not my friend, but it's relevant to my friend's dilemma . . . maybe you can wrap your supersize cerebellum around it?"

"All right, Alex. I'm listening."

"This was in Ireland. At a lovely old ruin called Glin Castle on the River Shannon. I was six years old, an only child. I adored my mother and worshiped my father, an admiral in the Royal Navy, as you well know."

"A brilliant naval strategist and a fine man."

"Well, yes and no, Ambrose. That's the crux of my story. At any rate, for my sixth birthday, he took me on a boy's own adventure to Ireland. Just the two of us, you understand. Mother stayed in London. It was wonderful. Riding and shooting at Glin Castle, the home of his good friend Desmond FitzGerald. I think you know him?"

"I do. The Eleventh Knight of Glin, title dating back to 1066. Splendid chap. Lovely rose gardens there at the castle."

"Yes. And my father's closest friend. We were there for four days. I was just learning to ride horses and I loved it. We went for a long ride, hill and dale, out in the countryside. On the return ride to Glin Castle, we encountered a young Irish fellow out jumping fences and other obstacles on his horse.

"My father told me the boy was clearly an eventer, a show jumper, something my dad had also done at a young age. I don't remember all the details, but apparently he'd been very successful at the sport.

"We stopped to watch. Dad was silent for a few jumps, watching with approval at his clearing different fences and walls and obstacles. Then, I don't know why, he began criticizing the boy's style and technique. Very disparaging comments. It was the first time I'd ever seen a side of him I didn't like."

"I would say it was unnecessary, yes. But not necessarily something anyone should be ashamed of, his father behaving badly . . ."

Hawke shook his head. "No, no. It gets worse, Ambrose. Much worse."

"Sorry."

"At any rate, we rode over to a small pond where the fellow was watering his beautiful chestnut horse. Dad struck up a conversation with the young man, whom I remember as being very good-looking, a fine shock of black hair, blue eyes, about sixteen or seventeen. He told Dad his name, and Dad introduced me to him. His name was Seamus McBain. And the beautiful stallion was named Eamon, a gift from his grands.

"Father told Seamus how much he admired his fine looks and his skill and the courage of his horse. He said later that the boy had the most beautiful smile . . . winsome was the word he used.

"And that he, Father, was determined to make me a great eventer or show jumper some day. Then Dad told Seamus about a high farm fence in a meadow we'd ridden through earlier, about a mile or two from where we were then. He said it was deceptively challenging, but that he'd successfully jumped it. He asked Seamus if he'd like to see it and he said yes. We rode back to the fence and Seamus agreed it looked extremely difficult. It was old and crumbling—unstable. It was a high stone wall with wooden fencing laced along the top. Dad asked Seamus point-blank if he thought his mount could clear it.

"Seamus said he probably could, but that he didn't want to put his horse at risk needlessly. He and Eamon were out training for a big event next day. Perhaps in the future, when his horse was more mature, but not now. But Dad wouldn't stop. He kept pressing him, goading him on and challenging his manhood and . . ."

"And what?"

"Seamus was getting angry, I could see it, and I wanted to tell my dad to leave him alone, that I wanted to go home. But I didn't . . . didn't say anything. Father had a colossal temper. I was too afraid of him. Finally, Seamus said, 'Fine. Me good horse Eamon and I, we'll jump that bloody fence, if only to silence that mouth of yours, sir.'"

"Oh, god, Alex. Don't tell me he—"

"Dad said, 'Good for you, lad! That's the spirit! I was beginning to think you didn't have the bottle for it! We'll watch from that hillside beneath the trees. Careful of that top post, it's deceptive.' With that, we rode up the hill to the copse of trees at the top."

" 'I know what I'm doing,' Seamus said, as we rode off, still angry."

"Did he clear it?"

"I didn't want to look. I covered my eyes. But Father grabbed my shoulders, jerked me around, and made me look. We could see that Seamus was pushing Eamon very hard, gathering all the speed he would need to clear that damn fence. I was watching, sort of aghast at what was happening, afraid for him, somehow already knowing it would not turn out well and . . . Oh, it was horrible, Ambrose. He never had a chance to clear that damn fencing atop the wall. He and his horse slammed broadside right into the whole structure at a full gallop. I screamed and tried to turn away, but Dad had my reins and wouldn't let me."

"Good heavens."

"Yes, so I saw it all. I could see that poor boy's bloody and mangled body sprawled atop that wall, his head cocked at an odd angle. One look told me he was grievously hurt. Dad told me to stay put, that he'd go down and see what he could do for him. He rode down the hill at full gallop and right up to the wall. I watched him dismount and go to the fence.

"He just stood there and stared at Seamus, not saying or doing anything. In hindsight, I suppose he saw nothing to make him think he needed to check the boy's pulse. Then he bent over the boy's horse for a few moments, again, just staring at it. For a long, long time. Thinking god knows what. And then he got back up on his horse and came storming up the hill . . . his handsome face showing no emotion at all."

"Was Seamus alive? Please tell me the boy was *still alive*?"

"I don't *know*, Ambrose. I'll never know. Dad was the only one who ever knew. And he's long gone now."

"What? What did he tell you? He had to say something to you!"

"Yes. He told me, he said, 'There's nothing we can do for him. Or, his horse. It's too bad. Accidents happen. But it's late, and we need to be getting back to the castle. Desmond is a stickler for punctuality. Alex, listen very carefully to your father now and never forget what I tell you. I don't want you to ever, *ever* mention what happened here to a living soul. Do you understand me? *Never!* This is our secret. And we shall both carry it to our graves.'"

"Holy mother of god," Ambrose whispered. He was stunned. "How horrible for you, Alex. Unforgivable behavior on his part, I must say. Certainly not the man I thought I knew."

"Of course I never forgave Father for what he'd done that day. But I kept it all to myself. All these years. I was only a kid. But I knew what I'd seen. I'd seen my own father *murder* someone."

"Murder? I think that's a little strong, Alex. After all, your father had successfully jumped the fence and had no idea that the boy wouldn't do the same."

"No! That's the thing I'm trying to tell you. We had stopped and looked at that bloody fence, yes. Father thought about jumping it, sure. Galloped right up to it a few times, turning away at the last second. But he *never jumped it*. He never even tried. He lied to that boy. And he goaded him into committing suicide."

"Or, even worse, left him and his horse to die alone in the woods."

"Yes."

"So. What is your question? The question you want to help your friend with?"

"Forgiveness. That's my central question, Ambrose. You're a classically trained ethicist, so you see my moral ambiguity. My moral dilemma. Should I ultimately forgive my father for what he did? Should I forgive myself for keeping quiet about what happened all those years ago? And finally, as an officer of the law, can you forgive me for that? Isn't that accessory to murder? Hiding the truth about a crime for decades? And not even—"

"Alex, stop torturing yourself. Of course I forgive you. You were trapped inside a horrific dilemma. You loved your father, your parents. You didn't want to destroy their lives, their marriage, and thus your own life. I think I myself would have done what you did. Any boy would have done the same. You kept the deep dark secret and thus kept your family together. Your real fear was that your mother would leave your father if she knew what he'd done that day. And your family would be no more. You couldn't bring yourself to do that."

"It's that simple?"

"Some secrets are better kept than revealed, Alex. Moral relativism, they called it at Cambridge."

Alex was quiet, gazing out the window at the receding countryside. Finally, he said, "Yes. I think that's true, Ambrose. Some secrets are better kept than revealed. That's very helpful. Not only for me, but, for my friend as well."

"I hope you both find some peace."

"I do, too. We both could use a little at this point."

"Can you tell me who your friend is? Do I know him? Or, her, as the case may be?"

"At some point I will tell you, perhaps. Not now. For the moment, that's a secret better kept than revealed."

Congreve looked at him, his expression something approaching a wry grin.

"Always good to have the last word, isn't it, m'boy?" Congreve said, puffing away at his pipe with wry good humor. "I suppose."

CHAPTER THIRTY-FOUR

Light was pouring into the wood-paneled breakfast room. Through the soaring windows above, Joe could see the vast sunlit brilliance of ethereal blue skies and towering snowcapped summits of some of the world's most dangerous mountains. All marching down to the crystal blue lake.

The large round mahogany table was situated in a bay window that featured floor-to-ceiling leaded windows. Again, from where he was sitting, Joe could see the external rock-clad shutters. Protection and concealment on all the windows in the fortress. Simulated rock doors and window shutters that would instantly slam closed in the event of unwanted visitors on the ground or in the air.

He'd just joined the beauteous Miss Peek and the professor for breakfast. He was late, but not that late. Helped by the midnight schnapps, he'd overslept and somehow forgotten you had to take a train to get from the guesthouse to the residence some two hundred feet higher on the far side of the mountain.

"More coffee, Mr. Stalingrad?" Emma Peek said, lifting the silver urn. She was wearing a tight white sweater this morning, one that left little to the imagination. The woman, who had to be pushing forty, had a body on her. Jesus, Joseph, and Mary!

"Sure, sure," Joe said, smiling at her.

He had this feeling, he wasn't sure, exactly, but he had this gut feeling that this Princess Diana look-alike had the hots for him. Who knew? He knew he was no Brad Pitt. He was built like a Dumpster and had the pockmarked face of a famous mass murderer. But crazier things had happened. Stockholm syndrome? No, that wasn't it. But something, yeah. Some chicks had a thing for him, for sure. Ever since middle school, when he'd emerged as the class clown. You want a chick begging for it? Make her laugh.

Hell, Playstation had women in L.A. flirting with him all the time. Women on the beach at Venice, on the Santa Monica Pier, starlets on the set, women at Spago, Musso and Frank. Hell, women who'd been on *Entertainment Tonight,* for crissakes. Something about him drew women to him. Something like a . . . mystique, if that was the right word.

Yeah. That was it. He had a certain . . . *mystique.*

Emma filled his cup, and Joe, touching his napkin to his lips, said, "Delicious omelet, Miss Peek. Beluga caviar, no less. My compliments to the chef."

"Thank you so much, Mr. Stalingrad!" she said brightly, and headed for the kitchen. "I made it myself! See you at lunch."

"Can't wait," Joe said.

"All right, Joe," the ever-observant professor said. "Let's talk. I've got a busy day ahead of me. I think it's time for you and me to get down to cases. I know you come with a message from my old friend Volodya. Please tell me what's on the great man's mind these days, Mr. Stalingrad . . . and how it concerns me."

Joe sat back for a moment to gather his thoughts, staring at the bookish man across the table. The man he privately had come to call the Man in the High Castle.

"Certainly, certainly, Professor. Well, you see this all goes to a private conversation the two of you shared. It took place last summer, when you joined the president aboard *Tsar* in the Med for a week. On the last night aboard, you confided your plans for the future . . .

spilled your dreams of a new life to the president. That was the way the president put it."

"Yes, I remember that little chat very well. But tell me, what aspects in particular did you two discuss?"

"The president said that, after many long decades of solitude here, you were growing tired of perpetual seclusion inside of a mountain. Having achieved your eighth decade, you wanted out. You wanted fresh air and sunlight on your cheeks every morning. Wind-in-your-hair kind of thing . . . gardens dripping with fragrant blossoms, the sea at your doorstep."

"I can't imagine the Volodya I know uttering those terribly flowery words, Joe, but he may have inferred something of the sort from my comments, yes."

"Not those words, exactly. I'm paraphrasing for effect. I'm an actor, what can I tell you? But that was most definitely the gist of what he said. He told me he believed you envisioned a radical change of lifestyle. That four decades of voluntary seclusion inside this mountain may well have been enough for one lifetime. Am I wrong?"

The professor sat back from the table and clasped his hands, resting them on his rounded belly. "Well, I don't really know how to respond. I thought my words to President Putin were for his ears only. And after all, I don't know you, Mr. Stalingrad. We've conducted business in the past, but we've barely met. But I will say this. Due to the very fact that you have earned the respect and loyalty of one of the very few men on earth whom I trust, I'll take a rare chance. I will confide in you."

"I'm honored, sir."

"What he told you is true. I want to break out of this self-imposed prison I've created for myself. Overstayed my welcome. I have been looking into the purchase of a villa in the South of France. The Villa America in Cap Ferrat, to be exact. Paradise. If I would ever leave my beloved mountain, it would be to end my days there. The Villa America is where I want to live out the balance of my time on earth.

For a man of my age, I'm in very good health. I envision long walks on the beaches, long afternoons puttering around in my gardens."

"What's stopping you, if I may ask?"

"To be brutally honest, money. Horrid stuff. Ironic, isn't it? That the man all Europe acclaims as the economic genius of the age has money problems!"

"What kinds of money problems, Professor Steinhauser?"

"Well, for starters, the current owner of the villa in question, a Saudi sheik, Mohamed al-Arifi, is demanding a ridiculous amount of money. A lot of my wealth is tied up in this mountain. And should I ever be lucky enough to locate someone mad enough and rich enough to buy this Alpine fortress of mine, I still don't think I could raise the capital to meet the sheik's exorbitant price of two hundred million dollars. So as I told Volodya last summer, I've decided to forgo my dreams for the nonce. Who knows what might happen?"

"Professor, I understand your dilemma. But that dilemma is the very reason he asked you to see me. He is genuinely concerned for your happiness. He understands your feelings and frustrations. And to be honest, he wants to help. He considers himself a friend."

"Very kind. I'm well aware that he's the richest man on earth. Some forty billion or so, net worth. But still, however might he do that? The president of Russia wants to buy me a huge villa in the South of France? I rather doubt it, Mr. Stalingrad."

"No, Professor. He doesn't want to buy the villa. But he has come up with a way for you to achieve your life goals, and at same time, for him to achieve his. That's how he works. He wants to see both sides of the deal smiling when they leave the table."

"Very interesting, Joe. Please continue. Why are you here?"

"A real estate deal. I'm here to tell you that the president of Russia may be interested in acquiring your mountain fortress. More than interested. Determined, in fact."

"Tell me why."

"His life at the moment is in a state of flux. He has fallen from power. He has many enemies in Moscow and throughout the world.

Lethal enemies, mortal enemies. All screaming for his head. His life, prior to his disappearance, was in daily jeopardy. So he's seeking safety. He envisions this place as his safe haven at this point. Putin sees this unique fortress as his principal residence going forward. At least until such time as he is ready and able to make his victorious return to Moscow.

"You really think he might do that? Buy my mountain? Der Nadel?"

Joe laughed. "Yeah. He's already got this name he's going to call it."

"What is it, pray tell?"

"Falcon's Lair."

"Falcon's Lair. Well, I do like the sound of that."

"I am telling you that he's determined to have this property. Where else on earth could the man find this kind of invincible sanctuary? 'The safest place in the safest country on earth,' is how he put it. I am here acting as his real estate agent. He'd like me to have a firsthand look at the property and report back to him on its viability."

"Remarkable. Truly remarkable. He's willing to do that? Buy my mountain aerie? In its entirety?"

"He is, sir. And of course, after the transaction is completed, you would then have sufficient funds to acquire your dream. Two birds with one stone, as the Americans say, sir. You both win."

"Indeed. You've painted a very rosy picture. For both of us. I hope we can somehow come to terms. In the meantime, I shall ask Miss Peek to give you the grand tour! Top to bottom! I believe you're free this morning, are you not, Emma?"

"Free as a bird, my love."

"I'd like Mr. Stalingrad to see everything. And, Joe, please feel free to use your phone camera to capture anything you think our buyer might find interesting. From base to peak. We have no secrets from Mr. Stalingrad. Remember that, Miss Peek."

Joe couldn't wipe the smile off his face fast enough to escape the grin from Emma Peek.

CHAPTER THIRTY-FIVE

Although it pained Joe to tear his eyes away from Miss Peek's shapely bottom leading the way up the stairs, he had to say her tour was an eye-opener.

You had to see this place to believe it. Twelve separate levels, all accessible by high-speed elevators, like a vertical office building built inside a mountain. Except not an office building—unless you meant a *war* office. This place existed for one reason only. To live in comfort until the moment you have to fight a war and win.

At sea level, you had the secret underwater air lock where the three subs arrived at regular intervals, delivering guests, food, and everything required by the inhabitants, a population numbering somewhere around two hundred or more. On lower levels, you would find the vast storerooms for food and other supplies, freezers, HVAC equipment, pump rooms, electrical equipment, generators, and such. Sort of like the basement.

On the third and fourth levels were the dormitories. Very much in the naval military style, like something you'd find aboard an aircraft carrier, with hot sheet beds and hammocks, showers, and toilets for each of the single-sex dorms. Two kitchens and two messrooms. And one officer's mess.

On level five, arms and the artillery to defend the lower and middle levels from invasion were stored. Old 105mm howitzers, six of them in perfect condition, were mounted on rail tracks in the center of the complex. In the event of an attack, six gunports would open up and the guns would be rolled out onto firing platforms. Also on the platforms, to either side of the rail tracks, were batteries of mounted .50-caliber machine guns, giving you tons of firepower to rain down on anyone foolish enough to mount an attack.

Level six was the sick bay and office space for the various physicians on staff. A fully equipped hospital with the best doctors, surgeons, and nurses, recruited from all over Europe by Leopold Levin, the Sorcerer's chief physician. There too on level six were the physical training facilities, including a basketball court and a fully equipped gymnasium.

Level seven was the communications and computer center. State of the art, Joe thought, like you might see at the White House. Rooms and rooms of IBM servers, the whole enchilada.

Seven was where it all got serious. Seven was the hangar space for the squadron of White Death fighter jets, the pilots' residence, the home of aircraft and maintenance. The gleaming silver jets, perfect rows of them, sat waiting twenty-four hours a day, the pilots in a state of constant readiness.

Level eight was also the launch deck. High-speed aircraft carrier type elevators whisked the fighter aircraft up from the level below. The deck was very much like that of a carrier except for its shape—it was oval! Four high-speed catapults radiated out from the center, one due north, one south, one east, one west. On command, the four hidden doors opened in sync and fighters were catapulted out into the sky at ten thousand feet! This enabled air combat communications to launch four fighters simultaneously, every five minutes! Even Joe, ever nonchalant, was impressed.

Nine was food services. The Mess Hall. Freezer storage, prep, banks of ovens and stoves, the kitchen team racing about keeping everyone fed and happy. Overseeing it all was chef Millicent Montserrat, a Cordon Bleu chef the professor had lured away from Paris.

Ten was where the work took place. Secretarial, Accounting, Payroll. It was also home to the large auditorium in which all big meetings were held. There was digital projection equipment, and Hollywood's latest fare could be seen every Saturday night at eight.

Level eleven was dedicated to all things offensive and defensive. There was the Battle Ops center, the radar command post, tracking everything worth having a look at. And also the SAM missile batteries, mounted on platforms with retracting rooftops, capable of exposing the surface-to-air missiles at a moments notice.

And finally, level twelve. The Residence. This was the level that Hitler had dedicated to his personal needs of complete luxury. This is where he could dine in splendor, sleep on silk sheets, and delight in all of his stolen art and libraries of thousands of books. There were a number of smaller bedrooms to accommodate VIPs from Berlin and the Führer's female guests from all over Europe.

And of course the magnificent office that Speer had created for der Führer, now occupied by the Sorcerer himself!

TWO HOURS LATER, JOE WAS sitting with the professor alone in his office. A blinding snowstorm was swirling outside the windows and the light inside the room was soft and watery. Seated on either side of the fireplace, they were sipping tea.

"So, Joe. You've seen it all. Quite something, isn't it?"

"*Amazing* doesn't begin to cover it."

"You think he might find it sufficient to his needs?"

"I do. Beyond sufficient. This mountain will be become an unassailable fortress against the president's enemies. It's just what he's looking for."

"Good, good. But, tell me, how in the world do I begin to put a price tag on this unique real estate asset? It's a problem I've been wrestling with for years."

Joe smiled. He'd been waiting for this part.

"No need. He put a price on it himself, Professor. Half a billion dollars. That is his offer. And it's a onetime offer. No counteroffers. He has authorized me to offer you five hundred million dollars. Today, immediately wired to your accounts. Three hundred million to cover all costs involved in the purchase of Villa America and relocating your possessions to France. Plus an additional two hundred million goes into the bank account of your choosing."

"Half a billion dollars?" the Sorcerer said, suddenly dry-mouthed.

"That's what the man said."

"That would probably make it the largest real estate transaction in history."

"Well, that's what he's putting on the table, Professor. Half a billion dollars so you can live your dream. What do you think?"

"I think I need to think about it."

"Of course. You've got twenty-four hours."

Joe got to his feet. "Miss Peek, will you help arrange my departure?"

"Of course, Mr. Stalingrad," Emma said. "Are you sure you don't want to stay for dinner this evening? Spend one more night at the mountain? It promises to be something very special."

Joe paused at the door, turned to her, and said, "Did you say special, Miss Peek?"

"Yes, I did, Mr. Stalingrad. Very special."

He was scheduled to set a chopper down in a densely wooded area of southern France the day after tomorrow . . .

"I think I can squeeze another night into my schedule, Miss Peek." Joe Stalingrad smiled.

CHAPTER THIRTY-SIX

The French Riviera

Lord Hawke, Stokely, and Ambrose, aboard Hawke Air, had just landed at the Nice airport that morning. Harry Brock, surrounded by all his gear, was waiting on the tarmac. It was a short but scenic one-hour drive along the corniche to their destination, the towns of Antibes and Juan-les-Pins. Hawke, however, had arranged a much more expedient mode of transportation, one that would give his colleagues an added benefit: a better view of the geography of the rocky coastline that was soon going to be their new theater of operations.

The six-passenger chopper waiting for them on the tarmac was a shade of baby blue. Its color was almost identical to the glorious shades of sky and sea found along the sun-shot coast of the Riviera in the South of France on this splendid morning in January.

Alex, seated up front next to the chopper pilot, felt better than he had in the weeks since his son's disappearance. He was now taking active steps, positive steps that could lead to the rescue of Alexei. He was fighting on two fronts, but he had powerful allies in the battle.

Gazing down at the diffused light and the ghostly wash of the Mediterranean far below, he realized he had another cause for his newfound optimism and happy humor: Once more he found himself amid the bliss that was this uniquely beautiful part of the world.

He put his forehead against the cool plexiglass of the cockpit window, stared down at the flow of scenes racing by below, and just breathed it all in, the unforgettable beauty of the rocky, sun-splashed playground peninsula of the French Riviera.

How he loved it here.

They were now landing at the helipad provided by the casino. A minute walk from anywhere. Hawke stepped down onto the tarmac, took a deep breath of pine-scented air, and looked around.

Unless you were a spy, of course, or a Russian billionaire whose mega-yacht required a deepwater port, or a plucky paparazzo hotshot on the trail of Leonardo DiCaprio, you might have little reason to find yourself in Antibes, or its charming little sister village Juan-les-Pins, on this brilliant morning.

But the quartet of men who climbed out of the baby-blue helo and started out on foot into the town of Juan-les-Pins had plenty of reason to be here. If Vladimir Putin actually was still alive, and that was a very big if, then they might well be a few steps away from learning where he'd stashed little Alexei.

Hawke, quickly walking ahead of the others, couldn't wait another second. He whirled around and said, "Stoke, listen, could you and Harry Brock do the honors? Take care of getting all our gear and weapons to the hotel? Ambrose and I are going to run ahead and check out the harbor. See if that big red boat is still here."

"You got it, boss."

He'd found himself hoping, recently, that his son was held captive at the KGB complex in Siberia. His mother was there. And, the safest place on earth for him, oddly enough. Of course he and Stoke would have to mount a major hostage rescue operation, and he'd call in his friends Thunder and Lightning from Costa Rica. World's toughest paramilitary-for-hire force . . . but yes, he'd have the advantage because he'd been a guest at the Winter Palace, knew every square inch of that grand palace and—

He heard a big marine engine start and then moving water and he paused a moment to see a big blue yacht getting under way . . . and there she was! He found himself staring out at the massive red yacht out there, bobbing at her mooring.

Tsar!

She was still here after all!

The wind was up and the current had shifted. She'd swung around her bow anchor, so that she was now lying stern to.

He knew every square inch of that yacht, too. He felt a frisson of pleasurable expectation ripple up his spine. He was close. He was getting closer. His son might very well be aboard that goddamn Russian boat at this very moment . . .

ALL HAWKE WANTED TO SEE now was the owner's launch from *Tsar* leave the yacht and head in his direction. Of course there were many reasons why the launch would have been dispatched to shore. Fetch food, wine and liquor, et cetera. But to pick up the owner and spirit him over under cover of darkness?

That was certainly one of them.

And then, in Hawke's mind, Putin would magically appear here at the harbor, stepping out of a nondescript automobile. Hawke would see Putin's face as he stepped out of the darkness here on the seawall and into the light . . . and he would take the old monster by the throat and . . .

I want my son and I know you've got him aboard . . . Take me to him or I'll kill you right here and now!

"I'll torture the bastard if I have to," Hawke had told Ambrose on the flight to Nice. "I will, I swear I will. He thinks everyone who knows him wants him dead? I'll happily go to the head of that line, by god I will."

He heard someone behind him and turned to see Stoke reach over and squeeze his shoulder.

"Stowed the gear, boss. Came back out to see what's going on."

Hawke said, "There she is, Stoke, god help us, there she is!"

Stoke looked up. "Holy shit," he said. "Will you look at that! Is that our boy Vlad's machine?"

"Thank god, right?" Hawke said, "All morning I was trying to prepare myself in the event that she'd already set sail."

"Nah, boss, you got more luck than that, man. Always have had."

Stoke gazed out across the sparkling bay, where all the heavy iron bobbed on moorings. These were the big-boy toys, the personal fleet of the masters of the universe, all riding at anchor here in the Billionaire's Paradise. Here were assembled some of the truly great yachts of the world, most notably the enormous *Ecstasea*, built for the Russian oligarch Roman Abramovich in the early 2000s and reportedly sold several times, including once to the crown prince of Abu Dhabi. And closer in to shore, Larry Ellison's $130 million *Musashi*.

But there, in the overarching shadow of that Russian monstrosity, *Ecstasea*, lay another Russian yacht, not quite as large as the other two, but still famous enough around the world in her own right. She was over two hundred feet long on the waterline, one of the world's most photographed vessels, and she belonged to none other than Russian Federation president Vladimir Putin.

"You've been aboard her many times, is that correct, Commander?" Brock asked Hawke.

"Yes, I have. A couple of lengthy cruises as well as visits while she was moored here. Why?"

"In the event Putin really may already be aboard or is to board her soon, it will be good for us to get a firsthand look at her interior layout, especially below. We may have to board her at sea, sir. At night."

Hawke looked at Brock with a half-grin. "I was just thinking the same thing, Mr. Brock, but thank you." Finally, Harry Brock making sense and at the perfect time.

"Yeah," Stoke said. "You know, whether Vlad shows or not, I think we go out there and have us a little lookie-loo down below. Whether we get invited or not . . . Right, boss?"

"Oh, believe me, Stoke, we're boarding that vessel and searching her stem to stern. No matter what the hell happens."

Putin's $300 million yacht was here all right, but was Putin himself? Or even—dare he say it—his son, Alexei?

"We got lucky, boss," Stoke said to Hawke. "We got ourselves some good luck going now."

"Luck had nothing to do with my intel," Harry Brock said. Being normally snarky, for some reason he was clearly being on his best behavior. Stoke had probably screamed at him, telling him to keep his shit together or risk being sent packing.

"Luck is for losers, Brock," Hawke said, "but I'll bloody well take it this time. Your story holds up, at least this far. So stay with it. That's the hotel over there, along the seawall. Pretty, isn't it, Ambrose? You've been here before. My favorite hotel on the planet."

"Lovely."

The old edifice, ablaze with bougainvillea lit by spotlights, was truly beautiful, and full of architectural grace and history. A history that Hawke knew all too well, having hidden out here in this seaside paradise with various lovers over the years. And once for an entire summer with his beloved Anastasia and their child, Alexei.

The five-star seaside hotel was now called the Belles-Rives, but it had once been merely a small house where the famous American author F. Scott Fitzgerald lived and wrote. He, along with his nearly mad wife, Zelda, and their towheaded daughter, Scottie, had rented it for two years, when it was called the Villa St. Louis. Long a literary favorite of Hawke's, Fitzgerald had finished his masterpiece, *The Great Gatsby*, here, and had also begun his novel *Tender Is the Night*.

"Monsieur Hawke!" a voice called out from across the square. Hawke whirled to see who it was. A dapper silver-haired man had spied the three of them crossing the terrace in his direction. *"Bienvenue, mon amie!"* the fellow exclaimed.

It was an old friend of Hawke's, a rascal of the first order: M. Hugo Jadot, owner of the Belles-Rives Hotel.

CHAPTER THIRTY-SEVEN

Hugo!" Hawke said, and with his three comrades trailing a bit behind, he started walking toward his friend. Jadot was standing by the door, just inside the wisteria-draped porte cochere at the grand pillared entryway. Beyond lay a broad sunny deck cantilevered like an ocean liner out over a sun-speckled infinity pool.

Hawke let his eyes fall on the merry diners sipping icy white wine and enjoying their ridiculously overpriced salades Niçoise as massive multimillion-dollar yachts danced attendance on the sparkling waves.

Memories.

Hawke said, "*Bonjour, Maître!* Lovely to see you again, old friend."

M. Hugo Jadot opened his arms and literally ran to Hawke, embracing him with delight.

Hawke said, "Hugo, meet my partners in crime. This gentleman, whom I sure you'll recall, is Chief Inspector Ambrose Congreve and—"

"Of course I know him! The great genius and celebrated detective himself! How are you, Chief Inspector?"

"Very well indeed, thank you!"

"And these are Mr. Stokely Jones Jr. and Mr. Harry Brock, both reasonably upright citizens of Miami. And this, gentlemen, is Monsieur Hugo Jadot, notorious local scoundrel and owner of this divine establishment and de facto mayor of Juan-les-Pins."

"You flatter me, Alex. So! Is this a vacation, Alex?" Jadot said with a sly smile. An acknowledgment that Lord Hawke had never once stayed in his hotel unless in the company of exceptionally good-looking females.

"No, Hugo. Serious business. My son, Alexei, has been kidnapped. It happened at Christmas."

"My god. No. It's not true."

"I'll fill you in, Hugo. It's a nightmare, but it's certainly true."

"I'll be at your service, Alex. Anything I can do during your stay. I love that child like my own."

Hawke said, "I'll fill you in over lunch, Hugo."

"Well, at any rate, welcome, welcome, messieurs," the jovial little Frenchman said, shaking both of their hands, apparently, with instant affection. "*Bienvenue! C'est une tres beau jour, n'est-ce pas!* I'm so delighted to have you gentlemen here at the Belles-Rive! When Lord Hawke called to reserve your rooms a few days ago, it was cause for great celebration. He and his family are much revered by the staff."

"It's a beautiful spot, Hugo," Stoke said. "You should be very proud of it."

"Well, won't you all come join me for a drink in the Fitzgerald Bar? A bite to eat, perhaps? While we discuss how I may be of service in solving this heinous crime against my friend? There's a view to the sea, and by the time we finish lunch, all of your rooms will be ready. Sorry for the delay, I didn't not expect you quite so soon."

"We are at your disposal, Hugo," Hawke said, pausing at the doorway. "Please take my friends to the bar. I'll join you momentarily . . . I just need a moment to myself."

"*Mais oui, Alex! Allez! Viens avec moi,* my new friends."

Hugo and the three men disappeared into the cool darkness of the hotel reception entryway and then into the bar beyond.

Hawke paused, then turned back to the wide and curving arms

of the harbor. A body of water embraced by a necklace of white pearls—how he thought of the large villas that circled the harbor. Many of these were the grand homes once owned by his literary heroes, men like Jules Verne and W. Somerset Maugham.

He caught his breath. He found himself recalling happier times, all those joyous evenings with Anastasia and their little boy . . .

At night, when the Mediterranean Sea breeze wasn't blowing inland, Juan-les-Pins smelled faintly like North Africa. It's a strange concoction made up of diesel fuel, dust, cooking oil, and cloying flowers. Across the harbor lay the entertainment district. It has always had a seedy edge, he thought, with sidewalk seating at nightclubs like the Pam Pam and snack shops with all-American names—Monster Burger and Wall Street . . .

In the waning light of afternoon, he and his little family would join the natives at the cafés or play pétanque in the great dusty square near Parc de la Pinède, with its playground and the strange old round stone building charmingly signed BIBLIOTHÈQUE POUR TOUS.

Memories.

HE'D LIVED HERE, LIVED MOSTLY happily here, with Alexei and his beloved Anastasia Korsakova, Alexei's Russian mother. In his memory, those were the best of all times, the best time possible. The contrast between then and now was stark.

Hawke felt his heart race and lit another cigarette to calm his nerves. He drew the smoke down deep. Then he just stood there on the breakwater, staring seaward, and considered the status quo. The threats to Alexei had always been about Hawke himself—Putin's love-hate relationship with him.

When all was well, the wily Russian was the soul of goodness toward them all. But whenever Hawke dared to threaten Vladimir or when he derailed one of the Russian's endless schemes against the West? Then the long knives of the KGB came out, flashing menace in the sunlight, carving fear out of the darkness.

What was it Congreve had said to him the other evening at the Palace Bar? One of his many pearls about how to solve a crime . . .

Never forget the power of a good timeline, my boy, remember the timeline! Words of investigatory wisdom from the mind of the great criminalist, Chief Inspector Ambrose Congreve of Scotland Yard . . . Indeed, Hawke had the timeline in his head.

ALEXEI HAD BEEN TAKEN SHORTLY after Putin dropped off the planet. But Putin was already on the run weeks before that fateful Christmas Day. Hiding wherever he could, traveling by night and avoiding the day. A man in such dire straits could hardly afford to saddle himself with a seven-year-old boy for company. Could he? No.

So after months of planning the snatch operation from his Kremlin office, Putin then has his KGB goon squad execute the kidnapping on the mountaintop. They then fly Alexei to Italy and torch the chopper to destroy evidence. And then the question becomes: where on earth do they secret his son away from prying eyes until Putin resurfaces?

Could Volodya come up with a better spot on earth than that yacht out there? *Tsar*, with all her technology, security, and defenses, and with a heavily armed crew at the ready.

Hawke was not at all sure Harry Brock's intel was accurate. But for now at least, it was all he had. He had learned long ago to proceed with what you had, no matter how implausible the evidence might be. Brock, in his experience, was an unreliable CIA operative. But Brock's intel would have to suffice for now.

He turned reluctantly and headed back to the hotel, haunted by old dreams and old feelings.

Whenever I come here to the Alpes-Maritimes, I'm always attacked by the itch of antiquity . . .

Why is that?

Memories.

CHAPTER THIRTY-EIGHT

Hugo, my dear old friend, when was the last time you laid eyes on the president of Russia?" Hawke asked Hugo upon entering the bar. He loved this old gin joint. Loved the Fitzgerald memorabilia and the nautical design of the large harborside bar. Jadot had designed the room to be one that mirrored rooms aboard the great yachts bobbing just offshore. There hanging above the bar was the familiar photograph of Josephine Baker and her pet cheetah out on the dock.

Hugo Jadot appeared not to have heard him and waved him forward to join them in the melee that was lunchtime at the Fitzgerald Bar.

Waiters in striped French boater T-shirts buzzed about, delivering cups of Nescafé that cost ten euros apiece. Famous entertainment-world boldface names swapped lies with billionaires over icy buckets of Krug.

The owner of the hotel was seated at a round banquette beneath windows overlooking the harbor. A large bottle of Domaine Ott Rosé stood in ice inside a frosty silver urn. He knew it was Hawke's drink of choice in the South of France.

"Hugo," Hawke said, pouring himself a glass, "when was the

last time you saw our mutual friend Volodya aboard his big red boat out there?"

"Volodya? Here? Oh, I don't know. He comes and he goes. I get no advance notice, believe me. I remember the last time you and he were aboard *Tsar* out there in the harbor. He took you out in his submarine, I believe. To demonstrate his new secret explosive, yes? *Feuerwasser*, I believe it was called. This was right before he tried to set the whole world afire, moving his secret armies into the Baltics."

"Right. I had a hell of a time talking him into changing his mind about all that," Hawke said grimly. "He's never spoken to me since."

"You prevented a worldwide conflagration, Alex. Give yourself a little credit, my friend."

"It was two years ago," Hawke said, dismissing the compliment. "Ancient history. My question is, Who's aboard now? The captain? Is he aboard? Guards? KGB? Please be honest with me, Hugo. I know you keep an eagle eye on the yacht community? Yes?"

"I keep my eyes open, yes. Look, Alex, what can I tell you?"

"Hugo, the whole world believes Vladimir Putin is dead. I happen to believe that he is alive and on the run. And you, my good friend, *you* are uniquely qualified as a daily eyewitness to what would most likely be Putin's primary getaway escape route. What have you seen? These last couple of months? Anything out of the ordinary? Anything we should know about?"

"Nothing, Alex, I swear to you. The normal comings and goings of the crew, that's about all. Food and marine supply deliveries. Zero visiting celebrities, movie stars, whatever have you."

"So who the hell's out there, Hugo?"

"Well, let's see. That would be the captain, of course. And then the skeleton crew still remain aboard."

"And why, I wonder, would all these people remain aboard a moored yacht for such a long time? I mean, unless of course they are out there awaiting further instructions about their next destination?" Hawke asked.

"I—I've really no idea, my friend," Jadot replied. "As I said, he really doesn't make me privy to his plans, you see."

Congreve stood up and clasped his hands behind his broad back. "No recent trips over to the fuel docks, eh?"

"No, Chief Inspector. None."

"No large food shipments coming aboard? Cases of champagne? Caviar? Liquor?"

"No."

"All quiet on the Mediterranean front, is what you're saying, Monsieur Jadot?" Congreve said, his attention fixed on Hugo, watching for the telltale tics of a practiced liar. Small alarms were going off in the great criminalist's forebrain. The manner of the man was plainly coincident with the manner of all congenital liars . . .

"Exactly right, Chief Inspector. All quiet."

"Tell the truth. Full complement of crew aboard?" the chief inspector snapped.

"No. Captain, first mate, cook. I swear to you. That's it."

"How do you know that, Hugo?" Ambrose said. "Who's aboard and who's not, I mean?"

Hawke smiled. Good for Congreve.

"Oh. Yes. How do I know since I've not been aboard in months? I see what you mean. Well, it's no revelation that the yacht's captain and I are longtime friends. I get invited out there occasionally. And Ivar, the captain, comes ashore to the hotel for dinners or upstairs entertaining his numerous female acquaintances."

Hawke said, "What's his full name?"

"The captain? Ivar. Ivar Solo."

"Ah, yes, Captain Solo," Hawke said, pleased that Ambrose seemed to be making good progress.

"So you're saying no unusual activity at all?" Stoke said. "Since Christmas, let's say . . ."

"*Mais non, monsieur! Rien!* Nothing! She lies at anchor. She doesn't rock, she doesn't roll. *Tsar* is not your answer. Whatever you gentlemen have heard, this is not where miracles will happen . . . that Putin will appear in Juan-les-Pins out of the mist only to sail away into the sunset. I'm sorry, Alex. If Vladimir Putin is why you're here, I'm afraid you and your friends are simply wasting your time. You think he's alive. But I know he's dead. We all know that."

Hawke raised his glass to the owner.

"Well! Thank you, Hugo, for your unique perspective on our situation. Very interesting, indeed. However, my colleagues and I have no problem wasting our time. Especially here in your lovely hotel . . . Cheers!" Hawke raised his glass.

Hugo, chastened by Hawke's tone and manner, raised his glass and said, "*A votre santé!* And now I would think your rooms are ready! I hope you fine gentlemen find your accommodations to your liking, yes?"

"One more thing, Hugo," Hawke said, "if you don't mind. We need a boat of some kind. Fast boat. Highly maneuverable. I think I saw a Wally Tender down at the docks. *Too Elusive*, I believe she's called. Wally makes a good solid boat and fast as hell. That's the kind of thing I'm talking about."

"Sightseeing?" Hugo said.

"Something like that," Hawke replied. "Have a look around, see the sights. Mr. Brock here has never been to the Riviera before. Isn't that right, Harry?"

"I can't wait to see all its charms, boss."

"See what I mean?" Hawke said, smiling. "He can't wait."

"Very interesting. Well, as it happens, your lordship is in luck. *Too Elusive*'s owner is a good friend and a fellow business owner. He lets me use her whenever he's traveling abroad. Like he is now. When do you need access to the boat?"

"As long as I'm here. Is she fueled and ready to go?"

"Not sure. Haven't used her yet this week. But the keys are at the front desk with the concierge."

Hawke said, "Thanks, I'll take you up on that very kind offer,

Hugo. Can you excuse us for a second? I need to talk privately with my colleagues here."

"Certainly," Hugo said, getting to his feet and touching his white linen napkin delicately to his protuberant liver-colored lips. "I bid you fond adieu, gentlemen. I've had a word with the chef. We look forward to seeing you here for dinner with us this evening. Outside on the terrace? I'll book you a table on the water. Yes?"

"Yes, of course, Hugo, please reserve us a table right on the water with an unfettered view of that Russian yacht out there. Yes?"

"*Mais oui! Mais oui!*"

"Stoke, I want you and Harry to run that boat over to the petrol dock and have her fluids topped off. Make sure she's seaworthy. We may need that thing in a hurry. Also, stow all our gear aboard now. All weapons, everything, on board that launch and secured . . . And, Stoke, heads-up. These Wally Tenders are very, very exotic. High-tech and sophisticated. Fast as hell. So give yourself some time to get used to her. Maybe do a quick sea trial out beyond the breakwater? I want us to be ready to mount an overwhelming assault the very instant the time comes."

"Aye-aye, Skipper," Stoke said. "Don't worry. We're on it."

"Who's got the graveyard watch tonight?"

"Brock."

"I'm sure our friend Harry remembers that disastrous night he was supposedly on duty down in the Keys," Hawke said, with a smile that held more than irony but less than scorn." When we were chasing Scissorhands all over creation."

"He'll never forget it, boss. He screwed the pooch that night with the Cubans and he knows it."

"Good. Tonight, he stands his post and he keeps his bloody eyes open, right?"

"Always."

"There are only four of us. We will not be welcomed aboard that big Russian boat with hearts of good cheer and open arms. We'll likely need all the firepower we can muster, Stoke."

Stoke smiled. "This ain't our first rodeo, Skipper!"

Hawke looked at him and put his right hand on the big man's shoulder. It was like scratching concrete.

"I've got to make a long-overdue phone call, Stoke. See you later down in the bar."

As soon as Hawke got to his room, he sat down on the side of the bed by the telephone. He lifted the receiver and asked the hotel operator to ring Badrutt's Palace in St. Moritz.

"*Bonjour*," the Swiss operator said.

"Yes, I'd like to be connected to a guest in the hotel."

"Of course, sir. Who shall I say is calling?"

"My name is Hawke. Alex Hawke."

"Ah. Lord Hawke, of course, sir. Which guest would you like to speak with, please?"

"Fraulein Sigrid Kissl. She's in Room 303."

"Ah, yes, let me connect you with her straightaway . . . Hold the line, please."

Hawke's heart was pounding on the walls of his chest loudly enough to fill his ears with a dull thunder. He sat and watched the second hand on his watch spin round and round.

"Hello? I'm still holding. Is anyone there?"

"I'm terribly sorry, sir, she's not picking up, I'm afraid."

"Please try her again, will you?"

"Lord Hawke, I'm so sorry. I am just seeing a note from the front desk come up on my computer. It seems that Fraulein Kissl has checked out of the hotel. The doorman says she was in considerable distress."

"What? When? When did she check out?"

"Just this minute, sir. You just missed her."

"Did she leave any forwarding address? Was she going to the airport?"

"I'm afraid we don't know, sir. Sorry."

"Are you sure? Could you check again?"

"Lord Hawke, I have another client here, waiting. I'll call you back at this number if I learn anything more, all right? So sorry."

Click.

Hawke stared at the face looking back at him from the ancient gilded mirror hung on the wall.

"*And now you've lost her, too,*" he whispered to himself.

Bloody fool.

He picked up the phone to call Congreve, deciding what to say and not say. "You've lost your assistant," Hawke said.

"What?"

"She's gone. Checked out of the hotel in Zurich and didn't say where she was going."

"What happened, Alex? Did you two have another row? I'd so hoped you two could straighten things out between you . . ."

"Yes. So did I. She has a lot of personal issues. Maybe we just have to give her some time to wrestle them to the ground."

"I'm sorry, Alex. I know how much you love her."

"I'll be all right. I've got a bloody plateful of issues all by myself."

Some secrets are better kept than revealed, Hawke whispered as he replaced the receiver.

CHAPTER THIRTY-NINE

Geneva

Next morning Uncle Joe bade farewell to Horst, the happy-as-horseshit Swiss sub driver, and climbed back into the Mercedes. Two nights sitting out on the lakeside dock in subfreezing temperatures, covered in snow, and the Merc cranked right up. Traffic was light on the highway that encircles all of Lake Zurich, and he knew he could make good time.

Instead of hanging a left toward Zurich, he hung a right toward Geneva. About a three-hour drive, he figured, to his destination. The Beau-Rivage Hotel overlooking the sparkling blue waters of Lake Geneva.

There were now just one or two more errands on President Putin's hit list of all good things for him to accomplish.

He felt pretty good about how things had gone so far, with the Sorcerer at the top of the mountain. The man had agreed verbally to consider Putin's offer to purchase the Alpine fortress. Tonight, when he got back to his room at the hotel in Geneva, he had a call scheduled with Vladimir. A bring-him-up-to-speed call, short and sweet, and nothing but good news.

Joe chuckled. A mate of his once said Joe Stalingrad was the kind of guy who could make throwing up on the rug seem like some kind of blessed event.

Now, if only his next meeting, the one with the colonel, was as easy-peasy as the rest had been. But maybe not. Joe knew the man he was going to see had a reputation as a surly American soldier of fortune, and that reputation was justified. He was one tough hombre.

The American had crossed swords with Putin a couple of years ago, but was now back in Putin's good graces for one very simple reason. Without this key player, Putin knew he had almost no chance of realizing his dream of a new and glorious Soviet empire.

The man's name was Colonel Brett "Beau" Beauregard. There was a name for cats like him, and Joe whispered it softly to himself: *"Badass."*

First in his class at West Point, a highly decorated U.S. Army Ranger, Beauregard rose quickly through the ranks to the rank of colonel. He was as strong as a team of oxen and had been captain of the Army gridiron team that beat Navy to win the big game on Thanksgiving Day 1990. The guy was the real deal, and he'd earned Joe's respect when they'd worked together, putting a secret army together for Putin in Siberia.

Beau was the kind of guy more than happy to take a knife to a gunfight.

The colonel had gained worldwide notoriety as the founder of Vulcan International. Vulcan, basically combat warriors for hire, had started small in the town of Port Arthur, Texas. Eventually they became the largest private army in the world, working with governments of every stripe. At one time, they were simultaneously working with the United States, China, Russia, and Cuba. The colonel worked hard to build firewalls between his competing clients; at one point he was working with both the Iranians and the Israelis.

They provided military assistance to every country that could afford their services. To Beau's credit, they never played favorites, and politics never entered into the equation. As Beau was once quoted as saying in the *Washington Post,* "I'm a soldier of fortune, damn it, and this soldier is out to make his fortune."

VULCAN WAS SO SUCCESSFUL THAT by 2003, they were training upward of 80,000 soldiers and sailors at the Port Royal facility, a vast military-industrial complex that had increased in size to over seven thousand acres—more than twelve square miles.

And then disaster struck.

It happened at Fallujah. Five of Joe's contract players were accused by the U.S. government of having wantonly taken the lives of innocent civilians. The worldwide media machine pounced, and the whole world turned on Vulcan. The heroes of Vulcan, who had taken bullets for the Americans, were now labeled as wanton murderers, Wild West cowboys with neither scruples nor morality who would turn on anyone if the price was right.

Beau himself was an object of scorn and ridicule. In a Fox News Sunday interview with Chris Wallace that Joe watched, the colonel had famously said, "Did some innocent civilians get shot? Hell, yeah. That's why it's called war. Did we shoot first? My opinion? No, we did not. I've seen the evidence. I stand by my troops."

Beau Beauregard lost almost everything in his headlong fall from the pinnacle. But he had invested his earnings all over the world and done quite well. He gave up his PJ, what he called his private jet, and all of his houses, but he held on to his boat. A 150-foot yacht he had named *Celestial,* which he kept moored at the Royal Bermuda Yacht Club.

And just when it looked like he was finished, finito, dead meat, the colonel got a phone call. It was from Uncle Joe himself. All was forgiven, Joe said; the president needed ole Beau to come back into the fold. It was time to embark on a mission of historic magnitude. His life was about to get very exciting again. And he was going to get very, very rich.

There was a beat, and then Beau said, "Lemme ask you a question. Is it going to beat living on a big fat yacht in Bermuda with hot and cold running honeypots? I mean, come on, Joe, get real! Hell, ain't nobody shooting at me these days and I'm swimming in pussy."

Joe had replied, "Well, hell yeah, Beau. But are you rich?"

Smiling, he mashed the go pedal. He had to step on it if he wanted to be in time for breakfast.

JOE GAVE HIS NAME AT the front desk, and a phone call later he was rocketing to the top of the building. There was only one door up here and it said *PH*, so Joe leaned on the buzzer.

Beau swung the door wide. *"Hot damn! I'll be danged,* look who's washed up! If it ain't my ole pal Uncle Joe! Hey, Hollywood! Good to see you, son, drag that skinny ass of yours on in! Come on in, I said!"

Beau on happy pills? Joe wondered, Ritalin or whatever? He stepped inside and looked around. Beau was all over him. Moving in for his close-up, causing Joe to take a step backward.

"You ever think we'd be doing business again? Huh? The Gruesome Twosome? The Beau and Joe Show?" Joe said, laughing as he shook the colonel's hand and was swept deeper into the grand penthouse suite. It was moderately vast, celestial ceilings and wall-to-wall windows with breathtaking views overlooking Lake Geneva.

Joe nodded, gazing around the suite in awe. The decor of the interior was an overstated blend of Trumpian sculpted gilt and old-world grandiosity. But there was another breathtaking view at a card table across the room. There, bathed in sunlight beneath a sunny window, two young women of dubious distinction were sipping champagne and playing canasta at a mahogany game table.

"And, who might these fine lovelies be, Beau?"

"Well, that one there on your left is Martina. An actress from London. Calls herself the Human Trampoline. Says she still loves Harvey Weinstein and probably always will. 'He's a doll baby,' she says! And the other one, in the pink bra and panties, that's Violette, my French niece. Flew over with me from Bermuda. Ladies, where you leave your manners? Back in the barn? Say hey to my ole pal

Uncle Joe! He'll be joining us for supper this evening. Look at him! He's famous! He's a goddamn movie star, for crissakes!"

"Hello, Uncle Joe," they trilled in singsong fashion, smiling at the Playstation.

"Hi, honey," Violette said, arching her back so that her front caught the light, "Can I be in your next picture, sweetie? Here, I'm writing my manger's number down for you."

"Sure!" Joe said, "Could be a star vehicle for you. It's a remake of the old Russ Meyer classic called *"Faster, Pussycat, Kill! Kill!"*

"Groovy!" Violette said, doing a giggly little shimmy-shake right there in her chair.

That's when from somewhere behind him, Joe heard a muffled snore. There was someone else in the room, and he turned around to see who the hell it was.

CHAPTER FORTY

O ver in a dark corner was a tall, rangy guy, deeply tanned, wearing faded Levi's and a sweat-stained black cowboy shirt. Sound asleep, he was slumped back in his armchair. He had it rocked back on two legs, his long legs extended out before him. If looks could kill, it would only be because this guy had them in spades. On his left calf, he wore a bone-handled bowie knife, sheathed in a fancy Comanche Indian beaded holster. Looked sharp. Meaning the man *and* the knife. Cowboy boots too, expensive Tony Lama's, polished to a mirrorlike finish. Top it all off with a sun-faded black Stetson pulled way down over his eyes.

Asleep? Or dead?

"Who *is* that guy?" Joe whispered to Beau. "Aside from being that actor Sam Shepard's twin brother, I mean."

"That's my newly appointed head of security, son. Ex–Army Ranger, former TV rodeo cowboy star and the best-lookin', meanest sumbitch ever to come out of Hico, Texas. Walking death. C'mon over here, son, and I'll introduce you to him. Speaks Russian, too. Married a Russian gal in East Berlin when he was CIA. Said he'd lived with her ten years before he had to kill her."

"Wait. He's CIA?"

"Not anymore, son. He *was* CIA. Now he's just pure paid badass-ness."

"Maybe we just let him sleep, Beau," Joe said, taking a couple of steps back.

"Hell, no, he's all right. Had him a late night at the Million Dollar Cowboy Bar, so he's taking her real easy today. Wake up, cowboy!" Beau said, lifting the brim of the cowboy's sweat-stained hat.

The man said nothing and was taking his own sweet time about opening his eyes. But when he did, they were blue. They were the coldest, darkest blue-black eyes Joe had ever seen. Holes in his face like piss holes in the snow . . .

Like *dead* cold.

Beau said to him, "Want you to meet somebody, dude, that's all. Hollywood movie star here, goes by the name of Uncle Joe. Joe, say hello to my old pal here. Name's Shit Smith."

"Say again?" Joe said, looking quizzically at Beau.

"His name is Shit Smith."

"Shit?"

"Uh-huh."

"Good morning, sir! Very nice to meet you," Joe said, gushing. "Heard a lot of great things about you! Rodeo cowboy, huh? Man, I do love that rodeo scene. Especially the clowns. A great honor, sir! Very great honor, indeed!"

The cowboy lifted his brim an eighth of an inch and squinted at the squat little man standing before him with his empty right hand still extended. When the man spoke, it was in measured tones, in words that were barely audible.

"Calm. The. Fuck. *Down*," Shit said, Johnny Cash deep and low-down and barely above a whisper.

The guy's eyes, sharp now, sharp as a diamond cutter, bored holes into Joe's face. After a while, he finally stuck his hand out. Joe shook it with some temerity, worried about the delicate bones in his fingers. But expecting tough, gnarled calluses, Joe found the handshake was civilized, almost weirdly soft and gentle for a rodeo cowboy. Somewhere in the back of his brain, Joe heard a faint *ping.*

His gaydar? What the—silently pinging . . . *gay!* . . . *gay!* . . . *gay!* . . . Gaaayyyy?

Could it possibly be that this badass Texas dude could really be what Joe's Cuban ex-girlfriend, Juicy Lucy Musso, used to call, a *Madalena tímida*?

A long, soft muffin? Shit Smith? Say it ain't so, Joe!

"Ow!" Joe squealed, grabbing his right leg. Shit Smith had just kicked him in the shin just below the knee. Hard.

"Uncle Joe, huh? So, how's it hangin', pards?" Shit said. More awake now, the psycho assassin spoke with a deep, slow drawl, one that called up images of cattle drives and tumbleweeds, and dollar-a-shot whiskey.

"Hanging in there, hanging in there," Joe said, doubled over in pain and rubbing his shinbone. "What'd you say your name was again?"

"I didn't say."

"Sorry?"

"Hell are you anyway, dude? A total vagina? I said, 'I *didn't say*'!"

Beau jumped in. "C'mon, Shit, don't be so damn antisocial. Tell the man your damn name. And don't kick him anymore."

"Name's Shit Smith," he whispered, more to himself. He closed his eyes again. "What about it?"

"*Shit* Smith?" Joe said, his pale blue eyes full of wonder and fear.

"Somethin' wrong with that, little buddy? Got some kind of problem with it, do you, Mr. Movie Star?" Joe froze. He's seen Shit's left hand grab hold of that bowie knife.

"Me? Oh, hell no, no, *hell* no. It's great. Terrific name, don't get me wrong. Who wouldn't love a name like that? Just unusual, that's all I'm saying. So I gotta ask, is Shit your real name, or just a nickname?"

Beau looked at Shit and rolled his eyes, apologizing for all this cheesy New York–esque behavior on Joe's part.

Shit said, "Hell, I dunno. Folks been calling me Shit so long I've forgotten what t'hell I started out with. Ain't that right, boss?"

"You were Shit when I met you, that's all I know," Beau said, grinning. "And Shit you'll always remain, buddy."

"Well, there you go," Shit said, smiling at Uncle Joe for the first time, deciding to maybe give this hinky little dude a pass.

"Like your boots," Joe said. "Never saw anything like them. Can I have the number of your shoeshine man? Just kidding, just kidding."

"Polish up real good, don't they? Listen. You ever see me standin' up real close and personal next to some pretty little split-tail in a short skirt? Gal going full commando . . . know what I'm sayin'?"

"Yeah?" Joe said, into it. "She's full commando . . . and?"

"Yeah. So, you see me doin' that, Joe, you just plain know ole Shit has a reflected bird's-eye view of that little gal's snatch, that he's looking straight up at that pretty pink snapper courtesy of old Tony Lama and these mirror-polished kicks of mine."

"Damn! I had no idea. You mean you can really see all the way up to her goddamn—"

"Awright, awright, enough, Joe," Beau said. "Get some shut-eye, Shit. I'll talk pussy all day long, you know that. But me and Uncle Joe here got some serious-ass bidness to discuss."

Shit looked at his boss with a blank, empty stare that even Joe couldn't read. He said, "Beau, lemme ask you something. Is Joe your real uncle? Or just some cutesy shit uncle?"

"No. Not real uncle. No. No relation."

"Is he a real Hollywood star, then?"

"Oh, yeah. Totally," Beau said. "Tell the man the name of your latest picture, Joe."

"You mean *Flaming Pussies*? About the psycho arsonist in the New Orleans whorehouse?"

"No, no, that was porn. The army one . . ."

"Oh, yeah. At Paramount. It's called *Little Patton*. I play the lead."

"Little Patton? Is that what you said?" Shit said, or more like *hissed*.

"Yeah. Right. Bingo."

Shit said, "Fuck me. Seriously. *You* play General George S. Patton, my beloved hee-ro? *You?*" He was going for the knife again . . .

"No, god no, not the *real* George S. Patton, Shit. I'm sorry. No, not the real Patton at all! The *avatar* George Patton. From the future, see. It's a sci-fi pic. What can I tell ya?"

"Ava-whut? What in fuck-all is this ugly little fuck talking about, Beau?"

Beau put a calming hand on Shit's shoulder and said, "Oh, c'mon, you know these movie people, Shit, who knows what the hell they're going on about half the time."

"Well, hell, then," Shit said, pulling his black lid back down over his eyes, "have to say, he was pretty good in that *Flaming Pussies* movie. You boys go on, do what you got to do. Don't pay no never mind to me. I ain't feeling so social no more. Y'all best scatter now."

He lifted the Stetson back up an inch, yawned loudly, and said, "Y'know, my old daddy used to say you should treat yer body like a temple. Hell, I treat mine like a goddamn amusement park . . ." His voice trailed off and he started snoring softly.

"Nice to meet you, Shit," Joe said to him, happy to be getting out of this new friendship alive, with only a badly bruised shinbone to show for the encounter.

No reply. Shit was off to dreamland.

"What'll you have to eat?" Beau asked him, going over to a loaded buffet table in the dining room. "We got chicken salad, free range, but god knows, if I'm going to eat a goddamn chicken, I'd like to know where the hell it's been! We got potato salad, we got lobster salad, we got any damn kind of sandwich you want . . . everything except gluten-free. I don't even know what the hell gluten is . . . but I do like the fact that it's free."

"Nothing for me, thanks, Beau. I stopped for late breakfast on the way down from Zurich."

"You want a drink? Bloody? Ice cold beer?"

"Little early for me. But you go ahead."

"Oh, I will. Let me whip up a damn Bloody eye-opener and we'll take her in there in the library and have us a private little chat. That suit you?"

JOE FOLLOWED BEAU AND HIS Bloody into the wood-paneled library, where a fire was crackling.

"He's alive, is he?" Beau said, taking his seat and lighting a cigar. "Putin?"

"Yeah."

"Holy shit," Beau said. "I was kinda wondering about that . . . how many people know?"

"Him. Obviously. You. Me. And a Swiss financier. Four. That's it. The rest of the world thinks he's dead as you know, Beau."

"Well, that's why I was a little surprised to get the call. But, shit, Vladimir is one hard little dude to get rid of, ain't he?"

"I wouldn't bet against him. Don't forget, the pro-Soviet forces allied with him still run deep, both within the Kremlin and within the Russian population at large. He's left the seat of power, semi-bloodless coup, pulled off by disloyal oligarchs. But he's still a major force to be reckoned with, believe me."

"So. Okay, so what's his deal? Hell's he want to do now?"

"He sees himself as Napoleon exiled to Elba. But all the while he's secretly making plans for his triumphant return to Paris. Or, in Putin's case, Moscow."

"What kind of plans?"

"A comeback. For him and for an old-style Soviet government. Big-time. He plans to spend his fortune, his remaining billions, plus whatever else he can steal, to build a new private military force, loyal only to him. In total secrecy. He wants you to be in charge of the whole military show, Beau. The new Soviet army, he calls it. Or better yet, his Soviet Imperial Army. He sits around drawing uniforms all day, he told me."

"Soviet Imperial Army, huh? He fixin' to re-erect the Berlin Wall?"

"No, no. Nothing like that, Beau."

"What's his time frame for all this stuff? And what kind of compensation are we talking about here? I got me a pretty good gig going in Bermuda right now . . ."

"Yeah? Doing what?"

"I'm in the pussy business."

"Buying? Or selling?"

"Renting."

"Funny. Anyway. He calls his big idea Operation Overkill. He says he wants it done inside of one year. Got that? He wants to retake Moscow sometime in late October of next year. A new October Revolution, right? But he needs more cash, a lot more, and he needs an army. And now, apparently, he needs you."

"I get it. The October Revolution, right? Roll into Red Square on the anniversary of the Bolshevik Revolution, I mean? He's planning on celebrating that?"

"Something like that, yeah, but listen to me, Colonel. Pay attention. As soon as you complete phase one—create, arm, and train the army—your first mission will be to successfully complete the annexation of the Ukraine, then wheel your army and march on Moscow with overwhelming force. He'll pay you thirty million bucks, ten when you sign on, five when you're up and running. Fifteen when you've completed your mission."

"Thirty million, you say? Well, hell, son, where do I sign on for *that* deal?"

Joe pulled the contract Putin had sent him from his inside breast pocket and handed it to the colonel.

He said, "This is *movie star* money, Beau. This is *athlete* money. You better be good, is all I can say."

"Ah, hell, Joe, you don't need to worry about that. If I ever let you down, I'll just send my best buddy Shit Smith around to see you!"

CHAPTER FORTY-ONE

Geneva

The Eagle has landed," Joe Stalingrad said with a wide grin as Putin answered the sat phone call. He'd picked up on the very first ring next morning.

"What the hell is that supposed to mean?" Putin said. "What fucking eagle? Landed where?"

"Oh, sorry. American jargon. Sometimes I forget who I'm talking to."

"I advise you not to make that mistake with me."

"Right."

"I assume you have news? I haven't heard from you in a week."

"I do, Mr. President. And, it's not fake news, either."

"It better be good, Joe. For your sake."

"Oh, it is, sir. As to the Sorcerer's mountain fortress, first item on the agenda. Professor Steinhauser accepts with pleasure your offer of five hundred million U.S. dollars cash toward the purchase of his real estate holdings in Switzerland.

"So, he agrees to sell? Very, very good news, Joe. Excellent!"

"Soar with the eagles, Mr. President! It's all yours!"

"Excellent! Very, very good, Joe! How soon can he be prepared to move out?"

"He wants to know if you want to buy it furnished. If so, he can be out within a week."

"Furnished? A mountain? I hadn't thought about that. What's included?"

"He didn't say. Washer, dryer, I assume. And that Formica dinette set in the kitchen . . . plus the fighter squadron, I assume."

"I know you're only trying to be funny, Joe. Please don't."

"I believe he means everything, sir. The whole enchilada, so to speak. Household furnishings, the art on the walls, the entire contents of the weapons armory, the radar and missile installations, the fighter squadron, et cetera, et cetera. I'd guess not a lot of real estate transactions include a fighter squadron, but there you have it."

"We've probably just set a world record for highest price ever paid for a single residence," Putin mused, "Will he take cash?"

"Oh, I'm sure that would be most satisfactory, sir."

"All right, get confirmation of that. Pull the trigger. Make arrangements for the delivery to him of five hundred million U.S. with the assistance of my banker in Zurich, Heinrich. Next?"

"Next up, Colonel Brett Beauregard."

"You saw him?"

"Yes, sir, I did."

"How did you find him? Is he still railing against me for events in Siberia?"

"No, sir, not at all. All seems to have been forgiven and forgotten. He inquired after your health."

"Since I'm supposed to be dead, I imagine he did. You laid everything out for him? The scope of the mission? The timetable?"

"Yes, sir."

"And?"

"He didn't even flinch. I think our timing is good. He was running low on cash and looking for what to do next . . . and he wants his head of security to go on the payroll, too."

"Colonel Beauregard has a head of security now?"

"Yes, he does. A CIA cowboy named Shit Smith."

"Shit Smith?" Putin said. "What kind of name is that?"

"Yeah, I know. Some name, huh? Crazy."

"What about the salary offer for Beau?"

"Beau wants to know about benefits."

"What? What fucking benefits? He gets thirty million fucking benefits when he signs on."

"Just kidding, sir. No, sir, he's fine with the salary. I just finished breakfast with him and Shit at his hotel here in Geneva. His question to me was about where his base of operations would be. This is going to be a fairly massive deal to put together. He needs somewhere off the grid. Where he can put this all together, you know, the air and land components of the army. He wants a face-to-face with you to discuss options."

"Are you still there? At his hotel?"

"In the lobby, waiting for my car to be brought around."

"Good. Go back up to his suite. Tell him we spoke and that I am delighted to be working with him again on so magnificent a project. Tell him fine about his security guy. Tell him you asked about the base of operations and I said this: After lengthy consideration, I have decided that the very best location to base this is the abandoned secret KGB military base he operated out of in Siberia. It's all just sitting there, just as he left it, abandoned because of budget constraints demanded by my political enemies. The fighter wing was mothballed at my insistence . . . as was the tank division and a lot of light artillery. All waiting to be recommissioned as soon as he can get there."

"Got it."

"The military housing, the defensive missile perimeter, the communications—all of it just like it was the night the two of you betrayed me and fled Russia with that fucking traitor Alex Hawke."

"The colonel asked about that, sir. He said he hoped Hawke wouldn't be poking his nose into our business this time around."

"Okay, so good. Tell him that I have taken protective measures to ensure that Alex Hawke stays as far away from this as possible. And if he gets anywhere near it, I have loyalist KGB assets all over Europe ready to take him off the board."

"And the face-to-face?"

"It will take place at my new Swiss residence, Joe. As soon as I'm established there."

"Want me to give him a ballpark?"

"A ballpark? He wants a fucking *ballpark*?"

"It means a rough idea of when. When you want the face-to-face, I mean."

"We need to talk about that. You need to exfiltrate me soon."

"What's the best way to get you out? I've got your new car. Mercedes with blacked-out windows. Geneva's not all that far away from Provence, sir."

"No. Too risky. And there are no passable roads to where I am. Accessible only on foot. The only way in or out is a chopper. Night landing in the field adjacent to where I'm staying."

"Where are you staying if I may ask? Hotel?"

"Hardly. My new address is a woodchopper's cabin deep in the forest. Cordial fellow, this French woodchopper. Good company. We've become something akin to friends . . . I help him cut firewood every day. And he helps me with my drawings of uniforms for the new Soviet armed forces."

"This is still in France, right? You haven't moved?"

"Yes. Still in Provence. Do you have a pencil?"

"Shoot."

"I'm going to give you my geographic coordinates. Tomorrow you will secure a helicopter. Today is what? The last day of January. I want you to get me out of here day after tomorrow. At midnight, second of February. Tell Colonel Beauregard I shall be expecting him at Falcon's Lair this coming Wednesday."

"Falcon's Lair is—what, again?"

"The name of my new home high in the Alps. I just thought of it. Like it?"

"Falcon's Lair. I love it, Mr. President. It just screams Vladimir Putin to me."

"Good thing, Joe. You're going to be living there."

Click.

Living there?

Joe smiled. He Google-earthed the mountain to get a better feel for the neighborhood. Looking at the bleak alpine images, he worried that his new boss may have forgotten the golden rule of real estate. Location, location, location. Then he wondered if the beauteous Miss Emma Peek would be included with the household goods left behind.

CHAPTER FORTY-TWO

Juan-les-Pins

*T*sar is on the move! Let's go!" a drenched Harry Brock said, bursting into the almost deserted Fitzgerald Bar at the Belles-Rives. It was nearly midnight, and Hawke, Stoke, Sharkey, and Congreve were having a late coffee at a corner banquette. They were still going over Hawke's hand-drawn renderings of *Tsar*'s layout fore and aft, above decks and below, getting it locked in their minds before they did a forced search of the big yacht.

This, after leaving Brock out in the rain on watch. A fierce electrical thunderstorm had rolled in from the Mediterranean shortly after sunset, and curtains of howling rain swept over the little harbor. Visibility was nil.

"Just like that?" Hawke said, leaping to his feet at Brock's appearance. "They're leaving in this weather?"

"Yeah," Brock said. "I almost missed him. You couldn't see a thing out there in the dark, with all the heavy rain and mist. And the crew kept the engines at idle and all *Tsar*'s running and nav lights doused until they'd weighed anchor and gotten well under way. I got lucky this time. They just happened to cross in front of a big yacht that was lit up stem to stern. So, I was able to see the red boat's silhouette gliding by in front of that brightly illuminated boat."

"Good work, Harry," Hawke said. "Let's move out." Hawke leapt to his feet and made for the entrance. This was what he'd been waiting for since Alexei's disappearance. He knew his boy might not be aboard, but whoever was could bring him one step closer to finding him.

The five men had hung their foul weather gear on hooks inside the hotel entry for just such a situation. Donning the bright orange offshore kit, they raced out into the storm. The storm's icy cold ferocity was shocking after the warmly lit peace of the cozy bar.

The steps down to the dock and the sleek Wally boat were slick, but they all took them three at a time. Then they were pounding down the long dock at full gallop. *Too Elusive* was tied up at the far end.

The Wally One, powered by twin Volvo Penta SP 800hp engines, was capable of speeds up to fifty-two knots. She was roughly forty feet in length, with a beam of ten feet. The big Russian boat would be lucky to make thirty knots through the water in this weather. So speed was an advantage in Hawke's favor.

Brock, Hawke, and Congreve scrambled aboard and prepared to get under way. Hawke went to the helm station and switched on the batteries, the fuel pump, turned on the GPS and all the electronics. Congreve went below and powered up the nav station, where he would be monitoring radar during the hostage rescue mission at sea. Brock went to the weapons locker at the sternmost portion of the cockpit to get the arsenal sorted out.

Stoke and Sharkey remained up on the dock to handle the lines, meanwhile scanning the harbor with powerful night-vision binoculars.

"Final weapons check, Mr. Brock?" Hawke cried above the thunder and crash of lightning and the burbling rumble of the engines. He was in the midst of firing up the big Volvos.

"All set, sir." Harry was affixing silencers to the assault rifles and side arms, checking ammunition and assault gear.

"I see her," Stoke shouted through cupped hands. "*Tsar*'s at one o'clock! She's just passing through the breakwater at the harbor mouth, pouring on the speed and headed for open water."

"I've got the helm," Hawke said. "Mr. Brock, please join Stoke and Sharkey up on the dock to handle the lines. Ambrose? Can you hear me down there?"

"Aye, Skipper."

"Good. Lock on to that target and don't let go! Understood?"

"Affirmative!" Congreve shouted.

"Bowlines are free, boss," Stoke said from above, heaving the freed bowlines down onto the Wally One's foredeck.

"Stern lines and spring lines free!" Brock said, heaving his lines onto the stern. Before boarding, he and Stoke each put a foot on the gunwale and shoved the speedboat a few feet away from the dock to ease maneuvering.

Hawke looked around at his not so motley crew.

Congreve was busy below at the nav station, tracking the target objective and warning Hawke of boats, markers, and bell buoys that he might not be able to see for the downpour. Stoke stood at Hawke's side, also on watch. And Harry Brock was at the bow, his head and torso emerging from the forward hatch cover. He had heavy artillery up there, the big M14 machine gun cradled in his hands.

"Everyone strapped in?" Hawke asked.

"Aye aye, sir!" they replied.

Alex put his right hand on the big chrome throttles and eased them forward. He now had to thread his way through all the myriad of yachts moored in the harbor. All in practically whiteout conditions. He flipped on the powerful searchlight and twin spotlights atop the cabin, and three white beams streaked into existence.

"Boat! Dead ahead!" Stoke cried. "Hard right! Hard right!"

"Christ!" Hawke said, throttling back and cranking the wheel hard over to starboard. He'd never even seen the big blue yacht now rearing up just fifty feet ahead of him. *Too Elusive*, heeled over so far that her starboard rail was underwater, cleared the big yacht's stern by mere inches.

"Slow way down, boss," Stoke said. "A collision at sea could ruin your day. We'll catch *Tsar* out in open water, don't worry. I did a sea trial in this thing early this morning. Topped out at almost fifty knots in a light chop. We're good to go tonight. We'll catch that bad boy."

Hawke said, "Maybe we'll get lucky. But, I'm not sure we'll find Alexei aboard. Putin's smarter than that. Too obvious a location maybe. You think Putin could have slipped aboard tonight, Stoke?"

"Thinking the same thing. In all that bad weather? Perfect night to do it if he did, wouldn't it be? All he'd need was someone in a rowboat to row him out to the yacht under cover of darkness and the rain. No one would ever have seen him in this bloody deluge."

TEN MINUTES LATER, *TOO ELUSIVE* was free of the constraints of the harbor and roaring past the breakwater at full throttle in pursuit of the fleeing Russians. Harry Brock was still at the bow station with an M14 heavy machine gun and wearing night-vision glasses. He'd told Hawke he'd seen no sentries aboard *Tsar* while she was anchored. But, now, who knew?

Below, lit by the glow of all the instruments at the nav station, Congreve was hunched forward, tracking the movements of *Tsar* on radar and sonar. "Target vessel coming to new course two-eight-five, bearing away to the northwest. Range fifteen miles and closing . . ."

"Where the hell's he going, do you think, Constable?" Hawke asked, ducking his head down inside the companionway.

"Hard to say. If I had to fathom a guess right now? I'd say maybe Nice airport. Jet waiting on the tarmac, maybe? Could be headed to Monte Carlo, of course. Who knows?"

"How long till we intercept him?" Hawke said. "What's your GPS telling you?"

"At our current speed, and if this brief respite in the weather holds, we should be within visual contact range in about six minutes," Congreve said. "Just as she's entering the harbor at Nice . . ."

"Hold on," Hawke said, shoving the throttles forward. "I can't wait that long . . . I want to board her out here in open water. Away from prying eyes on shore."

"Understood," Congreve said.

Too Elusive surged forward, throwing huge bow waves to either side and leaving a massive and roiling wake trailing behind her. It was still raining hard, but visibility was up considerably. Hawke peered through the curved windscreen, waiting for the big red boat to emerge from the mist.

"I'm beginning to believe Hugo," Hawke said to Congreve. "There's minimal crew aboard. With a full complement, *Tsar* would have picked us up on radar leaving the harbor mouth. But they're not pinging us, are they?"

"Not yet."

"Because if they think we're a threat, they've got surface-to-surface missile defenses that we could never overcome. I've known Hugo a very long time. He was very close to Anastasia and Alexei. I'm not sure he's lying about *Tsar*, but you're right, he knows something else he's not talking about."

"I hope you're right, Alex. I'd hate to go up against a boatload of heavy KGB security once we board . . ."

"Hello, boss," Stokely said.

Having disappeared below twenty minutes earlier, he now appeared at the bottom of the steps. He was wearing his Navy SEAL frogman gear and looked like some incredibly fearsome alien being from beneath the sea.

"You ready to go, big man?" Hawke asked him.

"Born ready, boss man!"

"Good, it's time."

Their plan called for Hawke to put Stoke in the water within swimming distance of *Tsar*. Get aboard without being observed, get to the stern, and haul a grapnel line to Brock on the bow of *Too Elusive* approaching from the rear. The tricky part was that, initially, both boats would be moving when Stoke splashed down. *In the same direction. Hawke would have to time Stoke's insertion right down to the nanosecond!* At the critical location just ahead of the oncoming *Tsar*.

Hawke knew that there was a wide-open submerged hatch in the starboard-side hull of the Russian yacht. Putin had installed a three-man sub, a bright yellow SM300/3, launched and recovered from the aquatics deck below the ship's waterline. Stoke would swim up through the open hatch and enter the yacht unseen and undetected . . .

Or that was the plan, anyway.

CHAPTER FORTY-THREE

The wind was howling, the slanting rain was stinging, and the ride back at the stern was wild. Stoke, bouncing every which way but loose, was trying to stay seated on *Too Elusive*'s stern gunwale with his legs hanging down over the transom, his flippers resting on the swim platform. He was looking back over his shoulder at Hawke, waiting for his signal from the helm station.

Bucking-bronco hard to hold on to the damn boat, sure, but he'd secured a lifeline round his waist to one of the stern cleats.

Too Elusive was doing forty knots now, flying from wave top to wave top and moving over the water twice as fast as the Russian boat up ahead of him. Hawke's next moves were critical. Hawke would keep *Tsar* on his portside but maneuver first to pull abreast of her. Then exceed her speed to get just far enough ahead of *Tsar* that when Stoke went into the water, he had just enough time to submerge directly in the path of the oncoming vessel and find that hatch as she passed. His mission: somehow get up inside the damn boat. And do it all unobserved and unchallenged.

Stoke's next move, get Hawke and company aboard *Tsar* to conduct a thorough stem-to-stern search. And if they got really lucky, execute a hostage rescue.

Suddenly Hawke slowed the roaring speedboat, bleeding speed rapidly now as he judged the relative positions of the two vessels. Stoke, who had done Navy SEAL ops like this countless times, believed he had never done one quite as difficult as this one. Timing was absolutely critical to their success, both on Hawke's part and his own . . . he saw Hawke raise his clenched right fist!

"GO!" he heard Hawke's muffled cry over the roar of the huge engines. "GO!"

He pulled the tab on his cleated lifeline and hit the water perfectly. He grabbed a quick look at *Tsar* as the big red boat approached him bow on. Calculating the relative distance and speed, he picked his spot, dove deep, pumping his massively powerful legs. And swimming as hard as ever he had, he crossed the distance in half the time they'd planned on.

He'd gained about a twenty-second advantage.

He kicked rapidly to the surface and eyed the big yacht, ever closer now, bearing down on him at speed, her knife-like bow heaving massive waves of water to port and starboard. He began his mental countdown and submerged deep enough and soon enough to let the starboard hull pass just a foot or two above him and . . . here she comes . . . he could see the open hatch in the hull . . . wait for it . . . and . . . NOW!

The hatch was immediately above him when he kicked hard. The big man shot upward into the opening, both hands grabbing blindly for a hold on anything locked down. His left hand had gotten lucky, grasped the bottom rung of a stainless-steel ladder descending from the platform of the aquatics deck.

Finding his footing on the rung and scrambling up the ladder onto the deck, working in near-total darkness and silence, he paused to ensure he was alone.

He was. He switched on the LED lantern atop his diving helmet and the sub pen's space was sufficiently illuminated. No staircases that he could see, no more ladders leading upward to the higher decks. Then he saw in the pure white beam of light exactly what he'd been hoping for.

On a far bulkhead was the polished steel door of the small elevator Alex Hawke had told him about.

Bingo.

He removed his flippers and silently padded across the deck to the elevator, pushing the higher button in the steel bulkhead. A second later, the door slid open and he entered, scanning the buttons quickly and determining which one was most likely to be the main deck.

The lift slowed, then stopped moving, and the door slid open silently. Stokely Jones Jr. stepped out onto the rain-swept decks of the yacht's massive stern. Empty. Not a soul in sight. The rain had eased only slightly and visibility was still way down when he made it all the way aft to the stern rail.

He'd hoped to see Hawke's bow searchlight beam out there, see *Too Elusive* bobbing in the misty rain, but there was nothing visible, at least not yet . . .

He heard a noise behind him and whirled . . .

He had his 9mm side arm and an HK50 machine gun at the ready.

But there was nothing there; nobody to shoot. A rumble of distant thunder maybe, Stoke told himself.

His next move was fairly straightforward. Once Hawke had maneuvered his speedboat to within thirty feet of the Russian boat's stern, Stoke would heave a line to Brock, who would be positioned on the bow. Brock would then secure the line to *Too Elusive*'s bow cleats, creating a way for the invaders to scale the broad transom, which slanted down to a platform at the waterline. Basically, a rope walk up an incline.

When they'd gotten themselves within Stoke's reach at the stern rail, the big man would then extend his hand and haul them aboard one by one. Sharkey's job, then, was to helm the boat, to keep the speedboat on an even keel as she was towed through the water by *Tsar*.

Getting around on the rain-slick deck wasn't easy. The coiled hundred feet of rubber-sheathed twisted wire cable that hung from his utility belt made moving about difficult. But he made the tow line secure to the stern cleats and was able to survey his situation. Suddenly, from out of the mist, he heard the low rumble of the speedboat. Hawke, at idle speed, was closing the distance between the two boats. Fifty feet . . . forty . . . thirty! Stoke gave Brock an all clear with his right hand. He saw Hawke at the helm flash him a V for Victory sign.

Game on, Stoke thought, rock steady!

Implausibly, the captain had posted no guards or aft sentries to ward off unwanted intruders such as he himself. He stared aft into the misty rain, waiting to see the spotlight on *Too Elusive*'s bow as Hawke powered through the roiling wake and got within spitting distance of *Tsar*'s stern.

Minutes later he saw Hawke's lone bow spotlight, haloed, bobbing and weaving through the rain and sea and darkness. Hawke slowly maneuvered closer and closer. Stoke could now see Brock on the bow, ready to take the line Stoke would heave in his direction, but he would only get one chance . . .

Hawke and Congreve were at the helm station, Brock on the bow to receive the line. Sharkey, the veteran charter yacht skipper who would remain aboard *Too Elusive* to captain the speedboat, was behind them, watching Hawke's every move to get them in the correct position to board the Russian boat. Given the rough seas, strong winds, and blanketing rain, it was no easy task. But on they came . . . maybe twenty feet away now . . .

Fifteen feet . . . ten . . . five! Stoke gave Brock and Hawke an all clear signal with his right hand. No hostiles. He saw Hawke at the helm flash him a V for Victory sign.

Brock suddenly shouted and raised his right fist, the signal that he was in proper position to receive the line. One that would join the two boats. Stoke paused a beat, then heaved the heavy line out over the remaining divide, being as precise as he could in so much wind.

It would be a close thing, as a huge wave came from out of nowhere and smacked the bow of *Too Elusive* ten degrees to starboard . . . He could see Hawke spinning the wheel, playing the throttles back and forth like a nautical musician, desperately hoping to get back to the right spot before Stoke's line sank uselessly into the drink. A little less port throttle now . . . a quick burst of startboard . . . full stop!

The bulk of the coiled cable landed on the bow!

At least it was inside the stanchions. It ended up about a yard from Harry's feet. Brock quickly seized it, found the rubber-coated grapnel hook and locked it to the foremost cleat on the bow. Done and done.

Now that *Too Elusive* was secure to the Russian boat, Hawke left Sharkey at the wheel, stepped outside the cockpit, and carefully made his way forward. He was immediately followed by Congreve.

Up on *Tsar*'s stern, Stoke scanned the darkened decks above and below him for any sign of opposition. Nothing—not yet, anyway.

He stepped back to the rail and gave the signal that it was safe for them to use the secured line to make their way to the platform and then up the slanted transom and onto the main deck of the enemy vessel.

Like pirates of yore, they had boarded an enemy ship to see what treasures they could find. The missing president of Russia? Or even better, Hawke's kidnapped son, Alexei.

It was quiet, Stoke thought, with a grim smile on his lips, despite the storm raging outside on the decks.

Too quiet, as they used to say in the old movies.

Way too quiet.

The calm before the *real* storm that was brewing out there.

CHAPTER FORTY-FOUR

At sea

Hawke was the last man aboard.

The small hostage rescue team huddled together under a canvas deck overhang, trying to be heard over the deafening patter of hard rainfall, trying to keep out of the driving rain as long as they could.

"Good work, Stoke," Hawke said. "What have you got for us? No hostiles? How did you get up here from the sub pen?"

"That elevator right over there."

"No guards, nothing?"

"No. It's like she's dead in the water, boss! A ghost ship! No sentries, no lights on, no nothing, but she's steaming ahead at twenty knots. So we know we got folks up on the bridge, at any rate, driving the boat. Skipper and a mate, minimum. Posted sentries? Ordinary seamen? No evidence so far, but I've not been forward."

"Good. But we assume nothing. We begin the search right here. Mr. Brock?"

"Aye, sir!"

"Go below. Search the stern, all decks, all compartments. You see anything interesting, get on your radio, let us know. Got it?"

"Got it."

"Chief Inspector Congreve?"

"Yes?"

"You're amidships. Top to bottom. Treat it like the crime scene it may well turn out to be, Chief Inspector."

"Aye-aye, skipper. I'm on it."

"Good. Stokely, you and I will go forward. Our ultimate objective is to breach the bridge and seize command of the vessel. But we'll search the bow as well, if need be. Come forward to us as soon as you hear me say we're taking the bridge. But also should you find something or as soon as you've completed your search. Ready? Let's go!"

Brock, cradling his assault rifle, immediately entered the elevator below to the stern. Ambrose mounted a ladder leading up to the deck above. Hawke and Stoke affixed silencers to their HK5 machine guns and started moving cautiously forward along the portside, headed toward the bow.

Minutes later, they stepped out into the open and onto the rain-swept bow. Deserted, like the rest of the boat. Still they lingered in the shadows below the bridge deck, thinking their luck so far might not hold.

Speaking softly into his lip mike, Hawke said, "Stoke, listen up. You see that large superstructure just forward of the primary anchor windlass? That's a companionway leading below to the crew quarters at the bow. We'll search compartments there, stay belowdecks and make our way amidships to Putin's private elevator. Taken it with him many times. His shortcut up to the bridge in an emergency."

Stoke nodded his understanding.

Hawke continued, "It's about fifty feet across the deck, out in the open. We have to figure if there's any security at all, it's up there on the bridge. Armed sentries out on the exposed wings to either side. So stay low, keep moving, stay in the shadows and move as fast as you can. I'll go first and give you covering fire. Give me sixty seconds and then move out."

"Aye aye, bossman."

"Good luck, buddy," Hawke said, and sprinted across the deck in the direction of the huge anchors mounted to port and starboard on the foredeck.

The loud chatter of a machine-gun burst instantly filled the air. Rounds were striking the steel deck all around Hawke's feet, ricocheting every which way. He looked back and saw the source. Two armed guards. Up there on the bridge wings, one to either side of the bridge itself. He needed cover now!

Another staccato lightning burst nearly caught him, but he was in midair diving behind one of the two ship's anchors. The decks were oily slick up here, and his forward momentum kept him sliding when he hit the deck on the fly. He instantly slid right under the anchor, out into the open from behind the cover the anchor had provided!

Somehow he was on his feet again, firing up at where he had last seen a muzzle flash. At that moment, the bow turned to daylight, illuminated, bathed in pure white light. Angry bees of lead were swirling around him again and he ducked behind the other anchor.

What to do? "Stoke, that was close. Two tangos up there on the wings, one on either side of the bridge. Guy on your side is standing directly above you. You've got frags, right?"

"Brock has frags. I've got smokes and flash bangs."

"Perfect. Pull the pin on the flash bang, step out from under cover, heave the grenade straight up, arcing back. A three-count after you pull the pin should do the trick. On my signal . . . he's moving around . . . Go!"

The starboard guard drew back from the rail upon seeing the grenade suddenly appear before his eyes. He tried to react, but the thing exploded right in his face. He dropped out of sight . . . And Stoke retreated back under cover.

"Good work!" Hawke said. "I'm going to lay down suppression fire for you. Keep the head down on the bad guy to port . . . come to me when you're ready . . . and . . . go!"

Hawke stood up and started spraying lead at the portside bridge wing. He had his weapon on full auto and the hellish hail of lead in the air was relentless. He saw Stoke, bobbing and weaving and diving as he neared the anchor.

"Thanks," Stoke said.

"Don't mention it. Now, you return the favor as I get that companionway hatch door open . . . Say when."

"When!"

Stoke stood up with the big M14 and unleashed loud and unholy hell on the Russian guard trapped out in the open. A second later, Hawke had covered the distance to his target. The door was locked. Shit. He attached one of his trademarked Semtex specials to the lock, got down on the deck, and triggered the explosive. It took the whole door off.

"Got a tango down over there," Stoke said. "He popped up for a lookie-loo and got a head shot for his efforts."

"I'm going up there, Stoke. Keep me company."

Hawke disappeared into the darkened hatchway and Stoke was right on his heels, both men pounding it out up the steep steel steps into serious darkness.

"Next stop, the bridge," he told the team on his radio.

Hawke had caught a momentary glimpse of the silhouettes of three men behind the dark glass up on the bridge. The captain, obviously, and two mates? Because of the extraordinary kindness Captain Ivar Solo had shown to Hawke on a short cruise to the Maldives, he had sent a gift to Putin's captain upon his return to London. A lovely old Purdey 20 gauge side-by-side that his grandfather had given him for his twenty-first birthday.

His primary concern, his hope now was that Ivar Solo was still captain, still in charge of this vessel, despite the Russian president's fall from grace or power or both at the hands of the treacherous oligarchs. Who, Hawke knew well, might rightly be the new owners of Volodya's beloved *Tsar*.

CHAPTER FORTY-FIVE

The elevator stopped and the door slid open, the gloom of the bridge tinged with a reddish light emanating from the giant curved array of the various instrument panels.

Hawke stepped out first, his weapon at the ready. He quickly scanned the bridge deck from one side to the other. He was relieved to see his old friend Captain Ivar Solo at the helm, flanked by two rough-looking seamen of dubious origin. Other than those three, the dimly lit room appeared to be empty.

He signaled Stoke to follow him.

"Ah, Ivar, there you are!" Hawke said with as much joviality as he could muster. "Look who's here! Your old chum Alex Hawke. Terribly sorry to be dropping in on you like this at such a late hour, but it couldn't be helped."

"Lord Hawke," the Russian captain said, but could supply no further words at the moment. There was something in the man's eyes Hawke had no trouble reading. Fear. Fear of what? Certainly not of his friend Lord Hawke. So. The men to either side of him.

"I imagined you might show up at some point, sir," Solo managed to croak out.

"Indeed. Looking for my son, as it happens. Friends of mine said I might find him here. Aboard your ship, I mean. Is that true?"

"On the right!" Stoke shouted. "*Gun!*"

Hawke swirled to the right just as the burly crewman on the captain's right was bringing his side arm up to bear. He was about to fire when Stoke shot the man in the head. He dropped to the deck like a sack full of stones.

Hawke, barely missing a beat, turned to Ivar and said, "As I was saying, Captain, I'm inquiring after my son. Is he or is he not presently a captive aboard this vessel? Tell me where he is and you'll avoid what will be a most unpleasant search."

"He is *not* aboard," came a hard, furious voice from behind Hawke. It seemed to well up from within the darkness at the comms and nav rooms situated at the rear of the bridge.

Hawke spun, shocked to see a legless ghost gliding straight for him out of the dark.

Rolling toward him in a wheelchair, a man who looked to be someone once known to Hawke as Der Wolf.

It was him, all right. The infamous Russian KGB General Ivanov. The man he and Stokely had been sent to Cuba to assassinate. That joint CIA/MI6 covert mission into the Sierra Maestre mountain range had unfortunately failed. But a subsequent drone strike Hawke had launched from Gitmo had not. It was Hawke's belief that Ivanovich had died in the drone attack. Or, so he was told by U.S. Navy officers on the scene reporting on the strike to Hawke.

Ivanov was a big, bald man, with masses of muscle bunched about his neck and shoulders, and dark porcine eyes peeking out from beneath a prominent, some might say, neolithic brow. A man who'd first made his real scorched-earth reputation fighting rebels in Chechnya. Now one of the most powerful leaders of the Opposition in the Kremlin, General Sergey Ivanovich Ivanov was a savage butcher.

So who was this ghost but Der Wolf himself?

"You seem surprised to see me, Hawke," Ivanov said, rolling into the light. He was, Hawke saw, completely legless beneath the blanket puddled in his lap.

"No doubt you thought I'd not survive in that pile of smoking rubble you made of my headquarters. My men lost their lives that night, but not me. I lost only my legs."

"Congratulations," Hawke said, a cold fury in his voice that surprised even Stokely. But he knew the boss could never forgive the horrific and brutal torture the two of them had endured at the hands of this monster.

"And what have you lost lately, Lord Hawke? Anything of importance? Anyone? A small boy, perhaps?"

"Listen, you disgusting piece of filth, if you've got my son on this boat or have anything to do with his kidnapping, you'll lose your head next. Although that particular loss will amount to nothing, compared to your legs."

The man had his blood up at that. "I had *everything* to do with kidnapping Alexei, you stupid British fuck. Who do you think did it? Putin? Spare me. It was my operation all along! Quite brilliant, even the great Lord Hawke might agree."

Hawke remembered the photo of Alexei. And the note signed Der Wolf. He said, "Take me to him. Now."

"Oh, so sorry, he's not here. But you just missed him, bad luck. I saw intelligence you were headed to the South of France and had him removed to a new location."

"Where is he, Ivanov? I swear to god, you tell me right now or I'll rip your bloody beating heart right out of your chest."

"Really, Lord Hawke? That's your strategy? And then what will you do? I am the only man alive who knows where your son has been taken. Kill me and you'll never see him again."

"You know as well as I do that everyone talks in the end, Ivanov. Why subject yourself to—"

"To what? Torture?"

"Alex! Down!" Stoke cried. "He's got a gun!"

A small silver automatic protruded from beneath the Russian's blanket and spat out two shots in quick succession. Hawke felt the two rounds whistle past his ears as he dove for the deck. Reaching for his own weapon, he heard Stoke's M14 machine gun unleash a short burst at point-blank range, one that blew what was left of Ivanov and his wheelchair backward into the darkness. He was dead now, all right, dead as dead.

"You! Drop your weapon," Stoke said to the man standing on the captain's left. The man's pistol clattered to the deck. "He work for you, Captain?" Stoke asked as Hawke got to his feet.

"No. They both worked for the general. Paid assassins."

"And the two outside on the bridge wings?"

"Both KGB officers. Two of the four who boarded this ship with Ivanov and commandeered it two weeks ago. If the president knew how these animals treated me and my crew, he would have shot that bastard himself."

"Stoke," Hawke said, "get Ambrose and Brock on the radio. Tell them the ship is now secure. Join us on the bridge."

"I'm on it," Stoke said, adjusting his lip mike to speak.

CHAPTER FORTY-SIX

Hawke had his gun on the second KGB thug.

"Ivar," Hawke said to the captain, "any more macho boys like this skulking about on board? Including the two recently deceased outside?"

"No, Commander, that's the lot."

"Stoke, cuff this bastard and lock him back in the comms room with his headless leader. We need to search the rest of this boat now. On the off chance that Ivanov was lying, and Alexei is still aboard, we need to turn this ship upside down and shake it."

"With your permission, Lord Hawke?" Captain Ivar Solo said.

"Indeed. I'm truly sorry to say that he wasn't lying. But, if someone else could steer the boat, I could show you exactly where your little boy was kept for the last two weeks."

"So he was here, Ivar?"

"Yes, sir. For these last few weeks. Ivanov thought he could safely stow Alexei here until Putin resurfaced. Then they would decide what to do with him."

"You believe Putin is still alive, Ivar?"

"I really don't know. He has not contacted me. But I believe he is, yes. I have no proof of it. It's just a feeling. Knowing him as well as I did, and knowing his state of mind this last year, I doubt he'd sit on his hands and wait to be murdered by his many enemies or the KGB. Or worse."

"Did you hear anything that might help me, Ivar? An overheard conversation, perhaps? Gossip between themselves, or even some off-hand remark of Ivanov's?"

"One night . . . perhaps three days ago, yes. The general was in the radio room. He was arguing with someone on the radio. It escalated to shouting."

"What did he say?"

"At one point, he screamed. He said, and I remember this clearly, he said, 'Fuck you, Joe! Fuck you! This is my operation and I'll handle it any way I fucking want to!'"

"Joe? Had you ever heard anyone use that name before? Joe something or other?"

"Sorry, I had not."

"Well, thanks, Skipper. We'll see where that leads."

At that moment, Ambrose Congreve and Harry Brock appeared at the top of the staircase leading to the decks below.

"Hello, Alex," Congreve said, looking at the blood-spattered carnage that was the bridge as he and Brock entered. "Are you two quite all right?"

"Well enough, considering. Stoke and I had a short-lived reunion with an old friend of ours from Cuba. KGB general named Ivanov, whom I'm sure you'll remember. He's in there, dead, with two other KGB officers—one alive, one recently deceased. And two more outside, rather more on the dead side."

"You lads have been busy boys," Congreve said with a rueful smile. "Any luck?"

"Alexei was here, Constable. That is, until two days ago when his captor got wind I might be headed this way. We just missed him."

"Well, safe to say we're a lot closer to finding him now than we were, Alex."

"You didn't get anything out of them before they got shot?" Brock asked.

"No, Ivanov pulled a hidden gun on me and Stoke shot him."

Hawke said, "Stoke, could you take the helm so that the captain might take us below to view Alexei's quarters?"

"Absolutely, boss."

"Captain Solo, this is Scotland Yard Chief Inspector Ambrose Congreve. He's investigating my son's kidnapping for Interpol. He'll be wanting to interview you about everything you saw or heard since my son was brought aboard. I'm sure you'll be forthcoming?"

"Of course, I'll do anything I can to help, sir."

"One quick question," Congreve said. "You mentioned that the killers appeared aboard in the middle of the night. How did they get to the yacht from shore?"

"A speedboat."

"What kind of speedboat, Captain?"

"It's called a Wally. Very high tech. Named *Too Elusive*. On loan, clearly. Belongs to an old friend of mine, the owner of the Belles-Rives hotel in Juan-les-Pins. Do you know of him? Lovely man. Henri Jadot's his name."

Congreve looked over at Hawke and said, "Yes, we know him all too well, Captain, don't we, Alex? He's been lying to us since the moment we arrived."

"You were right about Hugo all along, Constable. Bloody liar. Hardly surprising, I suppose—he is a Frenchman, after all."

"We'll get to the truth somehow, Alex," Congreve said. "Let's go see what we can see, shall we?"

IT WAS A SMALL CABIN, V-shaped, the one nearest the bow.

Hawke entered first, followed by Congreve and the ship's captain.

The single-berth bed with its thin blanket had not been made since the child's departure. Hawke immediately sat down on it and buried his face in the boy's pillow, craving the sweet scent of him and trying as hard as ever he could to stifle the heartbreak that threatened. He said, "It's him, Ambrose"—tears brimming but not spilling—"it's Alexei. I know now that he was here."

"Look at that wall, Alex," Congreve said, pointing to the bulkhead above the child's bed. It was covered with a dozen sheets of white paper that featured stick-figure drawings. One of a little boy and his dog. Another with his father, still another with both his father and mother . . . the very same drawings they'd seen on the wall in the picture slipped beneath the door that night.

From Hawke, a sigh of profound grief.

"Sorry," Hawke said, looking up at Congreve and trying to smile. "Bit overwhelming, that's all."

Congreve sat down on the bed next to Hawke and said, "Don't be silly, Alex. You've every right to vent your emotions at a time like this. Captain, please take that chair. And tell me every single thing you can remember about the day Lord Hawke's son was brought aboard this boat."

"The general and his four men, all heavily armed, boarded us in the middle of the night, as I said. I was awakened by my first officer. He said more KGB men were on the boat. They had a young child with them, someone whom they referred to as a hostage. They said they had orders from the Kremlin to seize control of this yacht in the president's absence. They would be staying for an indefinite period.

"The next morning, the general ordered me to set sail with no destination. Once we were in open seas, twenty miles or so from the harbor, his men ordered me and my crew, meaning the first officer, chief engineer, cook, housemaid, and a young midshipman from Kiev, to line up at the stern rail.

"They were executed, Chief Inspector, consecutive shots to the back of the head. I was waiting for the bullet. But because they needed me to drive the boat, I was spared. And then their corpses—these were friends of mine, by the way—were unceremoniously tossed overboard like so much rubbish."

"My lord," Congreve whispered, looking away.

"Of course, I said nothing about it, fearing for my own life. We then returned to the harbor."

"My god," Congreve said. "I am so sorry, Captain."

Hawke shook his head in disgust, and said, "And tell me about Alexei, Ivor. What do you remember?"

The captain, shaken, took his seat and said, "The first thing I noticed about him was how much he looked like his father. And what a loving child he was, even in the company of these murderers.

"In the two weeks he was aboard, I insisted that every day I be allowed to walk up on deck with him, so that he got some sunshine and fresh air. I found an old rubber ball someone had left aboard long ago, and we would stand up on the upper deck and toss it back and forth . . . He had the most wonderful smile."

Congreve looked over at Hawke. "Captain, we'd like to hear more later. I'd like to know everything you saw and heard from your captors. Every radio communication, every whispered conversation. Every detail you observed in the days preceding our arrival."

"Of course, Chief Inspector. They had so little respect for me, they were not very careful about what they said and did in my presence."

"Excellent news," Congreve said, with a smile to Hawke.

"Thank you, Ivor," Alex said, reaching over to shake the man's hand. "Thank you so very much, sir, for your kindness to my son. And your bravery in the face of Ivanov. I won't forget this, sir."

Congreve saw that his friend's sadness had been replaced by a smile, the exact same smile that his son wore on his face every day of his young life.

That wonderfully beatific smile.

CHAPTER FORTY-SEVEN

Hawke stood in the darkness, looking down at the sleeping man in the frilly pink nightgown.

The fellow's chest, having been subsumed by his belly, was rising gently and rhythmically. His snoring made him sound as if he had a mouthful of feathers, like the cat who's just eaten the canary.

"Time to wake up, ladies," Hawke said, smiling in spite of himself.

"Wha—"

"I said, it's time to wake up, Hugo. Now."

"Go way . . . sleeping . . ."

Hawke had a half-full bottle of expensive champagne, Krug, in his hand. Holding the mouth of the bottle somewhere in the neighborhood of the Frenchman's yawning orifice, he upended the carafe. The contents poured into his mouth, overflowing and gagging him.

"Fuck! Fuck!" he sputtered, kicking his tiny feet in the air.

"This is what they call waterboarding Riviera style, Hugo. Don't worry, it's going to get worse."

"Alex?"

"That's what they call me."

"Hell are you doing? I thought we were friends. Are you crazy?"

"Yeah, I'm crazy, all right."

Hawke fished in his trousers pocket for his old steel Zippo lighter. There was a single candle on the bedside table, a tall taper in a silver candleholder. He lit it.

"How the hell did you get in my apartment? I locked all the doors . . ."

"I'm an English *spy,* Hugo. Spy. It's what I do. Be careful, this might hurt."

"What do you want—ow! What the fuck—"

"I'm going to continue dripping hot wax on your face until I see your feet hit the floor. Take your time . . . I'm rather enjoying this. Stick out your tongue for me."

"Jesus Christ, Alex! For god's sake, stop this insanity!"

"I will. When you get out of the bed, take off your pretty little nightie, and put your big-boy clothes on . . . I'm waiting. Oops, that one went in your eye, didn't it?"

"All right! I'll get up, for crissakes . . . Jesus."

Hugo swung his short fat legs over the side of the bed and sat up, trying to wipe the hot red wax from his face. He'd gone to bed drunk. Had he insulted Hawke down in the bar? He couldn't remember . . .

"Good boy. Your clothes are in a pile on the floor in the bathroom. But you're going to need a heavy overcoat. The storm has worsened and the temperature is dropping . . . could get nippy out there, Hugo."

"Out there? Why the hell are we going outside? You want to talk about something? Let's talk here. I'll get someone to bring up a bottle of whiskey from the kitchen and—"

"No, no, Hugo, you don't understand. We're going on a nice long boat ride."

"Now? In the middle of the night? In a fucking typhoon?"

"Yes. It's a poor skipper who doesn't test his mettle in a blow. Used to say that in the Royal Navy. It's true. You've got three minutes. Hurry up."

Hawke turned and walked over to the heavy armchair nestled against the hearth; the fire was almost out, but the coals were glowing. He sat facing the bathroom door and pulled his Walther PPK from the holster hanging beneath his left arm. If Hugo bolted, he planned to shoot him in both legs.

"Leave the door open, Hugo," he said.

"For fuck's sake, a man has a right to a little privacy, Alex."

"When a man puts on a lady's nightie, he forsakes a whole lot of rights. And one of them is privacy. One minute."

THE COLD RAIN BLEW SIDEWAYS. Hawke and Hugo walked down the length of the broad main dock, the wind howling around them, blowing great walls of seawater up over the boards, the water sometimes rising to their knees as they struggled forward. Fishing boats to either side strained at their moorings, bucking like Texas broncos in their stalls. They kept walking, heads down against the driving rain.

"Where the hell are we going, Alex?"

Hawke kept the man close, the muzzle of the lethal little Walther pressed deep into his ribs.

"Right here, *mon amie*," Stokely said, standing at the helm of the speedboat. He cranked the engines.

"*Too Elusive?* Why?"

"I need privacy too, Hugo. You and I are going to have a lengthy conversation. It might turn unpleasant. For you, I mean. At any rate, I don't want an audience. Now get in your damn boat, Hugo."

Hawke helped the fat man get safely aboard and seated at the starboard-side fishing chair. Then he went about loosening the fore and aft mooring lines on the dock, so taut and strained in the high winds. Then, gun still in hand, he boarded the speedboat and went to the helm to have a word with Stoke.

"Take her straight out, Stoke," he said, "Fifteen, twenty miles offshore."

That done, he went over to Hugo and pressed the muzzle of his pistol against the Frenchman's forehead.

"Be still. If you move, if you even cross your legs, you're a dead man. Do you understand me?"

"Jesus, of course. I don't want to die."

"That's a healthy attitude, Hugo. We'll put that to the test out there on the open seas. It could lead to a productive conversation."

"Put it to the *test*?"

"Are you secure? This little boat of yours is going to get thrown around out there tonight. I'd buckle up and enjoy the ride if I were you."

"Boat of mine? It doesn't belong to me!"

"It does according to our mutual chum Ivar Solo. We had a little chat with him earlier."

"Fuck."

"Exactly."

Hawke took the seat beside Stoke and said, "Hit it, Stoke. Hit the throttle hard."

"Aye aye, Skipper. Hold on to your hat," Stoke said and firewalled the twin throttles. The stern went down and the bow went up at an alarming angle. *Too Elusive* shot forward, powering through the waves at tremendous speed, headed directly for the harbor mouth . . .

CHAPTER FORTY-EIGHT

Conditions were moderately insane just outside the breakwater entrance to the harbor at Juan-les-Pins. The wind had increased since Hawke's earlier outing in *Too Elusive*. Stoke was now wrestling with the wheel, having a hell of a time keeping his bow up and right into the wind. This, so she wouldn't be broadsided by a rogue wave and capsized. Or take a really big one over her stern, which, depending on the size of these walls of water, could simply overwhelm and sink them.

Looking back at the shoreline, Hawke could just make out lights winking on the Croisette, the boulevard that circled the beaches at Cannes, lights strung out in the distance like a glistening diamond necklace, floating in the dark skies above the stormy seas.

Half an hour later, the winds had lessened considerably. Hawke looked at his GPS and saw that he was approximately fifteen miles from the harbor at Juan-les-Pins. And due to weather, there was little chance he'd be interrupted by another vessel.

"Throttle back, Stoke," Hawke said. "It's time for the little powwow with our guest of honor here. Bring her up into the wind and engage the autopilot. I'm going to need your help with this."

"What are you going to do?" Hugo Jadot said, looking a little green about the gills.

"Feeling all right? Seasick?" Hawke asked him. "Sorry, I'm afraid we're fresh out of Dramamine, Hugo, old sport."

Hawke had secured the man in the big chrome fishing chair at the stern, with a line tied around his chest and his wrists and ankles secured with dental floss, a little trick Stoke had learned from the Viet Cong when he was back in the shit. *Ouch.*

"What can I do, boss?" Stoke said, coming aft to help.

"Hold on a second." Hawke was opening hatch covers in the wide transom. "Here's what I'm looking for," he said, hauling out two white nylon lines, each about forty feet long.

"You going to tie his ass up?" Stoke said.

"Not exactly. Going to teach him a little trick I learned in the Royal Navy. How the splendid captains and commanders of yore used to deal with a recalcitrant midshipman or two. Get the lying little shit out of that chair, would you, Stoke?"

Stoke freed the little fellow and said, "What next, bossman?"

"Cut his hands loose. And his ankles."

"Loose?" Stoke said. "Why would we do that?"

"We're going to take him forward to the bow. And he's going to need his hands when we get there."

"Alex," Hugo said, "I beg you. As one of my oldest friends—you don't intend to torture me, do you?"

"Good heavens, no, old sport," Hawke said. "That would be politically incorrect now, wouldn't it? No, no. Just a little enhanced interrogation is what we have planned for you."

"I have rights! I'm a citizen of France!"

"Right, but then you put on that cute little pink nightie and—"

"No! You can't do this! I insist you—"

"Shut the F up, Hugo," Stoke said. "When the man wants you to talk, he'll let you know."

"*Merde,*" Hugo muttered. "Shit. Shit. Shit."

"I got an idea," Stoke said. "Let's just cut this little butterball up into bite-size Shark McNuggets and feed him to the fishies."

"I've got a better idea," Hawke said, tying one of the lines around Hugo's waist and knotting it securely.

"Oh, wait," Stoke said, "I know where you're going with this. That old Royal Navy trick you taught me off of Miami one day."

"Correct," Hawke said. "Hold on. One more thing." Hawke opened another locker in the transom, this one full of scuba-diving gear. "Here we go," Hawke said, handing Stoke the heavy lead-weighted diver's belt.

"Oh, yeah," Stoke said, smiling, and hitched the belt good and tight around the hotelier's considerable waistline. "Now we're talking. That's not too tight, is it, Hugo?"

But M. Jadot, literally paralyzed with fear, wasn't in the mood for idle chitchat.

"Okay," Hawke said, "now, the second line also goes around his waist. Loop it a couple of times. Two lines with him in the middle, with about twenty feet on either side."

"I remember this!" Stoke said. "Hugo, you're going to love this shit."

Hawke, tugging Hugo along, had grabbed one end of the line and was carefully making his way toward the bow. Stoke had the other end and brought up the rear. Jadot, in the middle, was giving every evidence that he was about to be sick to his stomach.

"Okay, Hugo," Hawke said, flipping a switch that turned on all the bow lights. Then as they reached the bow pulpit, he said, "Time for your helicopter ride . . . Stoke, will you do the honors?"

"You got it, boss," the giant warrior said. He then grabbed Jadot by the neck, and stepping out onto the stainless-steel pulpit projecting from the bow, he held the man out over the heaving black sea.

"No!" Jadot squeaked. "Please!"

But Stoke had let some line out. He was already swinging the man round and round his head, executing the dreaded "helicopter," before heaving him into the black sea. Jadot landed with a splash, disappeared, and surfaced finally, floundering and slapping at the water in an effort to stay afloat.

"Ready?" Stoke asked Hawke.

"Yeah. I'll ease my end of the line and you walk him aft to the port side of the wheelhouse. Keep him afloat with your end until I get in position to starboard."

Hawke eased his line some more and moved from the port side of the bow to the starboard side. As he slowly fed Stoke more slack, the line disappeared beneath the keel, now pulling in on his line.

"Take a deep breath, Hugo," Stoke shouted down at the bobbing man. "You're going to swim with the fishies. We're 'bout to keelhaul your sorry ass."

CHAPTER FORTY-NINE

Hawke tied his end of the line to the starboard rail and went aft to join Stoke to port with Hugo. He leaned way out over the portside rail and saw Hugo bobbing there on the surface a few feet below, kept afloat by Stoke's end of the line. They switched places, with Stoke going forward to take Hawke's end of the line.

"Hugo, I'm going to ask you some very serious questions. Every time I don't like your answers, you're going down under the boat for a while, understood? I can't hear you . . ."

"Yes, but please—"

"Shut up! First question, where the bloody hell is my son? I swear to god, I'll kill you, Hugo. And you know me well enough to know I mean that, don't you?"

"I swear, Alex, I don't know—"

"Wrong answer, you little shit. Next. Do you know a Russian named Ivanov?"

"No."

"Never met him?"

"No."

"Liar. You didn't ferry him and his KGB thugs out to *Tsar*? Aboard this very boat? You have ten seconds."

"No."

"Captain Solo says otherwise. I choose to believe him. One more time, Hugo. Where is my son? Tell me!"

"I don't—"

Hawke craned his head around and yelled to Stoke.

"Keelhaul!" Hawke shouted, and Stoke began pulling on his line, submerging Jadot and bouncing him against the hull, pulling him under until he was centered directly beneath the keel.

After a two-minute submersion, Hawke said, "Okay, let's bring him up."

The bald head appeared above the surface.

"We can play this game all night, Hugo. But the water temperature's below fifty. Do you know the meaning of the word *hypothermia*? No? It means that after twenty minutes in that water, your body will begin to shut down. Question: Do you know a man named Joe? Another Russian, acquaintance of General Ivanov's?"

"Yes! Yes, I do! Please! Just pull me back aboard, Alex. I'll tell you everything I know. Okay? Please!"

"Where did they take my son?"

"I don't know! I swear! I'd tell you if—"

"Sink him," Hawke said. "Drop him like a bloody stone, Stoke."

Another minute or two passed before Hawke and Stokely brought M. Jadot to the surface.

"No more!" he sputtered, flailing about wildly. "I can't take any-more!"

Hawke looked at the man for a few moments and made a decision. Some men just weren't comfortable out in the open seas at night while wearing a life jacket made of lead. His wide-eyed former friend was plainly terrified of drowning in the black depths.

He was ready to talk.

Maybe.

"Ready, Stoke?" Hawke cried, just in case Hugo needed a wee bit more convincing.

"What now?"

"There are only two ways to keelhaul someone. The bad way. And then the *really* bad way."

"Talk to me, boss."

"Right, I'm going to pull him all the way under the boat's keel with my end of his line. Slowly, very slowly. I want you to feed me just enough slack so that he clears the underside of the hull . . ."

"And the really bad way?"

"You don't cut him any slack this time. That way, when I pull, he gets his ass bounced and scraped along twenty feet or so of hull, of really nasty, razor-sharp barnacles."

"Sounds unpleasant."

"It is, believe me. We do this enough times, Hugo won't have much skin left. Ready? First time, give him slack. We'll see what happens . . ."

Stoke pulled on his end. The terrified Frenchman went down and disappeared under the boat on Hawke's side, Alex feeding Stoke line. Stoke, watching the sweep of the second hand on his watch, slowly stared reeling the man in. He counted off the last few seconds, waiting to see the little bastard reappear in the water just below him.

"Bring him up, Stoke. Now!"

Hugo surfaced, sputtering and cursing.

Hawke came over to the port rail where Hugo was spitting up seawater and twisting at the end of the line. He asked Stoke to put his light on the man's face and bent down to speak to him.

"I'm going to wait until you're through throwing up all that sea-water, Hugo, and then I'm going to ask you about another name. By the way, I don't wish to alarm you, but all that splashing about you're doing has a very seductive appeal for any sharks in this neck of the woods . . . Ready?"

Hugo nodded his head.

"One more name for you, Hugo. Putin. Where is Putin hiding?"

"No idea, I swear to you! He's not someone who you can—"

His head disappeared beneath the waves before he got it all out.

Stoke counted to thirty before bringing him up again. Hawke bent over the rail and barked, "Who the hell is this 'Joe' that Ivanov was arguing with? Screaming about whose operation it was. And what is the operation?"

"Joe is just some guy who works for Putin. I don't know . . . heard his name, never met him."

"Not Uncle Joe, is he? I know Putin surfaced long enough to make a call. One call, and it was to Los Angeles. Home of Uncle Joe."

"I heard him called that sometimes, Uncle Joe, yes, that's right."

"And the operation? What's that all about?"

"No idea, but—"

"You really want to go back down?"

"No! Please. I can give you the name of the operation! I overheard them speaking of it a couple of times while they were aboard . . ."

"Tell me."

"Overkill, that's the name. Operation Overkill."

"Helpful. And where did these bastards take my boy?"

"Alex, you've got to believe me! You think that under these conditions, I wouldn't tell you if I knew? I don't know what to—"

"Asshole . . . Haul him up where I can get my hands on the little shit, Stoke."

Stoke hauled him up to the port rail and kept him swinging there as Hawke reached out over the rail.

"*Where is my son*, damn you? Tell me what happened! I want the truth this time. Last chance," Hawke said, and grabbed the man by the throat with his big right hand. He squeezed with crushing force. Hugo began screaming and dancing like a puppet on a string, knowing he was about to die—

Jadot looked up at his tormentor in a pop-eyed way and said, "Please!" he begged. "I'll talk! For Jesus's sake, don't kill me, Alex!"

Hawke let go. "I'm listening," he said.

Hugo's voice was strained and raspy to the point of being almost unintelligible. "Okay, okay, hold on." He coughed, rubbing his ruined throat with his hands. "You're right. This Uncle Joe and some Russian guys came and got the boy, middle of the night the day before you got here . . ."

"Did you tell them I was coming to your hotel? You were the only one who knew that information, Hugo. So tell me the truth. Lie and you die."

"Yes, I'm sorry, I couldn't stop myself. They would have killed me."

"Pity. Missed opportunity. Did you take Uncle Joe out to Putin's yacht aboard *Too Elusive*?"

"No. Had his own borrowed tender. A launch from one of the other mega-yachts in the harbor. Clearly he was a guest aboard that yacht, using their tender. The yacht hauled anchor and departed the harbor an hour after Joe left *Tsar* with your son."

"Which one?"

"Which one what?"

"Which effing yacht, goddamn you!"

"*Troika*."

"Good. Owner?"

"Don't know. Some Russian oligarch billionaire. Vasily somebody or other . . ."

"Where the hell were they taking my son? Goddamn you! Talk!"

"If I knew that, I'd tell you, Alex. But, I don't. I swear I'd tell if—"

"Haul him again, Stoke. Take him under. No slack at all this time."

"Fast or slow, boss?"

"What do you think?"

"Slow."

Stoke hauled on the line, bouncing Hugo along under the boat and singing all the while his version of an old sailor's ditty:

"It's only me, from over the sea, said Barnacle Bill the sailor,
I'm all lit up like a Christmas tree.
In every port, a gal waits for me,
So good-bye, Toots, I'll see you when you see me!"

CHAPTER FIFTY

"Another croissant, m'lord?" Ambrose Congreve asked Alex on the morning following the long night of enhanced interrogation featuring the repeated submerging of the hotel's owner, M. Hugo Jadot, beneath the icy seas.

Hawke had awakened filled with renewed vigor for the task at hand. Knowing the extent of Putin's paranoia and what he was surely capable of, he was determined to speed things up. Every extra second that his son was in the hands of the Russian was a second too many. Thus his sense of renewed urgency.

He looked at Congreve thoughtfully and said, "You're always talking about the importance of a time line in an investigation, Constable. Well, this one is certainly heating up, isn't it, coming to a boil. I want a new timeline, if you don't mind. One where everything we now know is known, and one that can determine that our high-value actions between this morning and the day we bring Alexei safely home are done on a rapid-fire basis. Yes?"

"Yes, of course. I'm already on it, Chief."

Hawke smiled. "As if I had any doubt . . ."

Congreve dabbed his chin with his white linen napkin and got his first pipe of the day going. He then regarded his friend for a few moments before speaking. A sea change had occurred. Hawke's blue eyes were clear and untroubled. His strong jaw was once more jutting out like the fierce prow of some great warship. The tension in his musculature seemed to be melting away, and there was a clear and visible return of the intense warrior spirit so sadly diminished by the pain of his son's kidnapping.

The two friends were having a quick breakfast outside on the Belle-Rives's stone-flagged terrace. Quite early on that sunny Sunday it was, and bright sparkles of gold danced in attendance out on the incoming parade of wavetops.

Stoke, Brock, and Sharkey, meanwhile, were upstairs in the hotel, finishing up packing all of the team's gear for departure. The three of them were Miami bound, catching the first thing smoking out of Nice. The other two, Hawke and Congreve, would be aboard the high-noon flight of Hawke Air back to Switzerland, departing in a little over an hour.

The prior night's fierce storm front had moved on. Fleeing to the south, it had carried with it every trace of morning cirrus cloud and sticky humidity; the famously clear blue Riviera skies were beaming down on the town of Juan-les-Pins.

"Lovely day for it," Hawke said, smiling up at the sun while stretching his long legs out before him. Miraculous, but for the first time in a very long time, he'd felt great surges of hope welling up in his heart. Alexei is alive, and you will find him, his heart was whispering to his ear. And he believed it.

He had good reason to be happy. The trip to the Côte d'Azur had yielded a great deal of fruit, and he congratulated himself on his solid instincts about coming here. There were still many challenges ahead. As Churchill had once so wisely said, "Now this is not the end. It is not even the beginning of the end. But it is perhaps the end of the beginning.

"Well, I must say, Alex. You're certainly in a jolly way this morning. Whatever went on out there in the dark seems to have had a most salubrious effect on the psyche."

"We got what we came for," Hawke said, his prominent chin jutting forward once more, the man full of energy and determination. "We've got the villains in our sights now, Ambrose. They're running out of room to hide."

"Speaking of hiding, where is Monsieur Jadot now, Alex? I'd like to interrogate that duplicitous toad myself before we leave."

"Up in his room, I believe. Not feeling well. Swallowed a great deal of seawater, apparently. Under very mysterious circumstances. A midnight swim of some sort. Enhanced interrogation can ruin your day, as the murderous sons of bitches at Gitmo used to whine."

"Good. The little cretin deserves worse for his betrayal of your valued friendship. Have a croissant. They're delicious."

"Trying to quit, old warrior," Hawke said, polishing off his last bit of poached egg. "Carbs. Who needs them?" Despite his current travails, Hawke maintained an extreme fitness program, one identical to his Royal Navy regime of exercise and diet. Whenever he could, he swam six miles in open ocean every day.

"So you finally got the fat little hotelier to spill *les haricots vert*, did you?" Congreve said, slathering a bit of orange marmalade on his croissant. "The beans? I assume you must have, based on your somewhat boisterous disposition this morning."

"Indeed, I did, Constable! I know I dissuaded you from coming along last night, for your own safety, but I really wish you'd been there. By the time Mr. Jones and I were done keelhauling the little bastard a few times, we had him up on the bow, singing like a cage full of canaries."

"I only hope his avian playlist provided relevant information as well as musical entertainment."

Hawke laughed out loud. "*Avian playlist?* Is that what you said?"

"Every now and then, my boy, every now and then. Now, pray tell me what you've learned."

"You will recall that, up on the bridge, Captain Ivar Solo said he'd overheard a heated radio conversation between a screaming Ivanov and someone on the line who went by the name of Joe?"

"I do recall that, yes."

"Well, you're going to like this development, Constable. The name struck a chord with me when I heard it, and now I know why. As it turns out, this Joe that Ivanov was so furious with is none other than our old friend Uncle Joe from our time in Siberia."

"No. Putin's former right-hand man is back?"

"He is indeed. He has somehow rehabilitated himself in the eyes of the Russian president. Restored to power, as it were. This is the Joe that Ivanov was screaming at on the bridge radio. Putin's old henchman is back on the world stage. Working for Putin on something Hugo says is code-named Operation Overkill."

"Good intel, Alex. But Uncle Joe betrayed Putin. That's treason, by dint of helping you and me and Colonel Beauregard escape Russia. Sentenced to death. I'm surprised he's still alive. Much less that Putin would actually have him back."

"They seem to have kissed and made up. That's all I can say."

"You're finally convinced Putin is still with us?"

"I'm convinced Volodya is alive and plotting a return to power. Where is he? No idea. But we're going to find out where Uncle Joe is. And I'll wager that's where I'll find Putin. And that, Ambrose, is where I will find my one and only child, my beloved Alexei."

"Hmm, as I recall, you gave Uncle Joe a one-way first-class ticket to Los Angeles the night we all cleared out of Russia. And promised to introduce him to your friends in the Hollywood community."

"Good memory, Constable. On the assumption that he used that ticket, first thing this morning, I called my friend Brick Kelly at Langley. Told him we may have a live one in Putin, after all, and that a bloke named Joe Stalingrad in L.A. may be able to tell us why. And where the hell he's hiding. Brick's on it. He said he'd call me shortly with an intel update."

A HALF HOUR LATER, HAWKE was up in his third-floor suite, baggage in hand, headed for the door and the airfield, when the bedside phone jangled.

"Hawke," he said, putting the receiver to his ear. He heard the familiar Virginia drawl of the tall Jeffersonian figure who headed the CIA.

"Alex, it's Brick. We're encrypted, so speak freely. First. How are you holding up? Hanging in there?"

"Better this morning. I learned a lot last night. Putin hasn't been anywhere near his yacht. But, I've got hope."

"Can't wait to hear what you extracted. But let me tell you where we are on this Uncle Joe character of yours. I assigned Special Agent James Steck in the L.A. station to his case. One of our very best men. Ex–Special Forces, three tours. Crack shot. Speaks fluent Russian, majored in Russian history at the University of Michigan. I'm texting you a photo of Steck's early, very preliminary report. First of all, the guy now calls himself Joe Stalingrad. He's in the movie business at CAA, bit parts in low-budget films. Or was until recently. Agent Steck just completed sifting his apartment on Melrose. He left a computer that he'd taken a hammer to . . . we're looking at it. But he's gone all right, Alex. Next-door neighbor says she hasn't seen him around for two weeks."

"Is Steck going to see his employer? CAA?"

"He's all over that. He also found a recent bank statement in the apartment. Wells Fargo on La Cienega. He's going to interview the manager this morning, guy named Larry Krynsky."

"All good. Tell me something, Brick. Where would Putin go? Because wherever he is, that's where Joe is going."

"Someplace safe. Completely safe. You've pretty much ruled out his yacht, I take it?"

"Right. So. Where might he be?"

"Your guess is as good as mine. I have no idea. He's on very thin ice. A lot of people out there who'd like to see him dead."

Hawke thought, *Right, Brick, and I'm standing at the head of that line.*

"Joe has Alexei, Brick. They were keeping him aboard *Tsar*. I just missed him by twenty-four hours. Another thing—I got one other great piece of intel out of Jadot. The name of the Russian yacht that brought Joe to the Côte d'Azur. I assume that's where he first took Alexei."

"Terrific. I'll get the chief of the Nice CIA station on that track right now. What's the name again?"

"She's called *Troika*. Dark green hull. Two hundred feet plus."

"Did you get the hailing port?"

"Sevastopol. That's all I've got."

"You got plenty, Alex. Good work. So now Joe's got Alexei. The really good news is that you did Joe Stalingrad a huge favor once. Saved him from the wrath of Putin and helped him get out of Russia and a start in L.A. He owes you one, buddy, big league, as the president would say."

"Believe me, I'm aware of that."

"You know I go up to that little chapel in McLean every Sunday morning? St. Paul's. Just want you to know that you two guys are in my prayers."

"Thanks. But I'm getting close. I am the one who's going to save him, Brick. Not god."

"Do me a favor, tough guy. Let god help."

CHAPTER FIFTY-ONE

Skies over the Alps

"Wherever are we going, Uncle Joe?" the little boy said between spoonfuls of chocolate mint ice cream. Joe smiled. They'd disembarked from Putin's pal's yacht *Troika* at dawn. The boss had a little PJ waiting for them on the tarmac at Marseille aeroport. He'd loved this kid on sight. Hell, he loved all kids. But this kid was something special.

A bright light shone in his big blue eyes, one that spoke volumes to Joe.

Keen intelligence, great natural curiosity about the world and everything in it. And maybe the best part, a sense of humor always lingering in the background, delighting in the company of a born comedian like Joe himself. Close? Yeah, you could say that. Two coats of paint, this close.

"To the most beautiful place in all the world, Alexei, Switzerland. Look out your window. See those mountains down there? Isn't it pretty?" Uncle Joe asked him.

"What's that ginormous tall one with all the snow, Uncle Joe?"

"Very famous mountain. It's called the Jungfrau."

"Can we go there? Do they have ice cream there? On the Jungfrau, I mean?"

"You know I won't go anywhere unless I know they have ice cream. I mean, like, even to the bathroom."

Alexei giggled, "You are funny, Uncle Joe. My uncle Stokely is funny, but not as funny as you!"

In accordance with Putin's latest instructions, Joe had assumed all responsibility for the young kidnap victim. After the rendezvous at sea with the Russian mega-yacht *Troika*, Joe now had assumed permanent custody of Alex Hawke's son. Any fears Putin had held that the child might have suffered mistreatment at the brutal hands of General Sergey Ivanovich Ivanov, aka *Der Wolf*, could be allayed.

The seven-year-old boy was, like his father, extraordinarily beautiful. Same unruly head of jet-black hair, same jutting chin, same Arctic blue eyes. He seemed fit, well fed, and given the circumstances of his captivity and the horrific separation from his father, remarkably cheerful.

Joe, who was unabashed about his admiration for Alex Hawke (except around Putin), could see a good deal of the father already beginning to take hold in the son. High spirits, humor, quickness of mind and action, charm, the love of living dangerously, and a readiness for anything.

Joe attributed the child's good fortune to Putin's skipper aboard *Tsar*, Captain Ivar Solo. The man had not only protected Alexei from his thuggish captors, he'd made sure the child was both happy and healthy. And felt cared for.

"So, we're going to Switzerland?"

"We are, kid. Are you happy?"

"Sort of . . . My father took me to St. Moritz for Christmas. Are you taking me back to my daddy, Uncle Joe? Please say yes! I had fun on the big red boat, I really did, but I miss my father. I pray for him every night, you know."

"I'm sure he misses you too Alexei. You'll see him again, don't worry. Maybe not right away, but soon. Okay? He's a friend of mine, you know?"

"Is he really?"

"Sure he is. Your pop is a swell guy in my book, Alexei, just swell!"

"I . . . guess so. Now I'm sad."

"You are? It's hard to be sad when you're eating ice cream, isn't it?"

"I guess so."

"Why are you sad?"

"I miss Daddy an awful lot, you know. But I also miss Captain Solo. He was fun. He gave me no end of treats too, just like you."

"Would you like some more?"

"No, thank you. Well, what about Captain Ivar . . . Will I see him ever again?"

"You liked the captain, didn't you?"

"Better than the Russian who looked like a bear in a chair. He was mean. Always yelling at people. Hitting them, too. You know what? I saw him slap somebody! Right on his face! But Captain Ivar was always nice to me!"

"Aren't I nice, too?" Uncle Joe said.

"You seem very nice. And sorta funny too, but in a different way, I mean. But I haven't known you very long."

"I'll grow on you, kid, believe me. Back in America, I'm a movie star, you know."

"You are? A real movie star? Like Harry Potter?"

"Well, Harry Potter's not actually a star, per se. He's the character in—"

"I love Harry Potter! He's my favorite!"

"Right. But I'm an actual star, see? I've got a DVD of my latest picture, called *Little Patton*. I'll show it to you when we get to Seegarten tonight if you like. Maybe have some popcorn, too."

"So . . . a movie, huh? You play a good guy? Or a bad guy, Uncle Joe?"

"Bad guy, of course." Joe laughed. "Look at me! Do I look like a *good guy*?"

"Well . . . you sure look like a nice guy, Uncle Joe. To me, I mean."

Joe was silent. It took a lot to move him. But the kid had him choked up.

"What's a Seegarten?" Alexei said after a few moments.

"It means a house on the water. In German, I think. It's on an island. On a great big lake called Lake Zurich. Look! You can already see it, way down there! That island house with mountains in the distance and lots and lots of land and green grass and flower gardens all around. You can play outside every day with my dog, Laika."

"Laika. That's a funny name for a dog, isn't it?"

"It's Russian. Laika was the name of the first Soviet space dog. She was the first to be fired into orbit and very, very famous."

"A dog went up in space?"

"Laika did. Pretty brave dog, huh?"

There was a short burst of static on the little Bombard jet's PA system and then the captain said, "Starting our descent now, Mr. Stalingrad. We'll be on the ground at Zurich in less than fifteen minutes."

"Buckle up, Alexei," Joe said.

"You betcha," he replied.

CHAPTER FIFTY-TWO

Oxfordshire, England

The two friends sat alone in the spacious cabin of the big Gulf-stream jet. Having dropped off Stokely, Harry Brock, and Sharkey at the Aeroporto de Nice, where they were catching an early-morning Air France nonstop back home to Miami, they'd driven to the far side of the field. There was their Hawke Air flight on the tarmac, engines running, gleaming in the sun.

"Here, Alex," Congreve said, reaching across the aisle with a thick portfolio tied with string.

"What is it?" Hawke said.

"That new timeline you asked for, dear boy, a dossier. I daresay you'll find it good reading. I began building a dossier the very evening of Alexei's abduction. I've included therein every scrap of information, every scintilla of evidence gathered by the Yard and the CIA, Interpol, Swiss Polizei, as well as every fact, every fable, every far-flung surmise I could devise."

"Wonderful of you," Hawke said, smiling. "Splendid, in fact. Why'd you wait so long to apprise me of its existence?"

"It wasn't complete until events recorded during our sojourn in the South of France. Here, there are three copies. That one is for you. The second I plan to give to Sir David Trulove at our MI6 debrief tomorrow morning. The other one is for me to use in a debriefing I've scheduled with the lads at Scotland Yard tomorrow afternoon. I thought it the most propitious and expeditious way for us to bring everyone up to speed on our progress on the case thus far."

"A lot of work went into this, Constable. I appreciate it."

"Never have I taken a case more seriously than this one, I assure you."

"You must be excited to be getting home to Diana and Brixden House."

"Oh, I am, very much so. One feels home reaching out for one with long, beckoning fingers. And a wind soughing about the eaves moaning, 'Come to me . . .'" Hawke just sat and stared at his old friend for what seemed an eternity.

He said, "That's almost poetic, didn't know you had it in you. By the way, I forgot to tell you that I have arranged for Pelham to retrieve us at Heathrow upon arrival. I hope you'll let me give you a lift. I can easily drop you off en route to Hawkesmoor."

"Lovely. I was just about to ask the copilot to put me through to Brixden House to make arrangements. Here's a thought, Alex. Diana always has the kitchen prepare a homecoming feast for me whenever I manage to return alive from a mission abroad. Why don't you join us? Pelham can drop you off, continue homeward with the luggage and gear, and I'll spirit you homeward in the Yellow Peril after supper."

"Don't tell me that old heap is still up and running. I wouldn't be caught dead in that thing."

"*Thing?* Really, Alex. How insulting. That Morgan Plus Four of mine is one of the finest examples of the marque on the road. And don't worry, dear boy, there's scant chance of embarrassment. No one will see you riding in it. It will be dark. And at any rate, it's the seat on a horse that marks the difference between a groom and a gentleman."

"Did you just insult me?"

"I was certainly trying to. I'm not sure I got the exact phrase I was looking for . . ."

"Don't get tetchy on me, Constable. It's not the car I object to, it's the color. My dear lord! It is the oddest shade, you know. I suppose it's called canary yellow. But if it is, that was one very sick bird. I, on the other hand, have a beautiful new addition to my stables."

"Another Ferrari? Please, haven't you got enough of those bloody Italian jobs? I do admire the catholicity of your collection, but I think you are overstocked with some makes and models."

"Rest easy, it is definitely not a Ferrari."

"What is it, then, for goodness' sake?"

"You'll see. Just delivered from H. R. Owen in London. God knows I don't need more cars. But I needed *something*, anything, a distraction to help from obsessing over the loss of my son. Buckle up, we'll be landing soon."

IT WAS A BRAND-NEW ROLLS-ROYCE, Congreve saw, as Pelham, the stalwart family retainer, drove carefully around the portside wing of the aircraft. Mammoth. And a shade of deep blue that was just one step shy of royal purple.

"Purple?" Congreve said as Hawke's crew stowed all the luggage in the boot. "You've managed to acquire a purple Rolls-Royce, Alex? Seriously?"

"It is clearly *not* purple, Constable."

"Well, what is it, then?"

"It's a shade Rolls-Royce calls deep indigo."

"They would, wouldn't they? It looks expensive, I will say that. If that's what you were going for."

"Low blow, but I'll ignore it. What it is, is a brute. It's called the Phantom Conquistador. She weighs nearly six thousand pounds, three tons. She has a 7.4 liter engine throwing out 551 brake horsepower, top speed of 174 miles per hour, and she'll do zero to one hundred in merely 5.2 seconds. Am I right, Pelham? An almost iconic piece of machinery? Yes?"

"Indeed you are, m'lord. Extraordinary thing. I've never experienced the likes of such before. A bit intimidating, to be perfectly honest. A handful, one might say."

Congreve smiled and stuck his hand out to the octogenarian butler.

"Oh, hullo, Pelham, how wonderful to see you outside of prison walls! On furlough, are we?" Congreve said, embracing the white-headed old fellow and patting his back with enormous affection.

After the murder of Hawke's parents at the hands of drug pirates in the Caribbean, Pelham was granted custody along with the seventy-year-old grandfather. Now in his eighties, but at that time a young senior butler in the Hawke household, he recruited Scotland Yard's Ambrose Congreve to help raise the child. As a result, the two men had forged a bond that, for decades now, went far beyond friendship. Privately, the two men would say that they had always felt like Alex Hawke's parents . . . in loco parentis, of course.

"Have a successful trip, did you, Chief Inspector?" Pelham said.

"We made a lot of progress, yes. We're closing in."

"Splendid news! I'm delighted. I miss that boy so. Miss him bounding down the stairs every morning with his howling dogs in tow . . . Sorry, is everyone ready to go? The luggage appears to be stowed."

"Let's get on with it, then." Hawke smiled, very clearly happy to be standing with both feet on English soil once more.

"Would you like to drive the brute home, m'lord?"

"Well, I don't want to step on any toes, Pelham," Hawke said, already climbing behind the wheel. "But, if you insist, yes, I would like to drive home. You two jackanapes climb in the rear. I shall see you home in jig time, Constable. Sit back and enjoy the ride in a real automobile."

"Oh, well, if I must. I wonder, Alex. Does it come in canary yellow?"

"Don't be obscene," Hawke replied. "I'll stick to the back roads so there's little danger of your being seen . . ."

Congreve was rankled but made no reply. He finally said, "Pelham, a question about this new Roller, if you wouldn't mind?"

"Not at all, sir."

"As to the color. What color would you say this car of yours was? Purple?"

"I really couldn't say, Chief Inspector. I've never really seen anything like it before. It seems to vary with the lighting conditions."

"It's called deep indigo, Pelham," Hawke said. "And I'll thank you to remember that."

"Certainly, sir. Deep indigo it is and deep indigo it shall be for evermore, m'lord."

"Thank you. Any other questions about my pride and joy, Chief Inspector?" Hawke said, hitting the red start button and igniting all kinds of 12-cylinder hell under the bonnet.

"Any idea how the *Oxford English Dictionary* defines *indigo*, Alex?" Congreve said.

"No idea," Hawke said, engaging first gear and getting the brutish Roller rolling. "And I don't actually give a fig."

"Well, I know how. Indigo is a blue vat dye derived from the indigo plant. The principal coloring matter of natural indigo synthesizes as a blue powder with a copper, *purplish* luster."

Alex, downshifting to third for a descending radius curve on the country lane, had a huge smile plastered on his face. It was almost as if he had not heard a single word Congreve had said. And, in truth, he had not.

AN HOUR LATER, THE BIG car was rumbling up to the massive black iron entrance gate at Brixden House. A forbidding piece of architecture in and of itself, the structure was topped with numerous gilded eagles atop marble columns, the birds weathered enough down through the centuries as to be discreetly unobtrusive.

After a short wait, a plainclothes detective emerged from the small stone gatehouse. Upon seeing Congreve in the back of the Rolls, he opened the gates and waved them through. A twisting drive through rolling parklands then led to Congreve's home.

It was a winding lane, bounded on either side by hawthorn hedges. It wended through vast plantations filled with yews, pear trees, laurels, and rhododendrons, many soon to come into full pink and white bloom. Acres of ancient trees filtered late-afternoon light onto dappled grass.

The evening was clear and seasonably chilly, and in the far distance, where sunlight lay like great bars of gold on the surrounding hillsides, one could see the earth just going green, with leafy old forests, towering oaks, elms, and gnarled Spanish chestnuts many hundreds of years old coming out of retirement.

They rounded a corner and a wide vista opened up before them. The sight of his home always evoked strong feelings in Ambrose Congreve. Set high above the River Thames, with a far-reaching view over the countryside, the impressive main house of golden limestone reigned over the rolling landscape in an imperious and almost lordly fashion.

"Here we are," Ambrose said as the big car rolled under the covered porte-cochere at the entrance, "welcome, gentlemen, to Brixden House. Pelham, please come in for a glass of sherry before heading on to Hawkesmoor, won't you?"

"Very kind, Ambrose. But I'm afraid I must continue onward with my journey. I want to get all of his lordship's belongings unpacked and put away before he returns home after dinner."

Hawke, sad to leave, climbed out of the car and smiled at his beloved Pelham. "Be careful with the beast on the way home. She's all-wheel drive of course, but the back roads are slick with ice by now."

"I certainly will, sir. And I should be most appreciative if the beast will be careful with me."

CHAPTER FIFTY-THREE

Brixden House, Taplow, UK

I t's a house of secrets," Congreve had once told Hawke about
Brixden House. It was the ancestral home of Congreve's wife, the
former Lady Diana Mars. Located just off the Taplow Common
Road in Oxfordshire, it had borne witness to the doings of countless
forebears, many illustrious, a lesser (so it was said) number of the
nefarious, the notorious, and in the swinging sixties, the famously
decadent.

The magnificent Italianate palace stood atop great chalk cliffs
overlooking a graceful bend in the gently flowing Thames. Dusk was
soon to come, and every window, large or small, was blazing with
the yellow cast of interior light.

Ambrose had once confided to Alex Hawke the true nature of
Diana's family seat. "In earlier times it was a den of treasonous spies,"
he said. "During the Second World War, a circle had formed around
Diana's great-grandmother, the viscountess, a German. Brixden House
had become a de facto salon for a right-wing aristocratic group of
politically influential individuals. This Germanophile cabal was not
only in favor of appeasing Adolf Hitler, but also of England promoting
friendly relations with Churchill's sworn enemies, the Nazis."

"I remember reading accounts of that era, yes," Hawke said,
lighting a fresh Morland cigarette.

"Ah, but the best was yet to come," Congreve said. "The swinging sixties had brought fresh scandal to the house. It was apparently the scene of ardent sadomasochistic sex parties. Parties where naked prostitutes, ashtrays and drinks trays strapped on their backs, were paid to crawl on the floor amongst the besotted revelers, HM government types, aristocrats, and royals, gleefully careless about precisely where they stubbed out their cigarettes or spilled their whiskey.

"Parties including one where cabinet minister John Profumo met and bedded a beautiful working girl named Christine Keeler. A woman who just happened to be simultaneously sleeping with a Soviet naval attaché named Yevgeny Ivanov. The press had a field day of it, merrily summarizing kinky and scandalous goings-on inside Brixden House."

"And John Profumo went down in flames along with Harold Macmillan's tattered government," Hawke added.

"He most certainly did."

After being greeted inside the doorway by an aging butler, Hawke and Congreve made their way through the great hall, a splendid room with its grand fireplace, soaring ceiling, and the famous John Singer Sargent portrait of Lady Mars's great-grandmother, which hung to the left of the wide hearth.

"There you are, darling!" Diana trilled, making her way down the broad and winding stone staircase. "And you've brought young Alex! How delightful."

She took his hand in both of hers and pulled him to her, looking up at him with shining eyes. "Darling Alex, I've been utterly bereft at the news of Alexei's kidnapping. I am so very, very sorry. But, Ambrose tells me that my precious godson is alive and unharmed. Alex . . . is that right?"

"I'm delighted to tell you that it is. And we'll find him soon, Diana. Your husband and I. We've made a great deal of progress in one short week."

"Only a matter of time, darling," Ambrose said, putting his arm around his wife. "Only a matter of time."

Hawke said, "And, Diana, we've learned he's also in the custody of someone whom I once helped enormously . . . Joe Stalingrad."

"Understatement," Congreve interjected. "You saved Joe Stalingrad's bloody life, Alex. Without you, Putin would have had Uncle Joe impaled on a stake in the courtyard at Energetika Prison."

Diana, her eyes aglow, said, "So, Alex, that's a very good thing, isn't it? A comfort to know that he is in the care of someone who is beholden to you?"

"A small comfort. Who knows? Alexei's still a pawn in a very dangerous game. For all I know, Putin is dying to get his hands on him. And this friend whom I helped is either trying to protect him . . . or gain favor with Putin by delivering him into the lion's den. We really don't know the answer to that yet, but the sooner we find out, the better the chances for Alexei's survival."

"Of course, darling, I'm sure you'll find out soon," Diana said, and went up on tiptoes to kiss Alex on the cheek.

Diana's wanton beauty and glowing energy always gave Hawke a start. She said, "Well, who's hungry? Your timing is impeccable, darlings! Dinner is just about to be served. Come along, Alex, we've just enough time to have a quick cocktail. And we have a great deal to talk about this evening."

"You mean Sigrid, of course."

"Yes, Alex, I'm afraid I do."

Ambrose, hounded by hunger and the scent of lamb roasting somewhere in the innards of the house, had walked ahead. Hawke turned to her and whispered, "That will be a private conversation, I hope, Diana."

A sharp pang had struck him. She wanted to talk about Sigrid. And whatever had happened to Sigrid, the beauteous young law student who had formerly resided in Gardener's Cottage, a lovely little manse situated just down the hill from the house where they now stood talking.

"Of course, you darling boy," she told him with true affection. "Our world-famous detective always goes alone into his library for a postprandial brandy by the fire. When the coast is clear, we'll duck outside and take our drinks onto the terrace and have a chat there."

"If you don't mind," Hawke said, "I'd rather like to see the cottage where she lived. Have a quick look round."

"Happy to show it to you. And so happy you and the famous detective had such a productive trip. He rings me every night to say that you're very close to solving this puzzle. Is that right?"

"Well, you should hear my prayers some nights."

"I'm sure, poor dear. I'm quite sure. Now, what can I get you to drink, your lordship? Dinner will be served shortly."

"Rum, please. I believe you have the Gosling's Black Seal 161?"

"Indeed we do! Onward!"

She took Alex's arm and the threesome made their way through a long gallery to the main dining room. It was a generous rectangular space with high vaulted ceilings and blazing chandeliers. Large candelabra with flaming tapers illuminated the suits of gleaming armor that stood guard against the old stone walls. Walls that were hung with faded tapestries and large gilt-framed portraits of Lady Diana's long-forgotten royal ancestry.

The three old friends were oddly quiet for the first and second courses. They were each preoccupied with their own private thoughts. Then came the roast lamb, pink as a baby's bottom, the perfectly cooked veggies, and the delicious claret, as the British so fondly call the wines of Bordeaux, flowed, loosening tongues.

Diana, so lovely in the candlelight, her coiffed blond hair and diamonds gleaming, raised her wineglass. Then she looked across the table at Hawke.

"To Alexei!" she said, her voice filled with hope.

"To Alexei," Hawke and Congreve chimed in, raising their glasses.

AFTER DINNER, CONGREVE, AS EXPECTED, excused himself and retired to his library. Outside, a light misty rain had begun to swirl in the gardens during dinner. Hawke and Diana each donned a mackintosh for the stroll down to the Gardener's Cottage. Passing through a cherry orchard, Hawke felt the earthy, pungent presence of leaves and limbs dripping in the dark.

"Please take my arm," Diana said, "These stone steps are dreadfully slippery."

"I'd be delighted," Hawke replied, and they made their way through lush dark gardens, down to the place where Sigrid had last been seen. He hoped she was still alive, Hawke thought, suddenly recalling her vivid descriptions of her violent ex-lover and her thoughts of suicide. Sigrid said her stalker had died in an auto accident, but there was something he couldn't put his finger on, some aspect of her story that just didn't seem altogether believable.

Had she given up on herself?

Had she given up on him at last?

Gone back to the ex-lover, despite all her fears? This was his own fear, that she might be lost to him forever. He'd planned to visit the Congreve's small garden cottage once he'd returned to Britain, had done so ever since she'd disappeared. Wondering, hoping, that perhaps he'd discover some kind of clue, some kind of physical evidence of where she might have gone.

"Here we are!" Diana said brightly. "Isn't it lovely?"

It was a small *Wind in the Willows* stone cottage, painted white, Hawke saw, even though to him it looked a bit forlorn and dark.

Covered with climbing ivy, two stories, brick chimneys at either end of the roof's peak, sitting in solitary splendor in the midst of a traditional English garden. There was a gate at the front, an opening in the white picket fencing, and they pushed through and made their way up the flagged front walkway.

Hawke, trying to keep his spirits up, kept looking up at the house, trying to imagine glowing lights in every window, and smoke curling up from the twin chimneys . . .

Suddenly he was seeing her silhouette in her upstairs bedroom window, reading something by Graham Greene before retiring to her bed . . .

"Here's the key," Diana said, interrupting his reverie. "Just give me a second . . ."

And they were inside a small foyer that led to the sitting room.

"There's a light switch on the right, Alex," Diana said in the dark.

"By the door?" Hawke asked, feeling the wall, and finding the switch, turned the lights on.

IT WAS A CONFUSED LITTLE room that looked out on the rear garden, with china cupboards and bookshelves sagging under the weight of heavy leather-bound tomes on gardening, and near the hearth one large comfortable wicker chair for the gardener, nestled beside the steel fireguard. Worn chintz and faded gingham on the occasional upholstered furniture . . .

Hawke remembered a trick Congreve had taught him long ago: Upon entering a crime scene (and this could be construed as one), stand in the center of the room in total stillness. And then, Congreve had said in a letter:

Open your heart and mind to all the secret memories the room holds. Open eyes and ears to the stories rooms can tell; they are significant because here they remain. They are the stray symbols of a life, a life after all the tall tales and sad stories have slunk back into the unconscious past; and there they cry out for rescue like the survivors of a shipwreck.

Hawke tried the approach, but it was useless. Fruitless, despite his intensive efforts to summon the past.

"Did she leave anything personal behind, Diana?" he asked her. "Or did she clear out completely?"

They had moved on into the tiny dining room, turning on more lights.

"Oh, a few things. Books. Some clothing. Some of her photographs and watercolors are still on the walls of her bedroom. Go upstairs and have a look. I'll wait down here. Those steep stairs are murder."

He climbed the steep and narrow steps, forlorn and hopeless. He'd lost her, the house was whispering from every dark corner. *She's gone.*

Standing in the center of her softly lit room, the place where she'd slept and dreamed and wondered, he felt hot emotions boiling up inside his heart. He'd been trying to hold it all back. Stifling them, steeling himself, feeling sure that his fears about Alexei, coupled with worry about Sigrid, would surely overcome him.

It was then that he saw a photograph of himself. It was in a beautifully carved sterling frame from Asprey's. He was standing beside one of his horses in the paddock at Hawkesmoor, and it was drenching rain. But his love of Captain, for that was the big red stallion's name, came shining through his smile, piercing the very rain itself with luminosity . . .

He picked up the picture. On the creamy mat below the photograph she'd written something in her small, cramped handwriting.

Whether the weather be cold, whether the weather be hot,
we'll be together whatever the weather,
whether we like it or not.

He sighed, blinked back the sting, and lit a table lamp. Sinking down into the tired leather armchair, he picked up a book lying akimbo on the little round table. It was a book he'd given her just last Christmas. *The Honorary Consul* by Graham Greene, one of his favorites. With a sigh, he sat back and flipped through it.

A small blue envelope fell out and landed at his feet.

He bent to retrieve it.

There were three handwritten pages inside the envelope. A letter. The writing stopped halfway down the third page. The letter was unfinished.

But it was addressed to him.

"Diana, come up here," he said. "I've found something!"

CHAPTER FIFTY-FOUR

Seegarten House, Lake Zurich

You've arrived at the island, Joe?" Putin asked Stalingrad on the phone.

"Just got off the sub ferry and walked in the door, sir. Can't thank you enough. It's a beautiful house and—"

"Never mind all that crap. You can't schmooze me, Joe, if that's the word you people use. Do you have him? Or not? Is the boy safely inside the walls of the compound?"

"Yes, sir, he is. Everything went according to plan. He's running around outside in the gardens, happy to be back on solid ground, I think."

"Who the hell is watching him?"

"Two of your sentries. I told them never to let him get farther than twelve feet away. And never outside the wall under any circumstance."

"All right. Good, good. How is he? Did that bastard Ivanov harm him? Even slightly?"

"No. He was remarkably well cared for. And you can thank Captain Ivar Solo for that. He never let Ivanov get anywhere near the boy. The man's a saint, I'm telling you."

"Did Ivanov give you any trouble? Taking over the custody of Alexei, I mean."

"Let's just say he wasn't thrilled about it. He thought this was *his* operation. You had asked him to perform a Christmas miracle in St. Moritz and he had succeeded. He wasn't all that happy about you sending me to pull the rug out from under his feet. Not that he had any feet of course."

Putin said, "He's not very happy now, either. He's dead."

"What?"

"Somebody got to him aboard *Tsar*. I don't know who yet. But I will soon. Ivanov had a lot of enemies in the KGB forces still loyal to me. I'm having Captain Solo picked up for interrogation."

"Go easy. God knows what would have happened to the boy were it not for him, I promise you. And Ivar is still fiercely loyal to you. Trust me."

"I'll take that into consideration."

"Speaking of being picked up, are you ready to leave?"

"More than ready. But the Sorcerer is taking his own sweet time about moving out. I told him to take his toothbrush and get it done. With what I'm paying him for that mountain, he can buy anything he wants. I'm giving him a week. I'll call you when I'm ready."

"Wait. One more thing before you go. I'm thinking out loud now, spit-balling the thing, but my feeling is that whoever took out General Ivanov did you a big solid."

"Tell me why you say that, Joe."

"Just a gut feeling. But I always thought he was not a man to be trusted. Long on himself and short on you. When you ordered him to mount that epic abduction operation, I think he saw his golden opportunity."

"To do what?"

"To fuck with you. Big-time. I can't recall a single kind word about you coming out of his mouth. He was, as they say in Hollywood, a hater. Now that he's dead, I can tell you that I heard from sources he was secretly feeding information regarding your whereabouts to the oligarchs and their hit squads."

"What? He hated me? That miserable old fuck. He was nothing.

Whatever he achieved militarily was at my pleasure. But I thought at the very least, *he* was loyal to me . . ."

"The Americans have an expression for it, sir. He was very good at two things only. He knew how to kiss up. And he knew how to kick down. Consummate bullshit artist."

"So what was this 'golden opportunity' Ivanov thought he saw?"

"I think that when he actually got hold of Alex Hawke's son at St. Moritz, he thought he held all the cards. He knew how desperately you needed some kind of protection from Hawke going forward. Something to keep Hawke at bay, keep him from interfering in your plans. I mean, at some point in the future. He knew that only Hawke, and no one else, had the power and resources to ever pose a serious threat to Operation Overkill."

"You make a good point, Joe. I see where you're going with this."

"Sure. Think about it. Ivanov is on *Tsar*, right, up on deck every day, sunning himself and getting blow jobs down below while sipping Krug, and all the while he is thinking, well, you know what, I think I'll just disappear somewhere for a while. Just me along with the boy. Wait for Putin to call me. Won't take long. He'll be desperate. And then I'll give him a ransom number. Twenty million? Thirty? What will it take for me to hand over the boy to him unharmed?"

"Christ, I think you're right. That's exactly what he planned. Listen, Ivanov's dead. I'm not. I need you to keep your head on straight for these next few months, Joe. How's the vodka?"

"Yummy. Never better. You ever try Zyr? Liquid gold, trust me."

"Lose it, Joe. Not a drop more. You taking any kind of drugs? Prescription medications?"

"Only Advil and testosterone. Do those count?"

"You know something, Joe? You're a very funny man. And sometimes I actually find myself appreciating your twisted sense of humor. But now there's no time for it. Dead serious is what I want and need from you. Focus. We're about to make history together, Joe. You have a lot at stake here. As do I."

"I understand."

"The world can be ours, Joe. You understand that, too?"

"I'm on it, boss. Clean and mean. I don't want you to think I don't appreciate this opportunity, because I do. Anyone who wants to take you out will have to go through me. I swear it."

"Good to hear. Now, one more thing for you. There are two of my loyalists operating in Nice. Seasoned KGB officers, both. Krebbs and Zhukovsky. I will send their contact information by secure email. Speak to them. Tell them this is coming from the highest level. Tell them I want someone taken and interrogated by any means necessary. You have all this, Joe?"

"I've got it, sir."

"All right. Instructions. Tell them they are to drive to the harbor at Juan-les-Pins. Say there is a hotel there. It is called the Belles-Rives Hotel. Right on the harbor. I want them to check in. To surveil the situation there, with an eye toward taking someone somewhere quiet where he can speak openly, yes?"

"Yes, sir."

"Good. There will be a man in the bar, always flitting about, giving orders to staff. A man who knows the name of whoever killed Ivanov. If they have to kill that man to get that name, it is of no consequence to me."

"Understood."

"Call me as soon as you have that name, Joe, the man who killed General Ivanov. Now. The man I want interrogated is that fat-fuck little owner of that hotel. His name is Monsieur Hugo Jadot. Tell your men they're free to do anything they want with him. Take him up on the roof of his fucking hotel and threaten to throw him off, I don't care. When they get the name, then they can heave him over the side."

Click.

CHAPTER FIFTY-FIVE

Provence

"Where the hell are you, Joe?" Joe heard an irritated Putin say in his headphones.

"Chopper pilot says we're ten minutes out. You all packed up and ready to go, sir?"

"Hours ago."

"Listen. I spoke with your friend the Sorcerer late last night. He says by the time we arrive, there won't be a trace of him left inside that mountain. He'll be sunning himself at his new villa on the Riviera. He was—what's the word?—almost giddy. Like, boom, he's being let out of prison after decades in solitary confinement."

"I hope he left those fucking F-18s and their pilots and crews behind."

"Where the hell's he going to store an entire fighter wing at a cozy little villa on the French Riviera, Mr. President?" Joe said. And for maybe the first time ever in his life, he heard Putin laugh out loud.

"I guess you're right about that. What did the colonel say about the meeting at Falcon's Lair tomorrow morning?"

"Game on. He's arriving at the Park Hotel Vitznau tonight and I've got Horst picking the two of them up in the sub in Vitznau just before dawn tomorrow morning. They'll be here for breakfast."

"The *two* of them? I didn't authorize Beau to bring anyone with him."

"He's bringing your new chief of security, sir. The man he said you authorized him to put on the payroll."

"Christ, I forgot about that. So who is he? You met this guy?"

"Yes, sir. I met him all right."

"You trust him? Because if you don't, there's no way in hell I'll admit him to attend a meeting of this magnitude."

"I do. Tell you the truth, I think you're going to love this guy. When I say he is something else, I mean he is truly something else. A different kind of breed of cat entirely. Jesus."

"Meaning what?"

"Meaning special. Meaning you might just want to hire him yourself. He is one seriously qualified hombre, sir. Former CIA assassin, former U.S. Army Ranger with a chestful of medals, handpicked by Colonel Beauregard for his own protection and the elimination of his enemies."

"What's his name?"

"Shit."

"What? Just tell me his name."

"Shit. Shit Smith."

"Shit Smith? As in, Shit?'"

"Shit Smith. Yes."

"Shit? What kind of name is that? Shit?"

"You heard right."

"Christ. What a name."

"I think he'll live up to it, sir. In a good way, I mean. There's bad shit and then there's good shit. That's our Shit. A real quality addition to the team, my opinion."

"You've piqued my curiosity, Joe. You must be nearing my position, I think I hear your rotors up there."

"We have the LZ in visual contact. And I see smoke from a chimney coming up from the trees."

"That's my cabin. You're right overhead. Set down in that small field just east of the forest."

Click.

"KEEP THIS THING FIRED UP," Joe said to the pilot as the skids settled into the grass. "I'll be right back."

He jumped nimbly to the ground and disappeared into the thicket of woods.

"How the mighty have fallen," Joe whispered to himself upon seeing the less-than-humble home where the former richest man on earth had spent these many, many weeks. Humble was an understatement, he thought, making his way to where the log cabin stood in a small clearing enveloped by deep wood.

He stepped up onto the narrow porch and began rapping on the roughhewn wooden door.

"Come in, come in!" a smiling Putin said, swinging the door wide and grabbing Joe's lapel and tugging him into the room. "My dear friend Étienne and I are just finishing my farewell lunch! Have a glass of whiskey or wine, Joe! I'm drinking a potato vodka we brew in a still just behind the cabin."

"Not for me," Joe said, eyeing the boss. He'd obviously already had a couple, but he would still remember the promise of abstinence Joe had made.

A round little guy, even shorter than Joe, less than five feet tall, handed him a stubby glass of vodka and said, "*Bienvenue*, monsieur. Étienne Dumas, owner." Joe had to smile. The two of them together looked like a couple of Snow White's boyfriends, Happy and Grumpy.

"Joe Stalingrad, good friend of the man here. You two certainly seem to have been having a good time of it. What's the occasion, Étienne?"

"A farewell party for my dear friend, of course! We started at breakfast . . ."

"I take it you two have been having a good time?"

The Frenchman said, "Oh, you have no idea. The adventures we've had and—"

Putin grabbed Étienne's arm and said, "Tell Joe about the time we got caught stealing chickens from the little farm across the river! A barking dog gave us away, but we got the chickens anyway and Étienne got a load of buckshot in the ass and I had pluck them out with tweezers! It took two days!"

Putin threw back his head and roared at the happy memory.

Étienne said, "Ah, yes. And then there was the time we took in a woman who'd gotten lost hiking up the valley. Beautiful girl, late twenties, maybe. Long dark hair, superb figure. *Merveilleux!* During the dinner, she keeps staring at Volodya, no? Yes, and saying she thought they'd met before. He looked so familiar! After dinner, we all sat round the fire drinking schnapps and she got very friendly and asked me how many beds I had. Only two, I said, his up the ladder and mine over in the corner."

Putin jumped in. "And then she says, 'Two such handsome men, whatever shall I do?' She looks at Étienne, back at me, then back at him, and she finally said, 'I guess there's nothing to do but flip a coin!' So I pulled one out of my pocket, flipped it, didn't like it, flipped it again and again and again until I won! Ha!"

"Yes! Fair and square! Volodya won the brass ring!" Étienne sputtered, bent over with laughter. "And then, guess what, *mon ami?*"

"What?" Joe said.

"She stayed for a week!" he shrieked.

Joe had never witnessed such jollity. It was apparent that the president had been very, very happy here. Doing far more than just sketching imperial Soviet uniforms at the kitchen table, apparently.

"Mr. President, the chopper is waiting. I'll carry your bags out if you're ready to go, sir?"

"Thank you, Joe, I'll be right behind you. I want to have a private word with Étienne . . ."

Joe picked up the two bags and Putin's fur overcoat and said,

"Étienne, it's been a great pleasure. Thank you for taking care of him with such humor and bonhomie. I've never seen him so happy."

"Volodya, you told me once you were a policeman from East Germany . . . why does Joe call you 'Mr. President'?"

"I was a president once, Étienne. I was president of the greatest nation the world has ever produced. Mother Russia."

"*Le présidente de Russe? Mais non!*"

"*Mais oui, Étienne.*"

"You are Vladimir Putin? My god. All this time and I had no idea that you—"

"This is for you, Étienne. A satchel of gold. All the gold I have. Careful, it's very heavy."

"Gold?" Étienne said, peering inside the leather pouch. "Oh my god, this is a fortune, Volodya! I cannot accept this . . . *C'est impossible!*"

"I will tell you this. Put it to good use. Retire to the South of France, buy a little place by the sea if that is your wish. Still. I tell you, Étienne. It is not nearly enough to compensate you for the great friendship and joy you have brought into my life. These past weeks and weeks I shall always remember. Remember as the time I realized that all the power and palaces in the world are little enough compared to the simple pleasures I've enjoyed with you, Étienne. I say farewell with tears in my eyes. You are my one true and loyal friend in all the world."

"And you mine, Mr. President of Russia. Volodya. I shall never forget you."

"Nor I you. Nor will history. It will be recorded that this humble but historic cabin was where a great man once plotted and planned down to the last detail the greatest return to power since Napoleon's triumphant return to Paris!"

CHAPTER FIFTY-SIX

Falcon's Lair

That historic first meeting, wherein Putin laid out his vast plans for the military coup that would restore him to power in the Kremlin, took place in the large ballroom at Falcon's Lair.

The room was quite elegant, a creamy white rectangle with a high-vaulted and windowed ceiling that filled the room with morning light after the shades and external shields were retracted.

Parquet floors waxed to within an inch of their lives, a long oval mahogany table surrounded with Chippendale chairs, and soaring walls hung with the former owner's magnificent collection of American Western art. Frederic Remington, Albert Bierstadt, Thomas Moran, and N. C. Wyeth's magnificent illustrations for *Treasure Island*.

When Uncle Joe entered the room, ten minutes late, Putin was alone, his back to him, inspecting his new collection of artworks from the American frontier—one of many such art collections he had purchased along with Falcon's Lair. Dressed formally in a navy suit and tie, he had his hands clasped behind his back as he moved from picture to picture.

He considered himself to be the world's foremost art collector, having borrowed (stolen) many of the most priceless pieces in the State Hermitage Museum in St. Petersburg. Privately, Putin called the entire museum the Midnight Art Supply Company.

He considered himself a curator, an educated man with vast knowledge of the arts, from the Old Masters to the Impressionists, all the way to Art Moderne. But he had been unprepared for the glorious American landscapes and portraits he was now exploring for the first time. They were of such beauty as to almost defy the eyes as to what he was seeing.

"Splendid!" Putin shouted to himself, gazing up at a painting of cowboys around the campfire in the moonlight, one of Frederic Remington's epic pictures. It had been reproduced in a picture book he'd owned as a boy, reading voraciously about the American West, and he'd cherished the image. And now he owned it, by god, the fucking original.

A sterling silver coffee service had been laid out on the table, and Joe was pouring a cup when he heard the president's exclamation. "What is it, Mr. President?" he said.

Putin, startled, whirled about. "Joe! I didn't hear you come in. Come over here and look at my new painting."

Joe approached, sipping from his cup. "Wow," he said, looking at the thing.

"Wow? Is that all you can say? Do you have any idea at all what you are looking at?"

"Horses? Cowboys?"

"Joe, listen to me. I'm determined to educate you, despite the abundant evidence it's an impossible task. This, Joe, is a Frederic Remington. About 1900 he began a series of paintings that took as their subject the color of night. Before his premature death in 1909 at age forty-eight, Remington explored the technical and aesthetic difficulties of painting darkness. This one he called *A Quiet Moment Around the Campfire*."

"Just look at this thing! My god. It's filled with color and light— moonlight, firelight, and candlelight. It's also elegiac, reflecting Remington's lament that the West he had studied as a young man had by the turn of the century largely disappeared."

"It's beautiful. I mean it. The more I look at it, the more I dig it."

"Where are my two new colleagues? Did I not say ten o'clock sharp?"

"Let's sit down. Be here in five or ten minutes. Their sub is arriving at the air lock as we speak."

"Tell me more about this new employee of mine. Mr. Smith."

Joe sat down opposite the president's chair and said, "I don't want you to be shocked by Mr. Smith's appearance. He's a little frayed around the edges. He looks like the Marlboro Man, but his jeans are torn and faded. He wears a big black cowboy hat and he never, ever takes it off. Maybe in the shower, I don't know, but it's a thing with him. The colonel says it's a thing with all real cowboys like him. Only place a cowboy takes his hat off, Shit says, is the barbershop."

"Sounds colorful."

"Oh, he's colorful all right. That is, if stone-cold killers are your cup of tea. He's a full-blown psychopath. But functional. Beau says the CIA considered him a national treasure during the decade he spent as a field agent."

"Political assassinations?"

"His specialty. Never the gun, always the knife. Bowie knife."

"All right. If you and the colonel think we need him, I'll give him a chance to prove himself. If he's successful, I'll make him a permanent addition to the inner circle."

"Do you have targets?"

"What do you think I've been doing all this time in hiding? Of course, I have targets. On every continent. Dozens."

"Where does he start?"

"Hugo Jadot is dead, Joe. An accidental fall from the rooftop of his hotel by the harbor. But before he died, he gave up the name of the man who shot and killed General Ivanov aboard my yacht, *Tsar*."

"Don't tell me."

"Your friend, Joe, your friend who helped you escape my wrath and my vengeance. The man who set you up in Hollywood. Lord Alexander Fucking Hawke."

"You must have known when you ordered the boy's kidnapping that Hawke would come after his son."

"I did. Why the hell do you think I ordered Ivanov to effect the abduction?"

"To use the kid as a knife at his throat to keep him at bay?"

"No. To lure in Alex Hawke with the thought of killing him. Of course. And now that he's getting close," Putin said, "I've been looking for the right asset to go after him. And luckily for you, you might have just come up with a worthy candidate."

"Shit Smith?"

"Shit Smith. But we don't kill Alex Hawke first. We save him for last."

"So who's first?" Joe said.

"His two closest allies. Stokely Jones Jr. And that Scotland Yard man of his. What's his name, you know, Ambrose Congreve."

"You know, if you do that, kill those two, nothing will stop him from revenge. Nothing. He will come after you, Mr. President, and his rage will know no bounds. I don't think anyone alive could stop him."

"Until a few minutes ago, I would have agreed with you. But you may have given me a great gift. A powerful weapon for both offense and defense."

"Shit Smith."

"Correct. Two of my loyal field assets, Cubans who happen to be brothers, are in Key West and already shadowing our Mr. Jones. The Cubans have never let me down. We'll send them to kill Jones and keep Mr. Smith under wraps until I decide the time has come for him to make his debut. Understood?"

"Shit works for Beau, Mr. President. Only Beau can send him."

"Shit Smith *used* to work for the colonel, Joe. But, for now at least, he works for me."

"Ah, look who's here, Mr. President. Colonel Beauregard and his colleague, Mr. Smith!"

The two men were at the door and Putin got to his feet. He said:

"Welcome, welcome, gentlemen! We've just been talking about you. Singing your praises, to tell the truth."

Colonel Beauregard, with Smith in tow, strode across the floor toward Putin. Not willing to settle for a handshake, Beau embraced the president.

"Good to see you, Mr. President," Beau said, heartily. "Long time, yes sirree. Like you to meet a young fella who works for me, sir. He is my shield and my sword. Couldn't live without him. Wouldn't be alive without him. This here's a man out of Texas, name of Shit Smith."

Shit reached forward and shook Putin's hand. He said, "It's an honor and a pleasure. I been hearing all about you from the colonel here. President of Russia? Man! That's some résumé you got there. I wanna thank you for letting me join up with your outfit. You got something needs doing, you just put old Shit on it, sir. I'll git 'er done for ya."

Putin gave the cowboy his dead-eyed stare, taking the full measure of the man. He was tall and finely muscled like a star athlete. He was remarkably handsome, with a face like one of the romantic cowboy leads in Hollywood. What was that man's name? Oh, yes, Randolph Scott, in *Ride the High Country*, that was it.

And the man had the coldest black eyes Putin had ever seen. And that was something, coming from the man forever using his own cold-as-ice eyes to intimidate and threaten all and sundry.

"Interesting you should say that, Shit. As it happens, I do have some things that need doing. Let's sit down and talk things over. If we're going to turn the whole fucking world upside down, we'd better get started. You've both met Joe. He reports directly to me. And you both report to him. Understood?"

Both men nodded in the affirmative.

Putin pointed up at the painting he'd just been explaining to Joe and said, "Shit, a question for you. Do you recognize this painting?"

"Yessir."

"Know the artist?"

"That'd be Frederic Remington. Picture's called *A Quiet Moment Around the Campfire*."

"Welcome to my world," Putin said with a smile.

"Joe, I need to speak with the colonel privately for a few minutes. Why don't you take Shit down to the kitchen and introduce him to the staff. Tell them to send up more coffee. And whatever Shit would like to have for breakfast."

"Just grits," Shit said, "Only thing I like, pan-fried hominy grits. Okay, okay, I get the picture, I'm going."

"Movie star, huh?" Shit said to Joe in the elevator down to the kitchen.

"Oh, I stuck my toe in the water when I first got to Hollywood. Couple of small-budget pictures. But I'm a classically trained New York actor, so—"

"Whoa. I remember now. You played that sick freak firebug, right? A pyromaniac serial killer who liked to off hookers and strippers and shit. Right?"

"Yeah, that was me. I was Joey Gafuzzo, worked backstage at a strip club and a whorehouse in the French Quarter, New Orleans, offing hookers in my spare time. One night the club catches fire accidentally on purpose and I kill half the hookers and strippers in the French Quarter."

"Yeah. That was great. Heavy role, man. What was the name of that movie again?"

"*Flaming Pussies*," Joe said. "My title, I wrote the script. It killed."

"YOU TRUST THIS MAN, COLONEL?" Putin said, taking a seat across the table from the colonel. "This Shit Smith?"

"With my life."

"The fact that he's undoubtedly unstable and probably insane doesn't trouble you in the least?"

"I first hired him at Vulcan when he left the CIA. That was ten years ago. I just recently hired him again and I demanded his abject loyalty. I've never had the slightest reason to doubt it since. He would die for me and I for him."

"Why'd he leave the agency?"

"Terminated. He killed his wife. Court ruled it was a crime of passion. I asked him about that. He said there was no passion about the thing at all. He said he'd been wanting to kill a woman all his life. She just happened to get in his way. Ruthless does not begin to describe Shit Smith, sir. 'A highly functioning psychopath' is the way I've heard him described by mental health professionals who worked for me."

"I'm beginning to appreciate his talents. Here's what I want you to do first."

"Yes, sir?"

"I want Mr. Smith to remain here at Falcon's Lair for the time being. Part of the short-term planning process involves Hawke. Keeping him off-balance, keeping him away from me until I'm ready for him to enter the field of fire. I want to send the English spy a message or two and I want it done now. There's a man in Florida needs killing. He's in Miami. I can give you his address later. His name is Jones. Stokely Jones Jr."

"Stokely? I know the guy. He was with Hawke in Siberia. His best friend, far as I could tell. One serious dude. You sure you want to go there? You might just enrage Hawke even further than you already have."

"Don't argue with me, Colonel. Write this name and address down. Cisco Valdes. Lives with his twin brother Rodrigo in a rented condo on Key Biscayne. A dumpy building called The Claridges. Two Cuban assassins, run by KGB but still loyal to me. They call the pair of them *Los Medianoches*, for some reason."

"The Cuban Sandwiches?" Beau said. "That's weird."

"Actually, it means the Midnighters. Get in touch with them. Tell them you work for me. Tell them that Putin wants this Stokely Jones eliminated. Now."

And that, my friends, Beau thought to himself, is right about the time when the real serious shit got on a collision course with the fan.

PART TWO

Bellum

CHAPTER FIFTY-SEVEN

Islamorada, Florida Keys

Memories of Florida had gone sun-bright in Stoke's mind. Now, after the insufferably long and bone-cold days and nights in frosty Switzerland, he was back where he belonged. He'd been down in the Keys at Islamorada for a solid week. Nothing but sunshine and bonefishing aboard Shark's fish boat *Maria*. Heaven meant tracking the wily Mr. Bone around the Keys with Captain Sharkey Gonzales-Gonzales at the helm. Oh, yeah, manna from Havana, so nice they'd named him twice.

In his prior life, before joining Stoke in Miami at Tactics International, Sharkey had been a charter member of Los Marielitos, class of 1980 before becoming a charter fishing captain out of Cheeca Lodge, one of the best guides in the business and famous throughout the Florida Keys.

It was hot.

The tropical sun was beating down on Stoke's bare shoulders, drying up the powerful sweat he'd worked up on Shark's foredeck. He was religious about doing his daily U.S. Navy SEAL exercise regimen. He'd never felt stronger, or better, either one.

After all the crap they'd been through, Stoke was feeling about as relaxed as he'd felt in years, feeling the sun-warmed teak decks beneath the soles of his bare feet, and, on the radio, sweet memories of a golden oldie running through his mind . . .

> My woman's left me for some other man
> Oh, but I don't care, I'll just dream and stay tan

There was plenty of Kalik beer (the "Beer of the Bahamas") on board, but plenty of Stoke's good old Diet Coke in the cooler, too. Stoke grabbed a fresh one. "Need another frosty?" he called up to his fishing buddy, driving the boat from atop the flying bridge.

"No, man, I'm good. I've had hundreds."

He heard Sharkey laughing. He was at the helm, pounding Kaliks to stave off the heat and humidity. And skeets. Lots of damn skeets in the mangroves. Heat 'n' Skeet is what Stoke's old SEAL squad used to call this part of the world, back during those golden days spent in Navy SEAL training at the Truman Annex in Key West.

He and the Sharkman had been living aboard Sharkey's sport-fishing boat, an old Huckins 50 SF. A classic beauty, she was a fish boat from back in the 1940s. Shark had named her *Maria* just before his wife left him over the three-hundred-pound Seminole princess deal.

He'd bought the black-hulled fifty-footer with the unexpected windfall of all the work he and Stoke had been doing for Harry Brock at the CIA. A new administration had swept into Washington, and in certain sectors of the military and espionage communities, business was booming.

Tactics International, the counterterrorist company Stoke had founded with seed money from Alex Hawke, had been very busy lately. The new American president's focus on rebuilding the military and increasing border security hadn't hurt. Just two days ago, the two amigos had helped the Coasties in Miami locate and round up a bunch of Bahamian drug runners who'd been hiding out on No Name Key.

Shark backed the throttle down and let the big sport-fishing boat settle and then drift with the currents at idle speed. Stoke put the map down, stood up, and looked over the stern, out across the perfectly clear turquoise water of a small bay, studded with bright green mangroves. Fifty feet below his feet lay the wreck of the *Havana Star*. She was a cruise ship out of Miami and bound for Cuba when she went down with all hands in the great Labor Day Hurricane of 1935. The wreck was well known to Sharkey, as it provided some of the best reef fishing in the Florida Keys.

Sharkey slid down to the deck fireman style, using only his one hand gripping the stainless-steel ladder rail.

"The Land Shark has landed," he said enigmatically. "Man, I love this old boat, Stoke."

"You and me both, partner. This is the life, little brother."

"You love it?"

"Who wouldn't, Shark?"

"You know what? I'm serious now, Stoke. Anything ever happen to me? *Maria* is yours."

"What? Oh, come on. Ain't nothing gonna happen to you, Sharkey."

"I know, I know. But, if it does, who can I leave her to? No more wife, no kids. Seriously. Nobody enjoys this old barge more than you do!"

"Yeah, well, ain't happening, bruh . . . ain't never happening. Time to scuba up, little brother. You ever been spearfishing before, Sharkman?" Stoke said, donning his own scuba gear.

"Can't say I have. Never in my life," the former charter boat skipper said, wiping beer foam from his mouth.

"Well, it's easy. Just do what I do."

"You got two arms," said the wiry little Cuban, who'd lost his right arm in a horrific shark attack off Key West. "I only got one. Why I never took up spearfishing."

"Correct. But you're better with that one arm than most men with two. So just watch me. Listen and you shall learn."

"What are we after today, bossman?"

"Yellowtail snapper," he said, donning his flippers.

"Love that fish. How do I load this damn thing?"

"First of all, you make sure it's pointed in any safe direction that does not include me."

"Sorry, man," he said, swinging it away.

"Second, spearguns should be loaded and unloaded in the water only. This is the safety button. It should be in the safe position. When we get in the water, I'll show you how to load. Basically you put the butt of the gun against your chest, then pull the rear band back, notch it, then the front band. Cool?"

"I'm cool, yeah. But I'm hot, too. Let's get in the damn water, Stoke."

"Last one in." Stoke smiled and executed a backflip from the gunwale with the assurance of a former Navy SEAL with three combat tours to his credit.

He kicked hard, diving down to the wreck and the water wonderland that awaited him. It was his last day in this paradise and he wanted to make the very best of it.

He'd had a nagging feeling for the last couple of days. He couldn't shake it, no matter how irrational it seemed. There was no cause for it, nothing he'd seen or heard, but it was there, haunting him.

He had the dull feeling he'd never return from this trip. Never see his wonderful wife, Fancha, again. His beautiful home on glittering Biscayne Bay. Never again experience that joy his life's work brought to him, that filled him up with satisfaction whenever he won, whenever the good guys won and the bad guys lost, whenever the strength went to the weak, whenever to the victor went the spoils . . . the feeling that he'd made a real difference in this world . . .

Aw, c'mon, Stoke! Snap out of it!

What the hell was going on with him?

CHAPTER FIFTY-EIGHT

The fish, as advertised on those TV ads for the Florida Keys, were unbelievable. Schools of multicolored blue tangs, angelfish, midnight parrot fish, hogfish, and sergeant majors, in countless numbers, flashed in and out and around what remained of the sunken wreckage on the bottom.

It was noon, and the sun blazing overhead illuminated the wondrous sights, making Stoke glad that Fancha had okayed this boys-only vacation when he and Shark and Harry Brock had returned from Europe.

This is fun, he told himself. *Relax, for god's sake.*

The two men explored the rusty remains, swimming in and out of the *Havana Star*'s gaping hull for perhaps half an hour before turning to serious game fishing. There was no shortage of game, and within the hour, when Sharkey finally mastered his speargun, they'd bagged their limit.

Sharkey swam for the surface while Stoke remained on the wreck site and dealt with some pesky issues with his regulator. Times like this, equipment issues, Stoke couldn't help remembering his SEAL days, and his pal Woodie McCracken. He was a twenty-six-year-old SEAL from Asheville, North Carolina, who'd died in these very same waters. He was a good kid, a brother, and one of the funniest men alive.

Woodie had been Stoke's dive buddy and best friend at the Key West station, and the accident had happened during intensive dive training in preparation for an overseas deployment. Nobody ever knew what had happened to that kid. To this day, according to the Naval Special Warfare Group, the cause of death was unknown.

Did he have a heart attack? Stroke? Was it his *gear? His regulator? Christ, shake it off, Stoke!*

He finally got his damn regulator straightened out and swam for the surface.

THE SECOND SHARKEY'S HEAD BROKE the surface, some fifty yards from where *Maria* was anchored, he heard the high-powered crack of rapid rifle fire. Rounds blistered the surface of the water all around him as he whirled about, desperately trying to locate the source of fire and lay eyes on whomever was trying to kill him.

There!

A blue thirty-footer with a soaring white tuna tower. He saw her name and hailing port emblazoned on the transom and seared into his memory: *Wombat.* And, below that, *Key West, FL.*

The rifleman was atop the swaying tower, with another guy down at the helm, now bringing the bow around to close the distance to the swimmer. Sharkey knew the shooter would assume he was still alive, that he wasn't already shot dead. He saw the guy as he checked the wind speed and direction before proceeding toward his target.

It had freshened while they were down on the wreck. *Wombat* was now thrashing about in choppy, wind-whipped and frothy seas. So he'd caught a break there, at least. The pitching deck of a boat in rough water made for a very iffy shooting platform.

The wind effect, heavy swaying, was most felt at the top of the tower, Shark thought, as he dove back down. And that wind had been all that had saved his life. He pulled hard for the bottom. Had to warn Stoke that they had a shooter up top.

He met Stoke on the way up. Stoke was shocked by what he saw.

Sharkey's eyes, behind the dive mask, were as wide as saucers, and he used improvised hand signals, finally managing to convey the message of a shooter and the dire situation up top to Stokely Jones.

"Stay here! I'm going up to see," Stoke signaled.

"Roger that." Sharkey nodded.

"Give me your speargun," Stoke indicated, and Sharkey did. Stoke could load and shoot faster and more accurately than any man alive, Stoke had told him.

Stoke pointed to his dive watch, looked at Sharkman, and held up seven fingers for seven minutes. Then he pointed at the surface and pumped his hand: Surface in seven, Sharkey! Seven!

Stoke paused just below the surface, just long enough to notch another two spears into his twin guns. Hardly the ideal weapon to use against armed assassins but it would have to do, he thought, kicking hard for the surface.

The second his head breached, he saw them. Fortune favoring the bold, the assailants luckily had their backs to him for a moment, still trying to locate Sharkey while looking directly into the blinding sun.

Stoke looked at his dive watch. Shit—Sharkey would surface in five minutes!

Two men, one driving the boat, one high atop the tower with a rifle with a telescopic scope, swinging the barrel in an arc. The skipper at the helm station below was carving a wide turn to starboard at idle speed. The shooter had binoculars out now. They were in no particular hurry. Their prey would ultimately have to surface.

The veteran of many tours of underwater combat experience didn't need much time to calculate their best and probably only chance of survival.

One of them would need to surface for a moment, in plain sight of the bow, just as the other surfaced unobserved just off the stern. The stern man would have the only shot and he would have to mount the transom platform in order to take it. It was up to the bow man to provide enough distraction to give Stoke, the stern guy, a chance to kill the shooter on the tower with his speargun.

He swam hard, his powerful legs thrusting him forward in pursuit of the *Wombat*. Was Sharkey in position off the bow? he wondered. Six minutes and counting on his stopwatch.

SEVEN!

Sharkey surfaced.

Stoke ducked underwater when he saw the shooter spot him and raise the rifle. Looking for Stokely's bobbing head in the scope, finger itchy on the trigger. How the hell had the guy acquired him so fast? Shit. The sun reflecting off his dive mask! He ripped it down, letting it hang from around his neck. The guy locking him in the cross hairs and squeezing another round off just as the bobbing head disappeared beneath the waves.

He clawed his way down deep to where the sun don't shine.

From down there, he could see the thin white bubbly streaks as rounds struck the water like tracer bullets before running out of gas. He would stay down thirty seconds, kick hard for twenty yards to a new location, and resurface . . . the shooter would not dare take his eyes off this moving target . . . Stoke would have just time enough to do what he needed to do—he swam for the *Wombat*, bobbing on the surface some five hundred yards away.

STOKE, HIS ARMS MOVING LIKE great steel pistons, seemed to heave himself up out of the water and up onto the stern platform in a single fluid motion. The shooter, sporting a long black ponytail, was atop the tuna tower. He was facing forward, firing his assault rifle at Sharkey. Stoke saw the boat driver, same ponytail, same powerful squat body, advance the twin chromed throttles, slowly gathering speed. He was circling in the area of the Sharkman's last known position . . . closing in.

"Hey!" Stoke called out, just loud enough to be heard by the shooter upstairs.

"Wha—" The man spun round to see a giant black man standing on the stern platform. He had a speargun aimed up at his beating heart . . .

Stoke took dead aim and fired.

The spear flew straight and true. It struck with great force in the center of the man's bare chest, driving him backward, the spear going deep, finding his heart. Struggling to keep his balance, fatally wounded, he looked down, stunned. Then his heart exploded and he fell backward, falling, bouncing once, but hard, off the starboard gunwale, and then into the sea.

Seeing his brother's body splash into the seawater, the helmsman, tattooed over every square inch of skin, turned to see Stokely at the stern. The Cuban had a TEC-9 machine pistol in his right hand, his left on the throttles, shoving them wide open. The boat came up out of the hole and leapt forward, the twin 300hp Mercury racing engines roaring.

Automatic pistol rounds were ripping up the teak around Stoke's feet when he squatted for a millisecond, then used the massive oak trees he called his legs to power up and launch him up and backward onto the transom of the boat. The driver was whipping the wheel back and forth, hard, trying to dislodge Stoke from the deck.

Stoke, in serious danger of losing his balance, backpedaling to hold it as long as he could, dropped the spent speargun into the sea. He raised Sharkey's gun in a desperate attempt to fire a second spear. The helmsman leaned on the throttles! Aw, shit, he was going into the drink and . . . he fired.

Fired and missed! Right then a burst of heavy throttle brought the bow up at a critical angle and a pinwheeling Stokely was jettisoned off the stern transom platform. Worse yet, he was plunged back into the speeding boat's wake, where he'd likely get chopped into chunks by the twin screws churning like mad beneath the hull.

SURFACING IN THE MAELSTROM OF *Wombat*'s wake, Stoke did a quick 360, shielding his eyes from the sun glare, looking for his friend. Watching the blue sport-fishing boat come round to a course of due south, Tattoo probably headed for Key West. And Sharkey?

Nothing.

He suddenly spied *Maria* at his two o'clock position, about a thousand yards away. He swam for her as hard as he had ever swum, hoping against hope that the tough little Cuban fisherman had not sacrificed his life to save that of Stokely Jones Jr.

He clambered aboard Sharkey's boat and hoisted the anchor. Cranking the engines, he noticed what a beautiful day it was. He didn't feel beautiful, though. War is hell and this was war, Stoke thought, firewalling the throttles and putting the wheel hard over, setting a course for the last place he'd seen Sharkey . . . The sun was dancing on the water and made seeing well nigh impossible. He kept looking.

And looking.

But the Sharkey he knew and loved wasn't there anymore.

All that remained of the little one-armed fisherman were the circling sharks in a high fever of bloodlust, whipping up the surface water to a bright pink-tinged froth.

They got his right arm first, Stoke thought, heartbroken sadness washing over him in waves . . .

And now, fifteen years later, they've taken the rest of him.

CHAPTER FIFTY-NINE

London

London Town was crowded for a Monday morning, but Pelham maneuvered the massive Rolls-Royce Phantom Conquistador through the narrow streets with aplomb. They'd driven down from Oxfordshire via the A40 and M40 in far less time than the usual hour and a half they'd anticipated. And it had given them ample time to stop by Jack Barclay Bentley on Berkeley Square.

Pelham had noticed an odd whine from the aftermarket supercharger Hawke had ordered. It had been a tricky installation, performed by the German auto tuners, Mansory. The last thing on earth that Alex wanted was to do any damage to that beautiful 7.5 liter engine, a beast capable of putting out 543 bhp.

"Won't be but a moment, your lordship," Pelham said as they pulled majestically into Barclay's service bay. "I'll just look in on old Rob, the service manager. He's expecting me and will want to have a quick peek under the bonnet to see if there's a problem, sir."

"Good, good," Hawke said from the rear seat. "I'm very happy back here. Just checking my messages."

"Very good, m'lord," Pelham said, and shimmered off into the deeper shadows of the garage.

As he scrolled down his messages, an email from a name and

address he didn't recognize caught his eye. But he did recognize the white oval symbol with the black letters *CH*. Confoederatio Helvetica, better known as Switzerland.

Switzerland? Who the hell . . .

Someone had sent him a video. One with no note of explanation attached. He opened the file and touched play . . . and—

His heart caught in his throat and he stopped breathing . . .

It was Alexei.

"Hi, Daddy," his little boy said, smiling into the camera. He was seated on a plush olive-green Windsor chair. Hawke hit pause and brought his iPhone screen up closer to scrutinize. His son was wearing lederhosen with reindeer-horn buttons and old-fashioned lace-up shoes. In his lap was a small dog licking his forearm, a dog Hawke recognized as a West Highland Terrier.

And he looked, dare he say it . . . happy?

Yes! Hawke thought, feeling a frisson of happiness himself, shivering up his spine. He's not only safe and unharmed, but he's actually *happy.*

He pressed play.

"This is Joe, Daddy!" the little boy said, hefting the dog aloft for his father's inspection. "He's my new dog. I named him after Uncle Joe because I like him so much! And, Daddy, my new uncle wants me to say hello to you, too. He's very nice. He told me that he was a friend of yours and I like him very much, indeed.

"Oh! I think my puppy needs to go pee, Daddy. Uncle Joe said we'll make another movie for you real soon . . . and he asked me to tell you that he will never forget how kind you were to him, helping him in Hollywood . . . What's Hollywood, Daddy? Oh, and it's been raining . . . raining and raining."

And it was over.

Pelham opened the car door and slipped behind the wheel.

"Rob said there's a slight adjustment to the blower needed, m'lord. An easy fix, I just have to schedule an appointment and—are you quite all right, sir?"

He turned around and saw that his lordship was staring at his mobile, a look of sheer disbelief on his face. And strong emotions roiling behind those ice-blue eyes.

"Everything all right, sir?" he asked.

"Yes, Pelham," Hawke said, and now he seemed to be almost on the verge of laughter. "Everything's going to be all right. Everything is quite wonderful again!"

Pelham wondered whom Alex had heard from. But he knew that whomever had messaged him must have had something to do with Alexei.

"To Black's, Pelham," Hawke said cheerily. "Sir David is expecting me, as you know."

"Indeed he is, sir," Pelham said. "Expects too much of you, if you ask me, m'lord."

Hawke let it go. What was the use? Pelham had always been overprotective . . .

Sometimes he felt like he and his beloved valet of thirty-some-odd years had evolved into an old married couple. Pelham, the consummate man's man, fussed and worried over him like some maiden aunt. And he insisted upon using Hawke's title, something that Alex would never do himself if he could help it. Nor would he let others use it. "Just Alex is good enough," he would say.

Gazing out at the streets of London as they drove along Brook Street and past Claridge's Hotel, Hawke suddenly said, "Pelham, good lord, this isn't the right way to Black's! You know perfectly well I'm already running late and Sir David will be fuming."

"I know you're late, m'lord. That's why I'm not taking the right route. And why, on the contrary, I'm taking the *fastest* route."

"Oh, do calm down, Pelham. Your self-righteousness knows no bounds, does it?"

"No, your lordship, I don't suppose it does. And, rightfully so, might I add, sir."

The sigh from the rear was deafening.

CHAPTER SIXTY

Black's Club, midday

A rriving at Black's Club, Alex was happy Ambrose Congreve would join them for lunch. This, at the behest of Sir David, saying on the phone the day prior, "I need that super brain of his, Alex. Get Congreve for lunch. Your club."

Something clearly was up with the old man.

Certainly this would be a working lunch. MI6 had been an enormous help in the ongoing search for Alexei. And, Sir David had hinted on the telephone, he had something of a breakthrough in the strange disappearance of Vladimir Putin.

And Hawke for his part had promised to provide Trulove with newly updated details on Alexei's kidnapping as well as information regarding the horrific assassination attempt on the life of Stokely Jones. An act that had resulted in the death of one of the two assassins. And the tragic death of Stoke's friend and colleague, Mr. Gonzales-Gonzales, a colorful Keys fishing guide known as Sharkey.

Hawke always entered the crowded Men's Grille, on the third floor at Black's, with some trepidation. He referred to the assembled posh gentry, a crowd of gentlemen splendidly turned out in Savile Row's finest bespoke wardrobes, as the Hi-Hi Society.

This because, as one passed by the long oak bar en route to one's table, seemingly hundreds of hellos were exchanged, brief acknowl-edgments of the lads one had been with at Harrow or Oxbridge, or in Hawke's case, Eton (where he was a great winner of prizes both on and off the playing fields), followed by the Royal Naval College at Dartmouth.

"Oh, hi-hi," he said to them. "Hi-hi," they never failed to reply as he moved through their number. Ahead he saw Sir David at Hawke's long-held table, sipping his fortifier and reading the *Times*. The table was directly beneath the massive lead-paned windows that rose up into the darkness near the top of the room. The most beautiful light anywhere, anytime, he'd long believed. "Hullo, Sir David," Hawke said.

"You're late," Sir David said, barely glancing up at him.

Hawke had entered his old St. James haunt promptly at half past noon. Sir David Trulove suffered neither fools nor tardiness gladly. He affected a lack of interest in Hawke, sipping his gin cocktail and studying the front page of the paper. "I see the Americans are still at it, accusing their president of being a Russian spy. Bloody hell!"

Hawke looked at his wristwatch.

"Hardly late, sir. I believe we said twelve fifteen."

"Twelve sixteen is considered late in my circles. It's now, what, twelve thirty-one?"

"Sorry, sir."

"Sit down, damn it, and order a drink. We've much to discuss."

"Yes, sir," he said, and sat. Waitstaff was instantly at his elbow. "Oh, hullo, Digby! Didn't see you there. A rum, please. Gosling's of course. The Black Seal?"

"Indeed, sir."

Hawke smiled at the elderly gent and said to Sir David, "Where's Ambrose, sir?"

"Went to the gents," the chief of MI6 muttered. "He's right behind you."

"Oh, hullo, Alex," Ambrose said.

"Oh, hullo, Constable," Hawke replied, standing up to shake

his friend's proffered hand. Congreve, in a cheery mood apparently, executed a snappy salute instead, and said, "Welcome aboard, Commander."

"Oh, no need to salute, gentlemen, I'll be on the bridge all afternoon!"

It was an old line, delivered in the manner of a puffed-up popinjay of a Royal Navy flag officer. But it always made the boss laugh, nor did it fail this time. Sir David, in a positive change of mood moderated by gin, said, "Aren't you two the cheeriest of chaps today, Alex? What have you been up to, dear boy? The investigation is obviously going well. Making good progress, are we?"

"Oh, this and that, sir. I'll tell you about it later.

"I've just watched a video of Alexei, sir. My child is safe, sound, and about as happy a boy as ever I've seen. He's obviously being very well cared for. God, the relief after all this time of anxiety . . . I really can't express it."

Sir David broke into a wide grin and said, "Well, well, that is splendid news indeed! I'm very happy for you. It's been a nightmare. Splendid news! Isn't it, Chief Inspector?"

"Good lord, how wonderful, Alex! May I see the video? Can you get a sense of place from it? Who his captors are?"

"We'll go to the Library after lunch. I'll show it to both of you on the telly then. I can't tell you how relieved I feel . . . I don't know . . . boulders off my shoulders, as we used to say at Eton."

"Marvelous, marvelous," Trulove chimed in. "Now, do sit back down and order a drink, Alex. A toast to Alexei's health, shall we?"

"Indeed we shall, sir," Hawke said, signaling to the hovering Digby. "You two were early, I take it?"

"Yes," Sir David said. "The chief inspector and I just happened to run into each other at Lobb's shoe emporium. We decided to stroll over here a bit early, seeking reviving liquid sustenance from the bar. Don't worry, Alex, we've not been talking about you. Ambrose has merely been supplying further details about the terrifying attempt on the life of your old friend Mr. Jones."

"So you know all about it, Sir David? I was going to give you the particulars."

"I do. And, Congreve and I are in full agreement as to who was responsible. Isn't that right, Chief Inspector?"

"Right you are, Sir David," Congreve said, sitting back and getting his pipe going. "Alex, I heard via morning dispatches at Scotland Yard that the two men responsible for the attempted murders have been positively identified by the Miami-Dade police. A vile pair of Cuban DGI assassins, under the direct control of KGB in Havana. Cisco and Rodrigo Valdes. Twin brothers, they were, quite infamous for their butchery, apparently, and known throughout the Caribbean as *Los Medianoches*."

Trulove said, "Your friend Stokely did all of us at Six and CIA a great favor by taking one brother out, Alex. We've been after those two bastards for years. I had my man in Havana, intel officer Mario Mendoza, run a skip trace on their communications prior to their arrival at Key West. A call from a KGB splinter cell initiated the action."

"So," Hawke said, wearily, "it's Putin after all, is it?"

"I'll just say this. We have no proof of his involvement, nor even, apart from an unverified phone call that CIA picked up, if he's still alive. None. But the consensus of my inner circle on the Albert Embankment is that, most likely scenario, he's simply disappeared until the Kremlin heat on him eases up a bit. But now he may be back, ready to surface."

"So the attempt on Stokely's life was a shot across my bow . . ."

"I'm afraid so, Alex. If it's Putin, and I for one think it most likely is, he knows you're getting close. His strategy being, and obviously this is not the first time, to keep you at arm's length while he executes his nefarious plans. Even though Stokely survived and was able to take one of his two would-be assassins off the board, it was a clear signal aimed directly at you. Stay away. Your son is not safe. Your friends are not safe. *You* are not safe, Alex. That's what your old friend is telling you. He is saying, 'Beware.' "

"I am only too aware of that fact, Sir David," Hawke said. "That's precisely why I've got to find Alexei! Before that son of a bitch can get his hands—"

"Alexei will come into play only as a last resort, Alex," Congreve said. "They won't move against the boy, not now, not until Putin's out of viable options. Hence going after your friends, not you. Hence your video this morning. He doesn't want you breathing down his neck in a state of high anxiety. No, no. He wants you lulled into security."

"Meaning?" Hawke said.

"Meaning Stokely is still breathing. They were not satisfied with taking Mr. Gonzales-Gonzales out."

"And what about you, Ambrose? If they'll go after Stokely, then they obviously will—"

"Me? Oh, I'm quite sure my name appears on a Putin shit list somewhere. All we can do is be extraordinarily careful until we get to the bottom of this whole thing."

"He must have something big to hide, then, Sir David," Alex said, catching his superior's pale blue eyes. "Going after my friends . . . this is virgin territory, even for Putin."

"We're just starting to get a sense of what he's up to. My deepest, darkest Kremlin mole believes he's still alive and plotting a military coup to regain power. He still has a lot of loyal support at the highest echelons of the Kremlin and the Russian military. And more important, the hard core of the KGB, the older boys, what we call the 'old wood,' will stand with him no matter what he does . . ."

"Sir David, if I may. What is the mood inside the Kremlin walls?"

"Divided. Sometimes I think I know exactly what they're all thinking. Other times I feel like I'm wandering around like a fucking pirate with two eye patches."

"Excellent image, Sir David," Congreve chuckled.

Trulove, who mistrusted compliments, gave him a look. "Yes," he said, "there are those who supported the oligarchs' ousting of Putin in the coup. And there are beginning to be more and more who are disaffected by the new regime. The oligarchs are ruthless, as you well know. Now insulated by the overwhelming power they possess, their wrath knows no bounds. The Kremlin is full of formerly powerful ministers now constantly looking over their shoulders for would-be assassins."

"Putin will no doubt find a way to add fuel to that fire, sir. And the Russian public at large?"

"As you might expect, they long for Putin's return. He is still a great hero to them. The man who stands up for them in the world. In a fight, they'd side with the man, no doubt."

"I imagine the oligarchs have legions of killers out looking for him."

"Indeed. My source believes Putin disappeared only out of fear for his life. That's what he wanted everyone to believe. But he has much grander ambitions. He's spent all this time in hiding plotting away. The disappearance was just to give him a cover story while he marshaled his forces. His next big move? I don't know."

Ambrose said, "Perhaps a counter-coup? Is that really what the hell he's up to, Sir David?"

"Maybe," Sir David said. He lit his Morland gold-tipped cigarette and added, "You two remember a certain Colonel Beauregard, Alex? That rather outlandish chap from Texas?"

CHAPTER SIXTY-ONE

Beau? Good lord!" Hawke said. "Remember him? How could I ever forget that fellow? I actually came to admire the chap before it was all over. His morals are a mite shaky, but he's got the strength and heart of a lion, Sir David. I've always wondered where he disappeared to."

"Well, wherever he's been, he's back, apparently. Been living in a hotel on Lake Geneva for the last month or so. Living it up. Round-the-clock prostitutes and room service. Someone else is footing the hotel bills, Alex. And I think we could both guess who that might be. The colonel is flat broke. He's been living on and off his yacht in Bermuda, the only thing that remains of his old life. Sold everything else: the beach house in Costa Rica, the G5, the cattle ranch in Texas, and now he's living on the proceeds. A watch collection worth over half a million . . . automobiles, horses, whatever he had."

"Beauregard working for Putin? Again? I very much doubt it, Sir David. He burned that bridge long ago, when Ambrose and I were last in Siberia. Betrayed Putin to help Ambrose and Stoke and me get out of Russia alive. Surprised the KGB never caught up with him."

"Alex, think about it. Putin is bent on revenge. He desperately wants to return to power. How many men on earth do you know who could put together a massive private army, tank corps, air wing, arm them, train them for a swift and deadly blitzkrieg military strike? Something truly shock and awe? You could do it, Alex. You and Stokely and your two soldiers of fortune Thunder and Lightning down in Costa Rica. But who else? Anyone come to mind?"

Hawke shook his head. The man was right. Beauregard was certainly one of a kind.

"May I have one of your cigarettes, Sir David?"

"Certainly. Do you take my point, Alex?"

"I do. If Volodya's planning something of that magnitude, say, mounting a military coup in Moscow, he would have to forgive and forget Beauregard's treachery. He would be forced to. He'd also offer him so much money, the colonel wouldn't be able to refuse. Enough to guarantee his loyalty this time around."

"Yes. We're all on the same page. Remember Uncle Joe, Alex?" Trulove asked.

"One of the most memorable characters I've ever met in my life," Hawke said. "As you'll soon see for yourself on Alexei's video, Uncle Joe is most definitely back in the picture."

"Meanwhile, have a look at this picture," Sir David said, handing Hawke an eight-by-ten black-and-white photo. It was a hotel lobby, full of people coming and going.

"A hotel," Hawke said, and looking up at the white-jacketed barman, added, "I think I need another drink. Gosling's Black Seal, if you please, neat."

Congreve sat forward and said, "Look at the queue waiting at the front desk. The second man in line, specifically."

"No."

"Yes. It's definitely Uncle Joe, Alex," Congreve said. "He's wearing a fedora, but you can't mistake that stocky little build . . . and that nose."

"It's him, all right. What hotel is it again?"

"The Beau-Rivage in Geneva," Trulove supplied. "The very hotel where Colonel Beauregard has been ensconced in the penthouse for this last month."

"Putin is reassembling his old team," Congreve said, bright lights going on all over the myriad regions of his vast brain. "The game is afoot, Sir David."

"Indeed it is," Sir David said. "And now the question is, where and when and how does this bloody game manifest itself? Where's Putin going to find the resources to fund and mount a full-scale military operation against such an entrenched enemy as the oligarchs in Moscow? He's still rich, to be sure. But billions? No. He's going to need more than one of Beauregard's legendary mercenary armies. He's going to need fighter aircraft, he's going to need bloody tanks and artillery, for heaven's sake! Alex, what are you thinking? You've got that look in your eyes again."

Hawke said, "What? Oh, yes, sorry. I was just thinking that no one's going to *give* him the damn money. Hand him billions? No. So . . . his only alternative . . . is to steal it. So, who's got all the money, Sir David? The Americans. The Germans and Chinese . . . the Saudis . . . did I leave anyone out?"

"The Swiss?" Ambrose said, with a wily smile. "They've all that and more. Seventy percent of the world's gold reserves are hidden away beneath those Alps. But I ask you why, Alex? You know Putin better than anyone. Why not just sail away on the big red yacht of his? Leave the damn world in your wake and get on with living the good life?"

"I'll tell you why, gentlemen," Hawke said. "Two reasons, really. One, he's got a price on his head, probably a massive number. It's awfully difficult to hide oneself whilst sailing around the world on a big red yacht. Two is that massive bloody ego of his. Because he sees himself as the bloody Comeback Kid, that's why. He's down . . . but he's never, *ever* out. He ruled Russia with an iron fist. Seized Crimea, probably the Ukraine and the Baltics soon."

"Has he no fear of a revitalized America?" Trulove asked. "A strong president investing untold billions to rebuild her weakened military, a powerful leader who will brook no nonsense from the bad actors out there? Witness Kim Jong Un . . . aka Little Rocket Man."

"Oh, I think he has some trepidation, yes, but now he sees a once-in-a-lifetime chance to cement his place in history! Standing shoulder to shoulder alongside his two great heroes, Caesar and Napoleon. Caesar at his height of power, Napoleon at his finest hour. The Corsican Giant, escaping his miserable exile at Alba for his triumphant return to Paris, with his army massed behind him, ready to destroy anything that gets in his path. France, bow down! That's how he sees his future . . . Russia, bow down!"

"The scary thing," Congreve mused, puffing away at his ancient briar pipe, "is that he might actually be able to pull it off. You're right, the new American president won't like it much . . . or will he? A destabilized Russia might be just the tonic for him . . . hmm . . . after all the hacking and meddling in U.S. politics by the Russkies?"

"He just might move the mountain," Hawke said, thinking it through. "With the help of men like Beauregard, Uncle Joe, his many high-ranking loyalists in the KGB, military, not to mention the hard-core followers he's amassed at the top of the KGB, now desperate for his return to power . . . Yes, I can see it, if he can find the money. He could do it."

"With the majority of the Russian people behind him, he most certainly could, Alex," Sir David said. "That is, unless and until someone like you puts a bullet in his fucking head."

"Wait. Can I put one in Kim Jong Un's head first?"

Ambrose took a sip of his whiskey and smiled at Hawke. "No free lunch, dear boy, no free lunch!" he said.

"Tell me about it," Hawke replied. "Let's order some lunch. I'm famished."

CHAPTER SIXTY-TWO

Zurich

S ometimes I get so goddamn bored I kill folks just for practice," Shit Smith was saying. "I mean, you know, just for the sheer fuck-all of the thing."

Joe just stared at him. Thinking how much he looked like that movie star Sam Shepard. If looks could kill, he was thinking.

Shit and Uncle Joe were in Zurich, in the Altstadt, sitting at a corner table in a dark bar getting solidly beer drunk on a cold, drizzly Sunday afternoon. Shit had his chair rocked back on two legs, cowboy style, sitting there paring his nails with his ivory-handled bowie knife. Joe was thinking, That's an awfully big knife for doing your nails. Total overkill, that was, face it, the Shit Way.

"Sorry?" Uncle Joe said, all ears now. Kills for *practice*, this psycho friend of his says?

"Yeah. Let that little beauty sink in, pards," Shit said, lighting a soggy old stogie and cackling to himself. "I was married once, y'know. To a Russian woman. Met her when I was CIA in East Berlin. Ilsa? Elsa? Something like that. Anyhoo, I put up with her crap for, what, mebbe ten years before I had to kill her. Judge ruled it a crime of passion. Asked me what I had to say. I said there wasn't no passion to it. Said I'd been wanting to kill me a woman since way back afore I can even remember."

"Jeez, I dunno, Shit. I just don't know about that."

"Ask you a question," Shit said, "serious question. You ever been to Pirates of the Caribbean?"

"You mean the Johnny Depp movie? Sure."

"No, not the fuckin' movie, Joey!"

"Oh. You mean, like, the ride at Disney World? You're talking about Orlando?"

"Exactly. Orlando. Armpit of the country."

"Never have, sorry to say, Shit. Sounds exciting, though. Pirates. The Caribbean. You know. Good stuff."

"Huh. Well, guess what, Uncle Joe. For your information, killing child molesters? Mass murderers? And nasty fucking Russian women? Trying to convince you you're an alcoholic? Or worse yet, early onset Alzheimer's? See you next Tuesday! Hell, that beats the living shit out of that damn Disney Pirates ride! Beats it all to hell and back, Joe. And I mean you can take that straight to the bank, little buddy."

Uncle Joe just sat there and stared at that crazy sumbitch cowboy. Trying hard as he could to come up with a snappy comeback . . .

As sometimes happened, Joe found he could supply no further dialogue at the moment.

The big meeting was tomorrow, Monday morning. The first assembly of the loyalists, newly arrived from Moscow. Joe and the Colonel would be briefing the members on the president's grand mission.

The mission Putin called Operation Overkill.

"Hey," Joe said, quaffing his libation, "you want me to introduce you tomorrow morning at the big show? Get you up on the stage, get you in the spotlight, brother. I see you all in black . . . a bullwhip in your hand, silver spurs on the Tony Lamas and—"

Shit Smith looked at Joe like he was plumb crazy. "The spotlight?" he said. "Are you out of your fucking mind? I'm a hired killer. Hired killers stay in the shadows, not in the fucking spotlight!"

"Good point," Joe conceded, thinking maybe he'd had one or two too many icy steins of lager at this point. Order some food, maybe?

This joint was a *bierstube*, Joe had told Shit, what you called a bar in German. It was in the Altstadt, the oldest neighborhood in Zurich. They'd decided to get the hell out of Falcon's Lair on this cold and drizzly Sunday afternoon in early February. Freaking claustrophobic, Joe told Shit.

Shit Smith, a child of the prairie, also had had it about up to here with living inside a fucking mountain. "Ain't natural for folks to live like this, Uncle Joe," he was forever saying to his new best friend. A man needs room to roam around in, air to breathe . . . and, ever now and then, a little strange pussy to tide him over till the snow melts and the cows come home. You with me on that, Joey?"

"Can't argue with that, Shit," Joe said, hearing his own slurred words in his head.

"Can't argue with nothin' old Shit says, Joe. Cause Shit speaks truth to power, goddamn it."

Joe looked across the table at the tall Texan. He was still pushed away from the old wooden table, leaning his chair back precariously on two legs, still smoking a Cuban stogie that Putin had given him after dinner the night before.

"Bullshit, Shit," Joe said.

"What'd you say, l'il podnuh?" the killer said, although it took him almost ten minutes to get the sentence out, along with a cloud of blue smoke.

"I call bullshit. You can't sit over there philosophizing, telling me you kill people for fun."

"I cain't? Well now, that's weird. I thought I could. Who says I cain't, Joe? You?"

Shit slowly plucked the soggy mass of cigar from between his teeth, leaned forward nice and easy, and flicked his grey ashes onto Joe's still-warm beef goulash. Did it like he was casually sprinkling a dish with a dash of seasoning for good measure.

"Goddamn it, Shit!" Joe said. "What'd you go and do that for? I was just getting ready to eat that. Why are you always doing stuff like that, huh?"

" 'Cause I can, little brother, 'cause I can. Lemme tell you a little story, Uncle Joe, set yo wiseass straight about old Shit once and for all. Does that sound good?"

"Go ahead," Joe said, grabbing a passing waiter by the elbow and ordering them another round of beers and another order of *ungarische gulaschsuppe*.

"Well, all right then. This was mebbe a few years ago, y'know, when I was living over to Folsom."

"Folsom, as in jail? Alabama?"

"Keerect. So anyhow, there was this dude on my cellblock. You ever hear of something called Mara Salvatrucha?"

"Who hasn't? MS-13. Probably the most violently dangerous criminal gang in the world. Salvadoran, but sprang up in the Los Angeles barrios. Human trafficing, drugs, murder, torture, hit men, coyotes, et cetera."

"Well, yeah, that's about right. One of the leaders of the MS-13 gang was a cat went by the name of Li'l Chico Perez. One of them light-skinned Puerto Ricans, he was, told me once he was one-eighth Haitian from his mother's side. Forty-something, I dunno, tried to act like a younger cat. Big ole guy, bald-headed, with tats all over his damn face, like a circus freak. Not all that fat, y'know, but had a weird shape on him for a guy, kinda like a woman. Everybody said he was a switch-hitter. Either that, or that he liked little boys."

"Or both, probably," Joe said, into it. Shit could work up a pretty good story when you got him liquored up, all right. Loosened his tongue.

"You got it. One day out in the yard, I saw Chico chatting up a new boy. Fresh meat. Had his arm round the kid's shoulders and was stroking his pretty blond hair, nice and slow, whispering to him, y'know, sweet-talkin' him."

"Got the picture."

"So I walked over to where they was standing and introduced myself, nice and po-lite. Told Chico to get his hands off the boy. Asked him if he had a death wish. Said if I ever saw him do it again, I'd shove a knife so far up his fat ass, come out his nose."

"Damn."

"So a month or so goes by, Chico seems to be leaving the kids alone. Staying on the down-low. And then one night, all of sudden, the fat fuck sends me a message. Courtesy of my cellmate, a quiet type, white teenager from Norman, Oklahoma, all he ever did was read his books, 'never said word one to nobody' kinda kid, you know what I'm sayin?"

"Harmless. An intellectual."

"Uh-huh, something like that, and under my protection. One night, Chucky—that was his name, Chucky—he comes back from the showers, he's crying 'cause he's got blood pouring out of his ass."

"Jesus, Shit, that's terrible."

"Broom handle. I ask him who did it. I ask Chucky what happened. He says he got caught in the shower by three cons. Two held him down while the other ripped up his asshole pretty good. I asked him was the one who did that a fat Puerto Rican who looked like a woman, and he said, 'Yes, sir, Shit, he sure was.'"

"Chico."

"Chico. So the next day I see that lard-ass waddling into chow around lunchtime, getting his tray. Guards weren't paying any attention, shooting the shit with the women working the chow line, serving. Chico's back is to me. I walk up behind him with a shiv in my right hand, real slow. Got close enough to touch and told him to turn around.

" 'Hey, amigo, how you doin'?' I asked him.

" 'Wha—' he said, just before I cut him a brand-new smile just below his fucking chin. His head stayed on, I was surprised to see that, I remember. I thought I'd really done a number on him. I picked up his tray and walked over to get in the mystery meat line, all them MS-13 cons of his giving me the evil eye. I dint pay 'em any attention. I had my own gangbangers, inside the joint and outside the joint, you understand, just as bad as the Salvadorans were, if not worse, and Chico's crew wouldn't touch me. But the warden did. He slapped me into solitary and left me there in that black hole to rot."

"How long?" Joe said, eating his goulash and signaling for another round of lagers.

"Long enough, long enough. When I got out, he says to me in his office one day, he says, 'Shit, I cain't get anyone to tell me they saw you kill Chico. I cain't prove it. And I'm not sorry you did it. But you and I both know you did it.' "

" 'I don't recall,' I told him.

" 'Don't fuck with me, Shit. I'll throw your ass right back in the hole, you do this again. You just can't go around killing folks in my prison.'

"So time goes by, I don't kill anyone else in particular I can think of. But then I come back into the cell one night and find Chucky sitting on the toilet with a book in his lap, dead. Eyes staring wide open and his severed dick stuffed halfway in his mouth. Next day, out in the yard, I helped three MS-13 spics enjoy a one-way ticket to the afterworld."

"What'd the warden do?" Joe asked.

"Warden didn't do shit. Warden had left the day before. He was takin' two weeks off. Had him a cattle ranch down there yonder in central Florida, town named Ocala, near Orlando, you know. Disney World, like I was saying earlier? That old cracker fancied himself a cattle baron. He was real proud of his stock. But when the warden got down there, I just knew that old boy was bound for some major disappointment."

"What?"

"Seems that someone, far be it from me to say just who, had

somehow broken into his stables the night before he arrived, see, and decapitated his prize stallion, Boomerang. And his herd of prized stock? Well, that same person had . . . culled the herd, so to speak. Like every other one . . . damn. Must have galled him no end, right?"

"What did he do when he returned to Folsom?"

"What the hell d'you think he did?"

"Fuckall, I'd guess."

"Nothing, exactly. I goddamn *ran* that prison ever after that. Mara Salvatrucha? Shit, model citizens. And nobody was butt-fucking any youngsters either, nossuh, not after that, I can damn well promise you."

"Damn, Shit. You were a hero," Joe said, suddenly full of admiration.

"Hell, I ain't no hero, Joe. Something like that, though, I guess."

"But you didn't kill those cons for fun, Shit. Think about it. You killed those men for a reason. Revenge. Isn't that right?"

"Tell you what, Joe. 'Stead of me telling you how the old Shit feels about stuff, why don't you do *all* my thinking for me, huh? Yeah, you do it. Tell me what's fun and what ain't. Okay? How about that?"

Joe noticed that after all this time Shit still had the big knife in his hand . . .

"Shit, c'mon. I was just kidding you, man. Playing around. You can't take me seriously when I act like that . . ."

"You know what, Joe. I can't take you seriously when you act like a pussy. You get busy and grow a pair, you and Shit will be bosom buddies. Until then, amigo? You familiar with the old expression 'Go fuck yerself'?"

And then those two black eyes . . . twin tunnels straight to the fires of hell. Joe stood up, looking around the dimly lit bar.

"Will you excuse me, Shit? Gotta hit the latrine, man."

"Ain't no excuse for you," Shit mumbled as Joe got out of his chair. His eyes closed and he was off in Shit Land somewhere.

CHAPTER SIXTY-THREE

Falcon's Lair

Well, the stage was finally set for the first of what would be many orientation meetings for what Joe had taken to calling Putin's High Command here at Falcon's Lair. Now taking their seats in the screening auditorium was Putin's highly prized brain trust, comprised of men and women of all stripes, from every strata of Russian society.

Assembling in the ornate and gilded screening room, stadium seating, now reconfigured as the war room, were the newly reconstituted Putin loyalists, as they called themselves. The room was very luxurious, complete with fifty maroon velvet armchairs and a screen to rival IMAX.

These were men and women secretly plucked from the top ranks of Russian industry, Kremlin operatives, KGB intelligence and military operations officers, including some of the country's most revered military commanders on the ground and in the air.

Fifty handpicked men and women, a new Russian warrior class that would now gather intelligence inside Russia and out, analyze it assiduously, formulate an invasion strategy, plan the attacks, and lastly, implement phase one of Putin's ultimate objective: his triumphant return to power at the Kremlin in Moscow.

Joe Stalingrad, Putin's newly appointed chairman of the operations committee, and today, master of ceremonies, was backstage, peeking through the curtain as the room filled up. The space was buzzing with energy and curiosity about what many felt was sure to be a seminal event in the annals of political history. But what would it be and who had invited them all here? That was still the big mystery.

At one end of the room, there was a small stage. A gleaming mahogany podium was emblazoned with the solid gold Russian coat of arms, dating back to the fifteenth century: the imperial double-headed eagle.

Joe was a tad nervous about the wardrobe he'd chosen for today's grand event, to be honest. The president wanted this meeting to go off without the slightest hint of a hitch. And he'd made Joe run all the arrangements—the audiovisual stuff, the order of presentation, all that—by him. Even the place cards for the evening banquet.

But Joe knew showmanship, if nothing else, and he knew getting the audience revved up simply demanded you push the envelope a little, go above and beyond, as they say. And so he had decided not to run what he planned to wear today by the president. Privately? He thought Putin was a bit of a whack job. A conundrum wrapped in a mystery wrapped in bacon.

Besides, he'd wanted to wear something dramatic today. What was called for today was something that was . . . what was the phrase he was looking for? Showstoppery?

Yeah, that was it.

Showstoppery would do nicely, he told himself, trying to relax. Besides, he thought he looked rather dashing in his chosen costume. It was something that might even appeal to the lovely Miss Emma Peek, who'd had her left hand on Joe's thigh all through her dinner with Putin over on the island at Villa Seegarten last night . . .

Putin had noticed. Irritated, jealous, all night long, staring at the two of them across the table, watching the gorgeous woman (whom Joe knew Putin believed he was entitled to, droit du seignure and all that). Emma making goo-goo eyes at him all night. Joe knew he'd have to watch his step down this lovely road to love.

Joe Stalingrad's last picture, *Little Patton*, had been pitched to the media, *Deadline Hollywood*, *Variety*, et cetera, as a "star vehicle" for Joe's rising star. But it had never been released to the cinema, never seen by anyone other than crabby airline passengers packed into sardine class on Delta.

But, but, but. Some good had come out of it, he thought, checking his action in the full-length mirror.

His wardrobe mistress had forgotten to pick up his *Little Patton* costume after the film had wrapped. It was quite striking—namely, a khaki shirt, dark brown jodhpurs, and knee-high, mirror-polished riding boots. And, last but not least, on his head a highly polished chromed parade helmet!

All that were missing were the Sam Browne belt, the swagger stick, and the gold-plated Smith & Wesson .357. Those beauties he'd left on his bed back at Seegarten. A little over the top, maybe. What the French call de trop, too much, even for Joe.

So he'd wow 'em, all right, the audience, but how would the boss react to Joe's brand of Hollywood showmanship? That's the question he had on his mind as he prepared to part the lush velvet curtains and Little Patton stepped out into the spotlight.

De trop, certainly for Putin.

"What the fuck, Joe?" the wide-eyed president said, finding him backstage just before he'd gone out, mouthing the words so that only Joe could hear them. "You can't go out there looking like that! A Patton lookalike? What kind of a signal does that send, Joe? Tell me!"

Joe just waved this off and gave the boss a big smile just before parting the curtains and stepping onstage and approaching the podium. He grabbed the microphone dramatically, saying, "Cue the music!" with a signal to the AV guy up in the booth at the top of the steep steps.

Speakers everywhere boomed. Wagner's "Ride of the Valkyries" exploded inside the auditorium and the audience suddenly came alive, all eyes on the man in the strange costume at center stage.

"And good morning, everyone! Great to be with you!" Joe said with enormous gusto, speaking directly into the microphone. "For those of you who don't know me, I'm Joe Stalingrad and—"

A ripple of applause coursed through the crowd, rising to a swell as more and more recognized the president's formerly powerful henchman and aide-de-camp.

"Thank you! Thank you!" Joe said, with a smile a mile wide. "Thank you! I do see some familiar faces out there! How's everybody doing?"

More applause.

"For those of you I've not yet met, I'm the former Kremlin senior counsel and aide to our beloved president. Ladies and gentlemen, let me first take the opportunity to welcome you to Falcon's Lair. You have the honor of knowing you were handpicked to be here today for this historic conference. You've read all the materials. And the endless memos from yours truly. You know why we're here: because, ladies and gentlemen, we are going to make Moscow great again!"

A surge of laughter and applause that was music to Joe's ears. He hoped Putin was catching all this.

"Because, folks, we've got what it takes. We've got the skills to achieve something heroic here. We've got the talent. We've got the will. And we've got the epic courage that will be necessary to . . . take our country back! That's right. You heard me. What are we going to do?"

"Take our country back!" they screamed in unison. "Take our country back, take our country back!" they chanted until he waved them silent.

"But you know, there's just one thing missing, folks. One piece of the puzzle . . . and that's someone who is uniquely qualified to bring us all together. Tough enough to see us through the darkest hours. And see us on to victory!"

"Make Moscow great again!" they roared. "Take our country back!"

"And so now, ladies and gentlemen . . . are you ready for this?"

"Yes!" to the rafters.

"Are you *really* ready?" Cue the orchestra . . .

Cheers, whistles, and shouts.

Joe walked back to the velvet curtains and grabbed a handful, waiting for the suspense to reach the breaking point . . .

"Ladies and gentlemen, true Russian patriots all, it is my very great honor and privilege to introduce you to a man the whole world believes they've seen the last of . . . But! Guess what?" Joe said and cupped one hand behind his ear, waiting for the crowd to answer . . .

"What? What?" they cried, now on the edge of their seats. Joe grabbed the mike.

"Ladies and gentlemen! . . . *He's baaaaack!*"

That did it. The crowd lost it completely. Screaming and cheering for the hero they all thought they'd lost forever.

"You heard me right!" Joe said, grabbing a handful of velvet and whipping the curtain back. "Let's give it up for our beloved leader and great president, Vladimir Putin! Please come on out here, Mr. President, and take a bow!"

He stepped from behind the curtain and into the spotlight . . . and there he was, bathed in glory.

At first there was shocked silence. It took a moment for them all to process that the fallen leader was actually alive! Not only alive, but *here*. Was it possible? Was that really him? Here?

In their midst!

That's when Joe had his moment of inspiration. He stepped to the microphone and—

"Shall we ask him to say a few words, ladies and gentlemen? I know he's going to be back here on stage in a short time, but . . . Mr. President, the microphone is yours."

"My dear friends and comrades, it is the greatest honor of my life to stand here before you here today. And I will tell you this much.

Our enemies think they've won this battle. But they have no idea what they're up against! Because . . . *We have not even begun to fight!*"

A woman screamed. The next instant, the roar of the crowd was instantaneous and it filled every cubic foot of space in the room as they leapt to their feet. A standing ovation, everyone cheering and clapping as loudly as they could. Putin, unaccustomed to this kind of outpouring of heartfelt affection, was taken aback. He turned and faced them, raising his hands for them to stop, but not really wanting to . . .

"President Vladimir Vladimirovich Putin, ladies and gentlemen!" Joe shouted above the cacophony. "Take a bow, Mr. President, they love you!"

The roar, and it truly was a *roar*, had the audience cupping their hands over their ears for fear of losing their hearing.

When Putin was finally returned to his seat in the first row and the crowd had quieted, Joe leaned into the microphone, pushed a button on the podium calling up the first slide, the new Falcon's Lair logo, and said, "As your president has just told you, we are gathered here today to embark on a historic mission. An epic mission that will require all that's the best of the best of us. A bold, daring mission that will, ladies and gentlemen, restore Vladimir Vladimirovich Putin to his rightful position as the leader of our beloved motherland . . . the presidency of Russia!"

Back on their feet, and shouting oaths of loyalty, the loyalists again showed their fervor for the mission.

Joe's gamble had paid off. He'd been right: Play to vanity and you play to win.

He cued the Valkyries music again, the volume set at eleven, and hit the button that called up the second slide on the oversize screen:

Operation Overkill

CHAPTER SIXTY-FOUR

Operation Overkill!" Joe shouted, hardly needing the PA system now, both hands raised above his head in the old Tricky Dick, Nixonian "V for Victory" salute. "And Overkill is just the beginning of the long road back to Moscow. Because, ladies and gentlemen . . . wait for it . . . cue the video, please . . ."

Suddenly the giant screen was filled with a sweeping panoramic video of the Swiss Alps. It was an aerial view, shot on a crystal blue day, the mountains at their snowy, wintry best. Joe'd picked the footage deliberately, choosing a breathtaking view of the Great St. Bernard Pass, the highest in the country, in the canton of Valais.

"Here at Falcon's Lair, we call our sacred mission Operation Overkill because . . ." he said, bringing up a bright red title over the picture of the Alps . . .

The Road to Moscow
Runs Through Switzerland!

"The road to Moscow runs through Switzerland!" he shouted.

"And with that, I'd like to introduce you to the man who has been chosen by our beloved president to lead us down that road, the first leg of our epic march on Moscow.

"A gallant soldier of fortune, an American warrior of the first rank, a man legendary for his leadership skills, his granite-like determination to win, and his prowess on the world's battlefields. One European newspaper, citing his brilliant victories over jihadis in Afghanistan, called him the American Alexander the Great! I call him our own General George S. Patton for the twenty-first century! And I'm wearing this uniform today as a way of showing my enormous respect.

"So without further ado, may I present to you a man the president and I have come to respect and revere . . . ladies and gentlemen, I give you . . . Colonel Brett Beauregard! Come on out here, Colonel, give the delegates a good look at you!"

The maroon velvet curtains slowly parted as the music swelled to a cresting crescendo of martial splendor. Out strode the colonel. He was a hard-boned Marlboro Man, well over six feet, dressed in full battle camouflage and regalia, combat boots, and a battered Aussie battle hat, pinned up on one side. In a holster, a Colt Army .45 with ivory grips, no less.

His powerfully jutting chin, his barrel-like physique, and his wide, white-toothed smile had the audience in the palm of his hand before he even opened his mouth.

Guy's a rock star, Joe was thinking. Putin had called it right on this one. Beau, Joe knew at that very early moment, was going to pull off Putin's outrageous plans, about to be unveiled to the loyalists. Certainly he was the one man eminently capable of executing such a feat with any reasonable chance of success.

Beau grabbed the mike by the throat and let it rip: "Good morning! Good morning, Mr. President, Chairman Stalingrad! I want to say it is my very great honor and pleasure to be here on this historic occasion. I say *historic*, because we are about to embark on an epic voyage that will carry all of us and your beloved president home again. Home to his rightful place in the motherland, home to his rightful place on the world's stage.

"And that voyage, as the chairman has just informed you, begins today. When I told the president that he had my full support, he agreed to create a military force consisting of light infantry; an air wing; a paratroop division; and a lightweight, highly mobile artillery brigade. Folks, this is what I do for a living. And, I can guarantee you that as sure as I'm standing here, I will deliver on my promise to President Putin. You heard me. I'm going to build the greatest private army the world has ever seen! And we will—let me say that again—*we will put our hero back in the Kremlin! And we will destroy anyone who tries to get in our way!*"

The standing ovation for Colonel Beauregard lasted at least seven minutes by Joe's count. When it was winding down, Joe took to the microphone to call the house to order.

"Thank you, thank you, Colonel," Joe said. "Isn't he something else? I'm telling you . . . right, Colonel, take a bow. You deserve it . . . sensational, just a sensational guy, ladies and gentlemen . . ."

When all of them had returned to their seats, Joe brought up a new slide. It was a picture of a mountain of gold bars stored under bright lights in some kind of underground cavern.

"Gold, ladies and gentlemen, is the foundation upon which Operation Overkill will be built. Yes, *gold*, you heard right. Stolen gold, as you will learn in a few moments. Stolen from the president himself! In order for Colonel Beauregard to fulfill his mission, he needs money. A hell of a lot of money.

"Now, it's no secret that President Putin is still a very wealthy man. What many of you don't know is that a lot of his personal wealth mysteriously vanished during his last year in office. It was stolen. Let me be perfectly clear. The president's gold was stolen from his private Russian vaults right here in Switzerland by the president's enemies! Stolen and transferred to their own treasure vaults by the vile Russian oligarchy, men who, having ousted our president, are feverishly working now to seize the reins of power from Medvedev and thus the Kremlin.

"They are rushing to permanently secure the Kremlin before President Putin has a chance to gather his forces and return to defeat them! That's why this mission, Operation Overkill, is so urgent, ladies and gentlemen! That's why we need to act now! Let's talk for a moment about the oligarchy . . ."

CHAPTER SIXTY-FIVE

Yes," Joe continued, "the oligarchy, a tiny, insular section of the vast population of Russia, enormously wealthy, enormously powerful, and which now, having successfully removed the president from power, has expressed its determination to rule the country from behind a curtain, through the machinations of their traitorous cronies inside the Kremlin.

"This is why they forced the president to abdicate from his office.

"These oligarchs, these are the men, ladies and gentlemen, formerly loyal to the president when he was making them vastly rich, who are now responsible for the numerous plots, attempted coups, poisonings of men loyal to the president, and failed assassination attempts on the president's life.

"Now, when our enemies had the president back on his heels, what did they do? They robbed him blind! That's what they did! They stole all of his goddamn gold!

"These corrupt, treacherous, and vile human beings are our immutable enemies, ladies and gentlemen, and believe me when I tell you that they will rue the day they took up arms against Vladimir Putin. Of *that* I can assure you!"

After the applause died down, Stalingrad continued his presentation.

"I said that gold was key," he told them. "And then I ask you, 'Well, then, where the hell is all this gold?' Well, it's right here under your feet. Some of it, anyway. President Putin, will you please join me on the stage?"

Putin smiled and nodded his head. Clearly happy with the way the morning was going, especially the reaction of his loyalists to the team he'd assembled. That had been critical, and both the chairman and the colonel had done extremely well despite their somewhat bizarre apparel.

He got to his feet and took the microphone.

THE GREETING FOR THE PRESIDENT was immediate and wildly enthusiastic. When they finally quieted, he spoke. "Good morning, everyone, and welcome to my home away from home. I call it Falcon's Lair. I hope you're finding your accommodations comfortable and the food to your liking. I never imagined I would find myself an innkeeper. And I can only say to you, 'How the mighty have fallen!'

"I was forced into exile. I hid for a time in a tiny woodsman's cabin in France. But I never, not for one moment, forgot my mission—to one day regain power in the Kremlin. And so I spent those long and lonely days and nights putting together the plan to accomplish that mission. That's why I invited you here. To share that plan with you, hear any and all input this august body can bring to the table, and adjust the plan accordingly. You're all the experts in your respective fields. Your advice will be priceless.

"Here at Falcon's Lair, I have turned an outdated communications level into a place for you all to live and work in comfort. First-rate dormitories for men and women, each with its own kitchen and dining hall. As you'll be working here for a lengthy time, I've done all I can to make you as comfortable as possible."

He grinned and they loved him and he basked in the glow of it.

"The road ahead is long and treacherous and fraught with danger. And yet a finger of history beckons. And as you have heard this morning, that long, long road leads through Switzerland. Now why is that important?"

"Seventy percent of the world's physical gold lies within these Swiss borders. Within these very Alps! Beneath your feet! And that amount includes gold stolen from your president, worth many billions and subsequently smuggled out of Russia and hidden in various locations around Switzerland.

"So where is it? Deep inside hollowed-out mountain storage facilities whose locations are top secret, locations guarded ferociously by the Swiss army, the Swiss government, and the nation's seven-hundred-year-old banking establishment.

"But now it's time for me to share a little secret with my newly appointed Falcon's Lair loyalists. I know where it is! I already know where all this gold is hidden! Including vast stocks of gold that rightly belong to the president.

"You are wondering how I came by this knowledge. I will tell you how. There is a man of my acquaintance, an elderly man now, but once the most powerful man in all of Europe. They all called him the Sorcerer, because that's what he was. He was a wizard of wisdom and a great repository of secrets. There was nothing that went on in the world of high finance and global banking that he was not privy to . . .

"And he lived for many, many years—indeed, until very recently—right here inside this very mountain. This was his beloved home. And now it is mine. My refuge, my fortress, my castle. I will not tell you how much I paid for the privilege of living here. The number would stagger you . . .

"The acquisition negotiations were handled for me by your own chairman Joseph Stalingrad. When the deal closed, Joe handed the Sorcerer a sealed envelope. Even Joe did not know the contents. But inside that envelope was a document that stated that the sale of

Falcon's Lair was contingent upon, not only the previously agreed upon terms, but upon the signed agreement to my terms as put forth in the enclosed contract.

"I said I wanted detailed information about all of the various mountain vaults where the oligarchs had stashed my gold. I wanted real-time pictures of the actual sites where my gold was hidden. I wanted GPS coordinates of the vaults, I wanted access codes, I wanted detailed blueprints of every single security system. And I wanted to know the disposition of the guards, their schedules, and their weaponry. Were there SAM emplacements at some of the higher elevations? Radar? Sonar . . .

"I demanded everything. And I got it. Colonel Beauregard and his team have put together a short video, showing aerial footage of the three sites, their weapons installations, their disposition of military forces, their security systems, changes of the guards, and what lies behind all those thick titanium doors.

"This video lays out visually all of the targets to be looted in Operation Overkill. Complete details about each site's security, access codes, et cetera, are in the blue binders you found on your seats. So, Joe, I'll turn it back to you. And I want to thank each and every one of you very much for your loyalty, your commitment, and your time. I look forward to seeing all of you at the cocktail party this evening. Seven o'clock in the ballroom at the residence."

Joe took the mike. "And now I'd like to invite Colonel Beauregard back up here to the podium. The colonel here is on his way to Siberia in a few days. Build us a fighting force we can all be proud of. Come on up, Colonel . . ."

Beauregard, picturing himself as MacArthur returning to Corregidor, strode up to the podium, adjusting the mike to suit him. "Thank you, Mr. President. And now I'm going take you all through a visual timeline of Operation Overkill. We'll dwell for a few minutes on each target, discussing how best to breach it. Because, as you saw earlier, the road to Moscow flows through Switzerland!

"Roll the film," he said, and began his twenty-minute narration, revealing their targets and military objectives, outlining in detail the impending invasion of Switzerland . . .

The lights came up as the video faded from the supersize screen. Joe knew it was his time to rally the troops around his particular flag. He puffed out his chest and said, "We will get inside Swiss borders. We will fight. We will fight in the air and we will fight on the land; we will fight *under* the ground. And we *will never quit*. Not until we have located and recovered the president's stolen gold, his precious gold. We will then take all the money, however much it takes, take what we need in order to build our mighty new invasion force. And then we will get the hell out and begin the ultimate march, the march on Moscow!"

Cheers and shouts filled the stadium to the rafters, and an empowered Colonel Beauregard shouted, "Will Europe be shocked, shocked that someone invaded their precious Switzerland? Stole some gold? Certainly. Will the world be outraged? Of course. But I tell you this, ladies and gentlemen . . . It's my gold! And by the time they get their forces mobilized, our forces will all be gone . . . and en route to Moscow!

"And think of this. What the *hell* can they do about it?"

CHAPTER SIXTY-SIX

Hawkesmoor, England

Days passed, but all of Hawke's efforts to find his son, aided by the CIA, by Congreve, by INTERPOL, and a small team of Scotland Yard detectives, all on the trail of Uncle Joe and his young captive, had turned up nothing. One wild-goose chase had taken two detectives to Hollywood; another led to St. Petersburg in Russia, birthplace of Vladimir Putin; and still another to Moscow itself.

All for naught.

Midnight came and went.

Hawke lay on his back, hands behind his head, staring at the ceiling, where the dying embers in the fireplace cast their flickering orangish glow. The ticking of the clock on the mantel was incessant. He considered going over to the drinks table and pouring himself a slug of sleep potion, then pushed that idea aside.

He was trying to watch his alcohol consumption during this time of trial. He needed all of his faculties firing on all cylinders all the time. Sooner or later, he was bound to catch a break. Uncle Joe would trip over himself somehow, Hawke believed, reaching for his cigarettes and lighting one up, inhaling deeply, feeling the burn . . .

Ah, his only remaining vice.

He turned over, stubbed out the cigarette, and pulled open the drawer in his bedside table, fumbling in the dark until his fingers found the scented pale blue envelope. He withdrew it and clasped it to his chest for a few moments, letting his nicotine heart slow down a bit, hoping the unfinished and unsent letter inside would again bring him a trace of solace.

He flicked on the sconce on the wall above his head and began to read.

The Gardener's Cottage

My dearest darling,

I know you are still angry with me. If I could rewrite history, erase that horrid night in St. Moritz when I confessed all to you, I would do it. My fervent hope is that somehow, with the passage of time, your heart will soften toward me. But how shall I ever prove what is in my heart to you? How will you ever again see it as I feel it? I only know that no man was ever before to any woman what you are to me . . . and still—

Your angry words pierce my very soul. I am half agony, half hope. Tell me, darling, please tell me that I am not too late! That such precious feelings as we two shared are not gone forever. I am rent asunder by the loss of you . . . I have come unmoored.

Shall I offer myself to you again, with a tattered heart even less my own now than when you almost shattered it, all those weeks ago?

Dare not say that woman forgets love sooner than man, that her love has an earlier death . . .

I have loved none but you,

Sigrid

PS:

It's morning now. I've collected myself. Don't worry about me, darling. I shall soon disappear. Go off the grid, as you would say, Commander Hawke. I know a little place by the sea where I can hide for a while. Somewhere peaceful where I continue on the mission I have recently undertaken. A sacred mission whose success might yet bring me back into the folds of your loving heart . . .

Hawke, a solitary tear streaming down his stubbled cheek, folded the letter, fit it into the envelope, and replaced it in the drawer, his mind racing his heart for control of his emotions.

He saw words, phrases lifted from the letter drifting like scattered clouds before his eyes:

disappear . . . a little place by the sea . . . a sacred mission . . .

"Christ!" He sat straight up in bed, switched on the lamp, and reached for his phone. He was never able to memorize phone numbers, but this one he knew by heart.

"Hullo," came the sleepy voice of his new pilot, Artemis Cooper.

"Artemis, it's Hawke. Sorry to bother you at this ungodly hour . . ."

"Not a problem, sir. What can I do for you?"

"How's the fuel in the Blue Streak?"

"Tanks topped off, sir. Always. Where are we going?"

"Africa."

"Excellent. Which part?"

"Not quite sure yet, Artemis. Need your help. There's a small village in Morocco, just up the coast from Casablanca. I can't recall the name precisely . . . started with an *A*, wouldn't you know it, like a hundred other Moroccan villages. Alsalla? Something like that. Locate a strip somewhere nearby Marrakech that can accommodate the plane."

"Absolutely. I'll find it, sir."

"Good. Next, call the La Mamounia hotel in Marrakech. Book garden rooms for you, me, and the copilot. Three or four days, something like that. Get the concierge to have a rental car delivered to the hotel for our arrival . . . four-wheel drive, off-road capability . . . I'm going to need your help, Artemis, both of you guys. We need to cover a lot of territory."

"May I ask what we're looking for, sir?"

"Yes. We're looking for a woman. Her name is Sigrid Kissl. She flew with us once, from Zurich to England. Remember? Blond? Beautiful?"

"With all due respect, sir, how could I forget her?"

"Right, Artemis. That's my problem exactly. How can anyone forget her?"

CHAPTER SIXTY-SEVEN

La Mamounia, Marrakech

The lobby bar at La Mamounia is called the Churchill Bar for a very good reason. During World War II, the darkly paneled lounge had been the site of many top-secret meetings. This historic spot is where Franklin Roosevelt and Winston Churchill would meet periodically throughout the war. It was here, in this very room, at this very table, probably over a couple of whiskey Rob Roys, that the two giants hammered out options for the deepest military secret on earth, the impending invasion of Normandy.

Today, framed black-and-white portraits of the two heroes are hung with pride on all the walls. Rain-sweet air, wafting in from the gardens, pours through opened French doors, scented with ginger and orange blossoms. This room had borne witness to some of the most historic and momentous secrets in human history. And a memory of secrecy lingered yet, a tribute to the power of the towering human spirit, seen here in its finest hours.

They'd all three checked into their rooms, unpacked, showered, and shaved after the longish flight from England to Africa. The maître d' had showed them to a prize banquette table in a sunlit corner of the bar, one overlooking abundant gardens where rain dripped off the sour orange trees.

The three Englishmen turned a lot of feminine heads as they strode past the bar to their seats. Hawke, of course, one of those rare chaps who could well be considered beautiful as well as being among the most dangerous of men. Born in the calm eye of a hurricane, Hawke, all dimples and charm, was, as his father had announced at the hour of his arrival, "a boy born with a heart for any fate."

But also his lordship's two pilots were both ruggedly handsome fellows in their own right. Formidable men who carried themselves as befit their rank. They were young, recently retired RAF fighter pilots, veterans who'd completed special ops missions in Afghanistan with their counterparts at SAS. A pair of swaggering badasses, as Stoke would call them—cocky, yes, but agreeably cocky.

"What are you drinking, Johnnie-boy?" Hawke asked Johnnie Walker, his blond-maned copilot, after they were seated. At his signal, an elegant Moroccan gentleman in a green felt jacket with shiny brass buttons, hovering nearby, handed them lavish dinner menus and disappeared.

"Iced tea, sir. No sugar, please," said the un-aptly named Lieutenant Johnnie Walker, RAF ret., a wide white smile appearing on his deeply tanned and handsome face.

"Good. How about you, Artemis?"

"Same thing, please, sir."

"All right. Now that I've got that tiresome obligation out of the way, I can order myself a nice cocktail. Sun's over the yardarm somewhere in the British Empire I should think. Don't you gentlemen agree?"

Both men nodded and Hawke signaled to the barman to render much-needed assistance.

A waiter was summoned and Hawke gave the jolly little fellow in the bright red fez their order. Forgoing iced tea, he ordered his cocktail of choice, a Dark 'n' Stormy made with muddled lime, ginger beer, and Gosling's Black Seal 151. The best rum, Hawke believed, and Bermuda rum, of course.

"Question, sir," Johnnie Walker said. "If I may?"

"Fire at will," Hawke replied.

"That expression you used, sir. 'The sun is over the yardarm somewhere.' I've always wondered at that, sir. Could you please explain it?"

"Certainly. It's an old Royal Navy expression. Used by ships' officers on station in the far-flung corners of the once mighty British empire. Traditionally, a sailor never took a drink until the sun was over the yardarm. The senior officer who is saying the phrase means, if it's time for a drink in Singapore, it's jolly well time for a drink in the West Indies. Because, somewhere in the British Empire, the sun is most definitely over the yardarm of some Royal Navy vessel. Good for one, good for all."

"In what way, sir? Don't mean to be dense."

"The yardarm was one of the horizontal spars high up the stick on the old square-riggers. If the sun dips below the yardarm, that means it's past noon. Time for a gin and bitters, you see. Or in my case, a tot of rum."

"Ah, yes. Officers still allowed to drink on board, are they, sir?"

"Only in one instance, Johnnie. Upon returning to home port from extended combat duty abroad. The U.S. Navy has the same standard. Now, let's get down to cases. You've brought along your side arms, I trust?"

"Sir, just to remind you," Artemis said, "we are both well-armed at all times."

"Of course. One of the reasons I hired you, Artemis," Hawke said with a wry smile. "A chap never knows when a couple of extra guns might come in handy."

"Speaking of which, sir," Artemis said, pulling a map from the inside pocket of his khaki jacket, "I've brought along the map I've been using to plot out our route tomorrow morning . . . coastal towns with names that begin with *A* and are possible locations are circled in red crayon."

"Very low-tech, skipper," Johnnie Walker said. "A paper map? I like it."

"Yes, I'm old school. Okay, look here, sir, you see this is the nearest *A* town. Just about an hour out. What time shall we get started in the morning? First light?"

"Dawn. It could be a long day. You chaps should keep your eyes open out on the highway and open roads. Our Muscovite friend Vladimir has already come after the chief inspector and me once down in Italy. And just last week he sent two unsavory Cuban fellows to the Florida Keys in an assassination attempt, thwarted, thank god, by Stokely Jones Jr. Vlad is gearing up for something big and he doesn't want me or my associates putting their noses where they don't belong. If you see something, say something."

"Yes, sir," Artemis said. "Saw a chappie in the lobby when we were checking in that I didn't particularly like the looks of, Commander. He was sitting in the red silk armchair chatting up the concierge."

"Did you see his skin?" Johnnie Walker said. "His face looked like lacquered walnut meat."

Hawke looked at the two pilots. "Chechen, by the looks of him. Short and swarthy, forty-something, with pomaded black hair? Yeah. I made him, too. Anyway, caution is called for, gents. As my dear friend Ambrose Congreve would have it, 'The game is afoot . . .' "

"Aye aye, sir," Johnnie Walker said, "it is indeed."

Eventually they moved on to an early dinner outside beneath the orange trees. Hawke gave them a highly edited version of the story of Sigrid's disappearance here in Morocco. He purposefully left out his oft-recurring suspicions about her complicity in the matter. That she had perhaps murdered her torturer and extortionist out of sheer desperation. He knew people who had killed for less, much less.

By midnight, all three men had been sound asleep for three hours.

THEY DROVE INTO THE CENTER of the first *A* town shortly after dawn broke the sky wide open. A thick drizzle from the sky, like a curtain's sudden sweeping. A cold front sweeping in on the coast had brought thunderstorms and lightning, and sheets of rain made driving extraordinarily difficult. And dangerous. Visibility had been at a minimum most of the way to their destination. Hawke could not remember enduring a storm with such ferocity.

But it wasn't the visibility in front of them that bothered Hawke, who was behind the wheel of the Toyota Land Cruiser. It was the lack of visibility in his rearview mirrors. There could be a car tailing him a hundred or so yards back there and he'd never know it.

With some difficulty, they located the entrance to the town's little public beach, parked, donned their ponchos, and made their way down to the sea. Rollers were breaking high on the sand, and the wind was whipping up rooster tails all along the incoming parade of waves storming ashore.

"Small white house with a red peaked roof, right on the sea . . . that's what we're looking for," Hawke said, using his right hand as a shield in an attempt to keep the rain from stinging his eyes. He and Artemis had taken the lead, with Johnnie covering their rear flank.

"Not much luck with single houses here, mostly just these small tourist hotels," Hawke said.

"Yes," the pilot replied, shouting to be heard above the thunder. "Where the hell is Johnnie?"

They both turned at the sound of muffled voices back there somewhere, sources of which made invisible by the grey fog of rain swirling around them.

"I got a white house!" he and Artemis heard Johnnie cry. "Peaked roof, maybe red, can't tell from down here. Going up to higher ground to get a look at it . . . You guys go on ahead, I'll catch up."

And then, maybe less than a minute later, shots rang out in the fog.

"Good god, go see if you can find him, Artemis," Hawke said. "You go that way along the shorebreak, I'll go up along the dunes . . ."

CHAPTER SIXTY-EIGHT

Coast of Morroco

Johnnie! Johnnie!" Artemis shouted, racing off into the dense fog. He sprinted in the direction the shots had come from. More shots rang out, one, two more, and then there came the awful screams and cries of a horribly wounded man . . .

Hawke raced across the dunes, taking a different tack than the one Artemis had chosen, hoping to come up behind whoever was doing the shooting.

"Artemis, where are you?" Hawke cried, almost tripping over a piece of driftwood he hadn't seen until too late. "Any sight of Johnnie?"

"Keep coming this way, sir!" he heard Artemis cry out. "I'm moving along the seawall now, looking for—oh, god! Oh, Jesus Christ, no . . . ah, *fuck*!"

Hawke could just make him out a little now, kneeling on the sand beside Johnnie, who was on his back.

"Look what they did to him, sir. Look what they did to my friend . . ."

"Call an ambulance, Artemis. Call the Marrakech police . . ."

Artemis whipped out his mobile and made the calls.

Hawke dropped to his knees and felt for the boy's pulse, trying not to gag at the sight of his young copilot. Hawke had seen horrific battlefield injuries in his day, but he'd never seen butchery as savage or as frenzied as this, nothing remotely close.

"Did you catch sight of whoever did this, Artemis?" Hawke asked.

"No. But there was a boxy grey sedan idling up there on the road along the seawall. I heard a door slam just as I saw Johnnie sprawled on the ground. I looked up. I could only make out the silhouette of someone behind the wheel.

"A heavyset man, not tall. But the passenger, yes. He was tall and slim, wearing boots and some kind of western hat, black, with the brim pulled low over his eyes. Then the car raced away, disappeared into the fog."

"Think, Artemis. Could the driver have been the Chechen we all saw in the lobby yesterday?"

"Could well have been, sir."

The tall man had apparently used a knife. The shots fired in the mist had all been from Johnnie's 9mm side arm, still clenched in his cold, dead fingers.

A brutal blade had ripped him open from his sternum to his waist, then hacked at him until his torso was unrecognizable. Hawke looked at the corpse the killer or killers had left behind and knew instantly that, whoever they were, they were sending him a signal. Then he tore his eyes away from the gore and looked up at the house looming above them atop the seawall.

It was white, just as Johnnie had said right before he died.

And it had a peaked red roof.

Was this even remotely possible? Finding the house at the first village? Of course it was.

AFTER THE RAIN, NOW, BRIEFLY, SUN.

After the ambulance had removed Johnnie's mutilated body and the local constabulary's detectives had finished their exhaustive crime-scene investigative interviews and the collection of forensic evidence, Hawke and Artemis repaired to a small café on the shady square just opposite the little white house.

The front door was a shade of blue Hawke was pretty sure was called robin's egg. Could Sigrid be somewhere behind that door? His mind raced ahead. One way or another, he would soon find out.

They ordered coffee and soup and the chicken tagine, as it was nearly lunchtime. Alone with their thoughts, the two men ate in silence. Artemis was plainly grieving the heartbreaking loss of Johnnie Walker, but Hawke saw fury battling heartbreak in those clear blue eyes of his.

Hawke kept his eyes on the house across the square, convincing himself that at any minute Sigrid herself might step through that blue door over there and emerge into the dappled sunshine.

"The driver was the same meaty chap from the lobby yesterday," Hawke finally said to Artemis. "I can still see him."

Hawke knew his pilot was surely having the same thoughts he himself was having: who might have killed his friend and comrade-in-arms?

"Most likely the same bloke, sir. Followed us, do you think?"

"Easy enough for him to follow us all the way from the car park at La Mamounia without being spotted. Not in that downpour."

"Let's have a chat with that concierge when we get back to the hotel and—"

The blue door cracked open about a foot and then stopped.

"Artemis, the blue door," Hawke suddenly said, gripping the pilot's forearm and half coming up out of his chair. "Opening."

And then it opened wide. A child, a little blond girl of no more than five or six, stepped outside into the spotty sun, a large white cat in her arms. She bent over and carefully placed the cat on the stone flags. Something, a voice from inside the door, made her turn around.

Then Hawke saw a woman appear. She with the red-gold hair, burnished by the sun, appearing in the doorway. She bent down and swooped both the little girl and her cat into her sunburnt arms. She looked around carefully and then crossed the street to the shady side.

There she entered a baker's shop, child and cat still in her arms.

"It's her, isn't it, sir?" Artemis asked. "Sigrid Kissl."

"Yes, it is indeed," Hawke said, his Arctic blue eyes transfixed, his mind spinning. God, he thought, did she now have a child he didn't know about? A whole secret life here in this tiny village? A husband? Did she—

Minutes later, she emerged from the baker's shop. She carried only two baguettes in a paper sack. The child and her cat remained inside the shop. Pausing in the baker's doorway, pinning up her hair, she looked both ways before crossing the busy street.

She fished a key from her handbag, unlocked the blue door, and slipped inside.

CHAPTER SIXTY-NINE

W ait here," Hawke said to Artemis after downing what was left of his cold coffee. "Keep an eye out for the grey sedan. Just in case the Chechen and the cowboy should decide it's a good idea to return to the scene of the crime. It happens a good deal more than you'd think."

"Good idea, sir. Take your time over there. I know how much this means to you."

"Thanks. You see anything out here in the square I need to know about, my mobile will be on. I'm sorry about Johnnie, Artemis. I liked him a lot, too. But, you know, I can be an avenging angel when I set my mind to it."

"Thank you, sir. I'll keep that in mind," Artemis said, smiling as Hawke got up and left the table. The pilot watched his lordship cross the street and rap on the blue door.

A moment later, the door opened.

"Oh!" the woman said, taking a step back. "Oh, my god. It can't be. Alex . . . how did you—"

"I found this . . ." he said, pulling the pale blue envelope from inside his breast pocket. "Up in your bedroom at Brixden House Gardener's Cottage."

"Oh? Oh . . . Yes. I . . . I guess I never intended to mail it. But in my heart, I always prayed that you might be curious about my rooms at the Gardener's Cottage . . . that you might even find my unsent letter. Might try to find me and—"

"I've read it a hundred times. I had to come! Had to see if I could find you. I didn't care how long it took. I only knew I had to see you again . . ." He paused to look back across the street at Artemis, still sitting quietly at the café, sipping his coffee and reading the newspaper.

"May I come inside?"

"Oh, god. Of course! Please come in. Something's going on here, Alex. I heard shots near the house. There were police all over the beach and—"

"I know, darling, I know. I'll tell you all about it."

"You're not hurt, are you?"

"No. I'm not hurt. One of my pilots is dead though. Russians got him in the fog."

Sigrid had to restrain herself from licking the salt from Hawke's stubbled cheek when she kissed him. Salty, Hawke was—oh my god, delicious, like some soft hot pretzel. She remembered that she always went a little weak around him and felt a vertiginous wave wash over her at the scent of him.

He followed her into the cold interior recesses of the little house to the kitchen. The ceilings were impossibly low for his six-foot-plus height, and he had to duck going through doorways.

"Coffee?" she asked, opening a cupboard. "Something stronger?"

"Perhaps a rum? Or a whiskey? Only if you've got it, of course. The sun is, uh . . ."

"Over the yardarm somewhere?" she said with a shy smile, remembering.

"Yes. Thank you. I'm a little—"

"Me too, Alex. Me too. Please sit down. Are you hungry?"

"Me? No, no. My pilot and I were just having lunch at the café across the street . . ."

"Here's your whiskey, Commander," she said, placing the tumbler on the table.

He took a sip, grateful for the burning sensation down his throat. Water of the gods. "So. This is your house?"

"Yes, it is. The one I bought to try and rehabilitate myself and rid us once and for all of that addled monster who threatened you and Alexei and—"

"Please don't go there. Not yet. I just want to . . . I just want for us to be together for a little while. I've missed you horribly."

"Me too."

"And the little girl? With the cat?"

"What about her?"

"Well, I mean . . ."

"Is she *mine*, you mean? My child? Is that what you—Oh, Alex, how could you ever even think that I . . ."

He'd no idea whether she was about to laugh or cry. She did neither. She smiled and it was the dawn. She reached her hand toward him across the table. He took it in his own, feeling its smallness, its pale white perfection. He had forgotten the spray of freckles across her nose.

"No, she's not mine, silly. She's the daughter of my friends here. A young English couple who moved in across the street. She runs English Tart, the local bakery. Peter and Lily Pell. They came here from Devon after seeing a help-wanted ad in the *Herald Tribune*. 'Town on coast of North Africa seeks qualified baker . . .' Isn't that sweet?"

He looked across at her, his blue eyes searching hers, so close he could see her irises swallow her pupils, his mind seeking out where to go next, what to offer, what best to keep inside . . .

Suddenly they were on their feet, holding on to each other as if on a typhoon-tossed deck, feverish whispers and pleas for a love so long denied.

"*Breathe*," he said softly into her hair.

HER FINGERS DOWN THE BACK of his boxers seared his skin. Somehow they were in her tiny bedroom at the rear, the seaward side of the white house. Tall French doors opened out on to the rocks and the grey and still-storm-tossed seas. He'd stood at the end of the bed, stood helpless before her in a kind of trance, the promise of love and warmth so overwhelmingly life-affirming after the cold horror of death mere hours ago.

He was silent as she sat on the bed's edge, staring up at him and holding his eyes as she unfastened his old brown leather belt and withdrew it from the loops, unbuttoned his khaki trousers, slid the zipper down, in a hurry, yanking his trousers, pale blue boxers, everything down to his ankles. He was already hard and that sight of him caused a short breath to catch in her throat.

"Oh, Alex. Oh, dear."

"You want the belt?" he said with a smile, doubling the thick leather belt and gently slapping his naked thigh with it. It was part of a constant game evolving between the two lovers. Using sex to tell each other stories about their deepest feelings and hidden needs long gone unmet, seemingly since childhood. Over time, the games had forged a powerful emotional bond between them. The ties that bind.

Lately, there had been more than a few times when she'd wanted him hard and rough, when he'd obliged her darker, submissive side. If you want a woman, give her what she wants. Whatever the hell that is. Doesn't matter.

"Not now, darling. Just you now. This time."

She growled, a guttural syllable, and pulled him to her, beside her, and then pushed him backward on her unmade bed.

Under her pale blue silk top, she wore nothing else. Her gooseflesh had taken on a lunar blue, and in the cold wind off the sea, her roseate nipples had dimpled inward. On their knees now, although the sheets were rough and scratched. It didn't matter. They were reduced to mouths and hands. He swept her legs to his hips, pressed her down, blanketed her with his heat until she stopped shivering, made a sudden, violent arch of her back. Her raw knees were raised to the ceiling and she cried out.

How he longed for something wordless and potent: what? He wanted to *wear* her, to live in her bosomy warmth forever, as a man shall cleave unto his wife forever. People in his life had fallen away from him one by one, like dominoes; his every movement now was intended to pin her further, hold her down, so that she could never abandon him again.

He had a sun blazing in him anew. This splendid everything, this new world now laid out lavishly before him, like some tasting menu, all was beauty, all abundance, all rich with the promise of new and endless love . . .

He imagined a lifetime of screwing in this small room or on the beach, en-plein-air fucking, until they were like one of those ancient pairs of parch-skinned old birds like the aging couples he'd seen on the beaches of northern Germany, like two storks speed-walking into the morning sun, hand in hand . . . even when they were old and so very grey, he knew he would waltz her into the dunes and have his way with her frail bird bones, her full, healing breasts, her salty-sweet and swelling clit.

This, then, for all eternity: her soft eyelashes on his cheek, her warm thighs draped across his waist, this thing they used to do, once more . . .

It was over too quickly. When she shouted, the gulls hovering and whirling outside the windows exploded upward like buckshot blasted into the clouds. The two were pressed so close that when they laughed, his laugh rose from her belly, hers from his throat. He kissed her cheekbones, her clavicles, the pale of her wrist with its skeins of veins, a tracery of blue beneath her almost transparent skin.

She stretched her long arms over her head and there were little nests of winter hair in the pits. She could hatch baby robins in those things, he thought but didn't say, and took her hand. He kissed it, bitten fingernail to bitten finger, up the arm, the neck, and then, because the air was bright and the whirling birds beyond the French doors were surely watching, he kissed a long trail down her stomach . . .

His terrible hunger he'd thought would be sated was not. The end apparent in the beginning.

"My girl," he said. "Mine." Perhaps instead of wearing her, he could swallow her whole.

"Stop," she said. She'd lost her smile, so shy and constant that it startled him to see her close up without it. "Nobody belongs to anybody. We've done something bigger. Something new."

He looked at her thoughtfully and nipped the tip of her nose with his teeth. He had once loved her with all his might and, in so loving, had considered her transparent, a plate of glass. Now he could see through to the goodness at her quick. But glass is fragile; he would have to be careful. "You're right," he said, thinking no, thinking instead how deeply they belonged. How surely.

Between his skin and hers, the smallest of spaces, barely enough for air, for the slick of sweat now chilling. Even still, a third person, her brutal past, had crept in.

She looked at him in fading light slanting in from the sea. For the first time in a long time, all of a sudden, she *saw* him again. The dark whip at the center of him. How, ever so gently, he flicked the lash and kept her spinning . . .

CHAPTER SEVENTY

"Come here, Alex," she was saying later, kneeling on the floor beside the bed, stroking his curly jet-black hair. He woke with a start. Outside, he saw the winter light had begun to leach from the western sky. How long had he slept? My god, Artemis! What must he be thinking? He had to—

"What? Wha—" he said. "I've got to go find Artemis and—"

"Shh. I want to show you something. Be a good little boy. Follow Mama."

He got up, naked, and padded obediently behind her. She led him out into the small hallway at the top of the stairs. They came to a door with a massive bolt and multiple locks securing it. She had a key ring and soon had the multiple locks opened.

"Now you've got my attention," Hawke told her. "Seriously, Sigrid, what in the world is going on here?"

"In here," she said. "I'll show you." And pushing open the door, she flicked on the overhead LED light panels.

"Sigrid," Hawke said, surveying the tiny room, amazed by what he saw, "I mean, really, what the hell?"

It was a server room. Every square inch packed with server racks, vertical towers of them ablaze with blinking green and yellow lights and a rat's nest of interwoven red and blue wiring on each rack. All running, humming away, twenty-four hours a day, seven days a week.

One entire wall was taken up completely by an array of Belkin computer display screens ablaze with worlds of imperceptible bright green numbers scrolling by. Atop an old console table in the middle of the room, a battered wooden stool and a large Apple iMac computer and a printer and a shredder.

Sigrid sat on the stool and plugged in a hacking tool disguised as a USB thumb drive. The black iMac screen was suddenly filled with green text flying by. There was a rolling stool nearby, and she pulled it beside her. "Sit here, darling, and pay close attention."

"Seriously, what's this all about?" Hawke said.

"That day, the day I was moving out of the Gardener's Cottage for good, Ambrose came down to see me and say good-bye. He begged me not to go. He said you needed me now, needed me more than ever. And . . . Alexei did, too. But my mind was made up, darling. I knew I had to disappear. Even then I knew it might shatter that Ming vase of your precious heart into a million pieces . . ."

"But, why? We'd had that awful fight in St. Moritz, I know, but—"

"Shh. Just listen. I told Ambrose and Diana that I had to leave. That I was going to devote myself to finding a way back into your heart. That however long it might take, I would search for a pathway home to you . . . and you know what he said? Ambrose?"

"No, I don't."

"He said, 'I may have a way back for you, Sigrid. But, it won't be easy. And, it will probably be dangerous . . .'"

"'Anything,' I told him. 'I'll try anything.'"

"He said, 'The search for Alexei is not going well, Sigrid. Sometimes I fear the worst has happened. But I can never let Alex know that. I have to be there to shield him from the useless fears that threaten him every second. But you, you can go down roads he and I cannot ever travel, roads even Scotland Yard has trouble following . . .'"

" 'You mean . . . follow what exactly, Chief Inspector?'

" 'Follow the money, Sigrid, follow the money. That was your genius at Credit Suisse before you two met! Use it! Nobody has deeper access into the hyper-secretive world of Swiss banking than you do. Who was that friend of yours in Zurich? The head of the Swiss Bankers Association's cybersecurity division? Jon Levin, was it? He helped us get to the bottom of Her Majesty's troubles with Russian cybertheft, remember?'

" 'No, it was Helmut Koller.'

" 'Exactly. Go there! Go to Zurich. Meet with Herr Koller, privately and in the strictest confidence. Explain about the kidnapping. And Putin's possible role in it. Tell him we think Putin is alive and on the run. Desperate for a place to hide. Tell him you want him to help you get on Putin's financial trail. Follow his footprints. See where it all leads.'

" 'Because where Putin is, so too will we find Alexei.'

" 'Yes. Precisely, my dear,' Ambrose said. 'And if you can find Alexei, oh, my dear girl, you can certainly find your way back into that poor man's heart, can you not?'

" 'I-I hope so, god help me.' That's what I told dear old Ambrose. *Et voilà*, here I am, darling. With Helmut's help, I set up this entire room. Everything in this room is linked though Credit Suisse to the Swiss Bankers Association Ops Center in Zurich. I get to see things no one else in the world gets to see . . . including CIA, MI6, and Scotland Yard . . ."

Hawke, amazed at what she had wrought, scooted his stool closer to her, looking over her shoulder at the big screen. "This is all simply unbelievable! Have you gotten anywhere? Are you making progress, darling?" he asked, the hope in his voice almost heartbreaking.

"I think so, Alex. I do. I'm beginning to see things coming together that hold promise, I'll say that much . . . Here, look at this one! One week ago today, Putin transferred a huge sum from—"

"Darling, what you're doing is amazing. Can you just pause for a few minutes?"

Hawke was looking at his watch. "My pilot, Artemis Cooper, is waiting for me across the street, over at the café. I'd very much like him to see all this stuff . . . if you've no objection, I mean. He's on the team . . ."

"Of course. I'll wait until you're back, Alex."

CHAPTER SEVENTY-ONE

Hawke returned a few minutes later with Cooper. After the briefest of introductions, Sigrid placed another stool in front of the iMac.

"Show us what you've got, darling," Hawke said, placing his right hand on her shoulder and squeezing it gently.

"Well, gentlemen," she said, tapping away at the keyboard, "have a look at this, for starters. We're looking at Putin's accounts now. Here's an exceptionally large transaction, wouldn't you agree? Took place about a month ago. I'm still trying to find out where the money came from, where it went, and how it got there. But the point is, Putin entered into a transaction wherein this sum, on a single day, left the country for an undisclosed bank in the South of France . . ."

Artemis let out a long, slow whistle. Hawke, on his feet, said, "*Five hundred million dollars?* What the hell?"

"Right. And mind you, this is not big corporate money we're talking about. Some mega-corporation swallowing up another mega-corporation. No, no, gentlemen. This is a *private* transaction between two fabulously wealthy individuals with unimaginable firewalls, encryption, and cybersecurity prevention tools the likes of which neither Helmut nor I have ever seen before. At any rate, with his help, I was able to dig this deep. Are you with me?"

Hawke said, "Yes. Keep going, Sigrid. What's this one over here? Thirty million the very next day? The man is on a buying binge . . ."

"Good eye! That's what I was about to point out to you. This transaction is similar in nature, but varies in one very important way . . ."

"Tell me."

"The money comes from the same Swiss black hole as the larger transaction the day before. But, it doesn't disappear down the same rabbit hole as the prior one. Oh, no, not by a long shot it doesn't."

"Where does it go, Sigrid? Do you have any idea?"

"I do now. It goes right into the pocket of this man right here . . . you may well recognize him, Alex. He was in your life, and mine, for a brief time."

She tapped a key and brought up a grainy photograph that filled the screen.

"Good lord," Hawke said, instantly recognizing the face of the man in the photo.

Handsome, the man was standing inside some walled gardens on the shores of Lake Zurich. It was a brilliant sunlit summer day, all vibrant green grass lawns and blue water and bountiful floral displays . . . He was smiling into the camera, bouncing a beautiful little boy on his right shoulder . . . He was . . .

"Baron Wolfgang von Stuka," Hawke whispered under his breath. "I'll be damned."

"Yes, Alex. It's him, all right," Sigrid said.

"Who?" Artemis said.

"Von Stuka was the powerful Swiss army divisionnaire whom I had long suspected of being involved with the Russians in the looting of Her Majesty the Queen's Swiss coffers. Not to mention my own more modest accounts. My money, flowing to the Russian coffers . . . but I could never prove it."

"With these new tools, we may well be able to do so now, Alex," Sigrid said. Von Stuka was a sore spot between them and she knew it.

Here was a man who'd once stirred jealous passions in Hawke's heart. When first they'd met in Zurich that summer, Sigrid had told Hawke that Von Stuka had once pursued her romantically. Despite her protestations that she was never interested, she had accepted the gift of a massive ruby ring. She was relieved to see that Hawke at that moment was all business.

"Tell me about that second transaction, Sigrid," Hawke said. "Curious, I must say."

"Real estate deal, plain and simple. Baron von Stuka is selling Seegarten, his gorgeous island estate on Lake Zurich, to an unknown buyer for thirty million dollars. A week later, the baron had removed himself from the island to the family castle up atop Great St. Bernard Pass. Helmut and I are still trying to find out just what—"

But Hawke wasn't listening.

He was still staring at the photograph of Von Stuka, looking closely at the magnificent mountain in the background of the photograph. A mighty peak that stood on the farther shore, soaring into the skies above Lake Zurich. Der Nadel. The infamously cruel mountain peak where, like so many climbers before him, Hawke's own grandfather had lost his life. His bones were still up there. Some day, Alex vowed, he'd bring them down and back to England to be buried properly at Hawkesmoor.

Der Nadel was popularly known by the name surviving climbers had given it. White Death. Hawke knew the mountain literally, inside and out. For deep inside the massive mountain lay one of Switzerland's best-kept secrets. The mountain was home to a massive military complex of the Sorcerer. Dr. Steinhauser. The incredibly powerful man known to the financial world as the wizard who'd made the global economy tick like a Swiss clock for decades.

Sigrid looked at Hawke until she had his full attention. "Here's the thing, Alex," she said, "and this is important. Whoever was behind that five hundred million in outgoing cash? That was the very same account or individual who paid thirty million for Von Stuka's island paradise, Seegarten."

"Putin bought *both* in forty-eight hours?"

"He did."

Hawke looked at her, thinking. "The baron also has a schloss somewhere, doesn't he? A family castle?"

"He certainly does. Schloss Weisses Kreuz is its name. The White Cross. Primary family residence for five hundred years."

"Can you take us there, Sigrid? Get Artemis and me inside the White Cross so we can have a little chat with the baron?"

She smiled and said, "Well, if I can't, nobody can. He still wants to marry me, poor boy."

Hawke smiled, but he didn't find it very funny. "Where is this place, Sigrid?"

"In the stratosphere. High in the Alps. Far above Great St. Bernard Pass in northern Switzerland. But, there's no way to surprise him, Alex. This time of year, the castle can be accessed only by Sno-Cat up the back side of the mountain. He'll hear you coming . . ."

"Artemis, my friend, we're going back to Switzerland as quickly as possible. If you think it's the right thing to do, we'll take Johnnie's body back home on the plane with us. Chief Inspector Congreve could supervise the postmortem work at Scotland Yard?"

"Yes. I'd feel much better getting him the hell out of Morocco and back to his family. Thank you, sir."

"Alex?" Sigrid asked. "Am I back on the team?"

He stood and pressed her head to his chest, holding her close. "After all that you've been doing here? This incredible room you've created? This mission of yours? My god, darling. What with all you've already done? And all this? To help me get closer to finding Alexei?"

"Yes?"

"Oh, Sigrid. You *are* the team, darling."

CHAPTER SEVENTY-TWO

KGB HQ, Siberia

L ate afternoon in the middle of nowhere. At the sound of an approaching chopper, Beau Beauregard stepped into the frigid air outside the front doors of HQ to greet his arriving guest, Uncle Joe Stalingrad. He looked up into the bleak blue skies. Oh, god, here he comes, he thought, seeing the bright red chopper swooping in over the tops of the giant pines. Joe always arrived on the scene with a mountain of baggage—and not the kind you packed clothes inside.

Beau knew Joe was a political genius. Here on official business, namely, spying on Beau for Putin. But he was also a drama queen of the first rank.

Beau had nothing to hide. He'd been a very busy boy. He already had six hundred battle-hardened war fighters under arms, barracked and training twenty hours a day. He was well on his way to the first plateau Putin had established for Phase 1 of Operation Overkill.

"Hey-oh, it's Uncle Joe!" Beau said, striding out onto the pad to meet him as soon as the rotor dust settled. The two men, he thought, had really hit it off in these few weeks since that first meeting at the Beau Rivage in Geneva. Wasn't that hard to understand, either. Hell, they were kindred spirits in a funny way. Both show business, rock stars in their own way. All about the sizzle, the greasepaint and the razzamatazz and the funky Broadway . . .

"Colonel, good to see you, hotshot!" Joe said, giving the big man a good squeeze on his left biceps. "Had a hell of a time getting here though. You ever take that trans-Siberian train? The Red Arrow? Out of St. Petersburg? Man oh man, getting here was definitely not half the fun. I had a small private compartment, mind you, and it still smelled like the room where sick cats all go to piss before they die."

"Yeah, I hear you. Well, anyway, welcome to nowhere. Look at this place. Not even the middle of nowhere is sufficient to describe it. You look like a man who could use a drink. Come on in and I'll fix you up. Dinner's in one hour. I got the kitchen to whip up some beef stroganoff in honor of your arrival . . ."

For the last three or four weeks, Colonel Beau Beauregard had been bivouacked here in what felt like the back of beyond, also known as Siberia. Familiar territory. He was at his old stomping grounds, the top-secret KGB HQ, the place where he'd built a massive military force for Putin some years ago.

Now he spent mornings in his old KGB office, scouring the files he'd created back in the glory years. Those golden days three years earlier, when he'd been engaged in creating the most powerful, most highly trained, most well-equipped and well-armed private army on the face of the earth. When money was no object and he was working his way through screwing every fat-fannied Siberian nurse residing at the base hospital. His "Huskies" as used to call them.

Yeah, those halcyon days of yore. Back when he'd first been at the service of Vladimir Putin, his henchman and right-hand man. Back then, a geographically voracious Putin had been hell-bent on redrawing the maps of Europe and the Baltic. Revanchism, pure and simple. Restore the borders to the old Cold War status, pre–Fall of the Wall.

Beau, with unlimited funds, had built up his magnificent secret strategic military base in record time. And in heavy secrecy, he had effected a miracle on Putin's behalf.

He had molded raw and seasoned men into world-class storm-trooper-level infantry troops, paratroopers, spec ops divisions, an air fighter wing, tank battalions—everything Putin would need for a massive surprise attack that, were he successful, would amount to a restoration of the old Soviet empire. He had even threatened to use a revolutionary new weapon of mass destruction (that turned out to be fake) should anyone get in his way.

But it was not to be.

Putin's erstwhile friend, and now nemesis, Alex Hawke, had risen up at the last minute. And saved everybody a whole shitload of trouble. With Europe, the Baltics, and the West all trembling at the brink of a world war, Hawke had gone to Putin's private dacha in Russia to confront the president. Fully confident that Putin's much-ballyhooed secret weapon of mass destruction, called *Feuerwasser*, meaning firewater, was a complete hoax, foisted on the world by that brilliant salesman, Vladimir Putin.

But Hawke had humiliated the president, met with him for count-less hours, and finally convinced him that the Western allies—the United States, Great Britain, France, Germany—were united and not even slightly fooled by his phony X-factor explosive. And that they simply would not stand for his rash belligerence, knocking on the doors of every one of America's NATO allies.

Hawke told him the Pentagon was already on a war footing in anticipation of Putin rolling tank divisions into Estonia and the Baltic. In the end, Hawke had presented Putin with a treaty drafted by the American president and Admiral Charlie Moore, the chair-man of the Joint Chiefs of Staff at the Pentagon. By signing, Putin effectively agreed to withdraw all Russian troops back to the legal borders and ordered all of his military commanders on land, sea, and air to stand down effective immediately.

In the end, a weary Putin had backed away and abided by the tenets of the American treaty.

But now, Putin was out to make a major comeback. And Beau was back. And both men reunited with Uncle Joe Stalingrad. Joe was Putin's eyes and ears here in Siberia and wherever else he roamed. Beau knew the former henchman was only here to check up on how the colonel was handling his new assignment. And find out exactly what was required to mount Operation Overkill. But he was also here to see how he could help Beau pull this miracle off on schedule.

"How much money? How much time?' Joe asked him point-blank over vodka in the little library. This was where Beau spent most of his free time, reading reports in front of the warming fire.

"You wanna talk money with me, Joe?"

"I do."

"Well, I tell you what I've been working on all morning. Look at this topo map of the Alps. I'm going to need me some lightweight tactical tanks to break through these well-defended Alpine passes, Joe. Our tactical air support, the fighter wing at Falcon's Lair, will not be, I promise you, will *not* be enough to ward off the swarms of Swiss fighter jets raining fire and brimstone down on our tanks and ground troops. Our boys bottlenecked at the pass? No."

"Yeah, I see that, Beau," Joe said. "How many tanks you think you're going to need?"

"Hell, I dunno. Ten. Fifteen," Beau said.

"Main battle tanks? T-14 Armatas?"

"No, no, no. Airborne Light Tanks. The Sprut-SDM1."

"I'll talk to the boss. Shouldn't be a problem."

"You also need to help me figure out how in hell I'm going to smuggle all them damn tanks and troops inside Swiss borders in time for a P-day shootout without nobody noticin' nothin' . . ."

Joe said, "You said you wanted airborne tanks. I guess you para-chute them in, right?"

Beau said, "Man, get serious! If Overkill is ever going to work, this has to be a surprise attack. Get it? You don't think folks seeing tanks come spitting out of the rear of aircraft is going to raise a few eyebrows?"

"Yeah . . . lemme think . . ."

"How about in a train?" Beau asked him, the idea, having occurred earlier that day, blooming ever larger in his brain.

"A train?" Joe said.

"Yeah, a train," Beau said, "like a freight train combined with a
passenger train, right? I've been thinking about this. You're gonna like
it, trust me. First, we air-cargo every damn tank, artillery weapon, and
trooper from here in Siberia and drop them into Armenia. Off-load
the whole shebang at the Russian 102nd Military Base at Gyumri,
Armenia, north of the capital, Yerevan."

"Okay, and where do we get this miraculous train?"

"We steal us one! Steal a train somewhere and have it waiting on
the railroad tracks at the base. I've done this kind of shit before, for
the Iranians one time. Listen to me. Those tanks you want to get me
are small and light, right? About the size and weight of a C-Class
Mercedes sedan. You could hide two of them in every boxcar, so say
ten boxcars, twenty tanks. More boxcars loaded with troopers and
light artillery. Rolling across the borders of Europe in the middle
of the night on a speeding stealth train . . . fake papers, disguised
somehow . . . Hell, pull right into the Hauptbahnhof at Zurich train
station at two in the morning and off-load in a remote part of the
damn rail yard . . ."

"Yeah. I can see it," Joe said, thinking, *This* is why the wily old
colonel gets the big bucks!

Time and logistics, those were the issues now, not money. All the
members of the Falcon's Lair loyalists had taken to calling the date
of the Russian invasion of Switzerland P-day, with a tip of the hat to
D-day, the "P" obviously for Putin.

That date was only two months away now. The invasion was
scheduled for the first of May. And this time, Beau was convinced
he and Joe, and Putin, could succeed in redrawing borders, rewriting
the history books. Putin had a simple goal: he wanted, in the very
worst way possible, to rule the world. The West would bow down to

him first, and the rest of the world would follow. This, Putin, in his heart of hearts, believed fervently.

And old Beau? Well, in Joe's book, he was still the baddest of the bad, the badass beyond the beyond. His mission? Restore Vladimir Putin to the Kremlin. First, invade Switzerland and recover all the gold stolen from him by the oligarchs. Second, use that money to fund Operation Overkill, the triumphant march on Moscow, and lay waste to anything and everything that stood in his way.

That was the plan, at any rate. Now, you know, war had a way of turning around and kicking you in the balls when you least expected it.

And P-day was fast approaching . . .

CHAPTER SEVENTY-THREE

Great St. Bernard Pass, Switzerland

The big blue Sno-Cat churned up the steepest face, the north face, of the snow-packed mountain pass. Great St. Bernard is the most ancient pass through the Western Alps, with evidence of it in use dating back to the Bronze Age. It's also the third highest pass, and the road is negotiable only four months of the year, from June to September. Now, in early February, travel was an arctic nightmare.

Artemis cranked up the wiper blades to high and leaned forward over the wheel, peering through the thick glass. The wipers struggling to keep up with the snowfall up here, in the nearly whiteout blizzard conditions. But as Hawke saw to his relief, Artemis Cooper was clearly in command and comfortable handling the growling monster.

Hawke, seated on the passenger side, turned around to smile at Sigrid, seated on the rear bench, her seat belt cinched tight around her hips. She was humming softly, skimming a new *Vogue* magazine she'd bought for the ride back from Morocco to Zurich. This trip up to the pass was very obviously not her first rodeo.

He had to say she looked phenomenal this morning. Forget the vapid redhead on the cover of her magazine; Sigrid could easily have graced the cover of *Vogue* herself. Clad head to toe in tight polar-white Bogner ski attire, her ash-blond hair piled atop her head, her wide blue eyes sparkling with adventure, she would be the perfect picture postcard for all that was right and good about Switzerland.

For her part, Sigrid found herself amazed at the camaraderie and sangfroid displayed by the two men up front. Considering the horrific death of poor Johnnie Walker, and him not even dead two days. But a part of her knew a thing or two about men. Sometimes grief is only grist for the strong, who use all that emotion as extra fuel for burning on the battlefield.

"Everything all right back there?" Hawke said.

"Perfectly all right, thank you very much for asking."

"You've been up here before," Hawke said, trying not to make it sound like a jealous question when in fact that's exactly what it was.

"Yes, I have, as a matter of fact."

"And was our dear baron a well-behaved host?"

"Alex, please. It was at his wife's invitation. A weekend guest, you see. A house party."

"Ah. At his wife's invitation, you say. You two are very friendly, I take it? You and the baroness?"

"Not anymore. The baroness is dead."

"Dead?"

"Hmm. She died last year. She and Wolfie were heli-skiing in New Zealand. Apparently she got out over her skis and ran out of luck and experience at precisely the same moment. She fell a thousand feet to her death."

"I notice you use the word *apparently*. Was there ever any sign or evidence of foul play up on the mountain? Like, say, murder?"

"None. The ski chopper had returned to base and she and her husband were alone at the peak, last the pilot saw of them. Wolfie, according to his testimony at the inquest, was first to descend the upper portion. He claimed he was waiting for her at the bottom of a particularly treacherous descent. She simply never came down. He never saw her fall. Never saw her again. They never found the body. Police believe she fell into a deep crevasse."

"Was this explanation challenged?"

"Not at the hearing. Let's say people around town were talking, though. Her disappearance was topic A at high society holiday dinner parties around Zurich that Christmas. There had been troubles in the marriage for years. She often used the bottle to console herself. And . . . Wolfie had a reputation as, shall we say, an imperfect husband."

"Zipper problems?"

"Hmm."

"But he got away with it?" Hawke asked.

"The zipper problems?"

"No. His wife's death. If it was murder, it was obviously a perfect murder. No witnesses, no corpse."

"Hmm. Anyway, it's all ancient history now, Alex. Social gossip has a short shelf life around here. Wolfie is now seen as the ultimate catch. Switzerland's most eligible bachelor. Kind of a Swiss version of you."

"Should I take that as a compliment?"

"No, Alex. You should take it as a joke. He is nothing like you, nothing at all."

"I'm not a crook. For starters. Oh, and I didn't kill my wife."

"Alex, this is the most displaced case of green envy I've ever seen. He once gave me a ring. I probably shouldn't have, but I accepted it. That's it."

"Sorry. Consider the subject closed. We've still got some time, Sigrid. Could you give us a refresher course in Wolfie 101? Artemis here needs to know what he's up against when we arrive at Schloss Weisses Kreuz."

"Sure. Where to start? Let's see . . . Baron Wolfgang von Stuka. Patriarch of one of my country's wealthiest, oldest, and most noble families. A citizen-soldier and a businessman. And not without his problems. It's a little-known fact that Europe's twelve ruling families remain deeply competitive. Who has the swankiest palaces, the biggest yachts, the shiniest diamonds, the healthiest bank balances. An expensive business, you know, being a royal.

"And then there's our poor Wolfie. Poverty stricken by the standards of the Twelve Families. He keeps the Von Stuka family dynasty going by selling off land and art piecemeal, all the while frantically scouring the Riviera and other playgrounds for a wife who's vastly richer than he is. There you have it."

"What do you think, Artemis?" Hawke said.

"I think that when I meet him, I shall forgo the customary gentlemen's handshake and hit him solidly in the mouth."

"Well, that will certainly break the ice. How much farther now?"

"This is the last stretch of rough sledding. We'll be there in twenty minutes or less."

"Good, good," Sigrid said, peering out her window.

CHAPTER SEVENTY-FOUR

Schloss Weisses Kreuz looked like one of those fairy-tale castles you see when cruising down the Rhine. Very Germanic, with four crenellated towers, one on each corner of the main structure. The ornate towers, with banners snapping in the wind atop them, soared into the snowy skies. Alex Hawke looked at one, mentally calculating its height. Good lord, he thought, they had to be 150 feet high!

There were also flying buttresses and great arches, many with stone eagles carved into the keystones. It was, Hawke thought, somewhat impressive, even for someone like him, a chap who has rather seen it all.

"Park it here, Artemis," Hawke said suddenly. "Out of sight of the entrance. Let's do this right, just as we planned. Only Sigrid goes to the door. She makes some excuse for me . . . Sorry, Hawke and his business colleague Mr. Cooper are still in the Sno-Cat on a conference call to their bankers in London . . . okay?"

"I can do better, Alex, but yes, that's fine."

"Good. Give it ten minutes. Ask for champagne. Get him relaxed. Then say you think I'm being rude. You're going to call me and tell me so . . . That'll be my cue."

"Right."

"And remember this, Sigrid. The Sorcerer, the *éminence grise* of Swiss banking, was convinced that someone in Zurich was assisting the Russians in hacking not only my most vulnerable accounts but those of Her Royal Majesty, the Queen. That he was the missing link among the Russian hackers and the Chinese thieves. When I insisted on a name, he gave me one. Baron Wolfgang von Stuka."

"You never told me that. Wolfie was stealing from *you?*" she said.

Hawke smiled. "Well, I knew he was a friend of yours, for one thing. And I really didn't think you needed to know, after you and Congreve cracked the case wide open and the two of you were headed back to England. The good news is that once you and the chief inspector had exposed the primary culprits, there was also no need for Wolfie to know I was on to him. And that I knew of his role, abetting the Russian hackers. I thought I just might have to save his sorry hide for a rainy day, as it were . . ."

"A day much like today, sir," Artemis said, grinning.

"Precisely," Hawke said, and then to Sigrid, "Good luck, darling. I'll wait for your call."

Artemis swung open the door and Sigrid climbed down from the cockpit of the massive Sno-Cat, dropping the last couple of feet into the drifted snow.

The winds were high and swirling up through the mountain pass. Hawke watched her until she disappeared into a fog of whirling snow . . .

The world was precarious, Hawke had learned. People you loved could be subtracted from it with swift bad math. If one might die at any moment, one must live!

A LIVERIED HOUSEMAN SWUNG OPEN the great oaken doors. He stood just inside the archway, with two enormous matching Dobermans straining at their leashes. The man bowed from the waist and waved the two new arrivals inside. Two footmen took their parkas and they entered. The barking of the dogs and all the sounds of their own voices created booming echoes inside the great sunlit space that was the enormous hall.

"Your names, please, gentlemen?" he asked.

"I'm Hawke. He's Cooper," Hawke said. There was no reply, only a sullen nod.

Hawke turned and saw a great double curved staircase rising up into the darkness of the higher floors. Above, clerestory windows shifted the light of milky sunshine one to the other, light that fell to the medieval frescoes on the walls below. The walls to either side of the staircase were lined with full suits of ancient armor. And in much profusion, gilt-framed oils of fleshy white men. The roots of the baron's ancestral tree, no doubt, Hawke thought.

"If you'll follow me, gentlemen, they are waiting for you in the drawing room," the manservant said, his English thick with guttural Germanic undertones. And they followed, with the hyperactive Dobermans slinging loopy strings of saliva in every direction and leading the way.

"Ah, there you are, Alex!" the baron boomed as Hawke was shown into the book-filled library. "I'd heard a nasty rumor you might show up here!"

Hawke smiled at him, hiding his contempt for the fabricated bonhomie, the artificial soul that lay at the very heart of this man.

"Baron, I appreciate your time. I'd like you to meet my new business partner, an old RAF man, Captain Artemis Cooper. I've been telling him a lot about you and—"

"Don't believe a word he says, Artemis! Jilted lovers, they're all the same. Come sit down and have something to drink, won't you? Fräulein Kissl and I are sampling a dollop of Krug . . . something stronger?"

"Jilted lover?" Hawke said, staring at Sigrid. "Did I miss a memo?"

"Oh, darling," she said, "don't take him seriously. He's just teasing you."

Hawke was not amused. He was barely able to contain his anger at all this false bravado and the sleazy solicitous attitude toward the lot of them.

"Got any rum?" Hawke asked. "Gosling's Rum?"

"Sorry, old chap, we don't drink that Bermuda horse piss up here at Weisses Kreuz. Sigrid, pour this man a whiskey, will you?"

She looked at Alex who shook his head no.

"Captain Cooper, what can I get for you?"

"Diet Coke?"

"Diet . . . what?"

"Never mind—maybe a brandy."

Von Stuka shrugged, plainly irritated, and handed it to him. He returned to his seat next to Sigrid on the silk brocade settee and plastered on that smile again. It took all of Artemis's will to keep from putting his fist through that face.

"So, Lord Hawke, to what do I owe the honor of your presence here in my family home?"

Hawke, who was in the midst of lighting a cigarette, paused and took a long slow puff before he answered. "In point of fact, I am looking for my son, Alexei. He was kidnapped in St. Moritz on Christmas Day. You haven't seen him, by any chance, have you, Baron? Caught a glimpse of him, perhaps?"

"Me? No. Of course not. Why would you think that I had seen him?"

"Just a hunch."

"A hunch."

"I think the man who perhaps kidnapped Alexei is a friend of yours, that's all. A business associate, shall we say. And that you've been doing business with him lately here in Switzerland."

"I have no idea who or what you're talking about, Lord Hawke. But I deeply resent your coming into my home under false pretenses, and I resent your line of questioning. Perhaps you two should leave. Miss Kissl can remain here with me. I'll see that she gets home safely."

"This is not a social call, Baron. I am a ranking official of Her

Majesty's government. A senior intelligence officer with MI6 investigating a serious crime with international implications. You have two choices. You can answer my questions truthfully here or I can have you arrested for suspicion of collusion with the Russians in the theft of monies from accounts belonging to Her Royal Majesty the Queen . . . not to mention my own personal accounts."

"This is outrageous!" the baron shouted. "How dare you make these allegations!"

"It is outrageous, isn't it?" Hawke said. "Alas, you must answer to them. You'll remember my good friend Chief Inspector Congreve of Scotland Yard. He was here with me investigating the White Death affair, as I'm sure you'll recall. He is at the Yard, standing by now for a call from me. Ready with a warrant for your arrest for crimes committed against Her Royal Majesty and the United Kingdom."

"Out! Get out of my house," the baron shouted.

"Shut up and listen to me. If I don't hear exactly what I want to hear, there will be officers of the Swiss polizei and Scotland Yard detectives knocking at your door within the hour. Now, if you'll excuse me, I need to use the loo for a minute—no, no, stay put, Baron, I'll find it—"

Hawke stood, nodded at Artemis, and headed for the door. As he opened it, he heard Artemis say, "So, Baron, let's talk about your lovely island estate . . . Seegarten, on Lake Zurich? I believe that's what it's called."

"What about it?" he screamed, furious at his sudden impotence in the midst of his own domain.

"You sold it recently, Baron. Lord Hawke and I are here to find out why. And who bought it from you."

"None of your fucking business," the man said and leapt to his feet, yanking open one of the drawers in his desk, reaching inside for a gun.

"Put the gun down, Baron," Hawke said.

Hawke stood in the doorway, his own gun in his hand now, his old Walther PPK. He quickly crossed the room and sat on the arm of the couch, three feet from Wolfie, his weapon loosely trained on the man.

Artemis stood up. He had his Glock 17 aimed at Von Stuka's head. "I said drop the weapon!"

Wolfie turned his head and was staring down the muzzle of the Glock. His shoulders slumped and he let go of his pistol and slammed the drawer shut.

Hawke said, "Sit back down, please, Baron. No, not by her. I want you in the armchair over there beside the fireplace. If I have to shoot you, we don't want any blood on her pretty white jumpsuit, do we?"

Von Stuka removed himself to the chair, his handsome face livid with anger.

"It's called Good Cop, Bad Cop, Baron," Hawke said. "Only in your case it's called Bad Cop, Bad Cop. How do you like it so far?"

Sullen, with his head down, the man did not reply.

"I want to know, Baron, and I want to know now. Who . . . did . . . you . . . sell . . . Seegarten to? Tell me the name of the buyer now, or this is going to get really unpleasant."

This fruitless interrogation went on for ten minutes before Hawke stood up and said, "Let's take a break, you know, stretch our legs a bit. Get some fresh air. Come on, Wolfie, on your feet, boyo. Captain Cooper and I would like a little tour of your castle . . . Artemis, fetch our ponchos, would you please? It's cold out."

Sigrid, who'd been silent the whole time, said, "Alex, do you want me to call Chief Inspector Congreve? Tell him we need the Scotland Yard officers and polizei up here?"

"Not yet, darling. I'm going to give him just one more chance to save his silly ass. Right, Baron? You up for this? The captain and I want to see the view from the top of one of your four towers . . . it's going to be cold and windy up there, but we're all big boys, right? Ready? Come, let us away . . ."

CHAPTER SEVENTY-FIVE

The view from the tower at the top of the world was spectacular. The snow was not coming down as fast and Hawke could see for miles across the Alps-studded vista. He smiled at Wolfie and leapt up onto the narrow stone parapet, a low wall that encircled the very pinnacle of the tower. Looking down (never a good idea) gave him a start. Far beneath him was a massive crevasse, its stone jaws wide and deep.

"You two need to get up here and see this view!" Hawke exclaimed. "All right, Captain, if you'd be so kind, please help our host here up onto the parapet with me, would you?"

"Get up on the wall," Artemis growled, lifting him. "Get up there now."

"Give me your hand," Hawke said, reaching down to help Artemis lift him up.

With Hawke pulling and Artemis pushing, they got him, trembling and whimpering, up on the parapet. It was like the man had known all along that this was where they were taking him and—

"Take his belt off, Artemis, and hand it to me," Hawke said, and removing his own thick leather belt, he buckled it into a loop. He then took Wolfie's belt and made another loop connected to his own.

"Okay, Baron, showtime. Artemis here is going to be the good cop now. He's the one who'll keep you from falling to your death. Don't worry, we're professionals. We've done this parlor trick many times before. Once high above Times Square on New Year's Eve, in fact. Turn him around, Artemis, with his back to the crevasse, heels of his boots over the edge of the parapet. That's right. Now, Baron, listen up. I've got a good grip on this belt. You need to hold on to yours too, because I'm going to lower you out over the edge until you're horizontal above the ground. Sound like fun?"

"No, no, please!"

"Another foot, Artemis, that's right, I want him fully extended horizontal over the ground."

Hawke carefully extended his loop, lowering Wolfie slowly out until his only contact with the tower was the soles of his boots. He was now, literally, standing on the side of the tower, parallel to the ground below, a hundred and fifty feet in the air.

"Who bought Seegarten, Wolfie? You want to live, tell me. Tell me right now . . ."

"Hawke! I don't know, I tell you. You think I want to die like this? Bring me back up, please, and—"

"Who bought it? Just give me the name and I'll haul you up . . . You've got fifteen seconds . . . starting NOW!"

"Fuck! My lawyers handle everything and—"

"Now, I said! I'm going to give you a count of ten. Ready? Ten . . . nine . . ."

"I don't know, someone in the South of France. Never learned his name. Only an account number. Never! I swear it!"

"Eight . . . seven . . . Come on, Wolfie, you must have dealt with someone! Who negotiated? Who made the offer? Who arranged the bloody wire transfer of thirty million bloody dollars? Who was it? Tell me now or you're a dead man, Baron. I'm not bloody kidding— you lied to me. You stole from me."

"It was . . . shit . . . it was an American. Working for the buyer, I think, or just representing him here in Switzerland."

"And the magic name is? Five . . . four . . . three . . ."

"Joseph Stalingrad. Calls himself Uncle Joe. He's from Los Angeles, California."

"Where is he now?"

"Bring me up!"

"Where is Uncle Joe now?"

"Living at Seegarten. Now an armed island fort. Land-mined, attack dogs, and the walls surmounted with barbed wire. Apparently he keeps himself surrounded by guards twenty-four hours a day, snipers on the rooftops."

"I don't imagine your former neighbors are very happy about this. Doesn't sound exactly neighborly."

"Bring me up! I told you, for Christ's sake!"

"One last thing. What do you know about Operation Overkill?"

"Overkill? Jesus. Some kind of invasion, I don't fucking know. That's all. I swear to you."

"Invasion of what?"

"No idea. A major operation . . . massive."

"Who is planning this operation?"

"This Joe character and someone named Beau. The Joe and Beau Show is what he calls it. I don't know what the hell they think they can invade, but—"

"Haul him up, Captain Cooper. And let's get the hell down from here. Scared the living daylights out of me, so I can only imagine how our poor Baron must have felt . . ."

AS SOON AS THE THREE of them, Hawke, Artemis, and Sigrid, were back in the Sno-Cat and headed down the mountain, Hawke lit another cigarette and said, "All right, gentleman, lady, game on. Hostage rescue operation. Sigrid, you first. I'm going to need a base of operations. Compound on the lake. Walled. Fortifiable, and—"

Sigrid smiled. "Sounds exactly like Seegarten, Alex. Ready made. Why not just attack it and seize that place for yourself? Spoils of war sort of thing."

Hawke turned in his seat and looked back at her.

"Woman is a genius. Next, Artemis, I'm putting you in charge of the operation. Assemble the hostage rescue team in Miami. We leave tonight on my airplane. After you drop Fräulein Kissl and me off in Oxfordshire, your flight plan is Miami. Once everyone is assembled, ferry them all back to Zurich just as quickly as you can put this together."

"Who do you need?" Artemis asked.

"I need Stokely Jones and Harry Brock, CIA. Both located in Miami. And I need my mercenaries, Thunder and Lightning, who run their operation out of a castle called Fort Whupass on Martinique, Lesser Antilles."

"Who?"

"Friends of mine, Artemis. Stokely will call them as soon as you know what I want. T and L. Best hostage rescue team for hire in the world."

"With all due respect, sir, sounds like a bit of overkill, pun intended, for a single hostage."

"Stalingrad and Putin have turned Seegarten into a heavily armed compound. There will be heavy resistance. But I'm also thinking ahead, Captain. According to the baron, we may also have some kind of invasion on our hands. Putin's building an army from the ground up."

"He's hired a man whose specialty is building private armies. Colonel Beau Beauregard."

"Operation Overkill is real, then? What the hell is it?"

"That's what we're going to find out. But first I'm going to bring Alexei home."

"You really think he's in there? In Seegarten?"

"Yeah. I do. I strongly suspect that Alexei is there, and that he is under the tenuous protection of Uncle Joe Stalingrad. Things are heating up fast, and the danger level for Alexei from Putin is ramping up with it."

"He's not going to do anything rash right now, Alex. He's got too much to lose."

"Look, I know Putin. He gets rattled in times like this, times of international crisis. Distracted. Hell, that night I visited him at his dacha? Pentagon sent me to get him to sign that stand-down treaty for the joint chiefs? By the time I left with that signed treaty in my hand, he was so damn crazy drunk he could barely stand up . . . and he was shooting at me! Shouting that if I ever interfered with him again, he'd kill both my son and me."

Artemis said, "You need to put an end to this thing, sir. Once and for all."

"You think I don't know that?" Hawke said.

CHAPTER SEVENTY-SIX

Lake Zurich

Thunder and Lightning. That's the moniker the famous mercenary team had acquired in the mid-nineties, when they started making an international name for themselves. Before they became legend in the head-banging warrior world of the soldier of fortune. They were recruited on battlefields that spanned the globe. Usually it was the last man standing in the smoking ruins who got the nod.

Ex–French Foreign Legion, Ex-SAS, Ex-SBS, and U.S. Army Rangers, ex–Japanese 1st Airborne, ex–Royal Australian Spec Ops Command, you name it—all could be found among the ranks of Thunder and Lightning. The weapons they carried varied man to man. Most common was the MP5, the Heckler & Koch 9mm submachine gun favored by SEALs, and the Sig Sauer 9mm pistol. Both weapons fitted with what the Yanks among them called hushpuppies.

Stun grenades and Willy Petes hung from their camo web belts in what looked like grape clusters. Willy Petes were terrifying weapons, white phosphorus grenades that spread unspeakably intense heat and fire wherever they ignited.

Chief Charlie Rainwater was the one they called Thunder. He was a full-blooded Comanche, a true Plains warrior, and he held the distinction of being the best underwater demolition man in the storied history of UDT and the Navy SEALs. Team Six had nicknamed him Thunder, and the name had stuck.

In Afghanistan, the chief was known for always scouting barefoot, saving countless lives in the doing, always finding trip wires no one else could see, hearing enemy footsteps no one else could hear, and smelling an ambush a mile away. He'd earned three Bronze Stars and one Silver Star for his valiant efforts.

Chief Rainwater was nearly seven feet tall and bristling with muscle, with blazing black eyes and a long, narrow nose sharp as an arrow above his somewhat cruel lips. Shoulder-length raven-black hair fell about his copper-skinned shoulders. He fought bare-chested, with an old pair of buckskin trousers and a pair of beaded moccasins he'd sewn for himself as his uniform.

And then there was the man called Lightning. FitzHugh McCoy was a big, strapping Irish chap, ruddy-complected and weather-burned. Along with flashing blue eyes, he had short red-gold hair, which also dusted his bulging forearms. He was a veteran of Iraq and Afghanistan, earning his stripes as a Delta Force war fighter in both theaters. He was also a recipient of the Congressional Medal of Honor.

These days they ran their operations out of Martinique, located in the Lesser Antilles in the eastern Caribbean Sea. Lightning, as a student at Trinity College, Dublin, had discovered an old British fortress sited on a hilltop deep in the jungle while on holiday. He'd decided on the spot that he would acquire it one day and make it the home of all his operations.

And, on the day he and Thunder officially commenced operations, he'd offered a five-thousand-dollar bonus to the man who came up with the best name for their new home.

Thunder had won, hands down. The chief announced they would call it, from this day forward . . . Fort Whupass. And it stuck.

Their old fortress headquarters was incredibly well sited and gleamed white in the morning sunlight. Sitting atop one of the many heavily forested hills that parade down to the sea, Fort Whupass looked to be late-seventeenth or early-eighteenth century, most probably English. Colonized by France in 1635, Martinique had remained a French possession, save three brief periods of foreign occupation by Britain.

"Alex Hawke!" Lightning exclaimed when he heard a familiar voice on the phone. "Christ, man, I thought you broke up with me! Where have you been, your lordship?"

Hawke laughed. "In trouble, mostly, Fitz. How the hell are you? Holding down the fort at Fort Whupass?"

"Busier than a long-tailed cat in a roomful of rocking chairs, sir, and glad of it. Got a little gig in Syria coming up in about a month, should be interesting. That new administration in Washington has boosted morale to the point where working with Yank troops might be fun again . . . Tell me what's up."

"Hostage rescue. And the pressure is on."

"How many of my lads do you need, sir?"

"Fifteen, twenty, minimum. There may be another action following quickly on the heels of the rescue. It's a Putin thing. Big surprise, right? Anyway, I need you and Chief Rainwater and I need you now."

"Where are we flying into?"

"Flying? Don't tell me you've still got that old rust bucket C-130 Hercules of yours."

"Indeed, we do, sir. *Archangel* will be aloft long after this lot of us is gone. You remember how much runway she needs, though."

"I do indeed. I'll start looking for a nice quiet little airstrip for you today, in fact."

"Where are you?"

"Zurich. The hostage is being held captive in a fortified, walled compound on an island in Lake Zurich. CIA is now taking sat shots daily, thanks to our old pal Brick Kelly, who dedicated a bird to us."

"Attaboy, Brick!

"Who are we up against? Anybody good?"

"Russians. If I had to guess I'd say KGB spec ops boys, directly under Putin's command. Spetsnaz, KGB, FSB. The bad boys. You know."

"Fuck."

"I try not to use that word, but my sentiments exactly."

"I thought Putin was dead."

"He thought so, too. Turned out not to be true."

"Who's the hostage, Alex?"

"My son, Alexei. They've held him since Christmas. Putin's idea of a way to keep my lordly nose out of his business."

"I guess it's not working. I'm so sorry you're going through this, sir. Fucking Putin."

"It's been sheer, unmitigated hell, Fitz, believe me."

"We'll get him out, Alex. We'll bring him home. You know that."

"Yeah, I do know. But if Putin gets wind of us making a hostage rescue move in his direction, and somebody in that house pulls the trigger and—"

"Stop it! It's not going to happen that way. Have we ever let you down?"

"Of course not. But this thing's been pushing me to the edge, Fitz. I have to be honest. Feel like I'm coming apart around the edges a little bit. Too much booze, too many cigarettes, too little sleep. You know the drill."

"God, do I. Can I have twenty-four hours to put this all together?"

"Yes. Thanks for that."

"Weaponry?"

"Bring everything you've got."

"Holy Christ, Alex. Are you serious?"

"I am. I said there may well be a subsequent action. In the last few weeks, Putin has sent thugs to try and take out everyone close to me. Stokely Jones, maybe Ambrose Congreve next. They only got close with Stoke. He's all right, but they got his best pal. You remember Sharkey?"

"Ah, shit. They got that little Sharkman, did they? Only one arm, but all heart, that one."

"Listen, I've got to jump. The target is in a well-defended compound out on the water. Out on a point of a fairly isolated island. A thick forest screens it from the nearest adjoining estates. Lots of dockage. My thought is, we charter a few high-powered speedboats, as many as we need. There are gobs of the things on Lake Zurich."

"Sounds good."

"We go in full throttle, locate my son, kill anyone who gets in our way on the way in or out. Needs fine-tuning, this plan, but it's fairly straightforward. They sent me a video of him last week. I'll email it to you. He looks good, considering. Clearly not being abused, at any rate. You can see his room, the dimensions anyway . . . might help pinpointing its location inside the complex."

"Every little helps, Skipper."

"I know. Listen, Fitz, I don't need to tell you how much I appreciate this . . ."

"No, you don't. Go get some sleep. See you day after tomorrow, sir. Tell all the lads Fitz says hi."

ALL WAS STILL INSIDE *ARCHANGEL*, the old turboprop transport plane, built by Lockheed in the early fifties. Six hours earlier, the giant matte-black C-130 aircraft had lifted off from a secret airstrip buried deep in the jungles along the northern shores of Martinique.

Aboard were some of the most dangerous men on the planet, killers trained to within a knife's edge of their lives. These hardened commandos all had enormous respect, a feeling bordering on love in some cases, for Alex Hawke, the man who was leading them into battle once more.

On they flew, lumbering along through the sunlit clouds at thirty thousand feet, on a northwesterly course across the rolling black Atlantic, black as night below their massive black wings. The aircraft's entire fuselage, wings, and engine nacelles were always kept to a strict matte black for nighttime insertions or evacs.

There were no nav lights winking on her wingtips, no lights showing at her tail or nose. Even the lights inside the cockpit were a muted shade of red, barely visible from outside the aircraft.

FitzHugh McCoy was up front in the left-hand seat and driving the plane, with Chief Charlie Rainwater in the right-hand position.

T&L commandos sat quietly inside the cold and cavernous fuselage, chilled and cramped on the rows of canvas sling chairs, alone with their thoughts. Some of the guys had just spread out facedown on the greasy pallets on the deck, resting or snoring the long droning hours away. For long periods, no one spoke at all.

They didn't have to. They all knew what the mission entailed down to the last detail. And most important, they all knew, each and every one, knew in their hearts that whatever may befall them in the violent hours ahead, they would gladly give their lives to save Alex Hawke's only son.

Archangel was coming once again . . .

Archangel to the rescue.

CHAPTER SEVENTY-SEVEN

Lake Zurich

They would strike at midnight. The first black, moonless night since the team had first assembled at the Baur au Lac Hotel in the heart of Zurich. Buses had off-loaded the twenty-four-man hostage rescue team at Seepfadi Zürich, the old marina on the lakeshore south of town. Artemis Cooper had managed to locate and charter a half-dozen high-powered speedboats for the trip down the lake and back.

The boats were moored side by side at the dock farthest from shore. On their sterns hung the three engines, triple 300hp Mercury racing engines. Hang nearly a thousand horsepower off the back of one of these things? Get out of the effing way, brother.

And Artemis had identified the perfect staging area from which to assemble and launch the attack, a deserted warehouse right on the lakeside docks. He, Hawke, and Stoke had already commandeered the abandoned building. There the team would perform final weapons and equipment checks. Top off all the tanks with petrol. And have one last look at the intel gathered on the compound and the forces defending it.

Eleven P.M. They had all gathered around a large wooden table, now littered with laptops, communication equipment, physical maps, blown-up reference photos of Alexei on that fateful Christmas Day when he'd been taken, checklists for weapons and ammo and—

Alex saw someone enter through the rear door and instantly knew that the man had been heaven-sent. His friend and the director of the CIA, Brick Kelly.

"Good evening, Alex. Good evening to you too, gentlemen. Sorry to drop in so unexpectedly, but my friend Hawke here said I'd be welcome if I could make it. I'm attending the G7 summit over in Davos, so it was an easy hop over to Zurich."

Hawke strode over and shook his hand. "Thanks for making the time, Brick. What have you got for us?"

"Well, I've got a lot of brand-new CIA intel, including close-up sat shots of the target compound, thermal imaging of current guard changes, et cetera. May I?"

The seasoned warriors looked at each other, incredulous. They'd never seen anything quite like this in all their years of combat. The director of the CIA had just walked into the room and now he was going to brief them?

Brick put a heavy satchel on the table, leather worn thin by years of use. He withdrew a heavy black three-ring binder. A scarlet X on the cover identified the material as top secret. In a pocket inside the binder was an Apple MacBook Air in a hard rubber casing.

And a complete set of construction and elevation plans for most of the buildings inside the walls, courtesy of the CIA's secret digital construction crew.

Brick said, "Let's start with this. Have another look at the hostage video released two weeks ago by Alexei's captors and emailed to Alex. I put a team of analysts on it and they did some fine work."

Kelly hit the play button and Hawke and the commandos huddled in for a closer look as he froze the frame and zoomed in on a window.

"All, notice the sun in deep background. We don't see much of it, but we see enough to notice that it's settling behind those mountains in the far distance. Here I blow up that isolated image and you clearly see the Eiger. And nearby Der Nadel, the mountain called White Death. So, we now know the hostage's quarters are on the western side of the primary residence. With a direct sight line to Der Nadel.

"Now, I'll pull out to look out all three windows visible behind Alexei in the foreground. Two windows on one wall with another one on a perpendicular wall. *Voilà, mes amis,* we now have pinpointed a corner room. *The* corner room on the northwestern side of the building. That's where we'll find your son, Alex."

"God bless you, Brick," Hawke said, his heart racing. This man whom he'd once rescued from certain death at the hands of Iraqi prison guards had never once let him down.

Brick said, "Finally, the trees visible in the windows. Those are mature fir trees. Grow to approximately fifty or sixty feet in height, and we're looking at the very tops of them . . . Are you with me, now? We're looking at elevations . . ."

Hawke stretched his hand out across the table and seized the artist's rendering of the Seegarten compound in his right hand, one that showed the primary residence in great 3-D detail.

"Yes, Brick, we're with you. The top floor. You've correctly identified the exact room where we'll find my son . . . It's this room right here, the one I'm pointing at. Alexei is being held in the northwest corner room on the top floor of the house!"

"That's where you'll find him, men," Brick said. "I'm certain of it."

Hawke grabbed Brick by the shoulders and hugged him.

"Thank you guys for doing this last-minute stuff for us, Brick. You've cut through a ton of analysis crap for us tonight, and probably saved a lot of lives, too. You're the best, man. You want to come along for the fun?"

"I don't think so, Alex. Got to get back to Davos tonight, get a little sleep. My big G7 presentation is the first one up in the morning, so . . ."

"Understood," Hawke said and squeezed his hand in a good-bye shake. "Give 'em hell, Brick."

The man started to make his exit, then checked that thought and remained at the table.

"Hey, boss," Stokely said, a big smile on his face, "now that we know exactly where Alexei is hanging out, shouldn't we just go get his ass *out* of there? *Booyah!*"

"Gentlemen," Hawke said, looking at his combat watch, an old black-faced Rolex Commando he'd worn all the way through his Royal Navy combat tours in the desert. "Are we ready? Let me hear it."

"Ready!" they all boomed out in unison. "Born ready, sir!"

"Well, hell," Hawke shouted, "then let's crank up those damn motorboats and roar like hell down this lake and kick some Russian ass, boys!"

Brick said, "Alex, can I have a quick word? Outside?" They stepped out into the chilly drizzle. "Something's up in Siberia. We don't know what yet."

"Tell me."

"Sats are picking up major flurries kicking up at that old secret KGB headquarters in Siberia. Troops in battle formation, artillery rolled outside and being reconditioned, a damn fighter squadron being taken out of mothballs, et cetera. Preparation for an invasion of some kind, we think."

"Invasion of what? Not the Baltics again?"

"No, he's already done that and failed."

"Who then? The Kremlin oligarchs?"

"No. Your pal Vladimir Putin. He's up to no good again somewhere, that's for damn sure."

CHAPTER SEVENTY-EIGHT

Falcon's Lair

Uncle Joe couldn't sleep. Despite all the planning, all the vast amounts of money expended, all the highly trained members of the Falcon's Lair squads, and Beau's Brigade, all his own assurances to Putin that it was all "under control," that he and Beau were on top of things, he had this nagging feeling here on the very eve of battle.

A nagging voice right at the back of his brain was saying, "Is it, Joe? Is it really, Joe? Is it really *all* under control? I mean, think about it. Russia is about to invade fucking Switzerland!"

Tossing and turning, he kept playing and replaying the dinner conversation he and Shit Smith had had with Colonel Beauregard the night before Beau left for Siberia. There he would fine-tune the troops and ultimately oversee the movement of his mercenary forces across Europe and deep into Switzerland . . . and commence Operation Overkill.

Beau and Joe and Mr. Shit Smith had decided to dine together that night in the main dining room at Falcon's Lair. Putin had been invited but had not shown up. Joe learned from kitchen staff that he'd ordered his meal sent up to his quarters. Along with three bottles of Château Lafite Rothschild and a case of Krug champagne to go with his "Pheasant Under Glass" or whatever.

Beau was saying to Uncle Joe and Shit over dinner: "You know,

Joe, it's long been said that 'Switzerland doesn't *have* an army, Switzerland *is* an army.' You see, the Swiss have not fought a war for nearly five hundred long years, and they are determined to know how so as not to have to fight one!"

"Whut'd he say?" Shit said, already into his seventh beer.

Joe looked at the sullen cowboy, shook his head, and said, "He means they're determined to know how to fight a war so as to know how *not* to fight a war, Shit."

"Whut?" Shit said, still not all that clear on the matter.

"Pay attention to what the man is saying, for crissakes. Go ahead, Beau, continue," Joe said.

"Okay. So in Italy, it has been said of the Swiss army, 'I didn't know they had one.' Ha! When the Italian guy learns that the Swiss army vastly outnumbers Italy's, the guido says, 'That is not difficult.'"

"Funny," Shit mumbled.

Beau continued: "The Swiss army has served as a model for nations a lot less languid than Italy. Get this, the fuckin' *Israeli army* is a copy of the Swiss army. The Israelis, Joe! You think those bastards don't know how to fight?"

Shit said, "How big is Switzerland, anyway? Tiny little place, ain't it?"

"Switzerland is two times the size of New Jersey. New Jersey, by far, has the larger population. Nonetheless, there are nine hundred and fifty thousand people in the Swiss army. At any given time, most of them are walking around in street clothes like you or me, or in blue from the collar down. And at home, every damn one of them's got an assault rifle under the bed!

"I'm talking about a civilian army, Joe, a trained and practiced militia, ever ready to mobilize. They serve for thirty years. All nine hundred and fifty thousand are prepared to be present at mobilization points and battle stations throughout the country in considerably less than forty-eight hours. That's why I've been telling you and Volodya we gotta blitzkrieg this thing."

"Give me forty-eight damn hours," Shit said, "I'll go in and get your damn gold out. Listen, they got an air force? Prob'ly not . . ."

"Hell, yes, they've got one," Beau said. "But you will drive the length and breadth of Switzerland and you will never, I mean, *ever*, see an air force base."

"Where the hell they keep all their airplanes then?" Shit asked, reasonably enough.

"Inside the mountains. Deep beneath the ground. Inside giant hangars carved out of the mountains with high-speed aircraft elevators modeled after those on aircraft carriers, that's where. Elevators take the fighters up to the catapults at the top of the mountains and spit the motherfuckers out at fifteen thousand feet! And all over the country, there are hidden highways used as ground airstrips in remote regions for the Swiss fighters to use in the event of attack.

"Their air force keeps their airplanes inside the *mountains*?" Shit said in total disbelief. "With carrier elevators and catapults? Man, that is pure badass."

"Yes. Mountains everywhere are fighter bases. You'll be hiking in the Alps through some meadow of wildflowers and come across two paved airstrips—but no airport, no evident hangars, because the modern ones are deep under the meadow. And no evident airplanes, no refueling trucks, not even a wind sock to mark the spot of airborne operations . . .

"You see such airstrips in many mountain valleys, too. Near the older ones are World War II hangars that are nothing but subtle rises in the ground. They are painted in camouflage and covered with living grass. Other strips are more enigmatic, since no apparent structures exist at all!

"If you just happen to be looking, though, you might see a hole at the top of a mountain open up—might see something like an enormous mouse hole appear chimerically near the peak of an alp."

"Chimerically," Shit repeated, nodding his head.

"Keep your eyes open. Because shortly, out of that mountain mouse hole comes a wave of supersonic aircraft—a Tiger, a Mirage—all bearing on their wings the traditional Swiss white cross on a field of red. In a matter of seconds, squadrons are climbing into the air.

Manned by pilots who have been training and sitting inside the mountains waiting night and day, month after month, year after year, for someone to be stupid enough to invade Switzerland."

"Like us," Joe said, suddenly horribly depressed.

"No, not like us," Beau said. "I'm not stupid. At least when it comes to fighting and winning wars. Got a pretty goddamn good track record in that department."

"Hell, Beau," Joe said morosely, "what makes you think we can defeat a million-man army? And a hidden air force?"

"Speed, that's what. And, of course, surprise. We get in and out, with all our gold, in less than twelve hours. Way before the forty-eight it will take them to mobilize. We'll take heat, sure, but the advantage of surprise and our instant mobilization? That will win the day. Watch and see."

"I guess so."

Beau almost came out of his chair. "You *guess* so, Joe? You'll be sitting up here in your mountain fortress telling everyone else what to do. What'll I be doing? I'll tell you. I'll be right in the thick of it on the ground, leading the troops to hell and back, praying to god there ain't a bullet out there with my name carved in lead, that's what. Don't give me any more of your happy horseshit, Joe. I ain't in the mood for it."

Joe said, "You're getting paid millions of dollars to take this risk. Nobody feels sorry for you around here."

"And you're *not* getting paid millions? Gimme a fuckin' break, Uncle Joe."

Joe said, "All right, that's it. I'm going to bed. But I just want to say one thing, get it off my chest before I can go to sleep tonight. You listening, Beau?"

"Yeah, I am. But I'm the only one, Joe. Your little cowboy buddy Shit Smith just did a face-plant in his quiche lorraine. He's going to be in great shape tomorrow . . . Go on, say what you got to say, man. Get it over with."

"I got to say that it occurs to me, and it *really bothers* me, that you never gave President Putin your 'stupid enough to invade Switzerland' speech. Now, why do you suppose that is?"

"That's it?" Beau laughed. "Seriously? I didn't tell Putin? That's all you got, man? Christ Jesus, I'll tell you why. Got us a saying out in West Texas might help you out a tad, partner. You listening?"

"I'm listening."

"We say, 'Never ever tell the daddy of some rich gal you're aiming to marry that his little girl is ugly.' "

Joe stood up, wiped his mouth with his linen napkin, and threw it down on the table.

"Ah, great, Beau. That's really good. Very reassuring. So now you're saying to me our little girl is *ugly?* Christ, I hope you know what the hell you're doing, Colonel. Because you sure haven't rallied the troops round the table tonight."

"Go to bed, Joe. You'll feel a whole lot better in the morning," Beau said, pushing back from the table. He left the dining room.

Joe sat there awhile, digesting all the worrisome things he'd just heard, listening to Shit Smith snorkeling loudly in his soup. He'd take him to his room, let him sleep it off. Then fill him with hot coffee and take the sub back across the lake to Seegarten.

He and Shit had a mission tonight.

All day, and he couldn't say why, Joe had nursed a feeling that Alex Hawke might be coming. Tonight or the next night or the next. He had no idea. But if Putin got word of it, that wonderful little boy he'd come to love would be dead in a matter of minutes. There was nothing else for it.

Joe and Shit would spend tonight on the island.

He was determined not to let some KGB thug kill an innocent child who'd done nothing. Nor kill a desperate father guilty of nothing but wanting to save the life of his only son.

If he was right, and Hawke was coming to rescue his son tonight, Joe would make sure that Putin's assassin had to go through Joe Stalingrad and Shit Smith in order to pull the trigger.

CHAPTER SEVENTY-NINE

Lake Zurich

Six high-speed boats, all jet black, all deck lights blacked out, five men to a craft. Stokely, ex–SEAL commando, driving the lead boat at the tip of the spear, a tight V formation. Hawke and Artemis were both just coming aboard, along with Auguste François, ex–French Foreign Legion, and a tough little Kentucky war fighter, a legendary Ranger sniper everyone called Beetle.

Before firing up the three powerful outboard engines hanging off the stern, Stoke had killed all the lights aboard, and only the instrument panel was casting a dull reddish glow on their faces.

"Everybody strapped in?" Stoke asked his crew.

Affirmative *yo*'s all around.

"Stoke," Hawke said, "give me a heads-up when we approach the five-thousand-yard-out mark on our approach to the island. We want to drift in and out of the fog. Edging closer into the docks at dead slow, staying close to the parameters of the fog until we get a good look at what we're dealing with. If there's a major artillery piece on the dock aimed in our direction, I want to disappear back where I came from . . ."

"Aye aye, Skipper."

"Let the other five skippers know as well."

"Not now, but right now!" Stoke said, grabbing the VHF radio.

Powering through the thick lake-effect fog that lay over the surface, and traveling at racing speeds down the mirror-smooth lake, they maintained their strictly held V-formation. The lead boat's foaming white-water wake was enormous. Racing engines, each pumping out a thumping three hundred horsepower, were kicking up all kinds of hell.

Hawke was at the stern of the lead boat, mentally taking stock of his team fanned out back there.

After all the discussions about strategy, after all the endless poring over CIA sat shots of the island, the Seegarten compound, calculating the dimensions of the big docks that stuck far out into Lake Zurich . . . after all the long nightmare of wondering if Alexei was dead or still alive, Alex Hawke was at long last taking the fight to the enemy.

And taking the infamous warlords Thunder and Lightning along for the ride.

Every man of the five squads was kitted out the same. They wore dark camouflage tiger stripes, wore nothing at all reflective, faces blacked out with camo war paint. Thunder and Lightning would be invisible when the five boats slowed dramatically to a dead-slow drift out of the fog and toward the docks.

"Mark!" Stoke said. "Five thousand yards and closing . . ."

Hawke felt the boat shudder and slow dramatically as Stoke throttled back at the five-thousand-yard marker. Looking through the powerful Leica binocs, Hawke went to the stern. He was surveying the dockage space, the shoreline, and the outer perimeter of the walled compound. Boat one would arrive first at the long dock at Seegarten and—

"Shit!" Hawke whispered, whirling around and motioning for Beetle to come aft to him.

Two makeshift wooden guard towers had been hastily erected since the last CIA sat pass! One, the closest, gave a view to the seaward side, and the farthest one looked out over the forest at the rear, or, western side of the residence . . .

Hawke handed the binocs to Beetle.

"First tower dead abeam of us, Beetle. I count three guards, two searchlights up top. Stoke, stop the boat a thousand yards offshore. Beetle needs to take out that first tower trio of tangos before they pick us up . . ."

And so it began.

Alex Hawke, as the Alpha Squad leader, would take his men way south along the shore, staying outside the wall, before turning west and entering the deep forest at the rear of the compound. Covering his flank, and ultimately joining up with Alpha, would be Stokely and his Bravo Squad.

Once Hawke and his two squads were in place in the woods behind the house itself and ready to scale the wall, they would alert Fitz's Charlie Squad and Brock's Echo to commence combat operations at the lakefront entrance to the compound.

Chief Rainwater, a towering figure in the rarefied world of combat demolition, and his Charlie fighters would be rigging Semtex plastic explosives at the wide entrance gate and all along the base of the seaward wall. Once the wall was breached, Echo, led by Harry Brock, would race inside the compound, with Charlie and his guys hot on their heels, all obliterating anyone who was suicidal enough to get in their way.

At least that was the way it was supposed to work, Hawke thought, as the big black speedboat nosed through fog thick enough to choke you and smelling terribly of seaborne iodine. The engines, at idle speed, were burbling softly at the stern.

"I'm sighted in, Skipper," Beetle said quietly, a man at one with his gun, lightly gripping the forearm, right elbow rock steady on top of his beanbag . . .

"Range?" Hawke said.

"One thousand yards, sir."

"Elevation?"

"Fifteen degrees, plus or minus two."

"Comfy?"

"Yes, sir."

"Take them out," Hawke said simply.

And Beetle did just that. Easy. All head shots: *pfft, pfft, pftt.*

One. Two. Three.

Simple as that.

THE ALPHA ATTACKERS CREPT THROUGH the forest toward the rear of the compound, the sounds of their footsteps muffled by the dense layer of pine straw under the soles of their combat boots. A light rain had begun to fall and the dark and looming trees were dripping.

Hawke could see lights through the branches now, blooming yellow in the windows of the upper floors. He signaled the squad to halt just shy of the clearing on this side of the thick brick wall. Moments later, Stoke and Bravo Squad arrived and took up positions inside the trees.

Stoke was looking up at the barbed wire atop the wall, surveilling their situation, quickly making a decision. "No need to demo the wall, Skipper," he said quietly to Hawke.

"Tell me."

"I climb this tree right here, boss. The topmost branches look sturdy enough to take my weight. And those branches reach out pretty far into the clearing. I make my way out, heave a grapnel hook, catch the highest railing on that top-floor terrace, and secure it. We hand-over-hand it across the line, no noise to alert guards or—"

"Guard," Hawke said, "coming around the far corner of the house with his dog. Beetle? You on this bastard?"

"Aye, sir. I've got him."

"Take the shot."

Two barely audible puffs of soft sound and the threat was eliminated.

"Okay, Mr. Jones," Hawke said, "let's do this quickly before another one shows up."

Stoke was already well up into the tree, climbing surely and quickly and silently.

"Artemis, you're next. Then me. Beetle, you're last because I want you to remain in the treetops until it's all over, making that hushpuppy of yours bark whenever necessary. Yes?"

"Yes, sir. I was thinking that, too. Shooting starts, there's a really good field of fire inside the perimeter of the wall from way up there. Maximum effect of the weapon."

Hawke looked up, saw Artemis some twenty feet up and climbing fast. He pulled out his radio. He needed to get Brock and Chief Rainwater on the same page, pronto!

"Charlie, Delta, Echo, this is Alpha, Bravo. We are in position inside the woods west of the compound. Found a way to breach the wall and enter the top floor minus the explosives. Terrace up there. Once we're in position to insert, I'll signal. Everybody copy that?"

They affirmed and Hawke started to climb like a man possessed.

He could barely stand the pounding deep inside his chest that was his terrified heart. If all went according to plan, within an hour, Artemis would be aboard the *Blue Streak*, ferrying Sigrid and little Alexei home to England, to his beloved Hawkesmoor. But. What if Alexei was not there in the corner room, had been moved?

Or what if the incursion had been seen and Putin had already given the order to—No. You don't go there, Lord Hawke. You calm yourself down and you go through that door with the force of a million men and a thousand hurricanes. You find your son, and you keep him safe forever.

That's what you do, Lord Hawke, that is what you damn well do.

CHAPTER EIGHTY

Charlie Rainwater couldn't help but smile when he got Hawke's new plan of attack. Commander Hawke was not going to announce their imminent arrival inside the compound with a noisy explosive breach of the rear wall after all . . . no!

Alpha and Bravo were already inside the rear perimeter! All eight men were up on the top-floor terrace, northwestern corner, all without an audible shot yet to be fired. The chief's plastic C-4 and Semtex charges along the seaward walls were all rigged and primed, and he was just waiting for Hawke to give him the signal to pull the trigger that would launch a spear-thrust attack on Seegarten proper.

He, along with Harry Brock's Echo and Fitz's Delta, had rigged the entire seaward portion of the thick wall to blow inward; all that steel and concrete blasted backward into the faces of the enemy inside. The second Hawke heard the explosions over on the lake side, the two squads under his command would breach the doors and windows and get inside the house in a matter of seconds.

They would then locate the hostage while Charlie, Brock, and Fitz led an assault on the front of the house, striking in a classic pincer movement. Putin's KGB and Spetsnaz forces would be getting M60 hellfire and stun and frag grenades from two directions at once, and from overwhelming force, a Thunder and Lightning house specialty.

Static on Rainwater's radio, then: "Charlie, this is Alpha. Pull the trigger, boys, we're going in."

The chief keyed the radio transmitter as his two squads leapt from the seawall down to the dock to take cover. His idea was that they would commence the attack from this ideal cover and assess the resistance before mounting the seawall and rushing the holes in the compound walls.

The multiple explosions were deafening.

The eight men crouched on the dock hugged the seawall and waited for the smoke to settle. "I'll take a look," the warrior called Thunder said three minutes later.

He rose up and put the glasses to his eyes to survey a scene of horrific destruction. "Holy shit," he whispered, astonished at the effect of their charges. "They're either all dead or they're playing possum under all that masonry. But I'm not taking any chances. Break out the heavy artillery, M60 teams, and lay down a barrage of suppression fire on my signal." Charlie's two weapons were capable of firing several types of ammunition, including ball, tracer, and armor piercing.

"As soon as the dust settles again, we hit them with those big-ass M32 grenade launchers and we go up and over this wall . . . Commence firing!"

Those ten headbangers were up and over that seawall and charging through what was left of the perimeter wall. Desolation and destruction were everywhere they looked.

"Down! Snipers on the rooftop!" Brock shouted as he dropped and rolled, coming up with his weapon trained on the three tangos sighting down at them from high above. He squeezed the trigger and wasted them.

Now they were taking fire from inside the residence. Shooters on all floors at all the windows. They were only fifty yards or so from the front entrance to the mansion. And the ground was covered with a litter of blackened chunks of blasted wall. His idea to focus the charges inward had provided him with an invaluable gift . . . a lot of enemy dead and . . . cover!

"We're going in," Chief Rainwater barked on the radio. "Hammer the front of the house, all three floors, with merciless fire, M60 rounds and grenades to soften them up . . . we storm the front gates in three minutes, on my signal."

And then, sure as sun follows rain, sheer, unadulterated hell was unleashed on the Russian KGB troops guarding the compound from both without and within.

It was a beautiful thing to see, Chief Rainwater thought, just beautiful.

HAWKE LOOKED DEEPLY INTO THE eyes of every one of his two squads' teams. All were now gathered there on the third-floor outdoor terrace. He was seemingly in no hurry at all, staring at them patiently but relentlessly, one by one, unequivocally conveying to each individual the unspoken three-word message he always sent to his warriors on the very brink of battle:

Duty. Honor. Courage.

CHAPTER EIGHTY-ONE

From the lake, a horrific blast rattled the windows all over See-garten. Chief Charlie Rainwater had blown the entire lakefront wall, all right, fifty feet in either direction, apparently to smithereens by the sound of things.

On the terrace, Hawke paused at the primary door to be breached and said: "Go left, four through the door, and clear every room on this floor. Go in low, acquire, and shoot. No fancy head shots. We're firing heavy loads. Once you're clear, round up on me. Stoke and I are going straight for the hostage."

"Blow the east and west doors simultaneously," Stoke said. "Smoke grenades, stun grenades, and frags. Time to hop and pop, ladies."

A second later, the windows and doors exploded inward with the squad's carefully rigged C-4 charges. Jagged shards of glass would shred any enemy combatants foolish enough to be waiting on the other side.

"Go, go, go!" Hawke shouted as his men stormed through blown-out windows and doors, disappearing inside with their weapons blazing. Hawke had identified the exterior door he felt would be the closest exterior entry point to Alexei's corner room. He now said to Stokely, "Blow this door right here! Now!"

Stoke blew the shattered door inward and off its hinges with the thumping M60 machine gun. Seconds later, they were inside. A wide, windowed hallway with a central staircase leading down to the ground floor. The firefight inside was intense.

"Top of the stairs, boss!" he heard Stoke say, and then the muffled *brrrrp* of his HK submachine gun. The barrel smoking inches from Hawke's right ear. Lead from the tangos down the hall whistling past his head.

"Down!" Stoke shouted and Hawke went prone on the marble floor, putting the sights of his own HK on the guards huddled in the smoke of Stoke's grenade. When you can see them, they can see you, he reminded himself, and squeezed the trigger. He saw the reply, two twinkling yellow muzzle flames in the smoke, and emptied a whole mag in that direction, obliterating the enemy in the smoke.

"Behind us!" Stoke shouted as Hawke reloaded. "Coming up the steps!" Concrete and other debris was raining down on them as wayward enemy rounds from hostiles on the staircase tore up the ceiling and walls above their heads. And the enemy was on the move again, charging up the staircase.

Christ. Hawke's machine gun had gotten trapped under his body! He reached behind him and grabbed a frag grenade off his utility web belt, pulled the pin, and heaved it with just enough loft to let it bounce down the wide white marble steps. The fighters saw it coming and started to retreat in a crazy jumble back down the steps.

By then Hawke had his Sig Sauer 9mm pistol on them and was firing into the thick of them. The heavy loads were incredibly effective, men just crumpling at the bottom of the steps. Then the frag blew and nobody and nothing was moving on those stairs.

The loud exchange of automatic weapons' fire on the floors below assured Hawke that Charlie and Delta and Echo squads had entered the residence and were hard at work clearing the ground floor before ascending to the second. It was then that Hawke saw a flash of movement on the floor near Stoke.

"On your right!" Hawke screamed to Stokely, just before he brought his machine gun to bear on a wounded man faking death beneath a table. Hawke had the gun on full auto and he just shredded the man and the table as he and Stoke got to their feet and ran. They heard the sound of a shot being fired in the room at the end of the hall and raced toward it.

Hawke's heart stood still.

The shot had come from inside Alexei's room!

He looked at Stoke, both pausing before the closed door. "I'll roll right, you roll left?"

"Let's go," Stoke said, grabbing the knob and kicking the door in.

CHAPTER EIGHTY-TWO

They dove for the floor, rolling away from each other in opposite directions, leaping to their feet with their weapons extended, the knuckles on their trigger fingers white with stress . . . Hawke's eyes widened in the dimly lit room. Where the hell was his son?

A man in partial shadow sat on the edge of the single bed. Joe, sure it was! He had his arm around a small dark-haired child who was weeping. Hawke knew the sound of those sobs by heart. Those were Alexei's tears . . .

The room was nearly dark, only a small candle flickered on the bedside table.

"Turn on the lights, Stoke," Hawke said quietly.

A second later, all was illuminated.

"Alexei," Hawke said, gazing down at his little boy, near tears himself, "are you all right, son?"

"Daddy?" came a tiny whisper . . .

"Yes, it's Daddy. I've come to take you home, son."

"Is it really you?"

"Yes, Alexei, it's really me. It's your papa."

"I want to go home, Daddy. Please?"

"I know you do, son. Me too."

The boy looked up at his father, trying to smile through his tears. "Can Uncle Joe come, too? He's my friend."

Hawke took a step forward and his foot brushed what felt like a human form. He stepped back to inspect it.

"What happened here, Joe?" Hawke asked, staring at the dead man lying in the shadows, on his back on the floor a few feet from the bed, his throat a yawning maw of red and white and pink gristle. Thickening blood puddled on the floor. There was a still-smoking gun in his hand, a small Makarov 9mm automatic. KGB.

"Who the hell is that?" Hawke asked Joe.

"Anatoly Slivko. KGB political officer. One of Putin's most trusted lieutenants. He came here to kill your son."

"That was the shot I heard? He fired at Alexei?"

"No," Joe said, "he fired a shot at me because I had a gun on him and wouldn't let him get between me and the boy."

"You were here protecting Alexei, weren't you, Joe?"

"Been here all night. For some reason, I thought you might be coming. Maybe tonight, maybe the next, but soon. I don't know why. But I knew if you did attempt a rescue, Putin would send his assassins to the island as soon as he learned of the assault."

Joe lifted the sleepy Alexei up and offered him to his father. Hawke took his son in his arms and hugged him tightly to his chest, his cheeks gleaming with tears in the lamplight.

"Oh, Daddy, oh, Daddy . . . I missed you so much and—"

"Shhh. Just rest. We're going home now."

"Did you do that to him?" Hawke said to Joe, staring at the dead man bleeding out on the floor. "His head is almost severed."

"No. The man over there in the corner did it. Slashed him ear to ear as you can see. He came up behind the assassin just as he raised the gun to shoot Alexei and fired at me instead. The boy was still asleep in his bed . . ."

"What man?" Hawke said, looking around.

"Over there in the corner, boss," Stoke said, pointing at a tall man in black sitting in an armchair, wiping the blood off of a long-bladed knife. It sounded like he was whistling softly as he worked.

"Who the hell is that, Joe?" Hawke said.

"Name's Smith. Putin's new bodyguard and chief of security."

"You saved my son's life, Mr. Smith," Hawke said quietly to the tall man. "I cannot ever thank you enough."

"Well, hell, you know. Good thang I walked in when I did," the man said with a long, slow drawl. "I don't much truck with folks who'd kill a child laying asleep up in his own bed. No need to thank me, it's what I do."

"Joe," Hawke said, his mind racing, "how the hell do you explain all this to Putin without getting shot yourself?"

"Mr. Smith came in, saw Putin's assassin about to shoot me in the gut. There was a struggle for the gun and Smith slashed his throat. During the struggle Hawke snatched the boy and bolted . . . That's all I've got, and if he doesn't buy it—well, hell, I guess I'm fucked."

"Joe. Come with me now. It's your only chance! Putin will never forgive another betrayal. He will most certainly kill you for aiding and abetting Alexei's escape!"

"No. He knows his life is in my hands now and there's nothing he can do about it. He's paying me millions to help him return to power. He *needs* me, Alex! He's totally dependent on me and Mr. Smith over there, and Colonel Beauregard. He won't kill any of us, trust me. We're all that's standing between him and the next assassin's bullet from the Kremlin."

"You saved Alexei, Joe. You did. I can't tell you how—"

The house was rocked by another loud explosion from somewhere in the direction of the waterfront.

"Boss!" Stoke, who stood gazing out the window, said, grabbing Hawke's shoulder.

"What?"

"We got to go! Spetsnaz troops are out on the docks, pouring gasoline and rigging charges all over our speedboats. The first one just blew! If we don't withdraw right now and get the hell off this island, we'll be trapped out here!"

"He's right," Hawke said to Joe, and turned for the door. With his son cradled in his arms, he took one last look at Shit Smith, his black cowboy hat pulled low over his eyes.

"Mr. Smith, whoever you are, you didn't just save one life tonight. You saved both a father and a son. I shan't ever forget you."

"Won't forget you either, pards," Shit Smith said in his low voice, staring at Hawke with a hard look in his black eyes that Hawke would never forget. The man appeared to be literally *smoldering*. Then, he smiled.

"You look like the kinda hombre could put up a good fight. Tell the truth, I don't run across too many like that. You and me, we could really mix it up sometime, huh? You like a knife fight some day?"

"C'mon, boss! We got to go!" Stoke said, grabbing Hawke by the shoulder and dragging him away from the twisted cowboy.

"Good-bye, Joe," Hawke said, pausing at the door, Alexei sound asleep, his head on his father's shoulder. "Tell me one thing. Putin's holed up inside the Sorcerer's old mountain complex, isn't he?"

"Yes. He is."

"Mounting an operation called Overkill?"

"Correct."

"What is it?"

"Bottom line? Putin's pulling a Goldfinger. His enemies stole about all of his gold and he wants all his gold back. Use it to take out the oligarchs running the Kremlin. That's the plan, what can I tell you?"

"Stay safe, Joe."

ON THE DOCKS, A FIREFIGHT was raging. Hawke, with Alexei still asleep in his arms, was waiting for the final skirmish to end. He was seated in an armchair, peering out a ground-floor window. He saw one of his boats was already afire and sinking, stern down.

He feared the blaze could soon expand to the other speedboats, eliminating any hope of their escape from Seegarten Island.

But the tide was turning.

Charlie and Delta and Echo squads now had the enemy fighters diving off the docks into the water to escape the hail of lead pouring onto them. And then the Russians started taking fire from their rear.

Alpha and Bravo now opened up with everything they had, as Hawke's guys began to pour out of the building. The carnage was devastating, the day was won. When the shooting stopped, when the appointed medic in each of Hawke's squads had attended to the dead and wounded, carrying many to the boats by stretcher, after the fire aboard the sinking boat was extinguished, Chief Charlie Rainwater, Thunder, went inside the darkened building, now eerily silent after all the gunfire and explosions.

"Sir?" he said, spying Hawke by the window. "I think it's time."

"Thanks, Chief, I'm coming. It's clear?"

"All clear, Commander. We're loading our dead and wounded and starting the boats."

Hawke rose from the chair and turned toward the front door.

A MINUTE LATER, EVERY MAN on the deck stopped doing what he was doing. The reaction of the men was instant and filled with satisfaction and a love of their leader. Everyone started applauding, cheering loudly. All of them knowing full well what was coming. What would happen when that front . . .

Alex Hawke emerged from the smoking building with his son in his arms and started walking toward the men at the boats.

"Mission accomplished, gentlemen," Hawke shouted from the steps. And his men went wild. "Once again, duty, honor, and courage have prevailed."

The man had his son in his arms. He was alive. He was safe.

It was time to go to war.

OPERATION
OVERKILL

CHAPTER EIGHTY-THREE

Falcon's Lair

P-day minus one. The last of the Falcon's Lair troops on the mountain-top had been deployed just before daybreak. Joe Stalingrad supervised their deployment, standing before the soaring floor-to-ceiling window with a radio in his hand. Lead-paned and crystal clear, it occupied one entire wall of Putin's magnificent walnut-paneled office and gave a panoramic view of what would soon be a field of battle.

When he'd first been ushered into this office, Uncle Joe had wondered if this window overlooking the roof of the world was a good idea. Especially for a man who was determined to hide from the whole damn planet. That was before, upon inspection, he saw the massive steel doors set in the rock to either side, their exterior sides camouflaged in hyperrealistic but fake rock. Doors and windows built in this fashion were everywhere, and all would seal tight at the push of a button.

There were fine and faded Aubussons and Persian rugs underfoot; the walls were studded with Old Masters, while the bookcases proudly displayed vast leather-bound collections of everything from Goethe to Gandhi, from Dickens to Hemingway to, of course, Chekhov, Pushkin, and Dostoyevsky. There was also a leather-bound copy of Nabokov's *Lolita*, Joe's fave novel of all time.

On the massive mahogany partner's desk, that large Nazi swastika, made of highly polished sterling silver, was being used as a paperweight . . .

Since Putin had suddenly stopped using the office, for god knows what reason, preferring to keep to his bed, Joe had gladly exercised his squatter's rights.

He and the president had spoken on only a few occasions since Seegarten fell to Hawke. And the scary discussion about who was responsible for Hawke's successful rescue of his son. Joe had been right about Putin, however. Under normal circumstances, the president would have had both Joe and Shit Smith shot for interfering in the hostage situation . . . preventing the boy's murder.

But these were definitely not normal circumstances. Putin needed Joe to keep Beauregard's invasion on track. And he needed Shit Smith to protect him from Alex Hawke, should his nemesis manage to confront him once more. In the unlikely event that Hawke's men should manage to break through the defenses and storm the gates at Falcon's Lair, Joe and the president had a secret escape plan. A plan known to only the two of them . . . and though it was strictly against Putin's wishes, Miss Emma Peek, Joe Stalingrad's latest conquest in waiting.

She had been intent upon seducing him just the night before, but Joe had been distracted by impending events. Still, he knew a sure thing when he saw it coming. She wore ever-shorter skirts, and every time she crossed her legs, she managed to give him a quick glimpse of her invariably pink panties. He was already fantasizing about marrying the damn woman, for crissakes! Did he love her? He knew only that he would gladly crawl through a mile of broken glass just to drink her bathwater.

And the poor kid hadn't even gotten a good gander at Playstation's *junk* yet!

On the snowy crest below the window, in the pale pink glow of dawn, a group of six Falcon's Lair commandos, magnificent in their white Alpine combat uniforms, were just being towed up to a higher altitude by one of the Weasels, like so many water-skiers.

Small tracked vehicles, Weasels were heated and equipped with a canvas roof; they featured widely spaced tracks that made it possible to operate in light-snow Alpine conditions. But the troops liked it better when they were towed to the top behind the Weasel with a towrope.

Joe, after much consideration, had decided to position his defenses a thousand feet above and a thousand feet below the primary entrance to Falcon's Lair. Two thousand feet of hot death, at elevations from thirteen to eleven thousand—bring it on. Some of the men were just now establishing machine-gun nests at various altitudes and locations. Many of them would be dug into snowbanks, completely concealed, invisible to the human eye even at twenty feet.

When the attack came, and it was coming, he knew, as sure as night follows day, he was ready to put up a helluva fight. But the odds were with him. If ever anything as sure as an impenetrable fortress existed in this world, Joe thought, taking a seat at his desk, Falcon's Lair was certainly it.

"Kitchen, may I help you?" said the voice on the phone when he punched the number.

"Has Miss Peek called for her breakfast yet?"

"No, sir. She usually calls at six thirty."

"Hmm. Fifteen minutes. When she does, please tell her that I'm having breakfast in my office and would like her to join me."

"Of course, sir. And what would you like to order this morning?"

"Coffee, black, for two. In the silver urn. Cheese omelet with baked ham, Brie, and shaved truffles on top. And, uh, a Diet Coke for me, please."

"Very good, sir. Shall we say in twenty minutes?"

"Perfect."

He hung up, sat back, and put his feet on the desk, gazing at the sterling silver swastika. It put him in mind of another man who'd had big plans to invade the tiny country of Switzerland: Adolf Hitler. Joe and Beauregard had done endless research, studying Operation

Tannenbaum, the German war plans for their pending invasion. An invasion that was over before it commenced. Upon reflection, Joe had to concede that between *der Führer* and him, there were few similarities.

Herr Hitler had had the Wehrmacht, the most powerful military machine on the face of the earth. Joe had Colonel Beauregard and his mercenaries. Hitler had the Luftwaffe and Hermann Göring, winner of the Blue Max and founder of the Gestapo. Joe had Beau. Hitler had Rommel. Joe had Shit Smith. Hitler had Eva Braun. Joe had—well, Joe had Emma Peek, so when it came to snatch, he'd gotten the best of Adolf there at least, and—

"There you are, Joe, you naughty, naughty boy!"

Joe was snapped out of his troublesome reverie by the appearance of the golden-haired Lady Di at his door.

Or at least a dead ringer for her.

"Good morning!" Joe said, leaping to his feet and going to her. Emma Peek looked adorable in a short skirt and a tight-fitting, plunging V-neck pink sweater. Hugging her to him was always such a treat. Because of his height, when he held her close, his face was automatically enveloped between her glorious perfumed bosoms. Sheer heaven. He wanted to die in there.

"Am I naughty, Miss Peek?" he asked her, briefly coming up for air to give her a kiss.

"You certainly have been, young man."

"What was my transgression?"

"Well, for starters, you couldn't get it up last night. And then when I awoke this morning, I had big plans for you, mister. But you were gone from my bed without so much as saying good night. What time did you leave me? And more important, why? Do you not, after all this flirtation, find me attractive? It was my perception that you were quite hot to trot. Superheated, in fact."

"God, no, I'm crazy about you, baby. Couldn't concentrate, that's all. Worried about things, as you know. I went down to combat ops to see if they had any idea where Beauregard was. He was supposed to call me last night. Then I went to the hangar level, to check on the squadrons' readiness . . ."

"And?"

"Good, thank god. Half of the fighter jets are already in the tunnels and ready to be catapulted out into thin air. The other half are waiting down at the hangar level in the high-speed elevators. I feel like I've done all I can do for now, but then I wonder. Do you think I'm utterly mad to have taken all this on? I sometimes do."

"Perhaps a little, Joe. But if we can get out of this nightmare without getting killed, we're going to emerge with countless millions in gold. You can buy me a villa at Cap d'Antibes and a glorious town house on the Rue Faubourg Saint-Honoré in Paris. And a pied-à-terre in Beverly Hills. Oh, and maybe a pretty little white jet and a big fat yacht thrown into the mix for good measure. Happily ever after!"

"Thanks for reminding me, honey. Makes me feel a lot better."

"We'll all feel a whole lot better when we hear from that fucking lunatic Colonel Beauregard. Let's call him now. See where the hell he is."

"May I serve you breakfast, sir?" a pretty little thing in a white cap and matching white apron asked him.

He nodded yes and then plunged his head back into Emma's bosom.

If only he could hide here inside her soap-scented warmth forever . . .

CHAPTER EIGHTY-FOUR

Somewhere in Europe

You could feel her coming. Before you saw her, before you even heard her, you felt her presence. The wind trembled before her and the earth shook in her wake. Tonight, even as dark clouds scudded across the face of the pale moon, the birds and busy creatures of the forest went suddenly still and silent.

The gleaming twin rails began to hum and then to sing . . . she was gathering speed. Careful! She's getting closer . . . slicing through the dark heart of Europe like a speeding knife. Her destination, Zurich, in the tiny Alpine country considered for centuries to be Fortress Switzerland.

The Arrow flies. See her four great funnels belching brilliant showers of flaming sparks up into the black penumbra of the frigid night? Look now, before she enters the yawning maw of the looming tunnel and plunges ahead, diving deep into the winter-white Alps . . .

The Black Arrow.

The oldest, grandest, and most illustrious survivor of them all, the historic Trans-Siberian Railway trains. Under new ownership, the Black Arrow had, since leaving the Grand Maket Rossiya railway museum at Odessa, traveled through eight time zones. Fifty railway passenger cars, boxcars, and freight cars in all: sleeping and dining cars for the troops; freight cars for food, water, and vodka, and for the Mini Tiger tanks and the light artillery and, finally, automatic weapons for Colonel Beauregard's troops.

The whole length of the train, gleaming black with gold trim, and festooned with scarlet bunting, trailed behind the brutish machine at the head, had fifteen boilers putting out nearly 18,000 horsepower. This, then, was Goliath, as the famous locomotive was known in the history books, a rolling monument to the lore of the rail, mechanized art in iron and steel, an enduring tribute to Russian locomotive might, the fastest, most powerful locomotive ever. She was Beau's pride and joy. He'd located Goliath at a lapsed museum, he'd negotiated her purchase on behalf of Putin, and at the KGB's Siberian headquarters, he'd overseen the conversion to military rail transport.

And then he sat down to figure out just how the hell he was going to get the Black Arrow from Russia and into Switzerland.

He was a master of military logistics after all. If anyone could solve this puzzle, he was that person. He sat up late that night with a bottle of Beluga Gold Strike and his old Mount Blanc pen, scrawling down ideas as fast as he could throw them into the fire. And then, like he'd known it would, came an idea so good it made him want to get up and dance about like Baryshnikov!

Yes. He would rename his train! He would call it, what, the Black Arrow, of course. Yes! And he would disguise it. And create a plausible event around historical locomotives that the Black Arrow could star in. He would stage something in Zurich! A plausible event, something believable to all the border patrols he'd have to get through. And he'd call his festival The Great Railway Centennial. That just might work, he'd thought, and then he went to work.

Flags and pennants on every car announcing the Centennial. Flyers depicting the Black Arrow in all its glory. Beneath the polished bronze headlamp on the front of the smokebox, he would mount a large silver five-point Russian star flanked by two large crimson banners that read:

Celebrating 100 Years of Railway History!
THE BLACK ARROW
CENTENNIAL

AND SO THE BLACK ARROW commenced its epic race across Europe, taking dead aim at the heart—Switzerland!

The colonel's butt hurt. Try sitting on a steel chair with no cushion for a few days. He spent his nights with a bottle of ZYR vodka (100 points!) in his sleeping car just aft of the coal car. His days were spent in one of the two dining cars, grabbing chow and playing cards with his newly minted mercenary troops.

Or, right here up front in the locomotive with the engineer, a gargoyle of a man and his new best friend, Vasily. Vasily had let him drive the train a lot when they had first left Russia. Helped him pass the hours until he even tired of helming the the Black Arrow's badass locomotive called Goliath.

Also with Beau on this starry evening in March was his hand-picked adjutant, a young former Swiss Mountain Division lieutenant named Hans Blitzen. Blitzen, a military translator, had been recruited to aid the colonel in his work to make the Black Arrow's race across Europe go as smoothly as possible.

The Centennial cover story for this rapid-fire insertion of troops, tanks, and artillery into the historically neutral heart of Europe was eventually a joint creation of Beauregard and Blitzen. Putin himself had described the idea as genius, a word Beauregard never tired of hearing as applied to him.

The trickiest parts, he well knew, were the border crossings. Sometimes the border guards saw the fluttering pennants waving on the Black Arrow and just waved you on through. Sometimes you got the officious petit bureaucrat far more concerned with procedural correctness than necessary. That's when his decision to hire Lieutenant Blitzen paid off.

The man had also been the highest-ranking logistics officer in the Swiss army's Mountain Infantry Battalion 29. He knew all the details about the customs and border patrol documentation needed for inter-European railway operations. He'd spent a week with KGB forgers in the documents section getting all of the Black Arrow's official papers in order.

And now there was only one more border to cross. The final one, at Basel, Switzerland. It would be the toughest, both men knew. Customs as well as immigration officers were going to ask a lot of questions and demand a lot of paperwork. But the colonel had a lot of confidence in Blitzen and wasn't overly worried about getting the train across the Rhine.

"Border in nine minutes," Vasily said.

"Well, Lieutenant, I reckon it's showtime," Beau said.

Blitzen snapped to attention. "Yes, sir! As I've told you both many times, when they demand the paperwork, you and Vasily need to say as little as possible, sir. No matter what they say or ask you for, you just defer to me. With a simple nod of the head."

"Won't they think it's strange, the two of us riding up front in the locomotive?"

"A little. But we both have powerfully credible documents as high-ranking officials of the Black Arrow Centennial Committee. We can do whatever we want. They'll want to see Vasily's paperwork first. That's always the way. I gave him everything he'll need to produce, including a passenger manifest, and a bill of lading for the food and water aboard."

The speeding black train slowed coming around a wide bend in the fast-flowing river. The large white cement building that housed customs and immigration officers loomed up ahead, looking like an oversized bunker on Normandy beach. The large Swiss flag, red with a white cross in the center, was still flying above the rooftop, lit by floodlights below. Lieutenant Blitzen surveilled the scene with his high-power binoculars.

"Slower, Vasily," Blitzen said. "Slower. Shit. They're already lowering the crossing gate . . ."

"What does that mean?" Beau said.

"I'm not sure yet. I need to get a closer look at them. Okay, Vasily, you need to stop the train well short of the gate for them to board . . . We may need to get up a head of steam in a hurry."

The fat little ginger-haired engineer hauled back on the throttle, first halving the amount of steam pressure, then slowly reducing it to zero pressure on the big brass gauges above their heads.

The huge brakes squealed and clouds of steam billowed out from beneath the locomotive as two men emerged from the building and quickly descended the steps leading down to the tracks. Both were wearing uniforms of pale blue and highly polished black leather boots up to their knees. The colonel and Blitzen tried to read them as they neared the locomotive. They looked as if they took their positions at the border very seriously. Very erect, no readable expressions on their faces.

Lieutenant Blitzen opened the cabin door and smiled as the two officials came to a halt on the platform.

"Good evening, *mein Herr*," he said in German to the ranking officer. He stepped back and allowed them to board the train. "*Wilkommen*."

"Papers," the older officer said stiffly, regarding the engineer with mild curiosity.

"*Jawohl, mein Herr*," Vasily said in easy, practiced German, and handed the Centennial binder with all of his forged information to the officer.

The younger man smiled at Hans Blitzen and held out his hand for the documents. He scrutinized every word, it seemed, and he was in no hurry.

"This is a ceremonial train?" he asked the lieutenant. "Not commercial?" Blitzen smiled.

"It is, sir. A 100 Year Centennial celebration. A gathering in Zurich of famous trains from all over Europe. You may have heard of it? No. Ah, well. Have a look at this flyer, it gives you all the information about the festival. We will be the first to arrive, I made sure of that."

"So your final destination is Zurich Hauptbahnhof?"

"It is indeed."

"Well, all your paperwork seems to be in order. But I'm afraid I have some bad news. Due to an accident, there may be a line closure at Frankenkirch. Line replacement crews are now on their way. Your train will need to stop and be fully inspected there. Mandatory, *mein herr!*"

"When will they arrive? The inspectors?" Blitzen asked, trying to mask his anger.

"Assume sometime around five A.M."

"This is an extremely fast train, sir," he said. "We'll be well past Frankenkirch and at Zurich Hauptbahnhof by that time."

"You don't seem to understand. We have no way of knowing when the line will be closed in both directions. You are required to stop at Frankenkirch for inspection. I will call and alert the inspectors about your arrival and perhaps they can expedite the process so that—"

"No need for that," Colonel Beauregard said, suddenly revealing the small automatic pistol in his hand. He aimed it at the older officer's head and said, "You see, you're coming with us, my friend. We cannot afford to be late for our rendezvous in Zurich. My colleague here is going to handcuff you both to that steam pipe over your heads. If either of you resist, you'll be shot. I'm assuming you understand English."

"You cannot be serious," the older officer said with a smile.

"Oh, I'm deadly serious, I assure you. I eat men like you for breakfast. Now do as he says, or I shall kill you both right here and now and throw your corpses into the Rhine when we cross the bridge. Either way, doesn't matter to me. Get on your radio and tell them to raise the crossing gates. Do it now!"

"Do as he says," the immigration officer told his young colleague. "This is an outrage."

"It is, isn't it? But war is war, my friend, and all is fair."

"War? What war?"

"Your war, I'm afraid. The coming invasion of Switzerland. This train is the opening salvo. You are eyewitnesses to history, gentlemen. My congratulations!"

"Vasily, full head of steam," Blitzen said. "We want the train to blow right through those barriers at full throttle. Send a radio signal that she's coming . . . the Black Arrow."

CHAPTER EIGHTY-FIVE

Zurich

The Black Arrow gathered speed as it rocketed down the polished Swiss rails, racing ever closer to the postcard-pretty town of Frankenkirch. Beau grinned a private grin at his next thought: the customs officials would not exactly be awaiting them with open arms.

But, so what? With Goliath's enormous power and speed leading the charge, they would blow right through the border and cross the Rhine! He had his top-secret orders in a red leather envelope from Putin, with instructions that it was not to be opened until he was safely inside the Swiss borders. He'd planned to open it right after all the drama to come at Frankenkirch.

His heart had lifted in anticipation of the amount of detail in the plans the envelope surely contained. Russian sat shots of the high pass in the Alps, a place he'd come to refer to as the Vegas Strip. Drawings and elevations of the three vault installations along the Strip. Where the machine-gun emplacements were. Where the artillery was, where bridges and tunnels were mined . . . and how. In short, a treasure trove for a wily tactician!

Down to the thickness and combinations to massive steel vault doors themselves!

In the steam-shower heat inside Goliath's cab, tension weighed like a warm fog. The two prisoners of war were driving Beau crazy. Wouldn't effing shut the eff up. He finally spied a roll of black duct tape hanging beneath the instrument panel.

"See that tape, Hans, up there?" he asked Blitzen. "Hanging below the pressure gauges?"

"Yes, sir."

"Cut two strips and tape their goddamn mouths shut. If they resist, shoot these two assholes. I'm sick to death of them. First two casualties in the war, that's all. Hear that, boys?" he said, smiling at them and waving his pistol about. "You're gonna be the first! Hot damn. You're going straight to number one!"

Beau, chuckling to himself, leaned forward, military binocs raised to his eyes, and stared up the tracks, studying the situation ahead. His new pal, Vasily, had told him that, at their current speed, eighty miles an hour, it would take the half-mile-long train a mile to stop.

"We're not going to stop, Vasily. How many times do I have to tell you that? Can you go any faster, for god's sake?"

Vasily looked at him as if he was insane and shook his head no.

Suddenly a blurry white form on the track up ahead, still some distance away, resolved itself into a blunt reality.

"Vasily, is that the Frankenkirch station?"

"Yes, sir. I beg you to reconsider your plan. It could easily result in disaster. We will all be killed."

"Vasily, if I see that throttle eased even a billionth of an inch, I will put a bullet in the back of your head and drive this train to Zurich all by myself. Do you understand me?"

"I do."

As they sped even closer, Beau saw the station far, far up ahead. It was another big white concrete block of a building, all lit up like a national monument with a number of floodlights mounted on steel poles atop the walls that surrounded the complex. You could see a lot of people standing on the platform next to the tracks. Far too many for this time of night, so police or military or both.

As soon as they got within a mile, Beau saw what they were up against. It wasn't any lowered crossing pole. No! They'd put into place some kind of heavy concrete structures, the kind you see around embassies in Damascus or Tehran, secured to the track rails with heavy steel reinforcements.

"Changing your mind?" Vasily shouted to Beau above the roar of the train.

"Fuck no. When I'm in, I am all the way in. Lieutenant? What about you?"

"We've come way too long and too far to stop now, sir. Damn the torpedoes! Let's roll!"

Above the black tape patches beneath their noses, the eyes of the two customs and immigration officers were wild with fear. So too, Beau saw through his high-powers, were the frightened eyes of the men and women crowding the platform. The Black Arrow was inside a mile now, and she wasn't slowing down! The imminent collision would kill them all!

At a quarter of a mile and closing fast, most of those up on the crowded platform had jumped down onto the railbed or the tracks and were running for their lives. Vasily had completely lost it. Took his hands off the throttle and dropped to the steel floor, covering his eyes and screaming, "I don't want to die! I don't want to die!"

Beau was hanging on to a steel support brace on the roof, gripping for all he was worth with both hands . . .

"Brace yourself, Lieutenant!" he shouted. "Grab something secure! We're going to hit! We're going to hit . . . NOW!"

There was a horrific jolt, then a massive grinding and screeching noise as Goliath's nose impacted the concrete and steel abutments. The men in the cockpit were all thrown forward as the locomotive staggered, slowed . . . and then gradually regained its powerful forward momentum.

No one up in the cab was hurt save Vasily. His body had been thrown violently forward and his head had slammed into the steel bulkhead. He was instantly knocked unconscious, with a deep laceration to his forehead. Beau, who'd been studying the little fellow's every move for many long hours across the European continent, assumed control of the speeding locomotive. He looked at his watch. It was midnight. He firewalled the throttles.

At eighty miles per hour, Hans Blitzen calculated, they would enter the massive rail yards at Switzerland's largest train station . . . at three in the morning. It would be dead quiet and the massive yards would be virtually empty. That was his experience, at any rate.

NEXT STOP, ZURICH HAUPTBAHNHOF. THE beautiful terminal lies at the heart of the city, nestled on the banks of the River Limmat. Residents and tourists crowd together from morning to midnight, taking advantage of the many shops and restaurants. And it's just a short walk to the town's bustling Lake Zurich.

But, at three A.M., it's another story.

The Black Arrow had made the trip from the Russian border to the Swiss in record time, arriving a full hour ahead of schedule. As they rolled slowly to a stop on the side-yard tracks farthest from the terminal and least likely to be patrolled by railway security officers, Hans was thrilled to see that his assessment of the yard held true. Not a soul in sight.

Beau smiled at Hans, thanked him, and picked up his radio. Time to check in with the powers that be.

"Combat ops," the voice said.

"Falcon's Lair. Combat ops, this is Overkill. Do you read me?"

"Loud and clear, Colonel. Over."

"Good. Black Arrow has just arrived Zurich Hauptbahnhof and we have begun the unloading of T-14 Mini Tiger tanks, troops, and light artillery. What is the status of Falcon's Lair air squadron? Over."

"Certified airworthy. Fuel topped off and all pilots on the line, the first wave idling inside the elevators, awaiting cat shots and launch commands, sir. Over."

"Good. I may need air cover en route to the Vegas Strip when the

Swiss army catches wind of this. But hold some fighters in reserve and ready to launch initial fighters on my signal . . . over."

"Roger that, sir. Over."

"My logistician says at the current rate, the flatbed truck and buses will be loaded and en route to the mountains in approximately twenty minutes."

"Standing by to launch first-wave aircraft on your signal, sir. Over."

AT FALCON'S LAIR, THE MOOD was tense. Joe Stalingrad and Putin weren't speaking, and Uncle Joe was clearly worried about the impending hostilities with the Swiss army and air force. To make matters worse, Putin had started drinking early and was stomping around combat ops and the fighter squadrons' pilot briefing room, screaming at anyone who got anywhere near him.

All of their hopes were riding on the skill and battle expertise of Colonel Beau Beauregard—a man who had just recently given Joe a laundry list of why it would be sheer stupidity to invade Switzerland. Joe had considered relaying the essence of Beauregard's dinner comments to Putin, but at the last minute had restrained himself.

The stress of the last weeks had caused the former Russian president to seemingly come unglued.

Putin appeared to have believed Joe's version of the events leading to Hawke's rescue of his son, but Joe feared the loss of his prized hostage had been a tipping point for Vladimir Putin. Hawke was after him again, and that was never a good thing.

"You know what, Joe," Shit Smith had said to him, "we got us a Russian president who makes that damn Kim Jong Un look like Franklin Delano Roosevelt. I ain't lyin' either."

He wasn't wrong. Vlad had gone from mild neurotic insanity to full-blown whack job. President Crazy-Pants, he and Emma called him behind his back.

And that, my friends, did not bode well for Operation Overkill. Nor the colonel's imminent looting of the Vegas Strip . . .

CHAPTER EIGHTY-SIX

Zurich

The Vegas Strip, in the Alps south of Zurich, includes a section of sometimes treacherous and precipitously icy road that climbs high into the Alps. The other problem with this road, now facing Beau's convoy, was that it was the only way in and the only way out. The road dead-ended in a box canyon about a mile past the Golden Nugget, the last vault they would hit.

The twisting road, over some of the deepest natural crevasses in the Alps, had been built during the construction of the National Redoubt. With construction starting in the late-nineteenth century, the redoubt constituted the beginnings of what later became known in Europe as Fortress Switzerland.

The National Redoubt encompassed a widely distributed set of fortifications and labyrinthine underground tunnels and warehouses where the infamous "Nazi Gold" had been stored during World War II. All aligned on a general east-west line through the Alps, and centered on three major fortress complexes: St. Maurice, St. Gotthard, and Sargans.

These fortresses were erected primarily to defend against Alpine crossings between Germany and Italy, and excluded the industrialized and highly populated heart of Switzerland.

The National Redoubt was planned as a nearly impregnable complex of fortifications that would deny any aggressor passage over or through the Alps. This was done by controlling all the major passes and railway tunnels running north to south through the region. This defensive strategy was intended to deter an invasion altogether by denying Switzerland's crucial transportation infrastructure to any aggressor.

In addition to being defensive, the National Redoubt was intended to be a massive underground bank. The redoubt included vast numbers of cavernous vaults and tunnels built during World War II. These were critical as the Swiss hunkered down under threat of the much-vaunted Nazi invasion—Hitler's Operation Tannenbaum—that never happened.

The Swiss were saved from devastation primarily because of their brilliant use of the Alps as defensive weapons, and because Hitler's mighty Wehrmacht got unexpectedly bogged down in Russia.

It was here, in deep underground vaults, that the neutral Swiss government and banking institutions frantically hid the wealth of the nation, not to mention its legions of worldwide banking clients. The Queen of England, for starters, stows a majority of the royal family's wealth in the vaults linked to the Vegas Strip. Gold—billions and billions of dollars in gold and other precious metals.

"There is still a lot of gold in them thar hills!" Beau said to Putin one evening over dinner. Said it to the president of Russia, who never, ever got the joke, and said it to Shit Smith, who laughed his ass off.

Beau had no time for joking now. He was busy as hell, running up and down the length of the Black Arrow and the long line of heavy flatbed trucks waiting for the train to be off-loaded. He was ensuring that the speedy transfer of men, tanks, and artillery to the trucks was going smoothly. For the most part it was. The few rail-yard officials who'd shown any interest had been permanently silenced before they could raise the alarms.

Beau looked at his watch. His micromanaged plan mandated that he be in the fully loaded lead truck and barreling down dawn-empty streets of the city before five A.M. Since the Hauptbahnhof was located on the shores of the northern tip of Lake Zurich, five minutes from where the trucks were being loaded, Beau figured the whole damn convoy could be out of town and racing south along the lake and headed for the Vegas Strip before the sun came up.

Or at least that was his plan, anyway. War has a bad habit of getting in the way of even the best-laid plans. If you want to make War laugh, tell it your plans. There were seemingly endless potential catastrophes ahead. The road up to the Vegas Strip, if you could call it that, was probably replete with tunnels that could be mined and bridges that could be rigged with explosives.

The strategy he had devised with the other two squad leaders was simple and straightforward: the convoy would blow through those tunnels and over those bridges so quickly that the enemy never had the chance to react. The spans over some of the deepest crevasses, with roaring rivers far below, were quite long, and that in itself was troubling . . .

In the last briefing aboard the Black Arrow, Beau had rewritten the attack plan, keeping tunnels and bridges in mind. Instead of mounting three simultaneous attacks on the Riviera, Caesars Palace, and the Golden Nugget, the entire convoy would race directly to the end of the Strip and the Nugget.

The force would be overpowering in a shock-and-awe way. Once the Nugget's vault was breached and the security forces were no longer a threat, the gold would be loaded on the flatbeds no longer carrying tanks and artillery. The trucks would immediately race to the little town of Riga, on the lake, where Joe Stalingrad had rented a falling-down warehouse in the forest.

And there the offloaded gold would sit as the trucks went back up for more, all that gold waiting to be ferried over to Falcon's Lair in the larger of the two subs devoted to carrying supplies.

The unified force would then regroup and descend back down to Caesars Palace, gain entrance, and gold, and finally the Riviera.

Those two would be tougher with the new plan, he had to admit.

Primarily because the joint force would have given up the element of surprise. Joe's answer to that was to take as much gold out of the Nugget as he possibly could, with an eye to forgoing any subsequent attack on the Riviera or Caesars Palace . . . or both!

At 4:55 A.M., still scanning the skies for Swiss fighters, but still without having to call in air support from Falcon's Lair, Beau climbed up into the cab of the lead truck. Taking one last look at the convoy now formed up behind him, he squeezed behind the wheel. "Whoo-ah, it's showtime!" Beau said to the young commando in the passenger seat. The redheaded kid's HK assault rifle barrel was resting on the windowsill, switched to full auto. Beau too had an HK that he could fire out the driver's window with his left hand if need be. Around his neck hung bandoliers of ammunition. In a holster on his hip, his trusty old Colt .45 Peacemaker. Once owned and operated by lawman Wyatt Earp himself. He'd also strapped a Velcro bandolier of four thirty-round mags around his right thigh.

Beau stole a peek in the rearview, looking back to see if he still had all his little ducks in a row.

Four other heavily armed commandos were aboard his truck, having taken up positions in the rear at the four corners of the flat-bed. Each truck used the same configuration of firepower. They all carried HK MP5s with attached rocket-propelled grenade launchers as well as the frag and stun grenades dangling like grape clusters from the web utility belts.

"Time to head for the hills, sonny boy!" Beau cried, twisting the key in the ignition.

These were the moments he lived for. Pitting himself against formidable if not impossible odds for enormous personal gain. This by far the biggest yet.

CHAPTER EIGHTY-SEVEN

On the Vegas Strip

The colonel whipped out his old Zippo, lit his battered stogie, took a pull, and expelled a huge blooming plume of blue smoke. Then he cackled, engaged first gear, and mashed the go pedal all the way to the floorboard. The big truck lurched forward and sped down the myriad crushed-rock roads of the outer rail yard, finally rolling out onto a wide boulevard of rain-wet pavement, illuminated by yellowish fluorescent lights and virtually deserted at this early hour.

Hallelujah!

He picked up the radio. Time to call Papa Putin and check on his ill-timed descent into madness.

"Falcon's Lair combat ops center, this is Overkill, over."

"Go ahead, Overkill."

"Gimme the president."

"Uh . . . hold on a second."

"I ain't got time to hold on, son! I need to speak to him now, goddamn it."

"Uh . . . sorry, sir . . . we're trying to . . . He's doing a media event and—"

"*A media event?* What media event? You mean to tell me he's on the goddamn television now? What the hell is going on over there?"

"Not yet on the air, sir. He's in the Falcon's Lair media studio. He's taping a video announcing the invasion of Switzerland and—"

"You do not announce a fucking invasion that hasn't even happened yet, for fuck's sake! Have you people lost your minds?"

"No, sir, it's just that the president says he wants to get maximum media mileage out of this thing and—"

"*What?* Holy Christ on a jumbotron, what the fuck is he thinking? We're just launching our first attacks now! And he's announcing our arrival to get media coverage? You go get him. You pull the plug on this fucking video, you understand me, son? Or your fucking head is going to roll."

"Yes, sir. I, uh, let me go see what I can do, sir. Over."

"You do that, over. Tell me something. Is Joe Stalingrad in combat ops?"

"Yes, sir! He just walked in."

"Put his ass on the damn phone."

"He's, uh, here he is . . . Sorry, sir . . . It's Colonel Beauregard for you, sir."

"Beau, talk to me," Joe said. "What's your status? We're expecting to be attacked here any moment . . . Radar has picked up a formation of Swiss army helicopters carrying Alpine combat troops and headed in our direction—"

"What the hell is Putin doing, Joe? He's announcing the fucking invasion on *television*? Are you shitting me? I'm en route to the goddamn Vegas Strip and he's telling the world I'm coming? I mean, I cannot effing believe what I'm hearing out here and—"

"Calm down, Beau, calm down . . ."

"Calm down? Seriously, Joe? What the hell do you expect me to—"

"The cameras aren't on, Beau."

"What?"

"Not rolling. And I capped the lenses. He's talking to *himself*, for crissakes. Fucking lunatic."

"Jesus. Okay, okay. Good. I gotta jump, get this buggy convention up the side of this mountain now."

"What's your situation, Beau?"

"Overkill convoy is on the move, Joe. Minimal casualties disembarking the train. Had to shoot a couple of yard dogs, that's all. No opposition at all so far. Leaving the lake now, headed up, approaching the road up to the three Vegas Strip target destinations. Our good luck won't hold forever, so keep the candles lit on those goddamn fighter jets, Joe. Over."

"What's your priority target, Beau? All still as planned?"

"Roger that, little buddy. I'm the lead truck in the convoy. Once we get up in the mountains and enter the Strip, we will continue on straight to the entrance at the Golden Nugget and—Hold on, Joe. What the eff? Jesus Christ! Joe, launch airplanes! Now! I repeat, launch all aircraft NOW! I've got a single jet fighter—a Swiss army Northrop F-5E Tiger—buzzing me, buzzing the convoy . . . a scout . . . They officially know we're here, Joe. It's gonna get hot real fast . . . Wait! Here come two more!"

"All right. I'm on it."

"This is where it starts, pardner. Drop your cocks and grab your socks, ladies, we going balls to the wall now, goodness gracious me! From the Halls of Montezuma to the shores of Tripoli!"

"Yeah. All that stuff. Good luck, Beau. I'll deal with Putin. Meanwhile, it's all on you. Make it happen, goddamn it. And make it home, bring the gold."

"Back at ya, Hollywood!"

THE VEGAS STRIP INCLUDES PANORAMIC views down one of the most spectacular high mountain valleys in the Swiss Alps. But unlike the Strip in Nevada, there are no windows to take in the view. There is no neon—no slots, no hookers, no nothing.

Except gold. Lots and lots of gold.

And everywhere you look but cannot see are heavily armed men who are there solely to prevent you from stealing it. Burrowed into snow-covered .50-caliber machine-gun nests. Heavily armed sentries at the entrance gates to each of the three primary fortified underground vaults. Invisible sentries posted high up in the rocks, up in the treetops, and inside phony rocks all along the scenic roadway. Sorta surreal, Beau thought, the whole thing. It was like Walt Disney had decided to open a new Swiss Theme Park—and called it "War World." With Mickey and Goofy firing live ammunition!

These soldiers up here are patient, vigilant, and highly trained, and like the men who sit tirelessly and forever waiting deep beneath the earth in missile silos under the Kansas cornfields, they are spoiling for a fight that may never come every single second of every day.

Beau was well aware of all these facts, thanks to the KGB intel bigwigs back at Falcon's Lair. He knew what he was getting into. But he was counting on the element of surprise, he was relying on over-whelming firepower, and finally, he was banking on the idea that *a lot of tanks* rolling up this frozen and forbidden road would be the very last thing the enemy security forces would be expecting.

And yet here he was. Coming round the mountain when he came! The colonel and his boys were ready! Bring it and bring it hot.

The gradient was growing ever steeper, with longer stretches of black ice, and the truck's big diesel engine was showing some strain from the ascent. The purple-black eastern skies were fading up to a faint pink against the panorama of snowcapped mountains. At this altitude, he could see almost all the way to Italy to the south, but—

Gunfire!

Coming from emplacements high and low on both sides of the road!

He accelerated as the commando next to him opened up with the machine gun, firing up at them from the right side. Beau adjusted his lip mike: "Falcon's Lair, where the hell is my fucking air cover? Jesus Christ, all hell is raining down on us!"

Joe himself answered, "Beau, first wave is out the door! They should be in the skies above you in approximately three minutes . . . There was some, uh, unexpected trouble here."

"What now? Putin, again?"

"No. One of the high-speed aircraft elevators. Gear jammed. So we only had one."

"Christ. Back to work."

"Good luck. We need it."

"Luck is for losers, Joe. And I ain't no loser."

Now firing his HK out the window with his left hand, he got back on the radio to his drivers. "Caesar and Riviera, this is Colonel Beauregard. The lead vehicles up ahead of you are now coming under heavy attack. Repeat. The convoy is under attack by automatic weapons on both sides of the road. And artillery fire from the higher altitudes. Increase your speed to match my own. We are returning fire using RPGs, which are proving very effective, even against emplacements higher up on the mountainside.

"Expect Swiss aerial attacks any moment now . . . over. Our air support will be overhead in the next minute or so. I am now proceeding to the Golden Nugget as fast as I can and still stay on this road. Stay with me. When we reach the barricades at the Nugget's entrance road, we will power right through, unleashing a hail of hell as we go. I wish you all godspeed and good hunting. Golden Nugget, over and out."

That's when the first of the Falcon's Lair jet fighters appeared out of nowhere. Off to his left, streaking downward at supersonic speeds. It was in a steep dive, right on the tail of and in hot pursuit of a Swiss pilot. The air war for Switzerland had just commenced in earnest.

DESPITE HIS SHATTERED WINDSHIELD AND the dead commando seated to his right, half of his face blown away, and despite the fact that numbers of trucks containing artillery and tanks had been blown off the road, despite the fact that his men were now taking heavy artillery fire from on high in the surrounding mountains, Colonel Beauregard, with his remaining trucks loaded with light artillery and light attack tanks, and his buses loaded with battle-hardened troopers, carried on.

He would take this fight to the enemy and he would recover all that stolen Russian gold or he would die trying.

Simple as that.

CHAPTER EIGHTY-EIGHT

Above Falcon's Lair

Hawke looked at his watch, willing the red-sweep second hand to slow down. A very serious storm front was heading his way through the mountain passes, as evidenced by the stepped buttresses of black thunderheads towering up darkly to the east. And another bulwark of dark purple cumulus clouds to the west, veined with jagged white lightning.

The big choppers, en route to the LZ, were bucking and yawing, beset by winds from the cold front that had entered the mountain range.

And Alex Hawke? Especially here in this violent turbulence, where instant death was just one wind shear away? Stoke never stopped wondering at the sight of the man on the verge of battle. He was hardly the picture of a British lord in his mid-thirties. He was dressed in his Alpine combat whites. He carried a machine pistol and an FN SCAR assault rifle equipped with a grenade launcher mounted on the lower rail. Grenades dangling from his utility belt, yet the man seemed to grow more and more peaceful as the moments until touchdown passed.

Comfortable, at ease within his surroundings, and at peace with himself. Quietly smoking, staring down at his boots. Only someone like Stokely, who knew the man down to his bones, who had seen him in extreme situations for over a decade, could know what was going on inside.

Stoke alone, of all the men now flying into the face of danger, knew that behind the little half-smile on his face and the placid exterior, Alex Hawke was after all a creature of radiant violence. Congreve had once told Stoke that their friend was a "masterpiece of contradictions." Equal parts self-containment, fierce determination, and cocksure animal magnetism. You could see the force of him now on the faces of the eager young men under his command; they seemed drawn to him like water to the moon.

"Penny for your thoughts, boss," Stoke said.

Hawke looked up as if woken from a dream and said, "What? Oh. We need to be over that damn LZ right now, if not sooner."

He adjusted his lip mike.

"How far out, Skipper?" Hawke said to the lead chopper pilot.

"Seven minutes to the LZ, sir. Trying to make up time. Head wind and wind shear has been killing us up here! Sorry about the ride, sir."

"Less than ideal," Hawke agreed, clenching the overhead grab rail to keep his feet beneath him and wondering about the wisdom of picking this location for the insertion. He could just hear one of his old military tactics professors at the Royal Naval College saying, "In times of peril, try to avoid inserting your troops into locations with names like 'White Death.'"

Hawke had zero inclination to fight his way through Putin's defensive perimeters in the middle of an alpine snowstorm. In these raging storms, temperatures could sink to forty below, leading to conditions far worse than the North Pole. The combined effect of cold, wind, and altitude made conditions up here one of the most hostile environments on earth.

His lads were more than dressed for the occasion. All in white, including U.S. 10th Mountain Division military-issue Polartec cold-weather jackets, Polartec bibs, white Nomex balaclavas, body armor, and boots with crampons at the toe.

"Stoke," he said, "how long do you think it'll take us to get up to the ledge?"

At midnight, Stoke, Harry Brock, and Thunder and Lightning had come to Hawke with a novel approach to the intended assault on Falcon's Lair. Instead of *descending* once they were on the ground and taking on deeply entrenched and heavily armed fighters on the way down, they would do something completely unexpected.

They would climb up.

There was another ledge above Das Boot. It was five hundred feet above their location on the snowfield. Wide enough to accommodate a patrol in full Alpine combat regalia.

"Take the high ground," Hawke had said, smiling. "Pour our fire down the mountain, from a position right over their heads. God, you guys are good."

"Jes doin' what comes natcherally, bossman," Chief Charlie Rainwater said.

"So, Stoke, once we're on the ground, how long until we're in position and moving along the ledge, engaging from above?"

"Weather holds, twenty minutes, max. We got crampons and ice picks, boss. All these boys are climbers since childhood. This ought to be child's play for them."

"Yeah," Hawke said, thinking, Killing is never child's play.

Hawke had just this morning emailed recent Swiss recon flight photos to all of his men. Shots of Putin's fighters digging in roughly a thousand feet above the entrance to Falcon's Lair at 12,000 feet. The same number of men were now entrenched a thousand feet below the entrance. This in order to ensure against attack from below, or best case, to wage a pincer attack, thus pinning Hawke's troops from both above and below.

The stiffest defense he'd encounter, Hawke knew, would occur at the main entrance to the complex. At a place called Das Boot. That was the name early climbers had given to the wide ledge-like formation of protruding ice and rock hanging off the mountainside just above the treacherous Murder Wall. The rocky protrusion, crusted with ice, was so called because it resembled nothing so much as the broad, flat hull of a massive German battleship of the World War II era.

The outcropping of rock was roughly seventy feet wide and maybe fifty feet deep. It had occurred to Hawke that you could probably land two choppers right at Putin's front door on the thing! But your odds of survival from the withering fire that would greet you from within the complex made that option somewhat less than ideal . . .

THE TIGHT FORMATION OF FOUR Swiss army choppers, each ferrying six commandos, was now arriving at the snowfield. The landing zone was broad, with a soft bosom of snow bisecting it. It was roughly a thousand feet above the entrance to Falcon's Lair.

So far he'd seen no visible signs of a resisting force, but he was fairly certain Putin's forces would mount a do-or-die attempt to keep his men outside of the mountain complex.

Hawke felt a dip in his stomach as the chopper dropped and dove in over the broad white snow for the soon-to-commence FRIES. Meaning the fast rope insertion extraction system, a technique using a thick braided rope that was first developed by the British in combat during the Falklands War. Fast-roping, as the insertion technique is called, is ideal for deploying troops from helicopters in places where helicopters cannot touch down.

It's dangerous, but so what else is new? A guy with heavy equipment is especially challenged. The person descending holds the rope with his specially designed heat-resistant gloves and uses his boots and his legs to control his slide down. The technique is much quicker than rappelling and several people can slide down the same rope simultaneously, but the people on the rope have to stay ten feet apart so that each man has time to get out of the way when he reaches the ground.

It takes thirty seconds to fast-rope to the ground.

Hawke was first out the door and first on the rope.

Almost instantly, heavy automatic fire, sporadic at first, and then concentrated, erupted, aimed in his direction. Hawke hit the ground running and ran toward the sound of gunfire. Training his MP5 at the source of the incoming rounds, he was joined seconds later by Stokely and Harry Brock, who ran up behind him. They were all firing, determined to silence what they believed to be three .50-caliber machine-gun nests hidden inside the snow-laden rocks.

A round whistled past Hawke's head and he dove for the ground. The enemy had found their range . . . and another emplacement had erupted fifty yards away, firing at the commandos still fast-roping down from all four hovering choppers. Machine gunners inside the choppers trained their guns on the source of the fire, but it continued.

"Stoke! Down!" Hawke shouted, ducking for cover. "Form on me! Behind these rocks! Give me cover fire. I'm going to make a run for the boulder over to the right. Get within RPG range and take these bastards out . . ."

Snow had started to fall up here, and fall hard. This visibility would not last for long.

As Hawke got to his feet, he saw his lead chopper rise about fifty feet off the ground, carve a deep left turn. This so that the two heavy gunners in the opened starboard door could lay down suppression fire to protect the commandos still fast-roping to the snowy ground. It was instantly effective.

Soft snow on top of packed ice. It made running tricky, but he sprinted ahead to his objective, still taking incoming fire as he ran out in the open. Ten feet from his objective, he dove for cover, finally rolling to safety behind the looming rocks.

He swiftly got to his feet and surveyed the scene, and ducked back down again. The offending three-gun emplacement stood between his men and the ledge that was their immediate destination.

He quickly screwed a rocket-propelled frag grenade onto the modified lower rail of his weapon. It was a long shot, beyond his range, but he'd take it. He couldn't get any closer to the enemy, so what the hell.

Sensing the timing of the shooter and sensing that the moment was right, he rose up, located the muzzles of the enemy guns winking in the snow, aimed slightly high to compensate, and pulled the trigger. He waited, three, four, five seconds, thinking he fired too high . . . and then came a concussion-causing blast of sound and the small mushroom cloud rising above the enemy's gun site.

"Form up on me!" Hawke shouted at the cadre of commandos racing from the choppers and toward Stoke's and his position.

"Stoke," Hawke said, "cover these guys. Lay down a goddamn barrage with the M60!"

"My thought exactly, boss!" Stoke said, doing what he did best. The big thumping, whumping gun seemed to have the desired effect. You could feel the booming muzzle in your bones.

They took heavy fire racing for the ledge, but they gave as good as they got. And most of them made it.

The battle for Falcon's Lair was on.

CHAPTER EIGHTY-NINE

Approach to the Golden Nugget

Beau looked at the icy road snaking up ahead. Not pretty. Bodies in twisted piles, scattered pools of blood everywhere you looked, burned-out machine-gun emplacements, and piles of grey, rotted snow lay to both sides. Here the road began twisting up to the higher elevations, where it would carve deeply into the side of a mountain.

And there, where the road made a wide curve continuing to the far side of that mountain, was the fortified entrance of the Golden Nugget.

Keep your eyes on the prize, Beau, he told himself. He could almost smell that prize now, the brass ring was dangling before his eyes.

In the skies above, the Falcon's Lair Squadron, considerably diminished, was doing battle with Swiss air force fighter jets. "An aerial ballet," Joe said, "with the flashing silver jets of Putin's forces engaging the red-and-white-marked Swiss F/A-18s." The only good news here on the Vegas Strip that Beau could see was that the Falcon's Lair pilot, his squadron, had, until the Swiss fighter jets arrived, softened up the Swiss ground troops and artillery guarding this approach to the Golden Nugget.

And there, like a great gaping wound in the earth, lay the yawning maw of Bernese Oberland Crevasse. The last great obstacle to be overcome, two deep V-shaped vertical expanses of crumbling rock and ice, monumental buttresses scoured by storms, avalanches, and stone fall. The crevasse plunged a thousand feet down to a churning river, sending up billowing clouds of mist.

The great iron suspension span across it, one of the notable engineering feats of the early Swiss army engineering corps, had long been a source of civic pride in this region of the Alps. Majestic, soaring, and spanning a distance of nearly a quarter of a mile, the graceful Gletscherspalte Brücke, Crevasse Bridge, has long symbolized man's mastery over mountains.

Concentrating the forces of the convoy into one long entity, troops bristling with armament, lethal battle tanks, instead of dividing it into three components had been a stroke of military genius, if Beau did say so himself.

Had he encountered resistance? Hell, yes. Had he been giving as good as he got? Hell, yes

In the air, swarms of Swiss fighter jets, the secret hidden air corps, had come screaming out of mountain holes suddenly opening near the tops of the Alps. An eerie sight, seeing a gaping hole appear in a mountain top and then a succession of fighter jets, each one catapulted out of that hole at tremendous speed. And the jets dove deep into picture-postcard valleys that, come summer, would be dotted with red barns and chalets with red geraniums in every window.

The enemy planes had been buzzing and diving, strafing them in the early going as they made their way to the target of operations. Amazing to see the picturesque little Alpine villages, with all the quaint charm they could muster, now engulfed in armed warfare.

A shooting war on the ground, with dogfights in the skies above, the all-out mayhem in this idyllic setting, was an amazing thing to experience, Beau thought, reloading his HK5. Never in my life did I think I'd see anything like this, he thought, never. If I survive this damn battle, I'm going to take all that gold and hole up someplace beautiful but remote, just me and my French niece, Violette. Yeah, and then I'm gonna sit by a pool every damn day and write a book about all this shit. Make a helluva good movie, too!

It was bizarre, unreal, Beau thought, careening around a corner and over a small bridge, conjuring up once more the Disneyesque aspects of this battle. Waiting in line in the Magic Kingdom at Disney World and all of a sudden you saw the U.S. Marines storming up Main Street USA, engaged in door-to-door combat en route to a Cinderella Castle in flames while screaming fighter jets above took out Space Mountain and the Swiss Family Robinson's tree house!

It was getting pretty hot. But when Beau's gunners, and Tiger tanks, hidden inside tarps on all those big mother flatbed trucks, had opened up with massive machine gun and cannon fire, the tide in the battle had swiftly turned in Beau's favor.

And then there was the squadron from Falcon's Lair. It had been a huge disappointment to both Beau and Uncle Joe. Although the colonel had never expressed his fears about the pilots' 24/7 operational readiness for aerial combat, the performance was worse than expected. But he'd kept his mouth shut. Especially not saying anything to Putin for fear of further destabilizing the man's confidence in the entire operation.

God knows these pilots, living out their days inside a mountain, rarely got airtime, and then only when mountain storms would cover their maneuvers in the skies above Der Nadel. Or dogfight simulations out over the Mediterranean. True, Joe had assured him that they were motivated and briefed, but the results in combat had been mixed at best.

You know what? Fuck it. He whipped ass with his ground troops. Always his style.

On the other side, the Swiss artillery emplacements up at the higher elevations had rained hellfire and brimstone down on his convoy. Good news was, they had eventually been silenced by the ferocious pounding of cannon fire they received from Beau's Tiger tankers that had kicked ass, man.

The tanks, the goddamn Tigers, were the most powerful weapons in his convoy, and, aided by strategic bombing by the Falcon's Lair squadron, they had been strategically distributed among the trucks. Ground troop resistance along the roadway at this point had been reduced to nil by the superior firepower provided by the killer tanks.

At the barricaded entrances to Riviera and Caesars Palace, Beau had paused the trucks just long enough to let the tanks and aerial bombardment soften up defenses and make way for the troops who would be returning from the Golden Nugget. Breaching the vault doors and overcoming resistance from security forces both inside and out just got a whole lot easier.

"Bring home the gold, Beau!" he said aloud and powered ahead, blowing his horn for the sheer hell of it.

CHAPTER NINETY

Falcon's Lair

Hawke and company had dealt the enemy a serious blow. His evasive tactic had taken them completely by surprise. His men had knocked the enemy forces below back on their heels. Finding their positions on the mountainside completely exposed, with all hell raining down from above, Putin's forces could do nothing but scramble around in the snow, hastily retreating back down as rapidly as they could.

Hawke had sensed the moment and seized the advantage just in the nick of time. Life was simple: Carpe the Diem and the bloody day will take care of itself—that was his view of the world, anyway.

The storm system he'd worried about on the way in to the LZ had entered the Bernese Oberland in earnest. It was now howling around him. It wouldn't be long before they'd all be snow-blind.

"Hold your fire! We're moving out!" Hawke said. "We can be down there waiting for them at their front door if we run like hell up to that ledge now, before we can't see a damn thing! Go! Go! Go!"

Like Hawke said, they ran like hell, clawing their way along to the narrow ledge. Slipping, sliding, always with the danger of toppling from the ledge and falling to their deaths on the rocks below, the Thunder and Lightning boys held on to each other, grabbing the backs of their snow parkas, pulling their comrades back, inches from death, all twenty-four of them smoking down that mountainside like a runaway train.

They made it down to a spot directly overlooking the broad entrance to Falcon's Lair in fifteen minutes.

When Hawke, who was leading the charge up on the ledge, a dead cigarette clenched in the corner of his mouth, saw the situation at the primary entrance to Falcon's Lair, he raised his right hand and silently signaled a halt. He then radioed his three squad commanders, Harry Brock, Chief Charlie Rainwater, and FitzHugh McCoy, to give them a briefing on his immediate intentions. Intentions that were subject to change in the coming minutes . . .

DOWN ON DAS BOOT, SOMEWHERE in the swirling and blinding snow, the enemy was waiting for them. The giant ledge, where Hawke had briefly considered sequentially landing his choppers, was no doubt chockablock with armed fighters lying in wait behind the barricaded gates. Unaware of Hawke's men and their steady and stealthy approach overhead, these Russian fighters were most likely all facing up the mountain, rather than covering the approach from below as well.

Chief Rainwater, upon seeing how they were deployed, grabbed Hawke's shoulder and said, "Commander, look here. My guys on the ledge have still got the three M60s with RPG capability. No need for us to go down there and engage in any hand-to-hand combat. Hell, no, we can just blow up their shit from up here. Launch a bunch of grenades right in the middle of them and—"

"Hold that thought, Chief. Stoke, I'm putting you in charge here. The chief and I are going down there alone, stealth move. I want to personally scout the situation up close before I commit our guys in any way. If you hear shooting or we're not back in twenty minutes, come get us."

"You sure that's a good idea?"

"No. Not really."

"You're not worried about some snowman down there shooting your white ass?"

"Yes, actually, I am. Like Churchill, I always prefer to be shot at without effect. We'll be going now . . . Ready, Chief?"

"Chief ready."

"Stoke?"

"Roger that."

"I don't ever use that phrase, terrible cliché," Hawke said, and then he and Rainwater were gone, melting away into the swirl of snow.

Man was something else, Stoke thought, watching him fade away.

The two men proceeded along the ledge carefully now. The icy footing was atrocious and he was in no rush. Because now, for what Hawke intended, the snowstorm was his first and best ally. In the midst of a battlefield enveloped in a raging snowstorm, every man in white is just another man in white. Or snowman, as Stokely had said. Sow confusion among your enemies. Something a young cadet had heard in a classroom one day at Dartmouth Naval College.

They picked their way carefully down the icy face of the mountain, using the crampons on their boots and their ice axes. He was exposed here and it was bitterly cold. As he climbed ever nearer the giant ledge known as Das Boot, he could hear the rattle of arms and the faint murmur of troops ready for a fight.

Dropping five feet down to a snowy outcropping directly overlooking Das Boot, the two men were now only thirty feet or so above the heads of the snowmen gathering below for a fight. Rainwater had just caught a very brief glimpse of a cluster of heavily armed snowmen, guarding the entry to Falcon's Lair. He told Hawke they were indeed all facing up the mountain rather than down.

And what about all those troops initially deployed a thousand feet below?

He'd been right—the two men saw shapes moving upward in the snowfall, more Putin troops headed upward to reinforce existing units above and below and at the entry itself. It had been intended to be a pincer movement, with forces simultaneously attacking both flanks of Hawke's invading formation. But Hawke's formation was now above the fray!

"How many of them, Chief?" Hawke whispered to the big man crouched by his side.

"Think we're looking at a hundred or more right now . . . more still coming up and coming down. Call it one fifty, two hundred max."

"Against twenty-four."

"Not bad odds, considering."

"Considering what?"

"Considering our side has you and me on it," the chief said with a wicked grin.

"Got any big ideas?"

"I see big explosions happening down there. But then I think, no, I have a better idea, sir."

"Surprise, surprise. No RPGs?"

"Not yet, sir. I think we take knives to a gunfight. I mean, *literally* take knives! Know what a smart Indian warrior would do in such a combat situation, Commander?"

"No. That's why I asked you the question."

"Remember Little Bighorn?"

"I went to the Royal Naval War College, remember?"

"Kidding you, sir. So the Sioux have Sitting Bull and Crazy Horse and masses of hopped-up warriors whacked on weed, sitting on their horses high above Lieutenant Colonel Custer's crowd, the 7th Cavalry, you know. Two hundred and fifteen souls down in a valley who have no idea what they are up against. Soon to take on *eleven thousand* very pissed-off Indians."

"Got it, and we're Custer," Hawke said. "Only above instead of below."

"Yeah. But we also know what we're up against."

"Right. So?"

"Ready? Okay, Fitz, Stoke, and Brock, those three only, remain in place up there on the mountainside with the big-boy guns. RPGs rule. Everybody else? Down the hill, now, join up with us. On my signal, the RPGs and M60s rain shit down, hellfire, right? Death, destruction, confusion down there. Yeah?"

"Yeah," Hawke said, "and that's precisely when we go down there and, how do I say this, we insinuate ourselves, we *insert* ourselves into the enemy mass, slowly, invisibly, dissolving into the crowd of enemy troops, moving and melting into them with such subtlety they'll neither know who we are nor realize we're among them. It's all confusion and smoke grenades. And we're not shooting anyone or calling attention to ourselves in any way . . ."

"No, of course not, Commander. Brilliant. No, we're using our assault knives, hidden inside our parkas. A quick and silent thrust up to the heart, the bad guy hits the snow, and everyone assumes he got shot from above. We take out as many as we can without calling attention to our presence, and they are none the wiser . . . until it's too late . . . we're like killer ghosts among them . . . zombies."

Hawke said, "Meanwhile, Chief, while Stoke, Fitz, and Brock are decimating the enemy from above, you, me, and the rest of the squad are slashing our way forward toward the barricades at the entry doors, rigging C-4 charges that'll blow those steel doors wide open."

Rainwater said, "Yes, sir! And the moment when that happens, and our entire force is now within the mountain, inside the walls of the enemy camp, then all of us open up with automatic weapons, everything we've got, at very close quarters. We storm the interior like screaming banshees. They'll never know what hit them."

"And just like that, Falcon's Lair will fall to the invaders," Hawke said with a small smile, knowing the two of them might have just cracked the one very strategic military code they'd needed to gain entry: how to confuse and subvert an enemy mass five times larger than your own!

Chalk one up for Sitting Bull, Hawke thought, smiling at Rainwater.

The white killer ghosts would enter the fortress en masse, hidden amidst and amongst the withdrawing forces, now being used in one of the oldest military strategies ever invented, the Trojan Horse.

Hawke, sensing a victory at hand, said, "Get Stoke on the radio, Chief. Fill him in. We're ready. Tell him the Chief says we're all taking knives to this gunfight. He'll like that."

CHAPTER NINETY-ONE

The Vegas Strip

Visible from the road, the twin fortified entrances to the two massive vaults at the Riviera and Caesars Palace consisted of mountainous natural stone blockades and barricades. Flanked to either side by guard towers bristling with searchlights and snipers. Didn't look good for the home team.

Beau grabbed his radio. "Falcon's Lair squadron leader, this is Overkill, do you read? I need air support and I need it now. Got that?"

"Loud and clear, sir."

"I'm just passing the Riviera en route to the Nugget. I got two guard towers at each location, need to be taken out. And I mean now, son. I don't wanna see any of these bastards still standing on my way back down. Over."

"Uh, that's a roger, sir. I'm directly overhead now, have eyes on the targets and will engage, over."

"Give 'em hell, son. Over."

He saw the pilot execute a barrel roll and then go into an almost vertical dive, unleashing a storm of air-to-ground missiles as well as his 20mm Vulcan cannon on the enemy towers.

Beau could see that inside the entrances to the Riviera and Caesars

Palace were steel portals that opened down into the underground vaults. At least to some degree, it looked as if some of the upper portions of the interior fortifications had already been reduced by earlier aerial bombardment to smoking rubble.

"Softened up." Beau smiled and chomped down on his trademark soggy stogie. The Falcon's Lair squadron boys were about to make his life a whole lot easier.

Those final two targets would be easy pickings by the time he hit them on the return trip back down the mountain. Once he had relieved the Golden Nugget of all that stolen Russian bullion, he would immediately wheel his forces and charge back down the Strip. Beau was ready, freddy, make no mistake about it.

He had even pulled out his lucky twenty-four-carat-gold toothpick, the one he'd won in a crap game in Vegas. He stuck it between his teeth and admired it in the rearview mirror. He was feeling mighty good for a formerly washed-up soldier of fortune, half broke and down on his luck.

True, he'd been worried about their untested airpower. And true, he'd been worried about an unglued Putin on the loose, wreaking havoc inside their headquarters and destroying morale. And the brooding, sullen presence of the killer Shit Smith everywhere you went. Man was seriously dangerous. And to some extent, he'd been worried about Uncle Joe, too. Joe was a genius in a weird way, kind of an idiot savant about politics and logistics and global infighting. But he was in no way a military man.

And yet look at them now. They had a good fighting chance of pulling this sumbitch off! Going home with the gold! Putin be damned, he and Joe could retire to life of PJs, what Joe called private jets, yachts, hookers, and limos.

Sure, there was always one more battle ahead and one more river to cross. But, hell, things looked kinda like the good lord was on old Beau's side today, didn't they? And you know, he was still a young dude!

A strong, healthy man with a helluva lotta living to do!

He had entered the beginning of the wide turn that would carry him around to the other side of the mountain . . . and the final approach to the great bridge across the crevasse en route to the Golden Nugget!

He brought his radio mike closer to his lips, popped the transmit button, and said to the convoy troops, "Here we go! This is nut-cutting time, boys and girls! Don't go wavering, don't go faltering. Don't lose courage now no matter what happens. There's a huge payoff waiting for all of us at the end of this here rainbow! And more where that came from when we get back down the hill to the rest of the Strip. I'm proud of you men. And how you've acquitted yourselves on the field of battle today . . .

"But we've got a fight ahead of us, make no mistake about that! And this one won't be easy. I'm going to take this big fricking rig across that bridge like a bat out of hell. All guns blazing. And I want all you pencil dick headbangers to do likewise! To do otherwise would just be . . . well, hell, I know we're just Putin's paid dogs in this fight, but it would just be downright un-American, is what it would be. Let's take it to 'em. This here's Colonel Beau Beauregard, over and out!"

And Beau pressed on.

MOMENTS LATER, BEAU SAW THAT he'd just been dealt a very bad card. Nearing the approach and entrance to the great span arching over the deep gorge, he saw nothing but trouble. The Swiss forces guarding the bridge, clearly alerted as to what was coming their way, had positioned two giant Swiss army Sno-Cats nose to nose at the entrance to the bridge! Shit!

And, worse, out on the bridge proper, he could see that, behind this makeshift barricade of two bright red snow vehicles, there were mobs of Swiss army regulars ready to open up with automatic fire.

He grabbed the radio: "Falcon's Lair, Falcon's Lair, come in! I need air cover! Fuck. Where the hell are those chicken-shit flyboys of yours? Over."

"What's your location, Colonel? Over." It was Joe and he didn't sound good. "We're under heavy attack here! I ordered what was left of the squadron to return to base. I've got to stave off Hawke's forces assembling at the entrance! Must be a couple of hundred of them down there! Shit!"

"Golden Nugget. I'm at the Crevasse Bridge at—aw, shit, Joe, I got me two fuckin' Sno-Cats blocking my access to the bridge and a Swiss fighter jet diving straight up my ass! And more up there strafing my convoy. This is do or die, goddamn it! You want this gold? Give me some air cover over here! Give me one damn airplane! Now!"

"We've still got a couple of guys airborne, I'll see what I can do. Over."

"How long, goddamn it?"

"I'll get back to you . . ."

"Like fuck you will," Beau said, knowing the little bastard was lying through his teeth. He'd save his own ass first and leave Beau with his dick in his hand.

Beau ground his teeth, downshifted the truck, and mashed the accelerator pedal to the floor. With a good head of steam he might, with a little luck, be able to blow right between those two vehicles, shunting them to either side, maybe right off the bridge and down to the river. Fuck it. It was his life on the line, do or die. He was going for it.

The big diesel roared and gained speed. He centered the truck on the approach road and gripped the wheel with both hands, shutting out everything except the narrow strip of daylight between those two Sno-Cats and shouting to his troops in the rear over the radio: "Close up on me and stay tight, you bitches! Stay together! We're crossing this motherfucker as one unit, boys! Do or die!"

Rounds from the diving Swiss fighter's 20mm cannon were perforating what was left of his long hood—steam issuing forth in billowing clouds—and the cab's roof was full of holes, hell, even the seat he was sitting on and he could see the road beneath his feet! The cab was full of swarming angry bees of lead . . . and it wouldn't be long before ole Beau got stung bad. But as long as he was breathing . . . At this point, life is all about true grit . . .

The twin Sno-Cats loomed larger, filling the view through the shattered glass of his windshield. Going to . . . going to hit them . . . *now*!

He had tried to keep his eyes open at the impending impact. But the brain-stunning collision jarred him to the bone, hurt him so badly he almost lost his sweaty grip on the wheel. He was whipped about the inside of the cab—everything was flying about: his coffee mug, his maps—but still, and only god knows how, he got his arse back down in the seat and his foot back on the go pedal . . . do or die . . .

Suddenly he was aware of white-suited bodies flying up in front of him, all around him and bouncing off his windshield . . . slamming down hard upon his roof! He was ripping right through the mass of Swiss army regulars who'd been positioned behind the two Sno-Cats he'd just sent plunging down into the deep gorge below. Holy shit!

He'd made it through!

Yes! He'd blown the two big Sno-Cats off the bridge! He'd seen the one on the left in the rearview, hurtling down into the dark depths of the crevasse. And ahead of him? The expanse of bridge ahead was wide open all the way to the far side. No more troops up ahead waiting for him on the other side, no tanks, no fucking enemy fighter jets rattling his cage. Shit! Hellfire, it looked like maybe he was going to pull this bastard off, after all . . .

THE FIRST INDICATION THAT ALL was not rosy ahead was a thin line of white-hot fire rising up along the far side of the bridge. Fuck! Right where the last span was joined to its massive concrete anchor, a structure embedded deep into the mountainside opposite. Eyes wide with horror, Beau saw that the spiking fire was now turning along the center line of the suspension bridge roadway and speeding this way. Fire and smoke were growing in strength by the second, the deadly line of fire racing directly toward his Swiss cheese truck and—

He shot a glance at his outside rearview mirror, still intact. Christ, a good half of the Overkill convoy was out here with him on the burning span, tucked in right behind him! Just as he'd ordered. Not even enough time for him to warn them to jump down and run for it!

As he watched in horror, the fire seemed to whip and fling its blazing tentacles everywhere, wrapping itself around the roadway, licking up the bridge's twin support towers . . . sprinting along the suspension cables . . . ever closer! He downshifted and slammed his boot down on the accelerator. His only hope was to try to outrun the fire, get to the far side before it got to him.

"Hold on, Beau, hold on!" he heard himself shouting . . .

Suddenly the entire bridge was rocked with the blasts of separate explosive charges mounted under the superstructure. And now whole sections were exploding and collapsing, falling away and dropping down to disappear in the mist at the bottom of the gorge. The bridge was quickly losing any connection at all with the anchorage on the far side! All of it, everything solid disintegrating around him, over and under his truck . . . his doomed convoy.

It was then that he could feel the whole world falling away from beneath him . . . in free fall now . . . watching the truck's big diesel engine spinning in space in slow motion all by itself . . . and feeling the searing pain of his clothes, his skin on fire. Flailing away, clawing at the air . . . screaming all the way down . . .

And then, finally, and through no wish of his own, that old scoundrel Colonel Brett "Beau" Beauregard, along with all of his life-long dreams of guts and glory, was suddenly and most definitely . . . dead.

CHAPTER NINETY-TWO

The siege of Falcon's Lair

Pity about the lovely doors," Hawke said to his demo man, Chief Rainwater, as the top commando's finger hovered over the detonate switch. The ice-coated doors were just the first of many things Hawke had admired when he was first granted admittance into Falcon's Lair by the previous owner, the Sorcerer.

Custom-built by the famous Krupp Arms Company in Germany's Ruhr Valley, the primary producer of heavy arms for Hitler's Wehrmacht, the doors at the entrance to Falcon's Lair were solid forged German steel. They featured elaborately carved Alpine scenes designed by Albert Speer, the Nazi architect who'd worked on Falcon's Lair. Three feet thick and each weighing in at about two tons, the two doors were works of art—in Hawke's mind, anyway.

"Still time to change your mind, Commander." Rainwater grinned.

"Blow the damn doors, Chief!" Hawke said, whirling about to fire at a bloodied and supine enemy fighter raising his weapon against them. The resistance outside on the ledge had all been negated or had melted away down the mountain. At one point, Putin's men, recognizing that they had been badly deceived and knowing that their numbers were no longer in their favor, had folded their tents and run away.

Hawke's men had suffered, too. Four killed and five wounded. The remaining nineteen or so fighters, under the command of Stokely Jones, had all assembled outside the entrance to the complex.

"Aye aye, Commander," the chief responded and, depressing the button, blew those damn doors right off their hinges and into the semi-dark interior. As quickly as the smoke cleared, they were inside and saw—

Nothing.

No one, anywhere. A cavernous space, dark and empty. And it was so cold they could see their breath, all of them stomping their boots to warm their feet. *Colder than outside?* Hawke wondered. *How could that be?*

Stoke said, "Over here, boss! I got one. He's maybe just a little dead, though."

Hawke ducked into the high-vaulted corridor where Stoke and Harry Brock had gone in search of enemy combatants. Hardly any light in here. He flicked on his tactical flashlight and saw faint light coming through the doorway of the far room on the left.

"Stoke," Hawke said, "what the hell?"

"Yeah," Stoke said. He and Brock were standing over what was left of a butchered corpse that looked like it had swallowed a bomb.

"Knife wounds," Brock muttered. And Stoke said, "He's been gutted, boss. Why the hell would anybody do—"

Hawke bent for a closer look. He'd seen such wounds once before, on a beach in Morocco.

"Shit Smith," was all Hawke had to say.

"That weird cowboy dude?" Stoke said. "In Alexei's room with Uncle Joe?"

"Yeah, that's him," Hawke said. "Same bastard that chopped up my copilot, Johnnie Walker, in Morocco. Mr. Brock, go get our guys. Let's go find Joe. He'll be with Putin. Come on, it's this way. Putin's office is one flight up."

THERE WAS A BROAD STAIRCASE at the end of the corridor. It had huge bronze sconces all the way up the walls on both sides, but they'd all been extinguished. Still, you could see all the blood.

It was everywhere, spilling down the steps like a thick red waterfall and putting Hawke in mind of that great movie *The Shining*.

And then there were more freshly mutilated corpses—mostly civilians, oddly enough.

Bodies everywhere. Shit had gone on a killing rampage, Hawke thought, knifing anyone and everyone he could find. Hawke's commandos raced up the steps, leaping over bodies sprawled in their path. Hawke had a sudden sense of urgency. If Shit had truly gone insane, had he killed everyone? Including Uncle Joe, the strange little man who'd spared Alexei from Putin's wrath?

"This way!" Hawke cried out and ran up the stairs leading to Putin's office. "Come on, Stoke!" he shouted.

The door was open and they burst inside, weapons at the ready.

There was a heavyset silver-haired man seated at Putin's desk.

Not Putin, but a heavily decorated Russian military officer. A general? He had his eyes closed and was rocking back and forth in the chair, moaning. Hawke went to him and saw that he had his fingers interlaced across his belly, trying hard to hold his guts inside.

"Stoke!" Hawke said. "Get the medic in here to attend to this man. General, can you hear me? Can you speak?"

His voice was harsh and raw.

"Yes . . ." he croaked.

"I've come for President Putin. Get him to stop the killing."

"Too late," the Russian croaked. "They're all dead. Putin and the cowboy and a couple of others are maybe still alive. They killed all of us . . . lined us up against the walls and started—"

"Sir, where is Putin now? Please tell me, General. This man will sew you up, sir. Just hold on."

"Up in the residence. It's on the—"

"Top floor. I know. You think he's up there?"

"He was. Don't know now. He's been locking himself in there for two days . . . drinking . . . he and that crazy fucking cowboy friend of his."

HAWKE SPRINTED UP THE STAIRCASE. His men were right behind him, weapons at the ready. No blood here. But very still and quiet as a crypt. As if everyone inside the mountain was dead.

At the top, they found themselves in a great hall with black-and-white marble floors. Guttering candles in the sconces on the wall provided a dim, wavering light, and a huge crystal chandelier was illuminated as well.

Hawke had seen the Sorcerer's, now Putin's, bedroom on his first visit to Falcon's Lair. It had been lavishly decorated and nothing had changed, he now saw through the double doors that hung wide open. Except that all of the furniture had been turned upside down and there was blood spatter on the walls. He raised his right fist and the men behind came to a halt.

"I go in first," he said simply, and strode across the marble floors and into the dimly lit room. "Give me two minutes . . ."

He took three steps forward, then stopped stock-still and said, "Oh my god."

The entire bedroom looked like a war zone. Upended furniture, smashed mirrors, and two naked bodies, a man and a woman, sprawled across the huge expanse of bloody bedcovers, their arms and limbs intertwined as if killed in a moment of passion. They looked to be dead. He recognized the man.

It was the bloody ghost of Uncle Joe, still alive, his lips moving, his chest heaving, beckoning to Hawke with his finger . . .

CHAPTER NINETY-THREE

Hawke spoke quietly into his lip mike and said, "Stoke, I've got at least one still alive in here. Get the medic in here now!"

He heard a grunt from the bed and then: "Alex," Joe whispered hoarsely. "Come over here . . . please . . ."

"Joe," he said, going to him, taking his bloody wrist and feeling for the strength of his pulse.

"No, no. Not me, I'm going to make it. Check her, Alex, please get Emma some help. Shit was brutal. He raped her and then started slicing at her with that motherfucking bowie knife of his and—"

Stoke was at Hawke's side. "Talk to me, boss. What do we need?"

Hawke said, "You and the corpsman attend to the woman first. She's the most grievously wounded, multiple stab wounds, lost a lot of blood. I'll look after Joe here."

"On it," Stoke said and nodded to the young medic.

Hawke hurried into the bathroom and returned with steaming hot towels. He started by wiping the blood from Joe's eyes, from his face, out of his mouth. "Jesus, Joe. What the hell happened here?"

"Is she still alive, Alex? Tell me she is," Joe said through his pain.

Hawke looked at Stoke and the young medic. "Stoke? Is she breathing? Will she make it?"

"Maybe. She's got a slim shot, is my guess. Corpsman agrees. But at least a strong heartbeat, boss."

"Alex? Talk to me, for crissakes!" Joe groaned.

"Calm down, Joe. She's going to be okay. Heartbeat is strong. We're working to stem the bleeding."

"Oh, thank god. Thank god." Joe was weeping.

"Who is she, Joe?"

"Emma. Emma Peek is her name. We were going to get married after all this was over."

"Shh. You still can, Joe. Just hold on to that thought until we get you two all stitched up and into the sickbay, okay? Now, tell me what the hell's been happening here."

"A fuckin' nightmare, that's what. Putin and Shit Smith. They were drinking all last night and all day today. They feed off each other and they are both insane. Putin's anger at you for the failure of all of his grand plans, and the cowboy's fury at seeing his new mentor being humiliated by you once more . . . and rage at me for helping you rescue Alexei . . ."

"Where is he, Joe? Where's Putin? I'm going to add to his rage right now."

"You can't, Alex."

"Please tell me why not."

"They escaped. The two of them."

"Gone? How? What happened?"

"First, you were knock, knock, knocking on Putin's door, storming inside to take him. Then, when he found out that there would be no stolen gold, that Colonel Beauregard and half of his convoy got blown off the bridge en route to the gold vaults they intended to loot, the man came completely unhinged. Ranting and raving, wild-eyed, screaming at me and threatening to shoot everyone who got in his way."

"I knew he was losing it, but I had no idea, Joe."

"Who did? Emma came to me in near hysterics. She'd overheard Volodya and that goddamn Shit whispering down there in the kitchen. They were laughing, for crissakes, talking about murdering the two of us. Saving the best for last, was how Putin put it to the cowboy."

"Christ, Joe."

"Yeah. So Emma and I figured we were done for, right? What the hell? We raced up here and barricaded ourselves in this bedroom as best we could. Then we got into bed and decided we'd go out with smiles on our faces and then . . . and then . . ."

"Don't talk about it. I can only imagine what they did to—"

"The two of them, howling like maniacs, broke into the room, tore up the place. Putin had the gun, Shit had the knife. The president held the gun to my head. He was staring at Emma, ripped the sheet off her naked body, a horrible smile on his face. I think he always thought she should be his, not mine. It drove him crazy that she would pick me over him."

"Yeah, I can see it."

"Then he told the cowboy, he says, 'That bitch is all yours, Shit. Do whatever you want with her. Take your time, too. No rush . . .'"

"No more, Joe. Stop torturing yourself."

"Yeah, you're right. Sorry. But you need to know something, Alex."

"I'm listening."

"I heard Shit promise Putin that he would track you down and make you suffer before you died. He said he'd do it for free, but Putin said he'd give him five million for your head on a platter."

"Hold my hand, I'm scared," Hawke said, smiling at him.

"You gotta take this guy Shit seriously, Alex. He's a bona fide human death machine."

"Yeah, well, human death machines come and human death machines go, don't they? Tell me about Putin. Where is he? Right now?"

"He and Shit could be anywhere by now, Alex."

"The two of them left the mountain? How the hell did they get out?"

"Used the sub."

"The sub? The Sorcerer told me six months ago that he had shut that whole underwater operation down due to expenses."

"Yeah, well, Putin re-upped the whole underwater operation. He must have always known it would be his only escape hatch if it ever came to that. For the last two days, he's kept Horst in the four-man sub down there waiting for him at the underwater air lock. Waiting the whole time the massacre was going on. He and Shit left an hour ago."

"I'll find that son of a bitch. Where do you think he'd run?"

"I'm sure he went south to Italy. That's what I'd do. Keep the sub submerged all the way to the southern end of the lake, have a car waiting for them late tonight . . . Who knows after that? Closest airport is at Milano, maybe."

THAT EVENING, HAWKE AND STOKE dined in Falcon's Lair's formal candlelit dining room. They were all trying hard to make it some kind of victory celebration. But the smell and presence of so much recent death hung heavy upon the room, and it was rough sledding for all.

At table were a heavily bandaged Emma Peek and a recovering Joe Stalingrad, desperately holding hands with each other throughout the meal. Joining them were Artemis Cooper, Harry Brock, Chief Charlie Rainwater, and FitzHugh McCoy. As well as the much-restored General Ivan Spassky of the Russian army who was well into the vodka despite the medic's warning about it.

The gleaming mahogany sideboard was laden with a mountain of Beluga caviar, champagne, hillocks of potato salad with pickles, and best of all, chef de cuisine Stokely Jones Jr.'s own recipe for buttermilk southern fried chicken, showcased and steaming on heaping silver platters.

At eight o'clock, Stoke leaned over to Hawke and whispered, "Eight on the button, Commander. You asked me to remind you."

"Right, I did. I'll be right back," Hawke said, "please excuse me." He left the table and went directly to Putin's office, where he closed and locked the double doors. With a sigh of exhaustion, he took the red leather chair behind the desk, lit a cigarette, took out his mobile, and punched in the primary number at his primary residence, Hawkesmoor.

"Lord Hawke's residence, may I help you?" he heard Pelham Grenville say in his flutiest tones.

"Yes, you can help me, you old dickens. How the hell are you?"

"Very well indeed, m'lord. Awfully good to hear your voice, to be perfectly honest. You sound tired, my boy."

"Yes, but I'll be home tomorrow. Pelham, tell me, how is Alexei? Is he having a fun birthday? I'm so sorry to be missing it, but, you know, duty calls."

"I completely understand, m'lord. And I should say he is enjoying his big day most wholeheartedly, sir! That pony! He's beside himself! The animal arrived early this morning on a lorry up from Cirencester. What a lovely creature. And Alexei is already sodden with love for him. He and the groom, young Fellowes, have been out riding over hill and dale all day long. I literally had to drag him out of the saddle in time for his birthday party, sir."

"How many children came, Pelham?" Hawke said, beginning to relax with the happy sense that life was somehow returning to normal again.

"We had twenty-two, sir, including the Duke and Duchess of Kent, who stopped by with the children. I must say, Alexei and Prince George have become fast friends at Eton. Great fun, sir! Boisterous, I must say."

Hawke smiled. "Well, marvelous. Has he named the animal yet?"

"He has, sir. I'd told him the pony needed a name and he said he'd think on it. Blurted the name out loud whilst blowing out birthday cake candles."

"And?"

"It is rather odd. Your son wants to call his new pony 'Uncle Joe,' sir. Not at all sure why. In any event, sir, I suggested 'Dobbin.' Because unless I am very much mistaken I am not aware of any Uncle

Joes in the family, sir . . . and no one has a more extensive knowledge of the family tree than I."

"*Uncle Joe?*" Hawke laughed out loud for the first time in weeks. He said, "Good lord! Well, I suppose it's not the worst name for a pony I ever heard . . . Pelham, please put Sigrid on the line, will you? She's expecting my call."

"Certainly, m'lord. She's hovering right here, sir."

"Alex?" she said, sounding shy and tentative. "Is that you?"

"Darling," Hawke said.

"Are you all right? You're not hurt, are you?"

"No, no. Fully intact. Do you miss me at all, darling?" he said. "Even a little?"

"Not even a little. And if you don't come home to me immediately, I shall miss you even less!"

"Good timing, my dear girl. On my way bright and early tomorrow morning. Just want to wish my son a quick happy birthday. See you soon, darling!"

"Here's your boy, jumping up and down he's so excited!"

"Hello? Hello?" he heard the little boy say then, and it almost broke his heart. He said, "Alexei, it's your father. I'm coming home tomorrow! I'm so sorry I missed your big day, but I do want to wish you the very happiest of happy birthdays ever, son!"

"Daddy?"

"Yes, darling."

"Oh, Daddy, I miss you so! Please come home to us, please? Pelham misses you, Sigrid misses you! Even Uncle Joe says he misses you! Everybody!"

"Uncle Joe? Who in the world is Uncle Joe?"

"Oh, Daddy, you know . . . He's my new pony! Sigrid and I just came back up from the stables. We went out to wish him a good night. It's freezing cold here, Daddy, and I put his blanket over him. And Fellowes is going to spend all night with him, sleeping on the hay in Uncle Joe's stall!"

"Do you really like him, Alexei? I must say he was the finest of all the ponies I looked at."

"Oh, Daddy, he's only the loveliest present any boy could ever wish for . . . Thank you so much. Oh, sorry! Sigrid says it's my bedtime, Daddy, so I must go now . . . Good night, good night, good night! I'll see you tomorrow!"

"I love you, Alexei, with all my heart," Alex Hawke said.

"Thank you, Daddy, for the best birthday a boy ever had!"

And indeed, there was not a scintilla of him that was not filled with love at that moment. He had his family back. They were all safe once more. He would guard them with his own life forever.

And sooner rather than later, he would track down Putin's newest monster, Shit Smith. He would find him, and he would kill him.

And, as for Putin, let him run. Let the world deal with him now. He'd made good on his threat to kidnap Alexei. And he'd been within a hair's breadth of having his son murdered. Hawke had dealt with Volodya for nearly a decade. He had little stomach left for the man, nor his ever more bizarre and dangerous actions. The Americans had a new president. He claimed to understand what made Putin tick.

At least somebody did.

Let someone else deal with the world's madmen for a while. He was going to take his girl and find a beach somewhere. Maybe his little seaside home on Bermuda. Yes, Teakettle Cottage would be perfect for the two of them. Fall asleep in each other's arms each night to the soft rustle of wind in the palms and surf breaking below on the rocks along the shoreline.

Alex Hawke had just wound Putin up. Tight. Someone else would bloody well just have to wind that coldhearted bastard down this time.

Good luck with that, whoever you are . . . you poor bastard.

EPILOGUE

Bermuda, the North Shore

The sun was just about to kiss the far horizon of the world, and towering banks of western clouds were tinged with gold and red as two lovers emerged from the sea. Holding hands, they began the sandy trek homeward. The man owned a small home nearby, set atop a rocky bluff above the sea. The house, a former sugar mill, was surrounded by dense green jungle, thick with wildly colored birds and exotic foliage.

It was called Teakettle Cottage because of its picturesque profile; its white domed roof was a perfect pot, and the lurching white chimney resembled nothing so much as a spout. The cottage, oft depicted on Bermuda's postcards, had a long and colorful history. It had housed a number of legendary gentlemen down the decades, including movie idol Errol Flynn and the immortal Hemingway, who had written the final chapters of *The Old Man and the Sea* under this very roof. Now it was the beloved retreat of Lord Alexander Hawke, a wounded warrior come to bind up his grievous wounds and take refuge from war and violence.

"Hullo!" a high-pitched voice cried out from above. It was the ancient Pelham, Hawke's lifelong friend and gentleman's gentleman.

"Pelham!" Sigrid called up to him. "We had the most marvelous ocean swim! Three whole miles! You should try it sometime!"

Hawke laughed and waved up at the man, feeling the last rays of the sun warm on his shoulders. After two whole weeks of marinating in all this sunshine, Hawke and Sigrid were both glowing with health and radiant with happiness. It had been a perfect day. After a feast of lobster and icy Pinot Gris out on the terrace, they had just completed a three-mile swim in open ocean and—

"Nap time! Last one in the sack's a little pickle!" the woman shouted back to him, sprinting ahead through the receding surf and soft pinkish sand. Sigrid's lithe body, like his own, was a shade darker than copper, and they both reveled in the boundless energy they suddenly found within themselves.

A lot of that newfound energy was expended in the bedroom. His was a whitewashed room, with all of its many gleaming windows opening outward to the glories of the aquamarine sea and the azure skies of Bermuda. The floor was glazed red Spanish tile, and the furniture was minimal, save the bed. Oh, that bed! How it called to him—

The current master of the house had long ago fitted a massive eighteenth-century four-poster bed into the smallish room. He loved it not so much for the vast expanse of white linen and the goose-down pillows, but for the sheer height of the bed. He loved awakening in the cool dawn and inhaling the glorious views afforded him by a high bed amidst so many windows. And falling asleep each night with a thousand stars beaming down on him.

Hawke laughed and raced to catch up. These late afternoons were when the two made feverish love before falling asleep in each other's arms. As a rule, the first one to wake up jumped out of bed and headed to the bar where the evening's pitcher of Dark 'n' Stormys was waiting, courtesy of the octogenarian butler who made the world go round here at Teakettle Cottage.

They made slow sweet love in that old bed that very afternoon.

Then despite the soft cries of wind beginning to howl around the windows, they slept.

"EXCUSE ME, M'LORD," PELHAM SAID, pausing in the doorway. "May I shut the windows, sir? We're having a bit of a blow, a thunderstorm, as you can see. I kept thinking it would awaken you."

Hawke lifted his head and gazed at his old friend. "Of course, Pelham, even though, as you well know, I adore bad weather."

"Since you were a wee child, your lordship."

The elderly man floated into the room, making short work of shutting out the wind and rain, but neither the rumble of thunder nor the flash of lightning could be put at bay.

Hawke sat up, the sheets puddled around his waist. "Yes, yes. My god, what a breeze. What time is it, Pelham?"

"Going on half-six, sir."

"Six-thirty? What time are we expected for dinner at Shadowlands this evening?"

"Lady Mars's invitation called for promptly at eight, sir. Apparently a bridge on the coast road is out due to the storm. You'll have to detour en route to St. George's."

"It's black tie, isn't it? This bloody dinner party?"

"Afraid so, m'lord. Everything is laid out in your dressing room and—"

Hawke swung his long legs out from under the duvet and started to slide from the bed. "Sorry, darling. Have to hurry . . ."

"Get back in here, buster, and finish what you started," Sigrid said, her voice husky and filled with deep longing.

"Stop that," Hawke said to her, swatting her rather prominent bottom. "Pelham, I want to wear those gold studs given me by Lord Mountbatten tonight. Inspector Congreve always seems a bit covetous of those gorgeous nuggets, does he not?"

"He has mentioned on occasion that he would gladly kill you in cold blood for them one day, yes, sir."

Hawke laughed, jumped out of bed stark naked, and headed for the loo, grinning at Pelham. "Oh, and do me a favor, will you, old fish? Call your pal Ambrose Congreve and tell him that, due to weather, his friend Hawke might be running a wee bit late."

"Indeed, m'lord."

"Alex?" came a sleepy voice from beneath the duvet.

"Yes, darling?"

"Do we really have to go? Come back to bed."

"This dinner is in your honor, my dear. Remember? Very kind of Lady Mars and Ambrose Congreve, I should say. Now haul yourself out of that bed and slip into something smashing, will you?"

He went into the bathroom and pulled the door closed. He hated shaving and leaned into the mirror to see if he might avoid the mug and razor on this rainy night. He saw the face of a strange new man, clear of eye and miraculously free of pain and fear. These last months since Christmas, trying desperately to save his son, life had been hellish, depleting his spirit and his vitality.

The agony had affected Sigrid too, and in London one night, late over wine, he had proposed that they escape for a few weeks on Bermuda, just the two of them, and let the shining sun and the elements cleanse them and rekindle their spirits.

He rejoiced in knowing that Alexei was safe in the hands of the Yard's Royalty Protection Service, who were also safeguarding William and Kate's children, Prince George and Princess Charlotte. The celebrated couple had been delighted to take little Alexei in for a few weeks. The two little boys were becoming fast friends, classmates at Eton in an experimental program for gifted boys of a very young age.

Hawke smiled at the face in the mirror.

It was going to be a lovely evening. Candlelight and good claret, probably a roast of lamb. There in the dining room at Shadowlands, surrounded by his closest friends, cheery lads he'd known since college, with the beautiful new love of his life by his side . . . Well, he was a lucky man. Life was bliss once more and all was right with his world.

SHADOWLANDS, THE BERMUDA ESTATE NOW owned by Lady Diana Mars and her husband Chief Inspector Ambrose Congreve of Scotland Yard, was once the grandest estate on the island of Bermuda. It is a sprawling twenty-two-acre property in St. George's that once belonged to a business tycoon named Vincent Astor. The wooded Astor Estate, with its gorgeous mansion, exquisite gardens, and many guest cottages, had once boasted a private narrow-gauge railroad, complete with Union Station.

Hawke was driving too fast, late again, and nearly missed the imposing wrought-iron gates that guarded the driveway at Shadowlands. The squall that whipped this part of the coastline was steadily growing in intensity.

"Slow down, Alex," Sigrid said, peering ahead through the foggy windscreen. "We're only ten minutes late. No need to kill ourselves."

"I know, I know . . . Is that it? I can't see a bloody thing!"

"Yes! Turn in here!"

Hawke managed to safely navigate the Land Rover Defender along the twisting drive through the rain forest that was Shadowlands. Moments later, Ambrose was standing under the porte cochere, a broad smile of welcome on his face, his hand outstretched to help Sigrid from the mud-splattered car.

And so to dinner . . . where Hawke was delighted to find himself seated at Diana's right.

She said, "You and Sigrid together again, Alex. I'm overjoyed to see the two of you so happy. I still remember that rainy night we were down at the Gardener's Cottage after she'd gone. I've never seen you so desolate and grieving. You were completely bereft."

"Yes."

"How are you, darling boy? We miss seeing more of you."

"Oh, I'm happy enough. But may I tell you something?"

"Of course."

"I sometimes find myself wondering if I'm outgrowing this life of mine, Diana. Weary of it. Living on the edge as I do. Constantly putting myself in harm's way the way I do. Putting even my only child in the eye of the storm. All the violence. All the bloody drama."

"Oh, Alex, you're still a very young man. Service to Queen and Country has always been your life's desire, ever since you were bouncing on Mountbatten's knee as a five-year-old."

"I know. It's true. It's what I was born for, I suppose. But these past two weeks here have been wonderful for me. I'm lucky to have such a refuge as that little cottage of mine. I always feel so safe there . . . so far removed from the evil that bestrides the world, the overwhelming danger . . . the—"

A young butler had slid up behind him and was bending to whisper in his ear. "M'lord, please excuse the interruption."

"Yes, yes. What is it?"

"There's a call for you, sir. In the library."

"A call? It's almost midnight. Who is it?"

"It's Pelham Grenville, sir. He says it's most urgent."

"Pelham? What did he say was wrong? I don't—"

"You'd best come take the call, your lordship. He didn't sound well at all and—"

Hawke put his napkin to his lips, rose up, and put his hand on Diana's shoulder, whispering to her.

"Please excuse me, Diana. Apparently Pelham is calling and something is dreadfully wrong . . . I have to go. Can you have someone ferry Sigrid home when the party's over?"

"Of course, darling. I'll bring her myself. I'm sure it's nothing."

Hawke ducked into the library where a fire was roaring and took the deep leather chair beside the hearth.

"Pelham?" he said into the receiver. "Is that you? Are you there?"

"Yes, m'lord," he said, and Hawke had never heard the man speak in such a strained and muted voice.

"What on earth is the matter? Should I come home?"

"Yes, sir, I believe you should. There's . . . uh . . . there's someone here. An unexpected visitor. He insisted that I call you and let you know."

"Someone? Who? Don't you know who it is?"

"No, m'lord, this man is not someone of my acquaintance. He is . . . how shall I say it . . . a bit unbalanced . . ."

"Has he hurt you?"

"Hmm. He—he cut my hand with his knife, rather deeply, to be honest . . . I don't know what to do, I just . . ."

"Pelham! Put him on the phone! Do it now!"

"Yes, m'lord . . . here he is."

"Hello?" Hawke said. "Who the hell is this?"

Silence.

"Tell me who you are, you bastard! What did you say? Speak up! I can't hear you."

The man's voice was a low-down and ugly whisper.

"I've come for you."

"What's that? Say that again! Who are you?"

"My name is Smith. Shit Smith. I've come for you."

Hawke dropped the phone on the floor and raced through the house toward the entrance, his own words ringing in his ears as he jumped into the Defender and roared off into the dark wet night: "So safe here . . . so far removed from the evil that bestrides the world, the overwhelming danger . . ."

ACKNOWLEDGMENTS

I would like to express my profound gratitude to my good friend and literary agent, the one and only Peter McGuigan, and his wonderful, talented team at Foundry. Claire Harris, for your unwavering cheery spirit against all odds. And, last but not least, to my film rights agent, Richie Kearn, who knows where all the land mines in L.A. are buried.